Legate of Rome

Book eight of the "Soldier of the Republic" series

By: William Kelso

Visit the author's YouTube site

William Kelso is also the author of:

The Shield of Rome

The Fortune of Carthage

Devotio: The House of Mus

The Veteran of Rome series (9)

Soldier of the Republic series (8)

Published in 2021 by KelsoBooks Ltd. Copyright © William Kelso. First Edition

The author has asserted their moral right under the Copyright, Designs and Patents Act, 1988, to be identified as the author of this work.

All Rights reserved. No part of this publication may be reproduced, copied, stored in a retrieval system, or transmitted, in any form or by any means, without the prior written consent of the copyright holder, nor be otherwise circulated in any form of binding or cover other than that in which it is published and without a similar condition being imposed on the subsequent purchaser.

A CIP catalogue record for this title is available from the British Library.

ABOUT ME

Hello, my name is William Kelso. I was born in the Netherlands to British parents. My interest in history and in military history started at a young age, when I was lucky enough to hear my grandfather describing his experiences of serving in the RAF in North Africa and Italy during World War 2. Recently my family has discovered that one of my Scottish/Northern Irish ancestors fought under Wellington at the Battle of Waterloo in 1815.

I love writing and bringing to life the ancient world of Rome, Carthage and the Germanic and Celtic tribes. It is my thing. My aim is to write 100 books in my lifetime. After graduation, I worked for 22 years in financial publishing and event management in the City of London, as a salesman for some big conference organizers. Working in the heart of the original Roman city of Londinium I spent many years walking its streets and visiting the places. The names of which still commemorate the 2,000-year-old ancient Roman capital of Britannia; London Wall, Watling Street, London Bridge and Walbrook. The City of London if you know where to look has many fascinating historical corners.

So, since the 2nd March 2017 I have freed myself from corporate life and become a full-time writer. It is one of the best decisions I have ever made. Stories as a form of entertainment are as old as cave man and telling them is what I want to do.

My books are all about ancient Rome, especially the early to mid-republic as this was the age of true Roman greatness. My books include, The Shield of Rome, The Fortune of Carthage, Devotio: The House of Mus, the eight books of the Soldier of the Republic series and the nine books of the Veteran of Rome series - Caledonia (1), Hibernia (2), Britannia (3), Hyperborea (4), Germania (5), The Dacian War (6), Armenia Capta (7), Rome and the Conquest of Mesopotamia (8) and Veterans of Rome (9). So, go on. Give them a go.

I live in London with my wife and support the "Help for Heroes" charity and a tiger in India.

To: All volunteer litter pickers

Dear Reader,

I hope that you will enjoy this book. "Legate of Rome" is the eighth instalment of the "Soldier of the Republic" series. "Book nine" will be published by December 2021. In total there are going to be twelve books in the Soldier of the Republic series covering the whole of the 2nd Punic War.

As an independently published author, I do not command huge marketing resources so, if you are so inclined, please do leave me a review or a rating. Also have a look at my short historical themed YouTube videos at

Feel free to contact me with any feedback on my books. Email: william@kelsoevents.co.uk

The story so far…

If you have not started reading the series "Soldier of the Republic" with book 1, then here is a short summary of what happened previously in the first six books. I would also suggest that you check the glossary and character list at the back; if you have forgotten "who is who" or you want to know a bit more about a particular topic or name.

The series "Soldier of the Republic" is set during the turbulent times of the Second Punic War between Rome and Carthage and involves three main characters.

Flavius is an ordinary but poor Roman citizen concerned with providing for his family but also much aware that he has a duty of service to the Roman Republic. Having fought against the invading Gallic tribes at the battle of Telamon he is a veteran and a family man who has known the sharp end of war. Readers from the beginning of the series will have followed him from his war service through to his decision to take his family north to join the hardy Roman colonists who are setting out to create a new home for themselves on the dangerous frontier in Cisalpine Gaul. From there we have watched him move from the fierce fighting in the snow-covered forests of northern Italy to the stinking slums of the city of Rome, to besieged Nola and Cumae and on to the magnificence of ancient Syracuse and Greece. Stoically facing the many daily hardships and dangers of Roman life Flavius is a rock that will not be moved. Father, soldier, spy and in his declining years legate of Rome. Now sent to the semi-mythical Tin Islands on a diplomatic mission Flavius is about to discover something more precious than gold.

Julian, Flavius's wayward son, runs away from home when he is just seventeen to join the legions after a clash of wills and a bitter dispute with his mother. His departure divides the family. We have followed Julian through the war in Spain and Sardinia as he learns his military trade and starts to rise through the ranks to become the closest thing the Roman Republic has to a professional soldier. Surviving the twin disasters of the battle of the Upper Baetis Julian has not seen his family in over seven years. With the arrival of a new commander in chief in Spain however the war is about to take a darker turn, one from which Julian will not be able to escape.

Gisgo is a proud prince of Numidia, an aristocratic horse warrior from northern Africa who is also bankrupt and suffering from the sins of his father who gambled away his inheritance. Seeking a way out of his current plight he signs up to join Hannibal's mercenary army as the Carthaginian prepares for war with Rome. We have followed Gisgo as he accompanied Hannibal into Italy and eventually to the battle of Cannae where Rome gambles all on a decisive victory. But Gisgo has never got over the mysterious loss, at sea, of his wife and young son. So, when an unexpected opportunity suddenly arises to find out what has happened to them, he must decide. A fateful choice that will have long lasting ramifications. On his return to Carthage Gisgo is imprisoned by his enemies and awaits his fate. Rescued by prince Masinissa Gisgo finds a new purpose and new respect, joining Masinissa in Spain as the war against Rome drags on. Soon with help from Masinissa's superb Numidian cavalry and Gisgo's military skill Carthage will stand supreme. But the Carthaginian generals are not united – bickering among each other. Caught in the political crossfire as punishment Gisgo is sent north to the edge of the world. The "Legate of Rome" picks up the story...

Chapter One – To the Edge of the World

Late summer 211 BCE – The Celtic Sea off the Isle of Ushant

Creeping along the rocky coast, the two Carthaginian ships were heading north their sails bulging in the strong breeze. Pitching, rising and rolling through the ocean swell the ship's timbers creaked and groaned, shuddering as the powerful waves sent ice cold sea spray crashing across the deck. Circling and swooping overhead, the shrill excited cries of the sea birds were relentless as the creatures soared over the tense and nervous looking Punic mariners. It was a beautiful clear morning and ahead to the north, Gisgo could see, lay the open ocean with no sign of land. Just an endless expanse of water, blue skies and white clouds. They had finally reached the most dangerous part of their sea-voyage, Bodo had told the sailors earlier. The most hazardous section of their journey from Gades to the Celtic port of Ictis – gateway to the Tin Islands. For from now on - for the next day at least – the Carthaginian diplomat had explained, they would not be within sight of land. They would not be able to anchor for the night and sleep ashore as they were accustomed to. They would be all alone adrift on the vast unpredictable swell, where storms were known to make ships disappear without trace. Where great sea beasts lived in the depths and the Carthaginian gods had no power. For the next day and night, they would be completely at the mercy of the elements, the tides and the whims of the weather. Bodo's words had silenced most of the young inexperienced crew, leaving fear and dread etched into their faces.

Standing on the deck, holding onto one of the mooring ropes, looking resigned and bored as the fresh playful breeze tugged at his thick black beard and waterproof cloak, Gisgo turned to peer at the small island to starboard. He did not really want to be here. Heading for the Tin Islands. To the very edge of the world. It had not been his idea to come. If he had been younger and seeking to make a fortune, he may have appreciated the adventure. But not now. There were better things he could have been doing in Spain. But he'd had no choice. This was his punishment Masinissa had told him. It had been unfair of course but he had to do the time. He had to do the job. To lead the small security detail, providing close protection to the Carthaginian diplomats on their irrelevant mission to the Tin Islands. A lowly position compared to leading four thousand Numidian horsemen into battle against Rome. But after being caught in bed with Sophonisba, general Gersakkun's daughter, and the debacle and spectacular fall out which had followed, Prince Masinissa needed him to disappear for a while. His boss needed him out of the way - at least until frayed tempers among the Carthaginian generals had cooled. Until the unfortunate episode with the Carthaginian princess had been forgotten.

At thirty-seven Gisgo looked fit and formidable with the easy confidence of an aristocrat. A man who had seen the world. A half-cast. An experienced Numidian soldier, Prince and veteran adorned with a strange mismatch of personal items collected from over the years. On his feet he was wearing sturdy Roman army boots. From his belt hung a broad bladed Roman pugio knife, while his expensive, finely crafted Spanish finger rings and African arm bracelets gleamed in the sunlight. His black hair and swarthy appearance were typical of the men of his Numidian homeland, while his blue eyes were a gift, a reminder of his mother's proud aristocratic Carthaginian lineage.

As the deck groaned under his feet, Gisgo turned his attention back to Bodo, who having finished his little speech to the crew, was standing nearby patiently gazing at the vast ocean that stretched away to the north - lost in thought. To compound matters, to make his punishment worse than it already was, Gisgo thought sourly, he had been assigned to protect Bodo. The tall, elegant looking Carthaginian diplomat who had been placed in charge of the mission to the Tin Islands was in his late forties. Wearing a simple woollen Punic sailors' cap, his eyelids were painted black like a woman and his fingers were bedecked by expensive gleaming rings. On being introduced to him in Gades, Bodo had claimed to be an experienced diplomat and sailor who had made the journey to the Tin Islands many times – boasting that he was thoroughly familiar with the local Celtic tribes and their customs. For a moment Gisgo eyed the man carefully hiding his thoughts. Maybe it was just bad luck. Maybe Gersakkun had placed a curse on him. Or maybe the goddess Astarte had been offended by what he'd done with Sophonisba. But fate had arranged for him to be tasked with protecting a complete dick. For that was what Bodo was. An idiot. He had taken an instant dislike to the Carthaginian diplomat. The man had not only displayed an arrogant attitude to his subordinates and unnecessary harshness to the ship's crew but what was worse – far worse - he was a friend of Hanno the Great. Bodo belonged to Hanno's political faction. The same people back in Carthage who had once thrown him in jail, intending to have him executed before Prince Masinissa had managed to rescue him. And the feeling of distrust and enmity appeared mutual for from the start. Bodo had taken a dislike to him as well. But none of it really mattered Gisgo, thought as he reached up to wipe the sea spray from his face. He had a job to do. He would just ignore Bodo. Misfortune came and went - such was life - and despite his personal opinion he had resolved to handle the situation in a professional manner.

"Gisgo," Bodo said, turning to look at him with his painted eyes. "At sunset tonight I am going to give a briefing to all the expedition officers in my cabin. Make sure you are present. I need everyone to be sharp and alert. If this wind holds we will be approaching Ictis within a day or two. Then our work begins."

"Very well Sir," Gisgo replied. "I will keep an eye out for sea monsters."

For a moment Bodo hesitated, as he glared at Gisgo with a suspicious look. "You do understand the importance of this mission, don't you," Bodo snapped. "Carthage wants these Celts to stop trading tin with Rome and their ally Massalia. If we can get them to agree to that we can strike a mighty blow against the enemy. Tin is a precious commodity, and these islanders are a major producer. We use the metal to harden copper into bronze. Denying the enemy this resource is just as important as what Hannibal is doing in Italy."

"I have no doubt Sir," Gisgo responded, his face giving nothing away. "But you did just mention sea monsters to the crew. As head of your security, I need to be alert to all dangers."

Across from him Bodo's eyes narrowed. Then shifting his attention to Xenocles who was watching the exchange with a bemused smile, Bodo licked his lips. For a long moment he eyed the Greek mercenary in silence.

"Sunset in my cabin. Don't forget. That will be all," Bodo growled at last, half turning to Gisgo as he stomped away across the moving deck to the small wooden structure at the stern of the ship.

"Sea monsters," Xenocles muttered raising an eyebrow as he came over to stand beside Gisgo. "Well, I thought you handled that very well."

"I shouldn't have brought it up," Gisgo murmured. "But I couldn't resist."

"I know," Xenocles said, quietly glancing back at Bodo. "That speech he gave just now has scared half the crew to death. Poor fellows. You know - it sounded like Bodo enjoyed scaring them. The man's a prick. Maybe I should go and tell the crew about the time you and I sailed to Kerne in the Punic Star.

How many days without sighting land did we endure? And not a single sea monster in sight. This trip to the Tin Islands is a leisurely stroll compared to that voyage."

"You are right. I can see Donis already shaking his head in disapproval," Gisgo replied with a little smile. Then abruptly his expression changed. "Look. I am sorry that I got you involved in this," Gisgo said, glancing at his old friend. "I know this is a shit job. Protecting a bunch of diplomats is far beneath what we should be doing. But I am glad you are here. It makes things bearable."

"I know. I know," Xenocles said breezily gazing out to sea. "Masinissa commands and you obey. I get it. But its OK. Masinissa is a good man. He is a worthy commander to follow, unlike so many others. You are lucky to serve such a man. Your goddess Astarte has been kind to you Gisgo. And as for me. Shit Gisgo. You don't have to explain yourself. I go where you go. That's how it has always been. You, me and Ablon are blood brothers, remember."

"Masinissa saved my life twice," Gisgo replied quietly. "I could not say no."

"Well, don't worry about me," Xenocles said with a relaxed yawn. "I get to see the world for free and being out here with you sure beats training recruits in New Carthage. I don't mind if it's a shit job Gisgo. I was born to be a soldier, a mercenary. I was raised to fight – for adventure. For the sheer fucking glory of it all. There is not much else that I am good at. I do believe that I am happiest going into battle with a good friend at my side."

"Well don't expect much fighting where we are going," Gisgo said glancing at the eight burly veterans he'd handpicked himself for the job. "We are to protect the diplomats and that's it. Simple and straightforward."

"From experience," Xenocles said cheerfully. "Nothing is ever simple."

For a moment Gisgo did not reply, as he gazed at his mercenaries, armed to the teeth, sitting about on the deck. Then lifting his eyes, he gazed across the water at the second Carthaginian ship that was ploughing through the waves parallel to their course. Onboard the naval vessel that was acting as their escort, he had twenty more mercenaries, mainly Spaniards but including a few slingers from the Balearic Islands. A tight knit, highly experienced group of soldiers - each one a battle-hardened veteran of the long war with Rome.

"Bodo refuses to tell me anything about these Tin Islands," Gisgo said at last in a resigned sounding voice. "I know nothing about the place where we are going. And the others, Phameus and Malchus don't want to talk either. It's like they belong to a club of which I am not a member. It's like Bodo thinks the knowledge of this land is something that must be kept secret. I don't get it. Why? We are all on the same side, are we not?"

"I think so," Xenocles said. "But the Carthaginians are secretive like that. Remember how when we sailed for Kerne - Donis did not trust me at first because I was Greek. He didn't want to share his navigational secrets with me. There has been a great mercantile and commercial rivalry between us Greeks and Carthage for centuries. Carthage has always tried to keep secret the details about their distant trade partners, to prevent the competition from muscling in. Maybe it's just force of habit," Xenocles added with a shrug. "Maybe that is why Bodo refuses to divulge what he knows."

"Maybe it's because he is an arsehole," Gisgo muttered darkly.

"He's the commander," Xenocles said quickly. "And commanders have the right to be arseholes. You should know that."

"Well, I did learn that the local Celtic tribesmen are friendly to us," Gisgo said ignoring his friend's smile. "Bodo is not expecting violence. Apparently the local tribesmen are used to visiting foreign tin merchants and sailors. But once we are ashore, we will keep the men together just the same. I don't want any fraternising with the locals until we have learned the lay of the land. Friendly or not, men are men. Misunderstandings can happen. I don't want any trouble. No fights, no gambling, no women. We are in a foreign land and if the men misbehave I will get blamed. Bodo may be a prick but he has connections, powerful friends in Carthage. The sort of friends who can cause us a lot of trouble."

"I am sure he has," Xenocles said still grinning. "Don't worry. As your deputy I will make sure the boys behave themselves."

Gisgo was about to speak again when a sudden warning shout from the lookout high up in the mast, made him pause.

"Ships. To starboard. Ships!" the lookout yelled, pointing.

Hurriedly Gisgo turned to gaze towards the rocky coast of Gaul just visible on the horizon. For a moment he saw nothing but the ocean swell and the circling seabirds. Then abruptly his expression darkened as he caught sight of the three small boats cutting through the waves towards him on an intercept course. The ships were small but fast – their bows rearing up over the choppy waves, their sails tight and bulging in the wind.

"Who are they?" A sailor shouted, as all eyes onboard the Carthaginian vessel turned to stare at the strangers.

For a long moment no one replied. Then suddenly a Punic horn rang out from the escorting naval vessel, its long monotonous blast reverberating away across the sea. It was the call to arms.

"Pirates," Gisgo yelled. "Get ready for a fight, boys."

As the mercenaries sitting on the deck leapt to their feet and reached for their weapons and shields - the ship's crew rushed to man their battle stations. Hastily Xenocles handed Gisgo a bow and a quiver of arrows and as he did, Gisgo was suddenly aware that Xenocles was singing softly to himself. A Spartan battle song. Cutting through the waves the Gallic raiders were coming on fast and as they drew closer and closer, Gisgo was able to pick out tiny figures standing upright upon the decks of the three boats.

"Damned pirates," Bodo swore, as he came staggering across the deck towards Gisgo. "But this time they have picked on the wrong target."

"This has happened before?" Gisgo said, shooting the Carthaginian diplomat a quick concerned look.

"Every time that I sail for the Tin Islands. Those bastards know how valuable our cargoes are."

"Sir," Gisgo growled in an unhappy voice. "You have been to the islands before. I have not. You know these Celts. I do not. As your head of security, I would appreciate it if you were to brief me beforehand on all the dangers that we are likely to encounter. We need to work together. It's important that we share all the information that we have. So that we can be prepared."

"I am in charge here. Security is your job," Bodo retorted as he peered across the sea at the raiders. "They said you were good. So, you figure it out. That's why you are here."

"Right," Gisgo snapped - looking away struggling to keep his cool. Onboard the Carthaginian vessel a sullen silence had settled upon the crew. And as the silence lengthened the tension grew. Suddenly the Gallic raiders appeared to turn away. They were changing course. Staring at the ships, Gisgo frowned. What was this? The pirates appeared to have given up. Quickly shifting his gaze to their naval escort, Gisgo grunted as he saw the reason why. Onboard the Carthaginian warship the marines had trained their naval artillery on the pirate vessels. The sight of the powerful Carthaginian harpoons appeared to have scared the raiders off.

"See. I told you that they had picked on the wrong target this time," Bodo said in a sneering voice.

***

The ship's only cabin was cramped and barely large enough to fit all five of the expedition's officers. Along one side of the creaking hut was the mattress on which Bodo slept, while from the ceiling a solitary glowing lantern swung gently in tune with the rocking deck. Standing with his back against the wooden wall, his arms folded across his chest, Gisgo was gazing at Bodo as the diplomat prepared to address his subordinates. Outside through a gap in the blanket that covered the doorway the daylight was fading fast. Out on the deck, where they also slept, Xenocles, the mercenaries and the ship's crew were huddled together quietly eating their evening meal.

"Gentlemen," Bodo said clearing his voice as he turned to his officers. "We are nearly at the end of our journey to Belerion. The Tin Islands. Soon we shall reach the port of Ictis. Now I do not need to remind you of the rules when we go ashore. You have all been here before. As chief diplomat for this mission I am in charge. I represent Carthage, and in that capacity, I shall be doing all the talking and negotiating with our hosts."

Abruptly Bodo stopped speaking as he turned to stare at Gisgo, who had moved to block the cabin doorway.

"Look I don't want to be difficult," Gisgo said, eyeing Bodo, "but no one is leaving this fucking cabin until I have been fully informed of what we are heading into. I am in charge of everyone's security. You may have all been to these islands before, but I have not. It is frankly ridiculous that I still do not know what to expect when we go ashore. So, I have some questions and I expect answers."

As Gisgo stopped speaking the Carthaginians hurriedly exchanged glances with each other.

"What do you think you are doing? May I remind you that this is a diplomatic mission," Bodo growled looking displeased. "You Gisgo are just here to provide security. Nothing more. You do not need to know anything. The details of my work do not concern you. You are just hired muscle to put on a good show for our hosts. To distract them with your exoticness while I get to work on the serious business. I am in charge of the diplomacy."

"No not good enough," Gisgo retorted shaking his head and standing his ground. "I have questions and I want answers."

"Bodo," Phameas exclaimed as the Carthaginian merchant quickly raised his hand in a conciliatory gesture. "It is a reasonable request. Let the man have his answers. What harm can it do now. He is a Numidian Prince. Not the enemy. He is here with us and he has a right to know."

"Even the Massaliots and Romans know about the tin mines of Belerion," Melchus chipped in, giving Gisgo a sympathetic look.

For a moment Bodo looked undecided. Then with an unhappy scowl he turned to Gisgo, folding his arms across his chest.

"Fine," Bodo said grudgingly. "If it ends your ceaseless complaining. But I must warn you. These are Carthaginian state secrets. They are not to be passed on to anyone else. Give me your word that you will obey."

"I will keep your secrets."

"So, what do you want to know?" Bodo snapped sounding annoyed.

"These Celts," Gisgo said quickly. "These tribesmen who control and operate the tin mines. What do we know about them?"

"They are called by various names," Bodo retorted, lowering his eyes. "The Romans and Massaliots call them the Cornovii. We however have always known them as 'the people of the horn'. That's because the land they occupy resembles a horn. Others call their land Belerion. They have traded tin with us for centuries. The trade between Gades and Ictis is most valuable. The Tin Islands used to be a trade secret known only to us but after Pytheas' voyage; the Massaliots eventually discovered the tin mines too. So now we share the knowledge and trade with the city of Massalia. And of course those fucking Greeks told their allies in Rome about the mines. The people of the horn are ruled by a woman. Queen Talwyn."

"A Queen," Gisgo exclaimed looking surprised.

"Yes," Bodo replied sourly. "These Celts are different to the ones in Gaul and Spain. They do not mind being ruled by a woman, if she is of noble birth which Queen Talwyn most definitely is. They treat their women as equals to the men. Some of the women even fight in battle. It is said they are as fierce and skilled as the best warriors. In that sense these people are very egalitarian. A simple society, technologically backward perhaps, but they love profit just like we do. They value the trade which they do with us. It has made them rich and famous. Tin ingots are shipped south to Gades while our merchants bring silver and Carthaginian manufactured goods north. Queen Talwyn likes us. We are welcome in her hall and long may that continue."

For a moment Gisgo said nothing. Then quickly he glanced at Phameas and Melchus. The two Carthaginian merchants, both in their forties with fat protruding bellies were acting as deputies to Bodo. But as he studied their faces, he could see they did not appear to dispute what Bodo had just told him. Finally, Gisgo glanced at Hanno, the stern looking captain in command of their naval escort, but he too appeared to believe what had just been said.

"So, this Queen. Talwyn," Gisgo said at last turning back to Bodo. "So, you trust her?"

"Of course," Bodo retorted. "I have spent years wooing her – turning her into a friend of Carthage. She is our friend and ally."

As Bodo spoke however Phameas shifted his weight uncomfortably, and lowered his eyes.

"I need to know the rules which my men will need to observe," Gisgo said, looking grave. "For when we go ashore. I have thirty battle hardened killers with me, whose main preoccupation apart from war is about getting rich and getting laid. I don't want any trouble with the locals. That would not do. So, I need to know the local customs. I need to know what laws these people live under, so that we do not break them accidentally. We are foreigners here. Guests. It would also be useful to know who and what these 'people of the horn' respect?"

For a moment, the cabin remained silent as the four Carthaginians warily glanced at each other.

"Look," Bodo said at last in an irritated voice. "You really do not need to worry about such matters. Just keep your men in check and stay in the background. You are just here to provide security and I doubt that your men's skills will be needed. Like I said we are welcome in this land. I will handle the Queen and the diplomacy. Queen Talwyn knows me very well. She respects me. Now if that is all – I would like to get on with my briefing if you don't mind."

"They love making a profit," Hanno said suddenly, speaking up for the first time as he stared back at Gisgo with a grave expression. "Profit makes them very happy and they respect their Druids. Their holy men. Whatever you do don't go insulting their Druids. That would be a big mistake."

***

It was dawn and Gisgo has been sleeping out on the deck when he was woken by a panicked cry. As he scrambled to his feet, his hand resting on his Roman pugio knife he saw Phameas staggering across the deck towards him. The merchant looked visibly upset, his face pale and fearful.

"Where is Bodo?" the Carthaginian merchant cried. "Have you seen him? He's not in his cabin or below decks in the cargo hold."

"What?" Gisgo said looking startled. "No. I haven't seen him."

Hastily Gisgo turned to look around at the crew, but there was no sign of the diplomat anywhere. A hundred yards away to starboard, the Carthaginian naval vessel was riding the swell secured to its sister ship by two thick ropes. And beyond in every direction there was nothing but the sea. But as Gisgo spotted Xenocles the Greek mercenary gave him a strange guilty look.

"Oh, this is a disaster," Phameas wailed, as he frantically raised his hands to his head in despair. "Where is Bodo? Where is he?"

"Could he have gone aboard the warship?" Gisgo called out, as around him the crew started to look at each other in confusion.

"No. He would have told me," Phameas cried in a voice bordering on panic. "He wouldn't have done that during the night and the little boat is still here. It has not been used. He's gone. Bodo is gone. This is a disaster."

"What about the lookout?" Gisgo retorted. Hurriedly he turned to look up at the figure seated high up in the mast. "Well, boy," Gisgo shouted. "You were on watch. Did you see or hear anything strange last night?"

"Yes Sir. I heard a splash," the boy responded from the crow's nest. "And maybe a cry for help. Something may have fallen overboard. But it was dark and I could not see what had happened. I thought the cry may have come from one of our men, calling out in his sleep."

"Shit," Gisgo swore as Phameas turned to stare at the sea with a horrified look.

"Overboard. Oh, great Baal. Oh, mighty Tanit," the merchant whispered hoarsely, his eyes bulging. "This is a disaster. What are we going to do without Bodo? He knew the Tin Islands like the back of his hand. He was our leader. He had so much experience. What are we going to do now?"

Taking a deep breath Gisgo turned to search the sea, his expression grim and for a long moment no one spoke. Then abruptly Phameas turned around to gaze at Gisgo, his chest heaving with emotion.

"We must turn back to Gades," the merchant wailed. "Without Bodo our mission is already over. We can't possibly carry it out now. We have to turn back. That is the sensible thing to do."

"No," Gisgo said with sudden resolve. "Bodo may have been our leader but he was just one man. The mission will continue. Those are our orders. We should not turn back now we are so close. Carthage wants this done and we can still complete the mission. You Phameas will just have to take over as our chief diplomat. You will have to handle the negotiations."

"Me," Phameas stammered. "No. I couldn't possibly do that. I am a tin merchant. I am not a diplomat, not like Bodo was."

"Then Hanno should take charge," Gisgo said grimly, staring at Phameas. "Surely he is qualified for the job."

"Hanno's orders are to only escort us as far as the port of Ictis, after which he is to return to Gades immediately," Phameas exclaimed. "He and his marines are not hanging around. As soon as we are ashore, he will be off. He won't be able to handle the negotiations, nor would he want to."

Swearing once again, Gisgo stared at Phameas with growing frustration. Then taking another deep breath, he turned to look out to sea again, his expression troubled and brooding.

"Fine," Gisgo said at last in a resigned voice. "Then I shall assume command and see this mission to its completion. Orders are orders. Carthage expects us to do our job and do it we shall."

Staring at Gisgo, Phameas said nothing, his lips working soundlessly. Then at last he nodded his acceptance.

"Very well," the merchant replied. "But if you want my advice - why don't we choose the easy option. Forget about trying to convince Queen Talwyn to embargo the tin trade with Massalia and Rome. It was always a shit idea. She is never going to agree to that proposal anyway. Why should she? No. Why don't we make our lives easier. We just go ashore, buy what the locals are offering and just leave it at that. We could be home before the winter sets in. No one will have to know. And as for Bodo, well accidents at sea happen all the time."

"No," Gisgo said sternly. "You are wrong. I would know. We are not doing that. We are going to stick to our original orders and I am going to need your help. We are going to bring a halt to the flow of tin that is being shipped to the Romans and their allies. We are at war. We are fighting for our very existence or have you forgotten that. Now, can I rely on you Phameas or should I be looking elsewhere for a deputy and adviser?"

Gazing back at him the Punic merchant's lips were still moving but no words were coming out of his mouth. Then at last he nodded. "I will help you as best as I can," Phameas stammered. "I know the way to Ictis. I can get us there and I speak the local language. The Queen is familiar with my face although she knows Bodo much better than she knows me. But I still think we should take the easy way out and just forget about this trade embargo. It's bad for business. If the Queen takes offence at our suggestion, it may come back to haunt us. She is a formidable lady, Queen Talwyn. Formidable and cruel. She has a temper. If there is one thing she lusts after over everything else, it is power."

"I am in command now and I will take responsibility for what we do," Gisgo replied aware that his mercenaries were watching him. "So calm yourself Phameas and get your act together. For now, I just need you to get us to the port. See to it. That will be all."

As he watched Phameas turn away, Gisgo lowered his eyes. What had he just done a voice was screaming inside his head? This was madness. He was way out of his depth here. He had no experience of the diplomacy required to pull this of. But it still felt like the right thing to do. Someone had to be in command. And now that he had put himself in charge, he sensed the lethargy he'd endured since leaving Gades, slipping away as if he had been released from iron chains. His old vigour and motivation were returning. He'd made the right choice. Once again he was in control of his own fate and it felt good. He was best when he was in command of his own destiny.

As his mercenaries slowly settled back down on the deck Gisgo turned to eye Xenocles, who was standing a few yards away. In response the Greek mercenary gave him a little silent and defiant look that spoke volumes. Coming to stand beside his friend, Gisgo paused for a moment as he gazed out to sea.

"An accident," Gisgo said quietly, cocking an eye. "Do you believe that? Do you believe Bodo accidentally fell overboard? Tell me what happened?"

By his side Xenocles was suddenly looking very philosophical.

"He may have fallen overboard," the Greek mercenary muttered. "Or maybe I threw him overboard. I didn't mean to. So maybe yes, it was accident."

"You threw Bodo overboard."

"Yeah, I think so," Xenocles replied, looking down at his boots. "Like I said I didn't mean to. It just happened. Our leader is not a lady's man, if you know what I mean, and last night he thought I would do him a favour. I think he took a shine to me, expecting me to provide a sexual act in return for a lousy coin. Unfortunately for him he picked on the wrong man and now he is no more."

For a long moment Gisgo said nothing, as he gazed at his friend. Then slowly he shook his head.

"Well, this is a great start to our expedition," Gisgo murmured. "Before we have even set foot on land, we have managed to kill the one man we were all supposed to be protecting."

Chapter Two – Ictis

Rising steeply from out of the sea, trapped just offshore within the bay, the small mysterious island looked forlorn amid the dark brooding clouds. Surrounded by a ring of foaming white water, the grey black rocks along the shore looked interminably old, immovable and weather beaten. Surging over and battering into them with a dull constant booming noise, the waves came on undeterred, locked in an eternal dance, an intimate embrace between sea and land as the giants of nature battled it out for supremacy. They had finally reached their destination, Gisgo thought, as he stood on the moving, pitching deck of the Carthaginian ship and peered at the cone shaped island. They had made it to the tin trading port of Ictis in Belerion. The furthest north and west that he had ever been. But as he stared at the steep slopes and wooded summit of the island, he could see no sign of the port or of any human habitation. Nor were there any other ships about, like he had expected. This place was unlike the busy harbours of Gades and Carthage which he'd been used to. There was no one about except for the shrieking, swooping sea birds that had accompanied them across the sea from Gaul. The island appeared to be deserted. Carefully casting his eye along the towering, majestic cliffs of the mainland, that stretched away into the haze, Gisgo frowned. Even for late summer it was cold, and he could see rain was approaching.

"An unmistakable sight, no," Phameas said proudly as he came to stand beside Gisgo and gazed out across the sea at the island. "Don't worry. This is Ictis," Phameas added, noticing the look of concern on Gisgo's face. "The port is on the other side of the island, facing the mainland. It's a tidal island. At certain times of the day the sea retreats to form a narrow land bridge. Then for a few hours Ictis is not an island. It's the perfect place to trade and store valuable cargoes like tin. You will see what I mean soon enough."

"It's small," Gisgo muttered. "Smaller than I had expected."

"This is the edge of the world, my friend," Phameas said grandly. "Not many people live here. What were you, expecting."

"Sea monsters. Giants," Gisgo said with a shrug.

"Hardly," Phameas replied scornfully. "Bodo just liked to show off to a new crew. His stories are fables invented to scare children. No. The weather is our worst enemy here. It is violent and unpredictable. You never know what the weather will be like tomorrow. Hot, cold, dry, wet. It's shifting all the time. Not like Spain or Carthage where we are blessed by the sun. It will keep you on your toes - this unpredictable climate. You will see. And when it storms, the sea is truly transformed. It becomes a terrible sight to behold. A raging, boiling inferno. You don't want to be out on the water when a proper storm comes in from the ocean. I have seen ships driven onto the rocks and smashed to pieces with all hands lost."

For a moment Gisgo, said nothing as he stared at the island.

"They call it the Tin Islands," he said glancing at Phameas. "But I only see one island. Is Ictis the only port from which tin is exported?"

"There are others further along the coast to the east," Phameas replied in a careful neutral voice. "But Ictis is the main port. It is the one we have always used and the tin mines are not far from here. Like Bodo said, we have a good relationship with Queen Talwyn."

"Good," Gisgo said with sudden resolve. "Then once we are ashore, I would like to meet the Queen as soon as possible."

Glancing at him Phameas hesitated. "It is still not too late to change your mind," the merchant said at last. "Carthage is asking a lot from the Queen by demanding she embargo the tin trade with Rome and Massalia. In effect we are asking her to give up a very profitable business. She will not be happy. We are going to anger her, and she has a temper. Rome and Massalia are her clients too. If she takes our demands the wrong way, it may come back to hurt us. I do a lot of private business with these people. We are taking a risk by pressing our demands. Maybe it would be better if we just quietly forgot about the whole thing."

Standing on the deck gazing out at the land Gisgo did not immediately reply. Then slowly he turned to Phameas.

"Mention abandoning our mission again Phameas," Gisgo said quietly, "and I shall have you bound and tossed overboard. I do not want to hear any more objections. We have our orders. I don't give a damn about your private business affairs. We are here on state business to serve Carthage and we will carry out the task that has been entrusted to us. Now have I made myself clear?"

At his side Phameas was suddenly looking nervous. Hurriedly the merchant bowed his head. "Yes Sir, as you wish," he said quickly.

***

As the two anchored Carthaginian ships rode the gentle swell in the sheltered island harbour, the Briton horn rang out once again, the deep, mournful sound drifting away across the water and land. Onboard their ships, the silent Punic sailors and mercenaries were manning the sides of their vessels staring at the island, every man eager to get a glimpse of their destination. Across the water, the small native settlement clung to the sliver of flattish land beneath the rocky and forested hill that dominated the island. Ictis was tiny Gisgo thought, hiding his disappointment, as he stood on the deck among his men. It looked barely large enough to house a hundred people. But apart from that, it didn't look too different to some of the Celtic villages he had seen in north western

Spain. As his eyes swept over the settlement, he could make out a collection of thatched round houses, which were protected by a stout stone wall with an entrance gate facing the mainland. And manning the walls were an unusually large contingent of armed men for such a small place. From holes in the cone shaped roofs of the round houses, smoke was billowing forth and among the buildings. Out of sight, Gisgo could hear several barking dogs. Turning his attention in the direction of the mainland, a couple of hundred yards away, he could see that the tide was in and for the moment at least Ictis was an island again. At the water's edge inside the harbour, a crowd of barefoot children had gathered and were staring at the Carthaginian ships. Unlike the silent Punic sailors however, the children were making a racket, boldly calling out to the sailors, their shrill happy excitement plain for all to see.

"I told you they would be happy to see us Sir," Phameas said, standing beside Gisgo as he gazed at the children who were beckoning to the men on the ships. "When we arrive here we always give the children small presents. They love what we bring them. That is why they are so excited to see us. It's all about winning hearts and minds. It's just good business."

"So, this is where they keep the tin ingots." Gisgo said, as he carefully studied the native settlement. "This is where the trading takes place. Is that why there are so many armed men up on that wall."

"Yes, the tin is mined and beaten into ingots on the mainland. Then they bring it here and store it over there in that large building," Phameas said, pointing at one of the thatched round houses. "As for defence and protection…" Phameas's voice abruptly trailed off as he turned to stare at the figures manning the wall. For a moment he remained silent. Then the tin merchant frowned. "Odd," he muttered. "The tin is valuable but they don't normally have so many armed men here. Something must have happened to warrant the extra security."

"Xenocles," Gisgo called out quickly turning to the Greek mercenary. "See to it that the remainder of our mercenaries are brought across from Hanno's ship. The men are to arm themselves and take all their kit, weapons and belongings. We're going to go ashore. Look sharp, but tell the men to be friendly. The natives are to be treated with respect. They are our friends."

"Yes Sir," Xenocles replied.

"Melchus," Gisgo continued, turning to the fat Carthaginian tin merchant who was standing nearby. "Have the crew start unloading our trade goods and make sure those children get the gifts that we have brought them. I am also going to need to see the gifts that we have brought for the Queen and her entourage! What are we going to give her by the way? What was the original plan?"

"Gifts my lord," Melchus said - looking surprised.

"Yes, gifts. For Queen Talwyn," Gisgo repeated in a patient voice. "We have brought her a gift have we not? Good business and all."

"Yes, we have – of course we have," Melchus said, swiftly recovering. "I was just not sure when you wanted to give it to her."

For a moment Gisgo eyed the fat tin merchant in icy silence. Had Melchus been hoping that he would forget about the gifts for the Queen, so that he could pocket the prize himself.

"So what are we giving her?" Gisgo asked.

"It's in the hold Sir," Melchus stammered. "I will get some of the crew to bring it out right now."

As the fat man hurriedly turned away, Gisgo subjected him to a hard annoyed look. There was something deeply corrupt about Melchus. As if the man believed, that everything in life could be purchased. He could sense it. It made him unreliable. But right now he had more important things to concern himself with, than investigating the actions of a sleazy tin merchant.

It was a little while later when Melchus and a couple of the crew reappeared, carrying a iron barred cage. As he caught sight of what was inside the cage, Gisgo groaned and quickly ran his hand through his hair. Peering back at him through the bars were two baby lions.

"This is the gift?" Gisgo exclaimed. "This is what we are going to present to the Queen - two lion cubs."

"Yes Sir," Melchus replied, looking down at the creatures. "It was Bodo's idea. He said that none of these Celts has ever seen a lion before. He said they were going to love them."

"Good gods," Gisgo exclaimed as he stared at the caged cubs in dismay. "So I am going to have warn the Queen that these cubs grow up to become man eaters. That they are not like a friendly dog and that if she tickles them, she does so at her own peril. She is really going to like that, isn't she. Aside from that, the poor things look like they are going to freeze to death in this climate."

"Well, the only thing that matters is that they will be alive when we give them to the Queen," Melchus replied with a whiff of defiance. "Who cares what happens to those cubs afterwards. She can eat them for all I care. It won't be our problem. She can't blame us if they die from the cold. Once she accepts them, she is responsible for their fate, not me."

***

Hurriedly scrambling over the side of the small-crowded boat as it gently drifted into the stony shore, Gisgo's boots splashed into the shallow water. Straightening up, he turned to look at the small Celtic settlement. From the doorways of their simple stone round houses, the locals were eyeing him in wary silence. It had started to rain, and the afternoon was already well advanced. Clad in his chain mail body armour and Greek style Phrygian helmet, his cloak adorned with his proud coat of arms, (a white horse on a black background), Gisgo looked magnificent. A leader of men. As his mercenaries and the ship's crew began to stream ashore, wading through the water, the Carthaginians were immediately set upon by the group of excited children who came rushing towards them. The youngsters were calling out in a language he could not understand. But they were not shy and, as the Carthaginians and Spaniards hesitated the children milled about among them, reaching out to reverently touch their clothing. Then abruptly a sharp cry made the children run away and, as he turned his head, Gisgo saw a party of armed Celts advancing towards him. The fierce looking men were all of fighting age. Clad in tight fitting trousers with leather belts, their tunics were covered by long woollen cloaks held together by brooches. Standing his ground, Gisgo cautiously eyed the warriors as they approached. The man leading them appeared to be young, not much older than twenty. A handsome man - he looked brash and confident; his rugged face covered in a full-face tattoo of a wolf. His head was closely shaven around the ears, leaving a central dollop of thick blond plaited hair to tumble down to beyond his shoulders. On his belt he was carrying a sword and a knife, and a small round shield was slung across his back. At the young warrior's side, an older man, tall and in his forties, was gazing at the Carthaginians with a solemn expression. There appeared to be something tragic about him that defied explanation. The older man's neck was adorned with a polished bronze torc, while his long hair was tied into a tight bob that sat squarely on the top of his head. In his hands he was holding a carnyx, a long beautifully crafted boar headed Celtic trumpet made from wood and bronze.

"Are these the Queen's men?" Gisgo called out, without taking his eyes off the approaching party of warriors.

"I think so. I don't recognise the young warrior," Phameas said guardedly. "Maybe he belongs to the Queen's guard. But the older man walking beside him is called Aed. He is one of the Queen's closest advisers. A good man. A friend of Carthage. He will help us."

As the party of Celts came to a halt a few yards away from Gisgo and his mercenaries, a tense silence descended upon the shoreline. For a long moment no one spoke as both sides took their time to carefully inspect the other, taking in every detail about each-others clothing, appearance, bearing and weapons. At last Aed spoke up in his native language directing his solemn words towards Phameas. Responding with a few words, Phameas took a step towards the Celt and quickly embraced him and as the two men parted, the atmosphere abruptly lightened and the warriors relaxed. Cracking a smile at Phameas that showed he was missing several teeth, Aed spoke again in a language whose intonation reminded Gisgo of the Celtic language he'd heard spoken in western Spain. For a brief moment the two men quietly conversed with each other like old friends. Then Phameas turned and gestured at him and, as he did Gisgo was aware that every one of the fierce Celtic warriors had suddenly turned to stare at him.

"He says that we are welcome in Ictis and that he is pleased we have come," Phameas said, smoothly switching languages. "His people will afford us the customary hospitality given to the Phoenicians who live in the far south. He says Carthage is an old and reliable friend. I told him that you are our leader. He wants to know, if we have come to buy his tin?"

"Tell him that we are grateful for his hospitality," Gisgo said, gazing back at Aed who was watching him, "and that we have brought gifts for him, his people and his Queen. Fine glassware from Carthage. Silver from Spain and exotic spices from Egypt. Tell him that we are glad to be here back among friends and that we have come to do business with him and his Queen."

As Phameas translated, Aed studied Gisgo in careful and solemn silence before nodding and replying.

"Aed asks what has become of Bodo," Phameas said lowering his eyes. "He wants to know why Bodo has not come this time?"

"Bodo could not make it unfortunately," Gisgo said coolly. "They have sent me instead. My name is Gisgo, Prince of the Massylii. Ask him, Phameas, if he will take us to see Queen Talwyn."

In reply Aed remained silent as he carefully studied Gisgo. And as he waited for a reply Gisgo was again struck by the strange aura of sadness that seemed to cling to Aed. As if the man had suffered some great unspeakable tragedy. At last Aed nodded and spoke.

"He says he will take us to meet Queen Talwyn," Phameas translated. "He says she is at her summer residence. Its a few miles away to the north. He is sorry that Bodo has not come. He hopes his good friend is alright and that he will visit again on his next trip."

"Tell him that I am grateful for his help," Gisgo responded. "I am keen to do business with his Queen. But I have a question. Ask him Phameas. Ask him why are there so many armed men up on those walls over there. It seems excessive for a settlement of this size. Is he expecting to be attacked?"

As Phameas translated, the fierce looking Celtic warriors suddenly stirred and a murmur arose from their ranks. Gazing back at him, Aed suddenly looked pained as if Gisgo's question had embarrassed him. Then gesturing at the armed figures up on the wall Aed spoke again.

For a moment Phameas hesitated as he listened. Then, looking grave and alarmed, the tin merchant quickly turned to Gisgo.

"All is not well in Queen Talwyn's realm," Phameas said. "Things have changed since my last visit. The Queen is at war with her husband. Civil war has broken out. It has split the loyalty of the people. Aed says that her husband wants the crown for himself, even though he has no legitimate claim. He is just her consort after all. But he has already stolen half the Queen's kingdom. All the land to the east of Ictis is under his control. The men on the wall are however loyal to the Queen. They are here to protect Ictis and the tin that is stored here - from her husband."

"Civil war. A fight between husband and wife," Gisgo exclaimed, raising his eyebrows.

Phameas was about to reply when the young rugged Celtic warrior with the full-face tattoo of a wolf stepped forwards and spoke, his eyes fixed on Gisgo and gleaming with the easy confidence and arrogance of youth.

For a moment Phameas did not respond as he listened. Then the tin merchant half turned to Gisgo.

"He says that his name is Galchobhar," Phameas translated. "He says that he leads the Queen's army and that he is going to personally kill her husband for her. He says that we should not be afraid. For we are now under his protection and no harm will come to us. He and his men will escort us to the hill fort at Trencrom, to meet Queen Talwyn."

"Oh that makes me feel much better," Gisgo murmured sarcastically. Then in a louder voice. "Tell him that we will be honoured to accompany him as soon as we have unloaded our gifts and trade goods."

Quickly Gisgo turned to Xenocles, who was standing a few paces away, gazing in silent fascination at the braided hair worn by the Celtic warriors. For their hairstyles were not too different to his own carefully braided Spartan locks.

"Xenocles," Gisgo called out sharply, speaking in Greek. "I want you to stay here in Ictis with fifteen of the mercenaries and guard the ship. I will take the rest of our men and go with these Celts to the Queen's residence. Stay alert and look sharp. Things are not as peaceful as they look. Civil war has broken out among the locals. It's wife against husband."

"Wow," Xenocles exclaimed. "So which side are we on?"

"The Queen's, you idiot," Gisgo growled.

Chapter Three - Queen of a Divided Realm

It was getting late, and the sun had already vanished below the western horizon, as the small band of Carthaginians and their Celtic hosts headed inland on foot. Led by Galchobhar and his fierce looking warriors, the Punic mercenaries were carrying their trade goods and gifts, stashed away in sacks and long terracotta amphorae. The men were silent, keeping their thoughts to themselves and for the moment the only noise came from the steady patter of the rain and the scrape of the warriors' boots on the rocky path. As the party finally reached the crest of the steep hill, Gisgo turned to gaze back the way they had come. From his vantage point he had a fine view of the small island out in the bay and the port of Ictis, nestling along its shore. Riding at anchor along the wild and spectacular coastline were the two Punic ships and connecting the island to the mainland, the narrow land bridge, that had appeared from out of the sea as if by magic. It was still there. For a moment Gisgo's eyes lingered. Then turning away, he resumed his path following the Celts into the green forest. Eyeing his hosts Gisgo, said nothing. The island Celts were taller and bigger than his own men and they appeared to be wilder and rougher too. Living on the edge of the world seemed to have lent them a natural savageness. As if their nature had been conditioned by the elements. Their iron weapons looked solid and their rectangular shields, decorated with mysterious swirling Celtic patterns were of good quality, but he sensed that the men were individualists. Warriors accustomed to fighting on their own. They seemed to lack the training and discipline to fight together as a cohesive unit in the Carthaginian and Roman fashion.

Wiping the incessant rain from his face, Gisgo turned to gaze about as he followed his hosts deeper and deeper into the dark secluded wood. The country around him was so green. Green like he had never experienced before. How unlike his native Numidia or southern Spain. Even Italy had not been this green. And there was no one about. Apart from Ictis he had seen no other native settlements. Belerion appeared to be sparsely populated. Ahead of him, moving along the forest path, one of his men was carrying the cage containing the two lion cubs. A blanket had been flung over the cage so as to keep the nature of the gift a surprise, but he could still hear the two young lions whining anxiously. They too appeared on edge in this strange wet land.

Catching sight of Phameas and Aed quietly conversing with each other as they emerged from the forest, Gisgo eyed the two men warily. Melchus he could handle he thought. The Carthaginian tin merchant may be corrupt and unreliable but he knew how to deal with men like that. Melchus was a known quantity. Phameas on the other hand was much more complicated and unfathomable. He was utterly reliant on Phameas for translation and for advice on the locals. There was no one else who could do that job, which put Phameas in a powerful position. If the Carthaginian decided to betray him or make him look like a fool, there was little he could do to prevent it. For a moment Gisgo eyed the two men with an unhappy look. But he had taken upon himself the leadership of this expedition and he could not back out now. Nothing was ever perfect and he had a job to do. He would just have to trust Phameas and judge the situation as best as he could. He had no choice.

As the warriors and mercenaries trudged across a forest clearing, heading north, Gisgo caught sight of a shepherd standing in the field surrounded by his flock of nervous, bleating sheep. The old man was clad in a simple, long white woollen cloak and he was barefoot. In his hands he was clasping a wooden staff. Eyeing the Carthaginians as they silently moved on past, the shepherd's rugged weather beaten face betrayed no emotion.

Suddenly Gisgo heard a shout. It was swiftly followed by the blast from a Celtic Carnyx - the deep mournful sound drifting away across the countryside. Up ahead, Galchobhar had come to a halt and was pointing at something in the distance. Raising his head Gisgo frowned as he spotted the circular fort perched on top of the summit of a hill, some way to the north. It looked small. Not much larger than Ictis but the site appeared to be well chosen for the high ground upon which it sat dominated the countryside. A thin solitary column of black smoke was curling into the sky from one of the buildings. Moments later an answering trumpet rang out from the hill fort.

"Phameas, walk with me," Gisgo called out.

As the Carthaginian tin merchant fell in alongside, Gisgo peered at the distant fort, gesturing with his head.

"Is that Trencrom," Gisgo said. "The hill fort where the Queen has her court. Where we are, going?"

"It is," Phameas responded. "In summer she lives there. In winter she moves to her residence at Caer Bran. Which is further to the west."

"I see," Gisgo said guardedly. "And where is Queen Talwyn's husband and his rebel army?"

"I spoke to Aed," Phameas said smoothly as the party plodded across the field towards the hill fort. "He says that the Queen's husband and his rebel forces control all the land east of here. They have set up camp at another hill fort, Carn Brea. It's about fifteen miles away over in that direction."

"And what about Aed," Gisgo said fixing his eyes on the tall man walking ahead of him. "What's his story? He seems to be sad all the time. He rarely smiles. Can we trust him?"

"Aed," Phameas exclaimed as he glanced at the man. Then he sighed. "He is a good man. Loyal. Yes we can trust him. He is a friend of Carthage and of Bodo. As to his sadness. When he was younger he lost his wife and son in an accident. The tragedy still haunts him. He feels responsible for what happened. I think he still blames himself. Bodo told me that Aed has not looked at another woman since he lost his wife."

"I understand," Gisgo muttered lowering his eyes as he remembered Gissa, his own wife. "I know how that feels like."

For a moment Gisgo remained silent. Then at last he shifted his gaze to Galchobhar who was leading the party of warriors at a brisk pace.

"And what of the Queen's army and our dashing young protector over there," Gisgo said gesturing at Galchobhar. "How many men does she command? Just so, that I know what I am dealing with."

"I would have to hazard a guess," Phameas responded, reaching up to rub his chin. "Bodo would have known everything. When I was here last the Queen could muster about a thousand fighting men. But that was before she fell out with her husband and civil war broke out. Aed says that both sides are roughly equally matched in numbers. So, I would say the Queen could probably muster four or five hundred men right now of which a hundred or so will be professional trained warriors like Galchobhar. The rest will be peasants, farmers, fishermen, craftsmen and tin miners who can be called up in an emergency. Her husband appears to have a roughly similar sized force. These islands," Phameas added. "We are on the edge of the world here. They do not support a large population. Wars here are more like a neighbourhood gang fight in Carthage. But this civil war. It's bitter. It has divided the people, families and brothers. Aed says it's the worst conflict that he has ever been involved in. He also says that there is stalemate right now. Neither the Queen or her husband have the strength to crush the other."

"No doubt," Gisgo said sourly as he fixed his eyes on the hill fort. "So, no chance then that Queen and husband can be reconciled?"

"No," Phameas said quickly shaking his head. "Aed told me that the feud between husband and wife runs deep. Queen Talwyn will not forgive this rebellion. She and her husband are stubborn like mules. She will not be satisfied until she has her husband's head on a spike and the feeling is apparently mutual."

"Right," Gisgo said. "A fight to the death then. So, what else have you managed to learn so far?"

"Well," Phameas said carefully taking a deep breath. "I know why Galchobhar has been given command of the Queen's army and why he appears so cocky and self-assured. She is sleeping with him. But Galchobhar is a brainless fool. Aed says the Queen has made it a habit of picking out young handsome men for her bed. But then eventually she gets bored of them and they are thrown out. The Queen is just using him."

For a moment Gisgo considered what had been said in silence. "What else?" he muttered at last turning to Phameas.

"A delicate matter," Phameas replied cautiously. "One that we are going to have handle with care and tact. Aed says he has the ear of the Queen as one of her closest advisers' but he is not the only adviser that she listens to. There is another. A nobleman named Morcant. He appears to be a rival of Aed's. My impression is that both of them are battling for influence and favour with the Queen. Aed says that Morcant is a man who harbours ambitions for himself. So, this is where things get tricky," Phameas added, giving Gisgo a wary glance "It's important that we always take Aed's side. That we support him. He is our true friend and an ally of Carthage. He has our interests at heart. He is our man."

"Your friend and ally," Gisgo retorted. "Why, what is wrong with Morcant? There is nothing wrong with an ambitious man. Why can we not make friends with him as well?"

"Because Sir; "Phameas said in a weary voice, "Morcant is a friend of Rome. He favours increasing trade with Rome and Massalia. Aed says Morcant is unabashedly pro-Roman. I suspect that he is going to argue against our presence here. He is going to speak out against us and cause us trouble. Now do you see what I mean about handling this with care?"

***

It was growing dark, and the moon had become visible in the evening sky. As the party began to ascend the steep slopes of the rocky hill on the final stretch towards the summit and the gate leading into the circular hill fort, Gisgo suddenly felt the wind start to pick up. Coming from the west, the cool powerful gusts had started to tug at the men's clothing and beards with playful and naughty curiosity, driving the rain into their eyes. Ahead in the fading light, the earthen embankment and the fort's wooden stockade were protected by a ditch, which gracefully curled away to disappear around the back of the hill. The settlement held a commanding position, perched on its windswept exposed summit, and as he approached Gisgo suddenly sensed that this place was old. Very old. People had occupied this spot for a very long time - lending the settlement a certain majesty. Above the gate a solitary armed lookout, his shield and spear silhouetted against the sky, was standing guard. A moment later a Celtic horn rang out, deep and long.

Following their hosts into the settlement, the Carthaginians remained silent, their subdued nature in stark contrast to the boisterous confident Britons, who now they were home, had started to call out to their kin. Coming to a halt, Gisgo turned to look around. Clustered tightly together inside the protection of their circular ramparts, the Celtic round houses, made of stone, wattle and daub with thatched conical roofs looked simple and unsophisticated. The hill fort appeared to barely hold a hundred inhabitants. Smoke was rising from holes in the roofs and a dog was straining at its leash, barking at the strangers. Beside the gate, a wooden pen enclosed a flock of sheep and goats and further away another pen contained a few cows slowly chewing grass. Coming towards him across the muddy open space carrying two buckets of water, a woman hesitated as she caught sight of him. Ignoring her Gisgo, turned to stare at the blacksmith's workshop and furnace. The blacksmith and his apprentice were hunched over their work bench. The smiths iron hammer rising and falling - creating a distinctive ringing metallic noise. Stacked in a corner of his shack was a pile of silvery white tin ingots. Sniffing the air, Gisgo caught the scent of wood smoke and the pong of human excrement. As his eyes swept across the small community, he noticed that people, women and children had emerged from the doorways of their homes and workshops and were staring back at him. But apart from the barking dog, the locals appeared to be indifferent to the arrival of the party of foreigners - as if they were used to them.

As his gaze settled upon the great hall at the centre of the hill fort, Gisgo paused. The building appeared to be larger and more opulent than the other homes and from an opening in its roof a narrow elevated wooden walk-way extended across to give direct access to the defensive ramparts.

"The Queen's hall," Phameas muttered helpfully, as he came to stand beside Gisgo, his eyes taking in the village scene.

Gisgo was about to speak when he was interrupted by Aed and Galchobhar. As the two men came up to him, Aed addressed himself to Phameas, speaking in his exotic Celtic language. The Queen's adviser looked solemn and dignified, his neck torc gleaming in the dying light.

"He says we will go and see the Queen now," Phameas translated. "Afterwards he will bring us some food and show us where we can sleep."

"Tell him that I am grateful for his hospitality," Gisgo replied glancing at Aed. "Tell him that I am impressed by the defensive qualities of this fort. His ancestors chose a good location."

As Phameas translated Aed inclined his head in a graceful appreciative gesture.

"He says Trencrom is not only a defensive post," Phameas replied. "He says that once you crossed the boundary wall and entered into his home, you are in a magical and special place whose peace and sacred tranquility must not be disturbed. For the spirits of his ancestors still live here within these boundaries. If he looks carefully he can still see them lurking in the shadows."

"My men will cause no trouble," Gisgo replied quickly, returning the polite gesture.

Scrutinizing him for a moment, Aed paused looking sombre and thoughtful. Then he spoke.

"Before we meet Queen Talwyn," Phameas translated. "Aed would like to know the nature of the business that you wish to discuss with the Queen. So that he has a chance and the time to properly advise her."

"You haven't told him?" Gisgo growled, glancing at Phameas.

"No that's your job," Phameas shot back. "I just said that we were generally interested in his tin. I kept it vague."

"Fine," Gisgo said, turning to look at Aed and then at Galchobhar who were both waiting for him to speak. It was clear who was the brains among these two. The young handsome warrior, rugged and fierce-some as he was, would not be the leader when it came to the coming negotiations. Turning his attention to Aed, Gisgo eyed him for a long moment in silence, trying to penetrate the sad mask behind which the Queen's adviser hid his thoughts. "Inform Aed," Gisgo said at last, "that I am here to ask the Queen to stop trading with Rome and Massalia. Tell him that I have come to ask her to embargo the tin trade with Rome and that I hope he will help me in this endeavour. I have heard he is a good friend of Carthage and Carthage is well known for rewarding her loyal allies."

Looking unhappy but resigned, Phameas turned to Aed and spoke and as he did Aed's reaction appeared to be negative. Frowning the tall man hesitated for a moment before turning to Gisgo with a scowl and quickly spitting out a response.

"He says he will do what he can to help us, but he is not sure that the Queen is going to like this request," Phameas replied. "The tin trade is good for his people. Barriers to trade are no good to anyone. He is not happy. I did warn you."

"We have travelled a long way to get here, and it is getting late. I would like to see the Queen," Gisgo said calmly ignoring the protest. "And when I do, I will explain to her why it is in her interests to agree."

***

Sat upon her throne, a simple straight-backed chair draped in soft animal furs, Queen Talwyn was waiting for them as Gisgo and his companions followed Aed and Galchobhar into her great hall. Carefully placing their trade goods and gifts on the floor the Carthaginians turned to look around. In the dim firelight from several burning braziers, Gisgo could see that the hall was spacious, with a massive central column holding up the roof. A small silent crowd had gathered, and the floor was richly covered in animal furs, while in a corner a ladder led up to a small secluded sleeping area beneath the roof.

Turning to the Queen, even sitting down, Gisgo could see that she was a tall woman. Around forty, she was athletically built and her long black hair was studded with colourful gleaming glass beads. Over her tunic she was wearing a long spotless white woollen cloak which was fixed near her throat with a smooth bone fibula. Her arms and fingers were adorned with rings and bronze arm bracelets engraved with swirling Celtic patterns and a golden torc gleamed around her neck. As he was led towards her, Gisgo could see she was no beauty. But there was nothing plain about her either. As the Queen coolly observed the Carthaginians, Gisgo became aware of a brooding energy and craftiness, a temper that appeared to be simmering just beneath the surface like a volcano. Immediately picking him out, as the leader the Queen's eyes turned to him and as they did he suddenly sensed her power. This was no weak-willed woman. No pretender to the throne. This was a woman firmly in charge of everything that that went on in her hall.

Lying slumped at her feet, two sleek hunting dogs had raised their heads and had turned to look at the foreigners. Standing out among the figures gathered behind their Queen, his back straight as an arrow, was an old one-armed man of around fifty. Sporting a great drooping moustache, with his spiky jet-black oiled hair the man was glaring at the party of Carthaginians with unmistakable hostility.

Calling out to the Queen, Aed was the first to speak and as he did so the Queen remained silent, listening, her eyes still firmly fixed on Gisgo, willing him to look away and show weakness.

"The one-armed man standing beside the Queen, the one with the moustache," Phameas whispered. "That's Morcant."

Remaining silent as the party of Carthaginian mercenaries halted before the throne Gisgo stared back at the Queen. Caught up in a subtle and silent battle of wills the monarch appeared to be challenging him. Trying to dominate him with her eyes alone but as he gazed at her Gisgo refused to back down.

At last Queen Talwyn spoke gracefully gesturing with her hand, and as she did Gisgo was suddenly aware that all eyes had turned to look at him.

"Queen Talwyn says we are welcome in her hall," Phameas said nervously. "She says that the traders of Carthage have always been welcome here since long before she was born."

"Tell the Queen that Carthage is always pleased to do business with her and her people," Gisgo said in a dignified manner. Then gathering himself he inclined his head to the Queen in a respectful and courteous manner. "My name is Gisgo," he continued. "I am a prince of the Massylii. Of Numidia. Like the Queen, I too am of noble blood. Tell her that we are grateful for her hospitality and that we have brought her a special gift."

And as he finished speaking Gisgo gestured for the man carrying the cage containing the two lion cubs to place it before the Queen. As the man did so a stony expectant silence descended upon the hall as all turned to stare at the cage and the blanket which hid the cubs from view. For a moment no one made a move. Then suddenly as if they had scented the two baby lions, the hunting dogs scrambled to their feet and gingerly approached the cage. An icy silence followed as the dogs sniffed the blanket and as the two sets of animals became aware of each other a little strangled warning growl escaped from the cage. As the tension started to mount, Phameas emitted a little groan of despair. The attempt to offer the gift to the Queen was in danger of going spectacularly wrong. As another warning growl seeped out from under the blanket, it was followed by a defiant hiss. Then abruptly Gisgo took a step forwards and lifted the blanket from the cage revealing the cubs. As they caught sight of the lions the hunting dogs barked and backed off, which elicited another round of feline whining and hissing.

Startled by the strange sight, for a long moment no one in the great hall said a word as all stared at the caged cubs. Then Gisgo turned to the Queen.

"Phameas. Tell the Queen that these animals we bring her are Kings and Queens in the land from where they come from," Gisgo said. "They are lords over-all. No other animal dares to attack them. No other animal hunts them. No other animal will dare take their territory from them - nor steal their kill. Tell her," Gisgo continued, "that it is the female of the species who does all the work of hunting and should be most feared. The male is bigger, but he is lazy and enjoys preening himself in the sun too much."

As Phameas began to translate, Gisgo could see that the Queen's attention was completely taken up by the cubs. Then at last she turned to Gisgo, eyeing him carefully and as she did Gisgo suddenly grinned. For a moment the Queen regarded him coolly. Then abruptly, she too broke into a pleased smile and immediately the atmosphere in the hall started to lighten.

"The Queen says the beasts you have brought her are adorable," Phameas translated, his relief plain for all to see. "She says they remind her of a cat, but larger and coarser."

"Tell her," Gisgo responded, "that these are no cats like she knows. When they are fully grown these animals are killers, man eaters. In the arena back in Carthage they are used to execute criminals. It's a horrible death, to be torn apart and eaten by one of these creatures."

Sat upon her throne Queen Talwyn remained silent and thoughtful, staring at the lion cubs as Gisgo's words were translated for her. Then gesturing for the cage to be taken away she turned her attention back to Gisgo and his band of Carthaginian mercenaries.

"The Queen says she is grateful for your gift and will find a suitable way in which to employ these fine looking creatures," Phameas said hurriedly translating as the Queen spoke. "But she is a little confused. She wants to know where Bodo is? Why has he not come to visit her this time?"

"Bodo could not make it I'm afraid," Gisgo said in a straight face. "Instead, they have sent me to do business with the Queen."

Looking disappointed at Gisgo's reply Queen Talwyn gazed back at Gisgo.

"Business?" The Queen suddenly exclaimed, using the Punic word as she arched her eyebrows.

"Yes," Gisgo nodded. "Carthage has sent me here with an official request. We wish to ask the Queen to suspend all trade with our enemies, Rome and Massalia. I know their traders frequent these islands too. We would like her to put an end to the trade in tin which she conducts with these peoples. It is a very important issue for Carthage. That is the sole reason and purpose of my visit."

As Phameas translated Gisgo carefully watched the Queen's reaction but if he had been expecting anger and hostility he was surprised by her reaction. On her throne the Queen suddenly burst out laughing.

Looking uncertain and caught off-guard Gisgo glanced at Phameas for an explanation. But he too appeared to be at a loss. Then the Queen was speaking again, her eyes smoldering with amusement.

"The Queen says that she has heard about the great war which is taking place between Rome and Carthage to the south beyond the sea," Phameas said translating in a chastened voice. "She says that the war must be going badly for us, if we have come to her with such a request."

"The war swings between victory and defeat," Gisgo said diplomatically. "But Carthage is not losing. Our great general Hannibal is most feared by Rome. None dare to fight him in battle."

"Hannibal," Queen Talwyn said carefully repeating the name before continuing in her own language.

"She says she has heard of this Hannibal," Phameas exclaimed. "She says she would like to meet him one day, to judge whether he is as great as they say he is. She wants to know if it is true that he has just one eye?"

"It's true. I was with him when he lost his eye," Gisgo replied. "It was in Italy after we had crossed mountains as high as the sky. I fought in a battle where we killed fifty thousand Romans in a single afternoon."

"And yet here you still are, asking me to ban trade with Rome," Phameas said hastily translating the Queen's mocking retort. "It does not sound like the war is going well for Carthage. It sounds like you are desperate."

"If the Queen were to agree to Carthage's request, to ban all trade with Rome and her allies," Gisgo said in a sombre voice, "we would make it worth her time. Carthage is willing to buy up all the tin that she would have normally sold to the Romans, at double the normal asking price. We will pay in silver coin and as she knows Carthaginian silver is of high quality."

"Double the normal price," Phameas said rapidly translating as the Queen leaned forwards on her throne, her eyes fixed on Gisgo. "Why not triple? Why not ten times the normal price? If she were to agree to our terms, she would offend Rome and Massalia and that would be bad for business - especially if Rome were to win the war."

"We will pay her double if she agrees to ban trade with Rome and Massalia," Gisgo said simply. "I cannot offer more. It is a good proposal."

As an awkward silence once more descended upon the great hall Gisgo stood his ground feeling slightly foolish. The Queen's reaction had unsettled him, and she had still not given him an answer to his request. At last, seated upon her throne, Queen Talwyn stirred and spoke with sudden dignity.

"Carthage has long been a friend and reliable trading partner of ours," Phameas said translating her words. "Since anyone can remember, your ships have been visiting our shores and bringing us many wonderful things. The city that was founded by Queen Dido shall always be our friend. She appreciates that you have travelled far to get here. She says she has no intention of insulting you and your men Prince Gisgo, but she is going to need some time to decide on this matter. It is a weighty decision which requires careful consideration. In the meantime, you and your men will be welcome to stay here as her guests."

Staring back at the Queen as Phameas finished speaking, Gisgo remained silent for a moment. Then gracefully he nodded his acceptance.

"The Queen is wise to take time to consider my request," Gisgo responded as he prepared to play his trump card. "We shall accept her offer to stay here as her guests. My men and I are soldiers. We are skilled in warfare - so tell the Queen, Phameas, tell her that if she agrees to my request, I shall help her defeat her husband. I and my thirty men will fight for her in battle."

Chapter Four - The People of the Horn

Standing waiting alone on the summit of the barren rocky windswept hill, Gisgo was gazing southwards. It was afternoon and in the dull sky the clouds had blocked the sun, while the cold wind moaned, tugging at his beard and toying with his cloak. From his vantage point he could see both the southern and northern coast of the peninsula, the distant sea calm and majestic. Looking grim, his eyes were fixed on the unmistakable island out in the bay. Riding at anchor at the port of Ictis, he could only make out one Carthaginian ship, the tiny speck of wood and canvas, insignificant among the vastness of the ocean that stretched away to the horizon. For a moment Gisgo's gaze lingered on the ship. Then, with a resigned sigh he turned to search the fields and forests but there was still no sign of them. Patiently, he half turned to eye the Briton hill fort, a hundred paces away, but everything appeared to be normal. The locals had been hospitable - offering him and his men a place to sleep in a barn and bringing them food and drink. But despite her generous hospitality, the wily Queen had made no response to his offer to fight for her. She had given no indication of her intentions or thoughts. The lady appeared to be keeping her options close to her chest.

Suddenly, to the south, he saw them. Hurrying across a clearing heading for the hill fort at a steady jog, carrying their shields and weapons. Grunting in relief, Gisgo watched the small party of armed men. Then, as Xenocles and his fifteen mercenaries approached Gisgo, raised his hand and called out to them. Looking perplexed but pleased to see him, the Greek mercenary returned the greeting as he and his men covered the last few yards.

"Any trouble?" Gisgo called out.

"No," Xenocles replied shaking his head. "We came as soon as we received your summons. Everything alright here?"

"Yes, the locals are friendly and hospitable," Gisgo said, turning once again to eye the hill fort. "I have met the Queen. She is going to consider our request, but it may take some time before she comes to a decision."

"Great," Xenocles said looking dubious. "By the way, Hanno sailed away this morning. He has set out for Gades. He said he is going home. I tried to convince him to stay but he was adamant that he follow his orders and return."

"I guessed as much," Gisgo said gesturing at the sea to the south. "When I got here, there was only one ship out there. It's a shame he had to leave. I could have used those marines of his, but his departure is not unexpected. It can't be helped. We'll manage."

"Maybe," Xenocles responded. "And what about Melchus? Are you sure you want to leave him alone back at Ictis. I don't trust that weasel. He is as reliable as an Athenian politician at election time. If he decides to sail away too, we will be marooned here. We will have no way of getting back home."

"I know its a risk to leave him behind," Gisgo growled. "But we don't have a choice. I can't afford to have you or any of our men keeping watch on him. I need you here. There are only thirty of us and it is his ship after all. He is the captain. But my guess is that he will not venture out onto the sea without an armed escort. Remember those Gallic pirates which we encountered. They are constantly on the lookout for our merchant ships. Melchus will be too afraid to sail without us being there to protect his sorry arse."

"If you say so," Xenocles said. "So, what's the plan?"

"The plan," Gisgo said, turning to eye the mercenaries who had gathered to rest on the rocks. "The plan is to convince the Queen to agree to our request. I have offered to fight for her. In this civil war of theirs. Against her husband."

"Fight for her?" Xenocles exclaimed looking startled. "I thought we were just here to protect the diplomats."

"Well, the situation has changed. If we need to fight for her to get an agreement then that is what we shall do," Gisgo responded. "We are all mercenaries here. We are paid to fight and against who, well it doesn't really matter does it?"

"Fair enough," Xenocles said puffing up his chest. "You are right. Against who we fight really does not matter. But there are only thirty of us. What difference can we possibly make in this civil war."

"Thirty highly experienced and trained warriors can make all the difference," Gisgo replied. "This is not the Roman army we are facing. Most of the fighting men here are just peasants. I am told that the Queen only has a hundred or so properly trained and equipped warriors. The rest are conscripts. Her husband's forces are apparently of a similar size. But remember the whole point is to get the Queen to agree to our request."

"Great, so when do we start?" Xenocles said, turning to eye the ditch and ramparts that enclosed the hill fort.

"This afternoon," Gisgo said carefully, "we will gather all our men together for a bout of training. I want to give the Queen a demonstration of our martial abilities - to impress her. So we had better make it look good."

"Impressing the ladies," Xenocles said, as he cracked a grin. "Oh boy, Gisgo. Now you are taking me back to my youth."

"Just make it look good," Gisgo shot back. "And for the gods' sake, do not mention Bodo's name. Everyone here is asking about him. They want to know why he has not come to pay them a visit. He seems to have been a popular figure. How he managed that I do not know."

"Right," Xenocles said, as his grin abruptly vanished.

Gisgo was about to say something else when he hesitated, as he suddenly caught sight of the young woman, carrying two heavy looking buckets, heading towards him from the entrance of the hill fort. The woman was accompanied by an older man clutching a wooden staff and sporting a huge white beard. As they approached Gisgo frowned - noticing that the buckets were filled with frothy milk. The woman's demure submissive expression contrasted sharply with that of her old and grizzled escort. The man was studying the mercenaries with a bleak unfriendly gaze as if he were doing something he did not agree with. Carefully placing the buckets of milk on the ground before him, the woman turned to Gisgo and spoke quickly in her own language, gesturing at the milk. For a moment Gisgo hesitated. Unsure about what the young woman wanted. Without Phameas there to translate it was impossible to know what she had said.

"I think she has brought us the milk as a refreshment," Gisgo said at last, quickly turning to his men. "So tuck in gentlemen and be sure to thank her for her kindness. A nod and a smile will do. Come on. We need to be on our best behaviour while we are guests here."

As the band of mercenaries rose to their feet and came round to inspect the buckets, Gisgo quickly glanced at the old man. The Briton's white beard was truly spectacular, the longest beard he had ever seen. But as the man boldly gazed back at him in silence, Gisgo was suddenly aware of a strong sense of disapproval.

"I get the impression he does want us here," Gisgo said speaking in Greek as he turned to Xenocles.

But at his side Xenocles did not reply - oblivious to his friend's words. His eyes were fixed on the young woman, as if he had just encountered a goddess who had enchanted him with her spell.

***

Across the barren rocky open space just outside the hill fort, the Carthaginian mercenaries had formed into fifteen pairs and were engaged in mock hand-to-hand combat, their shields and weapons clashing, their voices raised. Outside the gate a crowd of silent locals had gathered to watch the demonstration. Standing a little apart from his men, with Phameas by his side Gisgo, looked on as Xenocles put the men through their paces, shouting instructions as he moved up and down the line like the seasoned drill instructor that he was.

"You appear to have made a good impression on the Queen," Phameas said quietly without taking his eyes off the struggling, clashing mercenaries. "Aed says that you handled the meeting well. He says Queen Talwyn does not suffer fools and that she has an explosive temper. But you gave her no cause to be angry." For a moment Phameas paused. "I have conveyed to him your determination to see the embargo implemented," he added.

"And yet she has still not agreed to our request or my offer," Gisgo replied, as he turned to gaze at the Queen who was watching the exercise from the top of the walls, her long black beaded hair blowing in the wind.

"Aed says he is working on our behalf to get the Queen to agree to the trade embargo against Rome," Phameas said quietly. "He is trying to convince her that it is the right thing to do, but he needs time."

"Well, we have plenty of time," Gisgo growled.

"She has a lot on her mind," Phameas said, carefully turning to glance in the Queen's direction. "I fear that the situation is more complicated and difficult than I had expected. Aed tells me that because of the civil war, the Queen is no longer in control of all the tin mines. Her husband has taken over the mines at Gwenap and Porthtowan. He is trading his tin now through the port of Mount Badden. A rival to Ictis - situated along the coast further to the east. So even if she agreed to our request, we would only be partially embargoing Rome and Massalia. We would only be partially successful."

"So, another reason to help the Queen in her fight with her husband," Gisgo snapped. "If we can defeat him, Queen Talwyn will regain control of all the mines and our embargo will be complete. Life is about choosing sides and I have picked mine. We are going to see this through to the end."

"As you wish Sir," Phameas said, politely inclining his head.

"Xenocles," Gisgo called out, as he turned his back on his adviser. "Form the men up into a testudo and let's see what the locals make of that."

"You have got me demonstrating Roman battlefield tactics," the Greek mercenary commander complained as he came over to Gisgo. "Close quarters fighting, shield wall. All we now need is a bloody eagle standard and we could be part of the fucking Roman army."

"Does it matter," Gisgo replied with a shrug speaking in Greek. "The point is to impress the locals. Get the men into formation."

As Xenocles turned to marshal the mercenaries into their compact unit formation, their shields forming an overlapping wall and covering their heads, Gisgo strode over to the crowd of silent onlookers. Placing his hands on his hips, solemnly eyeing the crowd he patiently waiting until his men were ready. Then stooping, he picked up a pebble from the ground and turned to the onlookers holding up the stone for all to see before swiftly flinging the pebble at the testudo formation. As the stone bounced off the men's shields and clattered away, Gisgo picked up another, gesturing for the locals to do the same. Among the crowd however, the only ones to respond were the children, who after some hesitation began to pelt the stationary mercenaries with increasing confidence. Within no time, the hail of pebbles had become a deluge as the children rushed to and fro, their excited shouts drifting away across the barren hillside. Stoically standing their ground against the barrage of stones, the Carthaginian mercenaries did not move, enduring the bombardment in impressive disciplined silence.

"Forwards - at a walk," Gisgo suddenly yelled.

Immediately the thirty mercenaries began to move in formation and as the ominous looking testudo began to slowly advance towards them, like some strange-armoured beetle, the children shrieked in delight.

"Break formation - charge," Gisgo bellowed.

A moment later with a great roar the mercenaries broke apart and surged straight towards the crowd of onlookers, the ferocity and speed of their charge catching everyone by surprise and scattering the children in panic and terror. As the mercenaries rushed up, brandishing their weapons and shields, laughing and hollering at the terrified fleeing children, Gisgo smiled, and quickly clapped his hands bringing the exercise to a close. For a moment he paused, as he gazed at the locals who appeared to be impressed. Then turning to look up at the Queen who had witnessed the performance from atop of the walls, Gisgo caught her eye and took a little graceful and theatrical bow.

"Alright that's enough for the day," Gisgo called out turning to Xenocles who was loping towards him. "If we had horses, I could show our hosts some tricks, but we will just have to settle for infantry work."

"It's like working for the theatre," Xenocles exclaimed, as he came to stand beside his friend. "But actually, I think the men rather enjoyed that. Who can resist a bout of showing off. But if we are to really fight Sir. Really fight. It would be wise to know how these locals conduct their wars?"

"Oh, I would say they will not be that different to how we fight ours," Gisgo responded. "But I sense that trained and properly armed soldiers are a rare commodity around here, just like tin in Carthage or Rome."

But when Xenocles failed to respond Gisgo quickly turned to him. At his side the Greek mercenary was staring at someone in the crowd of onlookers, and as he followed his friend's gaze Gisgo recognised the young woman who had brought them the milk. Standing at her side was the older man with the impressive white beard and disapproving attitude.

"Oh, I see," Gisgo muttered, suddenly looking displeased. "Something has caught your fancy, my friend. I agree she is beautiful but that man standing beside her looks like her father. Maybe he is a Druid. He looks like a Druid. And do you really want him as your father-in-law? That man does not want us here. Can you not see. He is never going to accept you with his daughter. Think about it. Think it through Xenocles. Messing about with their women will just get us into trouble. Forget about her. The trouble she is going to cause you is not going to be worth it."

"I have never seen a woman like her before," Xenocles murmured sounding strangely detached. "Not anywhere in the world and I have been everywhere."

***

The crowd had started to disperse and return to their work while the mercenaries were sitting about resting, when Phameas suddenly gave Gisgo a warning nudge in his side.

"Trouble," the Carthaginian tin merchant muttered. Turning, Gisgo caught sight of a one-armed man with a great drooping moustache and carefully oiled spiky hair coming towards him.

As Morcant approached, Gisgo sized him up, taking in every detail.

"Prince Gisgo of the Massylii, of Numidia," Morcant said and to Gisgo's astonishment the man was speaking in good clear Greek. "You are far from home but I must congratulate you and your men. That was a fine martial performance that you laid on for us just now. I am sure that Queen Talwyn will be suitably impressed. That was the purpose of the exercise was it not? To impress my Queen?"

"It was," Gisgo said guardedly, taken aback by the man's approach.

For a moment Morcant paused as he eyed Gisgo in an easy composed manner, intelligence blazing from his eyes. "Most foreigners when they meet me for the first time want to know two things," Morcant continued. "How I come to speak such good Greek and how did I lose that arm. Well Prince Gisgo, you may believe that you have reached the edge of the earth, but even here in sight of the world ocean there are men of learning and skill. As for my arm, it withered and died when I was child. Some say that I am cursed by the god's but I think I was blessed. The loss of an arm turned me to other more important matters, than tin mining and soldiering. It forced me to get an education. When I was younger I spent some time in Massalia where I learned to read and write like the Greeks do. I have done very well out of that education. Very well indeed."

"I am sure you have," Gisgo responded in Greek. "Was there something that you wanted to discuss with me?"

"Yes. Your man," Morcant exclaimed, gesturing at Xenocles. "From his appearance and dress, I would say he was a Spartan, a mercenary like yourself. I prefer the Athenian school myself, but I must give you a word of warning and friendly advice. People have noticed. The woman he appears to have taken a fancy too. Her father, the man with the white beard, is our Druid, a most learned and respected man in our community. Guardian of our ancient laws and all our knowledge. Conduit between the gods and man. He has influence with the Queen too. But he does not like foreigners or your gods. He hates them in fact. He fears that your gods will rival our own and lead us astray. If he had his way he would ban all foreigners from coming him. He would end the tin trade completely. Fortunately for you and me Queen Talwyn does not agree." For a moment Morcant paused carefully eyeing Gisgo. "So, you must understand," he continued at last, "that our druid will never agree to match his daughter to your man. There is going to be trouble for you if your friend insists on following his fancy. I just thought I should warn you. No one likes a diplomatic incident. Especially after your gallant display just now."

"My men will cause no trouble," Gisgo replied, quickly folding his arms across his chest. "But thank you for the advice."

Pausing again, Morcant turned to give Phameas a sudden hostile look before turning his attention back to Gisgo.

"He does not speak Greek does he," Morcant said gesturing at Phameas. "Aed's friend," he added with sudden contempt. "How ironic that a translator does not understand what we are talking about. But Greek is the language of the world. Would you not agree?"

"It is widely spoken yes," Gisgo conceded.

"Tin is the only reason why foreigners come to these shores," Morcant continued, as he studied Gisgo. "Without tin no one would ever bother coming here and we would be left in peace. You are far from home Prince Gisgo. You must be anxious to conclude your business and get home before the winter storms make the sea voyage impossible. Which is soon. The weather and climate here is not like what you are accustomed to. So I have a proposal for you. I am prepared to pay you and your men in tin ingots if you were to leave right now and not come back. You will find me a generous man."

"You want to pay me to leave?" Gisgo responded raising his eyebrows. "In my native language that is called bribery."

"Call it what you like," Morcant replied. "But I am willing to pay if you leave right now and do not bother my Queen again with your silly requests. My people do not need a trade embargo against Rome and Massalia. It would be bad for business. Bad for everyone involved. So, take my deal and sail away while you still can. It is a fair offer but."

"No," Gisgo said firmly shaking his head. "You misjudge me. I have not come here to enrich myself, so I am afraid that I will not be taking up your offer. The Queen will come round to my request. The trade embargo against Rome will be implemented. That is my answer to you."

Looking displeased, Morcant took a deep breath, sucking the air into his lungs. For a moment he looked away with a pained expression, before he turned his eyes back towards Gisgo.

"That was the wrong answer Prince Gisgo," Morcant snapped. "You should know that this is not going to end well for you and your men. You have chosen badly. Aed will not help you. Your mission is not going to succeed. You should have taken my offer."

Chapter Five - Unorthodox Methods

Using a spoon to eat his porridge and milk breakfast, Gisgo stood outside the barn in which he and his men had been billeted, gazing at one of his men who was sitting on a stool receiving a full face tattoo from a local. It was morning and in the blue skies the sun had reappeared, radiant and glorious. Around him the people of the hill fort were going about their daily routines. Inside his workshop, the blacksmith was taking receipt of a fresh cart load of tin ore from a miner, whilst his apprentice was readying the ore to be smelted and turned into ingots of pure tin. The Celts appeared to be arguing about something. Shifting his gaze to one of the nearby round houses, Gisgo's eyes settled on an aged man, too old to work, who was sat on the ground hunched over a board game, which he was playing with one of the Carthaginian mercenaries. The game appeared to be about strategy and its chequered surface and simple coloured glass counters needed no common language in order to play. For a while, as he ate his breakfast, Gisgo stared at the players with an absentminded look. Then finishing his food, he quickly slipped his spoon back into his tunic and turned to survey the nearby cattle pen where the women were milking the cows. Stashed away nearby, were some amphorae and as he studied them a sombre resigned look appeared on Gisgo's face. The pottery was not of Punic origin. It appeared to be of a Greek design. For a moment Gisgo's eyes lingered. There had been other indications too that the people of the horn had extensive trade contacts with the Greek colonists in Massalia. The wine they had been given the other day had come from Massalia. In the Queen's hall he had noticed a hand mirror that was of a Greek design and the blacksmith had what appeared to be Roman knives packed away in the back of his workshop.

"Morning," Xenocles muttered as he emerged from the barn and came to stand beside Gisgo - idly turning to look around at the hill fort.

"Have you noticed," Gisgo said, gesturing at the amphorae. "How so much of the foreign stuff in this place here comes from Massalia. Everywhere I look I can see imported Greek shit. The Massaliots appear to be edging our merchants out of the market. But how? They must be better negotiators, for their goods are no better than ours."

"Yes, I noticed," Xenocles replied, with an unconcerned yawn. "But there is nothing wrong with Greek shit. I am Greek. Doesn't it just mean that the Punic traders need to up their game?"

"You are missing the point. Don't you see. It means that the Queen has a difficult decision to make," Gisgo retorted with a concerned look. "If she grants our request and cuts trade with Rome and Massalia she will be halting the flow of these trade goods. Her people will not be happy about that. We need to be aware of such things. Her problems are our problems and if we solve them for her - we win. That is how we are going to succeed. By helping her win."

"If you say so boss," Xenocles said, sounding a little disinterested.

Glancing at his friend Gisgo remained silent for a moment.

"I need to speak to you about that woman you have taken a fancy to," Gisgo said at last in a sober voice. "Your interest in her has been noticed. I have received a warning - telling you to back off. She is going to be trouble Xenocles. We do have enemies here in this place. People who don't want us here. They could use this against us. I know it. You know it. Everyone knows it. You need to back off. Don't make me order you to do so. But I can't afford any incidents that will undermine our position."

"A warning," Xenocles said, raising his eyebrows. "Wow. Lest I remind you Gisgo," Xenocles added in a changed voice. "We are here precisely because you couldn't keep your hands off a woman. And we are not going home any time soon because you are so anxious to please another woman. In fact, it seems everything we do is being determined and controlled by women. Well, if that is to be our fate, then so be it. But do not lecture me Sir on women. What I do with them is none of your or anyone else's goddamn business."

And with an angry scowl Xenocles stomped away.

Watching the Greek mercenary depart, Gisgo looked surprised. Then he turned to look away. It appeared that he had underestimated his friend's determination and the depth of his feelings for the woman. But Xenocles's anger was always skin deep. It would not last.

Suddenly a furious scream rent the hill fort, making the hair on Gisgo's neck stand up. Hurriedly, looking alarmed, he turned to stare in the direction from which the noise had come. For a moment all remained silent. Then once again the angry yelling and screaming erupted. It was coming from the Queen's hall. Standing frozen to the ground, dread building in his stomach, Gisgo was unable to move. What was this? What was going on? A moment later a man appeared, hastening out of the great hall, making straight for the gate, his face pale and drained, his arm shaking uncontrollably. He was followed out of the hall by a torrent of angry words. As he stared at the miserable figure hurrying away, Gisgo suddenly remembered what Phameas had told him about the Queen's famous temper. The poor man must have incurred the Queen's wrath for some reason. A moment later Queen Talwyn appeared on the narrow-elevated walkway, stomping down it in a flagrant rage, her long black hair blowing in the cool breeze. As she reached the ramparts, she turned to gaze to the east in the direction of her husband's encampment at the hill fort of Carn Brea.

"Don't ask," Phameas said quickly, shaking his head as he came over to Gisgo. "You don't want to be on receiving end of the Queen's temper. I have seen grown men wilt before her. Whatever that poor soul did to anger her, he is not going to forget it for a very long time."

"Right," Gisgo replied, as he stared at the Queen, standing alone atop of the embankment gazing out across the countryside. "Any progress on our case. What does Aed say?"

"Nothing. No more progress at this point," Phameas said with a sigh. "He is working on it. We need to be patient. But there is something else you need to know. We are under time pressure. If we leave it too late, the weather will prevent us from returning to Gades. We will be trapped here for the winter, at least until spring. I thought you should know."

"Understood," Gisgo grunted. "And Morcant? What is he up to? I don't think our conversation went very well. He tried to bribe me."

"Morcant appears to be biding his time," Phameas said, carefully turning to look around as if he was afraid someone would be listening in. "He is an ambitious man. He will be working to a plan. He seems to be waiting for something, but what I don't know. Aed says that Morcant is advising the Queen to refuse our request. He argues that the people will suffer from a trade embargo against Rome. He is complicating matters and making her decision harder than it need be. I believe that he is stalling her."

"Well that was to be expected," Gisgo retorted. "The question is why? What is he hoping for? How long can he keep stalling her?"

"Who knows?" Phameas said suddenly looking glum. "But maybe he is putting time pressure on us by threatening to keep us here for the winter. Maybe he hopes that the fear of getting trapped here will cause us to leave before the winter storms arrive. It's cunning."

"I want you to keep an eye on that man," Gisgo said quietly. "I want to know everything he is up to. A man like that. Intelligent, wealthy, corrupt and ambitious. I have seen his kind before. He's dangerous."

"I will do my best Sir," Phameas said, looking grave. "But just so that you know. It is still not too late to head for home while we still can. You do not want to get caught here in winter. Its brutal. Cold, wet and dark, unlike anything you have experienced. I know Melchus is keen to sail as soon as possible. No offence Sir but we do know these waters much better than you do. Time is not on our side. Soon you will have to make the decision whether we stay or go."

Gisgo was about to respond when a sudden warning shout from the sentry on guard duty above the entrance gate caught his attention. Turning in that direction, a moment a later a solitary horseman came galloping through the gate and into the hill fort enclosure. The newcomer looked to be in a state of alarm and was frantically crying out in his native language, and as he did a sudden tension seized the locals. Up on the ramparts Queen Talwyn had wrenched her eyes away from the distant hill and was staring at the horseman. Then she was shouting at her people and hurrying back along the elevated walkway towards her hall. Around him, Gisgo was suddenly aware of a new urgency among the populace as they started to rush about, hurriedly finishing their tasks and jobs.

"What the fuck is going on?" Gisgo muttered.

At his side, Phameas did not immediately reply - peering at the rider. Then the Carthaginian tin merchant swore softly to himself, a blush suddenly spreading across his cheeks.

"Trouble Sir," Phameas gasped. "If that scout's right, then the Queen's husband is on the march with his army. They are heading straight for us here at Trencrom. It looks like there is going to be a fight."

"I am not sure we are invited Sir," Phameas protested in vain as Gisgo barged into the Queen's hall. "This is her hall. It's her war."

Ignoring the Carthaginian tin merchant, Gisgo caught sight of Queen Talwyn standing surrounded by a group of men. They appeared to be holding an urgent animated discussion. Recognising Aed, Morcant and Galchobhar among them, Gisgo boldly strode towards the group followed by a reluctant Phameas. But as he approached, an angry scowl appeared on Galchobhar's face and raising his hand the handsome warrior swiftly moved to block Gisgo's path, spitting out a few words in his own language.

"He says we should leave," Phameas groaned. "He says that this is a "Council of War" and we have no business being here. We are foreigners. This fight does not concern us. I did warn you."

"Tell the Queen," Gisgo retorted, his eyes seeking her out, "that my offer still stands. My men and I are prepared to fight for her. Tell her Phameas, that she needs all the help she can get."

But as Phameas translated Galchobhar stood his ground, shaking his head.

"Galchobhar says we should leave," Phameas replied. "He says that he and his men can handle any threats to the hill fort. He does not need us."

"I am not leaving until the Queen has given me her answer," Gisgo said stubbornly, folding his arms across his chest.

As a miserable looking Phameas started to translate, Morcant suddenly took a step forwards, his eyes blazing and a stream of words followed, none of which sounded very friendly.

"Morcant says we are to blame for this emergency," Phameas said, suddenly sounding indignant. "He says the Queen's husband has made his move now because he has heard about our arrival. He says, we have forced him to act. To bring his men to Trencrom. He blames us Sir for this emergency."

Ignoring the two hostile looking men, Gisgo's eyes were fixed firmly on the Queen. Studying him with her dark impenetrable eyes, Queen Talwyn's face looked like thunder, fearless and angry, but nevertheless she was keeping a tight control on her emotions. As a tense silence descended upon the great hall and all waited for her reaction, Gisgo was suddenly aware he was once again caught up in a silent battle of wills with the Queen. A battle to dominate him, as if she wished to conquer his spirit. Then at last the Queen spoke, her words arriving like the lashes of a whip slicing through the air.

"Queen Talwyn says she will accept your offer to fight for her," Phameas exclaimed. "She is grateful for your help."

But before Gisgo had a chance to respond, a chastened looking Galchobhar intervened.

"Galchobhar says if that is the Queen's wish, then so be it," Phameas translated hastily. "But he is in command of the Queen's army and if we are to join the fight you Gisgo and your men will fall under his command. He is the Queen's leading warrior. He will lead the fight. You will obey his orders."

Staring at the Queen, Gisgo saw that she appeared to be in agreement leaving him with little choice. For a moment he hesitated. Then turning to Galchobhar, Gisgo gracefully indicated his acceptance.

"Fine. We will follow the young warrior's orders," Gisgo said. "Now ask him Phameas, how many men do we have for the defence of the fort? How many warriors will be accompanying her husband? What are we going to be up against and what is the plan?"

As Phameas translated, Galchobhar eyed Gisgo with a wary but satisfied look before responding in his own language.

"He says he can have seventy or so warriors here before dark," Phameas muttered. "As for the Queen's husband. The scout says he is on march, with around three hundred men. He expects them to get here before nightfall."

"And then what?" Gisgo snapped, still eyeing Galchobhar.

Across from Gisgo the young warrior shrugged, his rugged face unconcerned.

"Galchobhar says," Phameas translated," that the enemy will most likely besiege the fort. They do not have the strength to get over the walls, even with three hundred men. But there is plenty of food here and the fort has its own water supply so a siege does not concern him. The enemy will run out of supplies long before we do. He intends to sit it out Sir."

"I thought the Queen could rely on up to four or five hundred fighting men," Gisgo said. "That is what I was told."

Watching him Galchobhar nodded showing a sudden and unexpected restraint. "Yes, it is true that we have more men," Phameas translated. "But if he calls everyone to Trencrom, it will leave all the other settlements undefended. That would be a mistake. It is just possible that the Queen's husband is hoping we do just that by coming here and forcing a confrontation. If the rebels were to manage to capture Ictis it would cut off all our trade. We would be completely isolated."

For a moment Gisgo did not reply, as he studied the young warrior with a new found appreciation.

"Looks like I may have underestimated our young commander here," he muttered at last.

In the evening sky, the sun was fast sinking below the western horizon, a red ball in a darkening world. Beyond the defensive embankment and ditch that ringed the hill fort, the rebels, bunched together in groups, were standing about, strung out in a ragged line that partially encircled the settlement. The Briton's round shield, spears, axes and swords gleamed in the dying light, while the cool breeze tugged at their rugged beards, cloaks and leather body armour. No one spoke as the two sides eyed each other in sullen bitter silence. Standing massed upon the ramparts of their hill fort, the defenders appeared to comprise everyone capable of holding a weapon. For among the seasoned battle-hardened warriors were women, young boys and old grizzled men. Their weathered faces, stoic and implacable, as they prepared to defend their families, homes and lives. The defenders were armed with a motley assortment of weapons, many of them tools of trade, while some of the children only had stones to throw. Standing beside the Queen and her bodyguard, Gisgo peered at the rebels with a sombre expression. The scout had been right about their numbers he thought. There had to be three hundred of them at least, but only a handful of horsemen and no artillery. Unlike the defenders, the rebels however appeared to all be men of fighting age and well-armed.

Down below, inside the enclosure, hidden from view, Xenocles and the thirty Carthaginian mercenaries were standing about massed near to the gate, armed and ready for a fight. For now, it would be wise, he had argued, not to reveal the defenders full strength and to his surprise Galchobhar had readily agreed. Glancing at the young warrior who was standing near to the Queen, Gisgo carefully reached up to rub his beard in approval. Galchobhar was proving to be more competent than he had been led to believe, which was a pleasant surprise.

Suddenly a figure on horseback, holding up a Celtic war banner, broke away from the rebel lines and urged his horse towards the hill fort. Halting some distance away, the solitary man paused for a moment, as his gaze swept across the ranks of the defenders up on the wall, before calling out to them - his words drifting away across the barren hillside. For a moment he received no reply. Then nearby, Queen Talwyn stirred, her face flush with anger. Wearing a magnificent coat of armour, clutching an axe in her hand, the Queen looked clad for war, her head adorned by a splendid double horned helmet made of bronze. As she cried out in response, the contempt in her voice was clear to all.

"What's she saying?" Gisgo said turning to Phameas, who was standing at his side.

"The horseman over there," Phameas replied, "that is her husband. He is demanding that the Queen send a champion to fight him in hand-to-hand combat. So that they may decide who rules this land once and for all. But the Queen is having none of it. She says, she is the legitimate ruler and that her husband is a maggot who is going to pay for his treachery."

Beyond the ramparts and ditch, the warrior on his horse appeared to have got the message for he'd fallen silent, his eyes still fixed on the Queen. Then with a little contemptuous gesture, he turned his horse around and rode back to his men with the Queen's furious insults pursuing him all the way.

As he looked on, Gisgo could see that the rebels appeared to be making no preparations to assault the hill fort. Instead, as their leader returned to their ranks the warriors began to settle down for the night. Gathering together in their clan groups to prepare an evening meal.

"Looks like it's going to be a siege then," Gisgo muttered.

Along the wall to either side of him, the defenders too seemed to have come to that conclusion, for the women and young boys had started to slip away back to their homes in the settlement. Watching them go and sensing the tension starting to dissipate, Gisgo suddenly looked thoughtful. When at last only the Queen and her warriors remained standing up on the embankment, Gisgo took a step forwards and reached out to tug at Galchobhar's tunic, catching his attention.

"Listen," Gisgo said, fixing the young warrior with an earnest look. "I have an idea. It's unorthodox but it could work. It's one of Hannibal's favourite tactics. Hear me out, will you."

As Phameas hurriedly translated, Galchobhar studied Gisgo, listening in wary but respectful silence. The young warrior too appeared to be on a steep learning curve when it came to Gisgo and his Carthaginian mercenaries. Showing that he was willing to listen and learn. Then, as Phameas finished translating, Gisgo gave Galchobhar an encouraging grin and after a moment's hesitation, the warrior's face suddenly cracked into a reciprocal smile before he spoke a few words.

"He says he likes the idea," Phameas said, raising his eyebrows in surprise. "It's bold and it could work. But he will lead. He will show you, Carthaginian, how it will be done."

***

It was dark as the gate creaked open and the band of Carthaginian mercenaries and Celts quietly started to slip out of the hill fort heading straight for the enemy campfires that dotted the barren hill side. In the night, around them all was quiet and peaceful, except for the distant howl of a lone wolf. In the sky, the moon and innumerable stars were out twinkling and gleaming with eager anticipation, like spectators in the arena. On either side of the gate, up on the ramparts, two burning braziers were sending clouds of red sparks shooting into the darkness. Standing there too, hidden in the darkness, Queen Talwyn was looking on, silently waiting for the fight to start. Clutching his Roman short sword and a shield, Gisgo led his men through the darkness towards the enemy campfires. The soft patter and crunch of the mercenaries' boots on the ground sounded horribly loud. The rebels however, appeared to be asleep, as he hoped they would be, for from the darkness no warning cry came. Ahead of him Galchobhar and twenty of his warriors were bunched together, holding their weapons in their hands as they fearlessly closed in on the enemy. The warriors were sporting pieces of white linen tied around their heads and helmets, to identify them as friendly to the Carthaginian mercenaries. Still the rebel sentries had not spotted them. Feeling his heart thumping away in his chest, Gisgo strained his eyes and ears. He was not used to fighting on foot, preferring to be on a horse, but it could not be helped. If the sentries did not spot them soon, the snatch squad would have a real chance. They would be able to fall on the enemy and catch them completely by surprise.

Closing the distance, the Celts and Carthaginian mercenaries came on with quiet murderous intent. Suddenly a startled shout rent the night as they were finally spotted. Wasting no time, Galchobhar's men raised a roar and charged, surging out of the darkness and into the flickering light of the enemy encampment, their weapons thrusting, hacking, and slashing about in frantic murderous activity.

"Find the Queen's husband," Gisgo bellowed as he too leapt forwards. "Ten silver coins for the man who cuts him down."

Rushing into the enemy camp, his men needed no further encouragement. As a startled Celt staggered to his feet, Gisgo swiftly caught him, driving his sword straight through the man's neck. Then he was kicking another man to the ground, before finishing him off, brutally stabbing him with his sword, which sent a spurt of blood arching into the air and splattering across his face. Straightening up, Gisgo gasped for breath, wiping the blood away as he hurriedly turned to look around. His plan appeared to be working. The snatch party appeared to have caught the rebels completely by surprise. Around him in the darkness and flickering fire light, a confused mass of brawling men were rushing about, screaming and shrieking, as they hacked, bludgeoned and cut each other to death. But where was the Queen's husband? The target of his decapitation strategy. Catching sight of one of his men who appeared to have got into trouble, taking on two rebels, Gisgo sprang to his aid, catching one of the Celts off-guard, and repeatedly stabbing the man in his back until he slid to the ground with a soft groan and his colleague abruptly turned and fled into the darkness. Where was the Queen's husband? Frantically Gisgo turned to look around. But in the swirling confusion and chaos it was hard to even pick out his own men, let alone identify their target. Swearing out loud in frustration Gisgo brought his boot down on a wounded man's neck, breaking it with a horrible cracking noise. His plan relied on speed and surprise, but once that had been achieved they could not remain here for long. The rebels massively outnumbered him and Galchobhar's small band of warriors. They had to find the rebel leader and quickly, before they would be overwhelmed - but where was he?

Suddenly Gisgo heard a shouted cry rising above the confused din and as he did, he frowned. It was the agreed signal word to retreat. Galchobhar was telling his men to fall back to the hill fort. The night assault was over. Had they already succeeded and killed the enemy leader?

"Back," Gisgo roared. "Back to the fort men. Retreat."

Falling back through the darkness towards the two burning braziers that indicated where the gate was, Gisgo continued to cry out to his men, guiding them, letting them know where he was. Around him he heard muffled voices, swearing and scampering feet but in the darkness, it was impossible to see whether he had left anyone behind. As he made it back to the gate, he suddenly caught sight of Xenocles. His friend had suffered a nasty cut to his forehead but otherwise he appeared to be unscathed. Standing by the gate holding his bloodied sword, Xenocles seemed to be counting the mercenaries as they appeared from out of the darkness - rushing back to the safety of the hill fort.

"Where is Galchobhar?" Gisgo shouted, as he strode the last few yards towards Xenocles. But in response the Greek mercenary just shrugged. Ignoring Gisgo, he grimly peered into the darkness in the direction of the enemy campfires, his lips moving silently as he counted.

Swearing softly, Gisgo came to stand beside his friend, his chest heaving, his face damp with sweat and someone else's blood. The rebels seemed not to have pursued the attackers. Across the dark hillside the night was still rent by shrieks and confused hollering, but there was no sign of a coordinated counter attack. The rebels must still be reeling from the shock of the surprise night time assault. He and his men seemed to have got away. Suddenly from out of the gloom, Gisgo caught sight of Galchobhar lumbering towards the gate, supporting a wounded comrade, whose arm was slung over the warrior's shoulders. The wounded man looked in a bad way, his cloak stained with blood from multiple wounds and as he staggered up, Galchobhar's face looked resigned.

"The Queen's husband," Gisgo cried out. "Did we get him. Did we kill him?"

But as Galchobhar limped past supporting his wounded comrade the young warrior said nothing.

"Twenty-nine," Xenocles called out at last as he came over to Gisgo. "I count twenty-nine of our men back. One still missing Sir."

Taking a deep breath Gisgo turned to peer into the darkness at the enemy campfires as the band of Celts around him hurriedly started to close the gate. There was no chance of finding out what had become of the missing man. There was nothing he could do about that.

"Shit," Gisgo swore as the gate crashed shut behind him. "Shit. The Queen's husband. The target. I don't think we got the bastard. We failed."

***

Dawn had come and with it clouds of eerie swirling mist were drifting across the barren rocky hillside, like ghosts, shrouding the horizon. In the growing light however, Gisgo could see that the rebels had gone, abandoning their camp, leaving only the blackened ashes of their campfires. They had even taken their dead with them. Standing upon the walls of the hill fort, together with Galchobhar and a few of his warriors, Gisgo looked tired, his cloak wrapped around his body, his hand resting on the hilt of his sword. At his side Galchobhar looked pensive, his rugged features neither gloomy nor elated. He'd not needed Phameas's help to understand the young warrior, Gisgo thought, when he'd asked him again whether they had managed to kill the Queen's husband. Galchobhar had seemed to understand, and the answer had been a shrug - he didn't know.

A moment later a young solitary warrior, bare chested and sporting his tattoos, appeared from out of the mist, jogging back to the section of the wall upon which Gisgo and the others were standing. As the man came to a halt beside the ditch that encircled the hill fort, he shook his head calling out to Galchobhar in his native language. For a moment Gisgo eyed the man. The warrior appeared to be confirming that the enemy had indeed gone.

"It was worth a try," Gisgo said turning to Galchobhar. "We forced them to retreat. That is good news. Now they will respect us."

Turning to glance at him, Galchobhar paused as he seemed to understand the gist of what Gisgo was saying, if not the actual words. Then he nodded before silently drawing a finger across his throat and somberly shaking his head. Gisgo was about to speak again when he suddenly caught sight of Queen Talwyn striding towards him down the walkway. The Queen was still clad for battle, wearing her magnificent two horned helmet, her battle-axe dangling from her belt. She was accompanied by Aed and Phameas, both of whom were looking triumphant.

Fixing her dark smouldering eyes upon Gisgo, Queen Talwyn eyed him in silence for a moment before addressing him.

"The Queen has come to decision," Phameas translated in a hurried voice. "She says that she is pleased by the work you did last night. She says her enemy may have escaped, but that we have hurt him. She says she has a proposal for you. It is her intention to settle this civil war and seek out her enemy in a decisive battle. She is mustering all her warriors and tomorrow-afternoon, she will ride out to confront the rebels. If they agree - there is going to be a battle. Queen Talwyn says she will agree to our request and terms to embargo the trade in tin with Rome and her allies. But on condition that you and your men help her defeat her husband once and for all. She wants to know what your answer is, Sir?"

Chapter Six - Motive

Leaning back against the barn wall, Gisgo watched his men as they sat about on the ground in small quiet groups - tending to their bruises, scrapes and cuts. It was evening, and in the centre of the barn a fire was crackling filling the space with light and warmth, its smoke drifting up and away through a smoke hole in the roof. The subdued mercenaries were carefully preparing themselves for the coming battle that was going to take place tomorrow. In a corner, four mercenaries were kneeling around the blanket covered corpse of their comrade, quietly and reverently performing the last respectful funeral rites. For a while Gisgo gazed at the men as they said goodbye to their friend. They had found the body of their missing colleague that afternoon, badly mutilated, left behind by the rebels on purpose - as a warning of what was to come.

Moving about among the Carthaginian mercenaries, the young woman was silently handing out pieces of coarse dark bread and filling the men's cups with milk. Her father, the tribal Druid and her chaperone was sat on a stool, beside the door gazing at the foreigners with a bleak unwelcoming expression; his staff balanced across his knees. The man must be hating this, Gisgo thought, as he eyed the Druid. Being forced to spend time with foreigners whom he despised and hated. All to protect his daughter's virtue. It had to be awful. Had Queen Talwyn made him do this on purpose? It would be like her to do so. To force him to submit to her will. To show the revered holy man who was really in-charge?

Shifting his attention to the woman Gisgo's eyes lingered. The girl, he had learned, was the Queen's handmaiden and she was barely eighteen summers old. Noticing Xenocles, Gisgo drew a deep unhappy breath as he saw the way in which the Greek mercenary commander was staring at the woman. His friend appeared not to have heeded his demand to back off and his interest in the girl was painfully obvious for all to see.

And to his horror the interest seemed to be reciprocated, for as she went about her task now and then the girl would slip a surreptitious glance in Xenocles's direction as if she was checking him out.

Abruptly Gisgo turned his head as Galchobhar entered the barn, the flickering light illuminating his rugged features and long braided hair. Without saying a word, the young warrior came to stand beside Gisgo, taking his time to look around at the mercenaries. Then carefully he pulled a gleaming knife from his belt and examined it for a moment, fondly running his fingers across the iron and the beautifully decorated handle. Then to Gisgo's surprise he offered the weapon to him, speaking a few words as he did. Hesitating Gisgo gazed at the knife. It looked like a finely crafted weapon, made by an expert blacksmith with a carved bone handle. Galchobhar appeared to want him to have it. Accepting the weapon, Gisgo frowned. Then pulling his broad bladed Roman pugio knife from his belt, Gisgo offered his own knife to the Celt in exchange. Taking the pugio knife, Galchobhar carefully turned the Roman blade over in his hand before looking up at Gisgo with a pleased grin and a short nod.

"Looks like you have made a new friend Sir," one of the mercenaries called out as the man observed the exchange.

"Maybe," Gisgo replied as he examined the Celtic knife again, before slipping it into his belt. "Get some rest boys. Tomorrow is going to be a long day."

Casting his eyes around the barn, Gisgo noticed that the Druid, sat upon his stool beside the door, appeared to have nodded off, for his eyes were closed and his head was leaning back against the wall. Then Gisgo froze. Where was the Queen's handmaiden? She had been here a moment ago but now she was not. The young woman had gone - and so had Xenocles. Hurriedly, with mounting alarm, Gisgo turned to look around but there was no sign of his friend or the young woman. The two of them were no longer in the barn.

"Oh shit," Gisgo murmured as he took a step-forwards.

But before he could do anything else a sudden cry of alarm and panic shattered the tranquil evening. It had come from outside the barn. The cry was swiftly followed by others, the alarm and urgency clear to all and, as he heard them, Galchobhar's face went pale and he immediately bolted for the door.

"What's going on? Are we under attack?" Gisgo called out, as he nearly collided with Phameas at the entrance to the barn.

Outside in the dark evening sky, among the cluster of thatched Celtic round houses all appeared to be peaceful, but at the entrance to the Queen's hall people seemed to be in a panic.

"The Queen," Phameas gasped as if he had been running. "She has been taken ill. She is in a very bad way. She may not make it through the night."

"What?" Gisgo exclaimed, looking startled.

A moment later the Druid went rushing past, heading for the Queen's hall.

"She's become very ill," Phameas panted, catching his breath. "That's all I know. The healer is with her now, trying to save her life."

Staring back at Phameas in shock, Gisgo was unable to say anything for a moment. Then pushing past the Carthaginian tin merchant, he was off - heading for the Queen's-hall at a half run. As he entered the hall, which was lit by flickering braziers, he saw that a group of worried looking men had already assembled. Among them he recognised Aed and Morcant. Standing guard outside a curtained off area at the back, Galchobhar appeared not to be letting anyone pass. None it seemed were allowed to see the Queen. The young warrior's face looked ashen but determined, his hand resting on the hilt of his sword and there was no doubting his intention to use it on any who disobeyed. From behind the curtain, Gisgo could hear groaning and sputtering as if someone was being violently sick.

"Will she live?" Gisgo snapped in Greek as he marched up to the group with Phameas trailing. "Will the Queen survive?"

"Her life hangs in the balance," Morcant replied, speaking in Greek, looking sombre as he detached himself from the group and came towards Gisgo. "The healer and our Druid are with her now. They are doing everything they can. Let them do their job. There is nothing else we can do right now. If the Queen makes it through the night, her chances will improve. That's all we know."

For a moment Gisgo said nothing, as he turned to stare at the curtain that hid the Queen from view. Then he turned to Morcant with an icy look.

"What happened?" Gisgo snapped.

"Is it not perfectly clear to you," Morcant retorted looking troubled. "The Queen has been poisoned. Someone poisoned her. Someone here does not want our dear Queen to live."

Swearing softly to himself, Gisgo looked away. Then swiftly his eyes returned to Morcant.

"You are saying that this is her husband's doing. But how? How would he be able to get so close to the Queen. Did she not take precautions? Was she not aware that this could happen?"

"Of course, we took precautions," Morcant replied. "But somehow someone managed to get through to her."

"Who? Who would do such a thing?" Gisgo said quickly. "Was it you? Was it you Morcant who poisoned the Queen?"

"Careful, Prince Gisgo," Morcant retorted his face darkening. "You are a guest here and an unwelcome one at that. You do not get to make accusations in the Queen's-hall. What happens here is none of your business and believe it or not I am not your worst enemy here. Our Druid would see you all shackled and thrown into the sea, if he had his way. But to answer your question. No, I did not poison the Queen. I may be many things, but I am not an assassin. I serve my Queen loyally and faithfully. It was not me."

"So, who?" Gisgo replied, lowering his voice as he turned to stare at the group of worried looking men hanging about near to the curtain that separated them from their Queen.

"I don't know for sure," Morcant replied grimly as he joined Gisgo in gazing at the men. "We must be careful about tossing around accusations before we have evidence. It will be a disaster if the Queen dies. You need to look for a motive. Who would want the Queen dead and why? All I know is that Aed was the last to see the Queen before she fell ill. He is her food taster. He checks her food, and it was he who brought the Queen her food tonight, and he was alone when he did. The cook has confirmed it already. So Aed could have slipped the poison into her food. He alone had the opportunity. He must be the prime suspect."

Looking troubled, Gisgo took a deep breath.

"Aed," he muttered. "Why would he want to murder his own Queen. I don't understand. What is his motive?"

For a moment Morcant did not reply as he shot Phameas a little contemptuous glance.

"Your friend did not tell you," Morcant responded raising his eyebrows. "Really. I am surprised. Well then let me tell you

Prince Gisgo. Aed has a good motive. Years ago, he lost his wife and son. Some say it was accident. Others claim that Queen Talwyn was responsible for their deaths. The truth has never come out about what happened on that day, but it is possible that Aed believes the Queen was responsible, and that killing her is an act of revenge."

Standing beside Morcant, Gisgo looked dubious. "But why wait until today," he exclaimed. "Why now just before we are to fight her husband. And if Aed had a motive, why would Queen Talwyn tolerate his advice so readily or make him her food taster. No. It doesn't make sense, what you are saying. I don't believe Aed would have done this."

"Believe what you like," Morcant said with a shrug, still speaking in Greek. "But the facts remain. Aed could easily have slipped that poison into her food. No one else had the access that he had. No one else could have pulled that off. Why is he still alive and breathing when the Queen is fighting for her life. Can you explain that? No of course you can't."

Looking increasingly troubled, Gisgo remained silent. Guarding the curtain, preventing anyone from seeing the Queen, Galchobhar looked drained and pale, as if the life had been knocked clean out of him. Shifting his eyes onto Aed, Gisgo hesitated. The Queen's adviser too looked worried, nervously swallowing and licking his lips as he stared at the floor. Then Gisgo caught sight of the Druid, his eyes gleaming darkly as he emerged from behind the curtain, where he had been helping tend to the Queen. Turning to the assembled men the aged holy man spoke rapidly, gesturing about with his arm in an irritated manner.

"He is asking if any of them have seen his daughter," Phameas said, standing at Gisgo's shoulder. "He is asking them to go and find her. She is the Queen's handmaiden, and she is needed here at once. Her job requires her to help tend to the Queen."

"Oh, great god," Gisgo groaned as he lowered his head into his hand. "This is turning out to be a fucking nightmare."

As he lifted his head, Gisgo was suddenly conscious that the Druid had spotted him and was staring at him, his eyes blazing with fury before a stream of words came hurtling towards Gisgo like a hail of arrows.

"He says," Phameas stammered, backing away with growing alarm. "That we have no business being here. The Druid says that he wants us out of the Queen's-hall right now. We had better go. If the Queen dies, we may no longer be welcome here. If he takes charge you may want to consider a hasty retreat back to our ship Sir. We may have to leave at once."

***

As an arm hurriedly shook him awake, Gisgo scrambled to his feet his hand dropping to his knife handle in a reflex. Through the barn entrance the light of dawn was growing in strength and from somewhere out of sight, a cock was crowing. Standing over him Phameas looked grave. Dark circles had formed under his eyes and his lip was trembling slightly with an excess of nervous tension.

"The Queen," the Carthaginian tin merchant said carefully clearing his throat. "She is still alive. Aed says she has a strong constitution. She is still very weak but Aed believes that she is going to pull through. She is going to make it."

"Oh thank the gods and their mistresses," Gisgo exclaimed, exhaling sharply with relief.

"Yes indeed," Phameas nodded, looking like he had not slept all night. "Aed says the Queen probably owes her life to the swiftness and skill with which her healer and the Druid attended to her. Both are well versed with herbs, potions and the workings of the body."

"Maybe her gods were looking out for her," Gisgo muttered, turning to glance in the direction of the Queen's-hall.

"Maybe," Phameas said glumly. "The healer has confirmed that she thinks the Queen was poisoned. She says all the symptoms point to a poisoning. Aed is leading a council meeting to decide what to do right now. But the Druid he insisted that we be excluded. He does not want us there. Maybe it would be wise to keep away for a while until tempers calm down."

"Now where did I hear that before," Gisgo muttered. Then nodding in agreement, he stared at the Queen's-hall, where an armed guard had been posted outside the door. For a moment he remained silent. Then he turned to Phameas with a troubled brooding look.

"So, the Queen was definitely poisoned," he said quietly. "So, she has enemies outside as well as inside this hill fort. Maybe it is not only her husband who wants her dead and gone. Morcant told me, he believes Aed is the main suspect. He is the Queen's food taster after all. He had access to her food and apparently he has a motive as well which you failed to tell me about."

"Aed," Phameas said looking pained. "I can't believe he would do such a thing. He would never ally himself with the Queen's husband. That man is a usurper and Aed is loyal to the Queen. As for his motive. I have heard the rumours too, but I didn't think them important. That's why I did not mention them. Aed never gave me any reason to suspect he believed the Queen was responsible for his family's death. He never mentioned it, to me or Bodo as far as I know."

"Well, he wouldn't, would he," Gisgo growled. "But Morcant has a point. If Aed was the Queen's official food taster, then why is he alright and she is not. And there is something else which I don't like. That Druid. He too has a motive. The Queen appears to be deliberately humiliating him - forcing his daughter, her handmaiden, to serve us, knowing how he hates foreigners. That is a power play. Showing who is in charge. Who wields the power? The Queen tried it with me too. She likes that kind of thing. So could that Druid have had a hand in all of this. Could he have poisoned the Queen in order to get rid of all of us?"

Hastily Phameas ran his hand through his hair in exasperation, and it was clear he had not thought about that possibility.

"Well, whoever did it," Phameas said, closing his eyes with a sudden tired look. "They failed to kill her. They failed. But it looks like our plans have changed. With the Queen in the state that she is in, we will not be marching out to meet her husband in battle today. Aed told me as much. The levies who will be arriving here this morning, will be sent back home. Aed says that the Queen must rest and recover which will take time. Galchobhar is not letting anyone near her, except for the healer and the Queen's handmaiden. That young wolf knows that if the Queen dies, his position and status goes down with her."

"Great," Gisgo snapped looking unhappy.

"And there is something else Sir," Phameas said in a weary reluctant voice. "But maybe now is not the time."

"No, go on," Gisgo said, quickly turning to the tin merchant. "If you have more news, I want to hear it."

"Melchus has sent word from Ictis," Phameas said lowering his eyes. "He is not happy. He wants to know when we are to sail for Gades. For home. He says he is worried that we are going to leave it too late."

"Oh great," Gisgo said in a sarcastic voice, reaching up to rub his beard. "Well, we are not yet done here. So, he will just have to wait. Tell him that I expect him to wait and keep his ship seaworthy and ready for when we return."

"As you wish Sir," Phameas said. "That's what I thought you would say. I will get a message through to Melchus."

Catching sight of Xenocles slumped up and still half asleep against the nearby wall, Gisgo's face abruptly darkened.

"And where the fuck were you last night," Gisgo called out in an annoyed voice. "You had better have a damn good explanation."

Chapter Seven - The Battle

In the blue afternoon sky, the sun ruled supreme. Picking his way across the green deserted fields, Gisgo peered at the low rocky ridge that cut across the country up ahead. Several days had passed since the Queen had been poisoned but today the waiting appeared to be over, he thought. Today it looked like matters' were finally coming to a head. But there was still no sign of the enemy. No indication that the Queen's husband had accepted battle. Clad for war, carrying his round shield, painted with a black horse on a white background, Gisgo's coat of chain mail body armour gleamed in the sunlight while on his head he was wearing his magnificent Thracian helmet, easily identifiable by its distinctive high and inclined apex. Following their leader across the fields the band of Carthaginian swordsmen and slingers too looked ready for a fight, white pieces of cloth tied to their arms to identify them as allies. While striding along at Gisgo's side, his hand resting on his sword pommel, Xenocles looked grim and uncompromising, his black braided locks carefully arranged for battle in the ancient Spartan manner.

Moving towards the ridge, spread out in a wide line, clumped together in their extended family clans, the five-hundred-armed men and boys came on in stoic silence. The Celts were clad in their woollen cloaks and tunics and leather boots, and most were bareheaded. The gentle breeze was tugging at their beards. Sporting green tattoos across their faces and arms, many had exotic amulets and good luck charms dangling from around their necks. The men were armed with a wide assortment of weapons of varying quality, swords, axes, clubs, spears, knives, bows, hammers and shovels. As he gazed at the Celtic army, Gisgo however could see that most of the men and boys had no proper body armour and many did not even have shields. Only Galchobhar's professional warriors were decently armed and equipped, but they made up less than a fifth of the total force.

Riding at the head of her army, resolutely leading the way across the fields towards the ridge, Queen Talwyn was clad for battle. Holding her axe, her head adorned by her splendid double horned bronze helmet, she was standing bolt upright in her magnificent chariot, which was being pulled along by two white horses. Accompanying her on foot, jogging to keep up with her chariot were her bodyguards, while her leading nobles, among whom was Morcant were riding horses. And bounding ahead of the Queen were a pack of eager war dogs, their barks drifting away across the deserted countryside.

For a moment Gisgo eyed the Queen. From his vantage point bringing up the rear of the army, he could not see her face. But he knew the effort she was making to be here leading her men. She had still not fully recovered from the effects of being poisoned and despite being told she needed to rest, she had insisted that she lead her men into battle. To delay any further would be seen as a sign of weakness she had argued. So they had lashed her legs and body to the side of the chariot to keep her standing upright.

"Where is Aed?" Xenocles suddenly exclaimed, his eyes hard as nails, as he peered at the small band of mounted men. "I don't see him among the other nobles. Should he not be here?"

"Aed," Gisgo replied stoically as he strode along across the field. "Aed will not be here. The Queen has placed him under arrest."

"Arrest?" Xenocles said, turning to Gisgo with a startled look. "I didn't know that. You didn't tell me that he was under arrest. Isn't he, our man?"

"Yes, he is. But the Queen has arrested him," Gisgo replied in a tight voice. "Aed is suspected of having poisoned her. The evidence all points to his involvement. He was her food taster, and he apparently had a motive. When this battle has been settled and if we win, there is going to be a trial and there is nothing I or Phameas can do about that. It is the Queen's decision."

"Shit," Xenocles muttered, looking away. "But that is bad news for us, right? Aed was our friend, our ally. If he goes, we will have no friends left here."

"So," Gisgo said, carefully raising his voice to convey his displeasure. "It would be helpful if you didn't make matters worse by pursuing that young woman. If her father, the Druid, were to find out what you have been up to our position here would become even worse. You are putting everyone in danger."

Moving along at Gisgo's side, Xenocles again looked away, his lip curling in sullen defiance but he remained silent.

Up ahead, as the Queen's chariot reached the top of the ridge, she came to a halt and for a moment she was outlined against the clear blue sky. A heroic figure standing bolt upright on her chariot, surrounded by her bodyguard and barking hounds. Then abruptly a Celtic Carnyx rang out, its deep, powerful and mournful sound travelling across the countryside. After a few seconds of silence, the trumpet rang out-again but no answering call came.

Reaching the top of the low rocky ridge, Gisgo quickly signaled for his men to come to a halt. Along the high ground the mass of armed Celts, clustered together in their family groups, had stopped as well and were silently staring across the gently sloping fields towards another low ridge line, a few hundred paces away. For a moment Gisgo peered at the deserted fields. There was no one about. Then he turned in the Queen's direction. But she was not moving. It appeared that this was the spot where she had chosen to fight. This was the place where the civil war was going to be decided one way or the other.

"What now?" Xenocles growled, as he turned to look around with a guarded expression. "Where is her husband and his army?"

"We wait," Gisgo replied coolly.

"And if the battle goes the wrong way. What then?"

"If it does," Gisgo said. "Then we will have to run. We run all the way back to Ictis and pray that Melchus and his ship are still there."

"Great," Xenocles muttered.

It was sometime later, when Gisgo suddenly heard the sound of a Carnyx. Hurriedly turning in the direction from which the sound had come, his eyes narrowed and he reached up to rub his beard. The noise had come from beyond the opposite ridge line. But still he could see nothing, except for the deserted green fields and barren rocky slopes. Massed along the high ground on either side of him, the Celts too had heard the sound and a sudden tension seemed to grip the warriors. Then Gisgo abruptly spotted dark figures appearing along the opposite ridge line and as the enemy swarmed into view and began to occupy the high ground, he saw there were hundreds of them.

"They are here," Gisgo called out to his mercenaries. "The enemy have come. We are going to fight. Prepare yourselves."

Among the Iberian swordsmen no one said a word. Along the low ridge the Queen's army too appeared to be getting themselves ready for the coming battle and a moment later a Carnyx rang out again. Among the Celts standing nearby, Gisgo suddenly noticed that the men had started to mutter to themselves, their voices like loud ominous whispers. As the whispering grew and was taken up by more and more of the Queen's army, Xenocles frowned.

"What are they doing?" He said quietly.

"I am not sure," Gisgo responded. For a moment he paused. "Maybe they are reciting the names of their forefathers and clan ancestors," he continued. "To tell their gods who they are and from who they come. To build up courage. They do it to honour their blood line. Phameas mentioned to me that it is customary before a battle."

"Interesting," the Greek mercenary commander replied. "I did not know that. Maybe I should give that a try next time."

"Next time," Gisgo said, raising his eyebrows as he turned to stare at the massed enemy ranks that were growing and forming up across the shallow green valley, a few hundred yards away.

"Well this is the moment of truth. Now we are going to see what our young commander is really made of," Xenocles exclaimed with a grim, sceptical look as he turned to eye the enemy.

Saying nothing, Gisgo suddenly spotted Morcant hurrying towards him. As the splendidly outfitted Celtic nobleman rode up, Gisgo could see that he looked tense.

"Prince Gisgo," Morcant quickly called out in Greek, restraining his nervous whinnying mount. "Galchobhar orders you to take your men and occupy the very end of our left flank. You are to remain in your position until you hear four clear short blasts from our trumpets. When you hear that signal - you are to advance around the enemy flank and fall on their rear. No mercy. Is that clear?"

"I hear you," Gisgo responded with a nod. "We will do as instructed. But the enemy are also the Queen's people. They are your people. What happens if they want to surrender?"

"No mercy," Morcant snapped, his eyes gleaming. "Galchobhar says this will be a fight to the death. There is too much at stake. We must win this battle or else we are all doomed."

"Right," Gisgo said nodding.

"Four blasts from our trumpets," Morcant repeated fixing Gisgo with a penetrating look, as he held up four fingers. "You do not move until you hear that signal. Whatever happens."

"We got it," Gisgo replied speaking in Greek.

As Morcant rode away back towards the Queen's chariot, Gisgo frowned as he gazed at the activity taking place along the ridge. Then suddenly he opened his mouth in surprise as he finally understood what Galchobhar was planning. A moment later he chuckled. "Oh, that's brilliant," Gisgo called out with growing admiration in his voice. "Xenocles. These Celts. They know what they are doing. I see now what Galchobhar is planning. He is going to envelop the enemy flanks and crush them just like Hannibal did at Cannae. Oh, its brilliant. See. Look he is thinning out his centre and reinforcing the flanks. Looks like the Queen and Morcant will hold the middle while we and Galchobhar will roll up the flanks."

"Maybe," Xenocles said, sounding less confident as he carefully studied the Queen's army that was forming up for battle. "But Cannae was touch and go. You were not there in the centre holding back that Roman infantry assault like I was. Our lines could easily have broken. That day is still the most terrifying day of my life." For a moment Xenocles paused as his face darkened. "To repeat that victory," he continued, "will require the enemy to play into our hands. If the Romans had crushed our centre before our cavalry could drive their cavalry from the field, it would have been a disaster and the end of Hannibal and us."

"The Queen," Gisgo said quickly pointing at Queen Talwyn who was standing bolt upright on her chariot, clearly visible for all to see. "She is the bait. Galchobhar is using her as bait to draw the enemy towards our centre. Her husband will not be able to resist. He will go after her. She will draw him in."

"But our centre looks awfully weak," Xenocles growled. "Most of these boys have no body armour or shields. They are just conscripts. Amateurs. How long do you think they are they going to be able to hold on before they break and flee? Galchobhar is taking a big risk."

"You never win without taking risks," Gisgo said quickly patting the Greek mercenary commander on his shoulder as he turned away. "Come on. Follow me. We need to get into position."

***

Along the enemy held ridge, hundreds of rebels had begun to advance, coming on at a steady walk, their ranks bristling with weapons and shields. In the blue afternoon sky the sun bathed the green fields in light while the wind had died down, as if it were holding its breath. Watching the enemy as they descended from the high ground, Gisgo's face darkened, his hand resting on his sword pommel, his other clutching his shield.

"Listen up lads," Xenocles called out, turning to the tense, grim faced Carthaginians. "We are soldiers. We live to fight. That's what we do. That is what we have chosen to do as free men. We fight for ourselves. For our comrades and for the mercenary flag. So stick together. Fight together. Rally to your banner and obey. Do this and we shall win. And for fucks sake don't try to be a hero. I want to see every-one, of you ugly mugs alive after this is done."

As Xenocles finished speaking and the silence returned, Gisgo began to tap his fingers against the pommel of his sword. Along the ridge to his right the Celts in the Queen's army had not moved and were stoically awaiting the enemy assault. Holding the centre, clearly visible for all to see, the Queen was standing up in her chariot, surrounded by her bodyguard.

"Looks like they are taking the bait," Gisgo said at last.

Across the field that separated the two armies, the rebels appeared to be converging on the Queen's position, drawing men in from the flanks and massing them together into a gigantic solid V shaped wedge.

"Yup," Xenocles replied.

Wrenching his eyes away from the advancing rebel force, Gisgo hurriedly turned to look at the Celts to his right. The thin line of men guarding the ridge appeared to be made up of the old and the very young, many of whom were just boys of fourteen or fifteen. Biting his lip, Gisgo studied them for a moment. The defenders were going to be of dubious quality and reliability and if they broke upon the first charge, he and his men would be cut off and isolated.

In the shallow valley the rebels came on. The tramp of their boots and the jangle of their equipment becoming louder and louder and, as they closed the gap, Gisgo could make out the warrior's faces, hard, grim and savage. The rebels too appeared to be in no mood to offer mercy.

Abruptly the afternoon was shattered by the sound of a Carnyx. Then another and another joined in, blaring away and, as the rebels steadily closed the distance the noise grew in crescendo. Along the ridge, the first arrows had begun to fly, whining away into the massed enemy ranks. Then across the valley floor the rebels abruptly raised a mighty roar and charged.

"Wait," Gisgo cried out to his men as he pulled his Roman short sword from his belt. "Wait for the signal. Wait."

To Gisgo's right, the rebels were storming up the slope towards Queen Talwyn. A wild, furious and terrifying charge. Holding the high ground however, the Queen's army was bravely standing its ground, braced to receive the charge, arrows whizzing through the air and hammering into the rebel force. Anxiously, Gisgo stared at the rapidly developing scene. The two sides were about to clash. The Queen had not moved. Standing bolt upright on her chariot she rose above her men like a white statue, impervious and immovable. Directly in front of Gisgo and his men there was no one. Galchobhar's plan to lure the rebels into the centre appeared to be working. But still the signal to attack did not come. What was the young warrior waiting for? He was cutting it fine Gisgo thought. If he delayed too long, the centre of the Queen's army could break and flee. As the two sides came crashing into each other, the whole ridge line instantly dissolved into chaos. Hacking, stabbing, lunging and battering into each other - a ferocious hand-to-hand combat had broken out and the afternoon was filled with blood curdling shrieks and cries. Tensely Gisgo peered at the fighting to his right. In the chaotic melee it was impossible to see who was winning or even who was on whose side. The Queen's men however, holding the high ground, had it seemed managed to halt the rebel charge - for there was no general flight to the rear. They were holding on. But for how long? Suddenly amid the screaming din, in the thick of the battle, Gisgo caught sight of Queen Talwyn, still standing upright on her chariot, the fierce bloody fighting swirling around her like a howling; shrieking-tempest.

Then Gisgo heard the Carnyx ringing out, four sharp and frantic bursts, summoning him into the fight.

"Follow me," he cried as he began to move towards the enemy.

Hastening forwards with his men following close behind, Gisgo began to close in on the rebel flank. Snatching a glance at the

Carthaginian mercenaries, he saw that a number of Celts, old men and boys, had joined his war band bringing his numbers up to around fifty. Ahead of him, seeing the developing threat to their flank, a group of warriors had detached themselves and were moving to confront the Carthaginian mercenaries. The men however did not look like seasoned warriors, and many had no shields or body armour to protect themselves. As the two sides closed with each other, Gisgo grimly tightened his grip on his sword, raising and pointing it at the enemy whilst covering his body with his shield.

"At them," Gisgo suddenly bellowed, as he lunged towards the Celts. Crashing into a warrior, Gisgo caught a furious sword blow on his shield. The momentum of his charge however sent the rebel stumbling backwards and before he could recover, Gisgo savagely drove his Roman short sword into his unprotected shoulder. As his opponent dropped his weapon and staggered backwards with a howl, Gisgo leapt on him, kicking the wounded man to the ground. Around him the Carthaginian mercenaries needed no further encouragement. Picking out their opponents, the Carthaginians and their allies charged into the Celts, their swords, stabbing and slashing at their poorly protected enemy. As he blocked a wild spear thrust with his shield Gisgo, cried out and drove his opponent backwards. Then he was set upon by a semi-naked man, clad only in trousers with crazy bulging eyes, swinging a double-edged axe about, over his head. The warrior was screaming in fury, spittle flying from his mouth. But as he came at Gisgo preparing to strike, one of the Carthaginian swordsmen rammed his sword into the man's exposed chest, sending him crashing to the ground with a groan.

Stumbling backwards clutching his bloodied sword, Gisgo's chest was heaving with exertion, his eyes darting about. But around him the fight was already over and the remaining Celts were fleeing, leaving the bodies of the slain and wounded scattered across the field. The rebels had been comprehensively cut to pieces - being no match for the more experienced Spanish veterans and the superior weapons they carried.

Grimly Gisgo reached up to wipe his face as he caught his breath. Ahead of him the great confused mass of snarling, struggling men were still battling and slugging it out for control of the high ground. But the rebel rear and flank were now utterly exposed. Then before he could act Gisgo, heard the Celtic Carnyx ringing out again, four sharp frantic bursts and the urgency was unmistakable. The Queen was under huge pressure. The defenders up on the ridge appeared to be barely clinging on. A rout could happen in a split second.

"With me," Gisgo cried out. "With me. Follow me."

Then he was off, racing towards the fighting and as the Carthaginians and their allies fell on the enemy rear all hell broke loose. Knocking a boy to the ground, Gisgo brutally stamped on his young face and was rewarded by a cracking noise and a high-pitched scream. Nearby, a wounded Celt was trying to stagger to his feet, but before he could do so Xenocles had decapitated him with a Celtic axe. The Greek mercenary commander, his face crimson with someone else's blood, appeared to have abandoned his sword and picked up the double-edged Celtic axe instead. Wielding it with dreadful efficiency and skill, Xenocles was causing absolute carnage among the enemy ranks. Pressing forwards, Gisgo lunged at another man who abruptly dropped his weapon and bolted. Coming face-to-face with a shrieking woman Gisgo blocked her frantic slashing knife with his shield before leaping forwards, and sinking his sword into her neck, killing her instantly.

Pausing to catch his breath, Gisgo gasped, his chest heaving. His assault on the enemy rear was working. He had caught the rebels off-guard, but they were not done just yet. Breaking away from the chaotic fight for the ridge line, a party of warriors came storming towards him, brandishing their weapons, crying out, their faces set in a savage and murderous expression. Narrowly avoiding a spear that was hurled at him Gisgo blocked a slashing sword blow. Then he was being driven backwards by the fury and momentum of the Celtic charge. Crying out, he thrust his sword at his opponents, his eyes darting about but his attack was rebuffed. The men facing him were proper warriors, carrying shields while their torso's were protected by thick leather armour.

Grimly Gisgo tried to stand his ground, jabbing his sword at his opponents, as around him the Carthaginian mercenaries struggled to contain the fresh attack - the clash of iron against wood reverberating across the shrieking field. Suddenly the enemy pressure however began to slacken and, in the confusion and chaos of battle, Gisgo gasped as he saw why. The rebels immediately in front of him were being attacked from the rear by a band of Celts who had appeared as if out of nowhere. For a moment the battle appeared to teeter on a knife edge. But then, as a Carnyx rang out, its deep blaring noise sweeping across the battlefield like a gale the rebels broke, and within seconds a mass panicked flight had started. Leaping forwards and crashing into a rebel, Gisgo drove the man backwards with his shield, his sword repeatedly jabbing at the warrior's face until at last, the steel blade punched into flesh and bone. As his opponent collapsed to the ground, Gisgo finished him off by driving his sword into the man's throat. Hurriedly, straightening up Gisgo staggered backwards in horror as he was abruptly splattered by a fine spray of hot blood. In front of him there were suddenly no more enemies. The rebels appeared to be in full flight, broken and running for their lives, scampering away, carried along by the infectious panic. Victory was close at hand. The battle was nearly over. Crying out to his mercenaries Gisgo tried to rally them for the pursuit. Then a few yards away, across the battlefield he suddenly caught sight of Galchobhar with a few of his warriors. The young handsome warrior's tunic and body armour were splattered with blood and gore as he and his comrades cut the fleeing rebels to pieces, screaming and yelling as they did. Spotting Gisgo, through the chaos, Galchobhar suddenly cracked a grin before swiftly raising his sword in the air and crying out in savage triumph.

Across the corpse strewn and blood-soaked field what was left of the panic-stricken rebel army was in full flight. Galloping after them in pursuit, Gisgo spotted a small band of horsemen - among who was Morcant, easily identifiable by his splendid coat of armour and helmet. The Celtic nobles were mowing the rebels down with their swords and spears, meeting no opposition but there were only a handful of them to complete the rout. Pausing, Gisgo grimly turned to look around at the bloody carnage strewn around him. His work appeared to be done. They had won. The battle was almost over. Cut off from their fleeing comrades, a group of men and boys were trying to surrender, having thrown down their weapons, their pitiful cries needing no explanation. But as the Celts closed in on their enemy, they showed no sign of being willing to give them mercy.

"Rally on me. Rally on me," Gisgo roared, making himself heard over the din.

As his mercenaries, looking tired, battered and bloodstained, silently and hurriedly assembled around him, Gisgo peered at the fleeing enemy but made no move to go after them. Breathing heavily, but saying nothing, Xenocles abruptly appeared at his side, still clutching his double-edged axe, his eyes still gleaming with savage murderous intent. Then, as if the wind had finally decided to finally release its breath, Gisgo felt the cool soothing breeze on his face again.

"You alright," Gisgo muttered, quickly glancing at his blood brother.

"Yes I am alright," Xenocles murmured.

Looking away, Gisgo suddenly spotted the Queen's chariot trundling slowly across the battlefield towards the desperate group of men and boys, who were trying to surrender. The rebel's fate appeared as if it were going to be decided in the next few moments. Still standing bolt upright in her chariot, the victorious Queen's face was pale and white like milk.

***

Kneeling before Queen Talwyn, in the middle of the great hall of the former rebel stronghold, the hilltop fort of Carn Brea, the rebel tribal elders looked miserable and subdued. Their heads humbly bowed towards their Queen - their arms outstretched in submission. It was evening and lining the walls of the building, a throng of armed warriors were looking on as the elders made their submissions to their Queen, begging for mercy. In the crackling firelight Gisgo could sense the sullen yet triumphant atmosphere prevailing among the assembled tribesmen. Standing directly behind their sovereign, Morcant and Galchobhar were gazing at the rebel leaders in stern silence, their arms folded across their chests. Meanwhile seated upon a wooden throne, with her war dogs lying stretched out on the floor by her feet, the Queen looked pale and unwell, keeping her composure by sheer force of will as she surveyed her subjects.

"The Queen's husband," Phameas said quietly leaning in to Gisgo. "It appears he has escaped the battle with a handful of his followers. But he no longer has an army. He has lost his power. The elders over there supported him - but no longer. They are here to make their peace with their Queen. To recognise her as their rightful ruler. The rebellion has been crushed. The elders are telling the Queen that her husband came here straight after the battle before fleeing eastwards. They say that he intends to seek asylum among the other tribes. He has taken the Queen's children with him as hostages."

"So, the civil war is not yet over," Gisgo growled, eyeing the Queen.

"It is for us," Phameas replied, his eyes gleaming in the dull firelight. "We have helped her win the battle. Now the time has come for her to repay us. It looks like we are going to get that trade embargo after all."

Standing among the assembled warriors Gisgo said nothing as the elders continued their humble supplication. The fight with the rebel army had cost him three of his men killed and six wounded, one of who was in a serious condition. But Phameas was right. He had done as he had promised. The Queen owed him and tonight he would get what he had come so far for.

As the elders at last stopped speaking, an ominous silence descended upon the hall as all eyes turned to the Queen, awaiting her verdict. For a long moment Queen Talwyn said nothing as she stared at the kneeling nobles. Then at last she spoke, her voice brittle but clear.

"She says that siding with her husband against her was a traitorous act," Phameas quietly translated, his eyes fixed on Queen Talwyn. "She says her people are one indivisible tribe and that she alone will rule. She says much harm has been done by this rebellion and that many are dead who need not have died. She says she will hunt her husband down, even if it means going to the end of the earth to do so. She says she is going to make him pay for his crimes." For a moment Phameas paused to listen as the Queen's quiet fragile voice filled the hall. Then at last the Carthaginian tin merchant sighed. "She says that she will let them live," he continued. "She is being merciful. But in punishment for their support for her husband, each man will hand over half of their wealth and land to her. The Queen says she intends to use this money to compensate those families who have lost their breadwinners today. She says that the wounds inflicted today - now have time to heal. She welcomes the end of the fighting and the return of peace."

Finishing her graceful reply - silence once more descended upon the packed hall. Then abruptly Galchobhar took a step forwards and raised his fist in the air, crying out in a loud voice. Taking their cue from the young general the assembled warriors broke into a great joyful cheer, stamping their boots on the ground. Swiftly the cheering turned to a chant and as the triumphant noise swept around the hall the atmosphere abruptly lightened and people started to relax.

"They are celebrating their victory," Phameas called out raising, his voice over the din, his face cracking into a pleased grin. "Long live the Queen. Long live the Queen. Now we celebrate with wine and beer!"

As the tension in the great hall melted away and the formal gathering began to break up into smaller groups, Gisgo left his post. Eyeing him in silence Queen Talwyn watched him approach.

"Phameas," Gisgo called out. "I would like to speak to the Queen. Tell her that I and my men have kept faith with her. That some of my mercenaries will never see another sunrise again. They fell for her cause. Tell her that now peace has returned I expect her to keep her end of the bargain. That there will be a complete and immediate embargo on the tin trade with Rome and her Massaliot allies."

As Phameas translated, Gisgo gazed at the Queen, steeling himself for the silent battle of wills in which she liked to indulge. But on this occasion the Queen appeared not to be interested in playing the subtle power game. Listening to Phameas she said nothing as she coolly observed Gisgo, her eyes flickering between him and Xenocles, who was hanging back. Then at last she spoke, her words imbued with a certain grace and respect.

"She says you kept your word Prince Gisgo," Morcant suddenly called out in Greek before Phameas had a chance to translate. "She says, you are indeed an honourable man and that she grieves for the loss of your soldiers. You and your men fought bravely today. So, she says that she will keep her promise. My Queen will honour the agreement she made with you. The trade embargo against Rome and Massalia will commence tomorrow at dawn - just like you wished for."

"Thank you," Gisgo replied in Greek, nodding at the Queen. "Tell her, that I am grateful and now that my mission is complete, tell her that I and my men shall shortly be returning to our homeland. Our job here is done. Our task is complete."

"Oh, you may have got your way today," Morcant cried, his crafty eyes gleaming. "But this is not over yet Prince Gisgo. You forget that with Aed under arrest, I now have the ear of the Queen."

"Tell her," Gisgo continued turning to Phameas as he ignored Morcant. "That we are grateful for the treaty we have made with her. Tell her that she has made a wise choice and that I am pleased. This is a great day for the both of us. Long live Queen Talwyn. Long live our new alliance."

***

Inside the great hall, the noisy victory celebrations were in full swing. Standing together with Xenocles and a few of his mercenaries, Gisgo was clutching a mug of frothy beer as he quietly observed the increasingly rowdy antics of the victorious warriors who were slowly getting drunk together. It was late and through the open doors the darkness of the night had come. Sat upon her throne, surrounded by her nobles and bodyguard, Queen Talwyn looked exhausted as she quietly observed her boisterous celebrating warriors with a weak but amused smile. At her feet her hounds were gnawing on bones, growling contentedly. Watching her from the crowd, Gisgo could see that the effects of the poisoning she had endured were still clearly visible across her face and body. Would she ever fully recover? Shifting his gaze, he suddenly spotted Galchobhar heading towards him. The young muscular warrior looked deadly serious and sober, giving no hint as to what he wanted. Coming to a halt in front of him the young Celt, studied Gisgo for a moment from top to bottom, like he had never seen him before. Then raising his chin in a provocative manner, he pulled his Roman pugio knife from his belt and quickly nicked his wrist so that a line of blood immediately welled up. Eyeing Gisgo, Galchobhar spoke, his eyes gleaming with a strange and sudden fervour.

"Phameas?" Gisgo said quickly.

For a moment the Carthaginian tin merchant hesitated as he gazed at Galchobhar in surprise.

"He says Sir," Phameas stammered at last, his voice affected by alcohol. "That today is a glorious day. He and you Sir fought side by side like brothers in a common cause. He is proud of having fought with you Prince Gisgo. He says that you are his friend and that he wishes to seal this friendship with blood. Will you give him your arm?"

"Blood brothers!" Xenocles exclaimed, as he took a step forwards. "He wishes to become your blood brother Gisgo."

Gazing back at Galchobhar, Gisgo did not immediately respond. Then slowly he extended his arm and nodded. Looking pleased, the young Celt did not waste time and quickly cut Gisgo's arm bringing forth a small amount of blood. Clasping hold of Gisgo's arm with his own, Galchobhar grinned as he allowed the blood from their wounds to mingle.

"Right," Xenocles said, pulling forth his own knife. "If the young wolf is going to be your new blood brother, then he is going to be mine too. Tell him Phameas - who I am and explain to him my illustrious background. Tell him about my great deeds in battle and the fame of my name."

It was a while later, with the drunken celebrations still in full swing, when Gisgo suddenly noticed the stranger rushing into the packed hall. Ignoring the rowdy party, spotting the Queen, the man hurried over to her. The stranger was clad in a long cloak splattered with fresh mud indicating that he had only just arrived at the hill fort. Feeling a sudden twinge of concern, with a frown Gisgo took a step forwards - gripping his beer mug in his hand. What was this? Something was going on. But what? Standing beside the throne the messenger was engaging the Queen in an urgent looking conversation and, as he spoke the tired, amused smile on the Queen's face slowly drained away. Then turning to her nobles, she raised her hand for silence.

"What's going on?" Gisgo said quickly, as around their sovereign the Celtic nobles had hurriedly started to call for silence in the packed hall.

Looking flustered, Phameas did not immediately reply. Then at last he stirred and turned to Gisgo.

"I am not entirely sure. The Queen," he muttered as the hall fell silent. "She has just been informed that foreigners have arrived and wish to speak to her. They are here, waiting to enter the hall. They have come from the coast."

"Foreigners?" Gisgo exclaimed.

But before Phameas could answer, four men had suddenly appeared at the entrance to the great hall. Emerging from the darkness they came into the flickering reddish firelight. And as they did, a hush descended upon the feast as all eyes turned to stare at them. Pausing for a moment to look around at the packed audience, the strangers hesitated. The newcomers were led by a stocky blond man in his fifties who was walking with a limp. Coolly picking his way towards the Queen, ignoring the hard-faced warriors, the man and his three companions approached and, as he did Gisgo felt a surge of alarm. The strangers were clad in Roman and Greek style cloaks and tunics. They were Romans. And the blond man - Gisgo thought as the blood suddenly drained from his cheeks. The blond man with a limp. He knew this man. He knew that face. He had seen him before - but where?

Coming to a halt before the Queen, the blond man paused before gracefully and respectfully inclining his head. Then he spoke in Latin and, as he did Gisgo gasped in dismay, struck by sheer horror as he finally remembered where he had seen this Roman before.

"He says his name is Flavius and that he is a "Legate of Rome," Phameas stammered, looking shocked. "He says that he has been sent here by the Senate in Rome - to agree a new trade agreement with the Queen."

Chapter Eight - Rome's Legate and the Clever Men of Massalia

Late summer 211 BCE - The Greek colony of Massalia, south coast of Gaul

Out on the sparkling and pristine waters the splendid port of Massalia was teeming with ships of all sizes. It was afternoon and in the spotless blue sky the fierce yellow sun was slowly baking the already bone-dry land. Anchored off the narrow harbour entrance, a Massaliot warship was guarding the port and the headland, its deck artillery and harpoons aimed out to sea. Lying at anchor within the sheltered natural basin, enclosed on three sides by land, were huge grain ships from Sardinia and Egypt, small, fast Italian and Greek liburna's and penteconters, local fishing boats, rafts and dugouts - while two Roman warships were undergoing repairs in a dry dock. Down beside the water's edge, the rocky beach and the rows of boat houses were a noisy hive of industrious activity, as cargoes, people and trade goods were ferried between the ships and the shore.

Leaving the busy port Flavius clad in a white Roman toga, limped along the narrow street and into the city, accompanied by Scoti who was carrying a brown leather satchel slung over his shoulder. The two men could not have looked more different in appearance and class. Looking grave, bareheaded, his blond hair cut short - at fifty-one Flavius appeared rugged and tough. His face deeply bronzed by a lifetime spent outdoors working as a carpenter, his hands rough and workmanlike. While ambling along at his side the bookish, highly educated looking Roman astronomer and Scipio's client, in his late thirties and sporting a hooked nose, was gazing about at the people and buildings with a curious and carefree expression.

"I always wanted to visit Massalia," Scoti announced, as the two of them made their way through the noisy, congested street towards the magnificent temple of Artemis, whose stone columns and sloping roof loomed over the sprawl of the city.

"Oh, why is that?" Flavius responded, without taking his eyes off the temple ahead.

"It's a city famed for its explorers and science," Scoti exclaimed. "I have read much about this place. The Massaliots were the first to raise the theory that the moon influences the tides in the seas which we now believe is true. Euthymenes explored the coast of West Africa long before the Carthaginian voyages of exploration. And then there is Pytheas. He was the first to penetrate the northern lands and find the source of amber. He too visited the Tin islands. A truly remarkable man."

Limping on down the street, a subtle and patient look had appeared on Flavius's face. Scoti liked to talk, he had soon discovered. There was no stopping him and O-boy, could the man talk? His travelling companion, highly educated and able to read and write, unlike himself, could recall endless stories and obscure details - and all he could do in return was listen.

"But I like it mainly because Massalia is an exciting city." Scoti continued, his eyes darting about, a pleased smile plastered to his face. "It has always had a place in my imagination. This polis - it is the gateway to the vast Celtic world whose heartlands lie to the north and west. It has a temple dedicated to Artemis. Now Rome knows her as the goddess Diana and Artemis is a fun god. She likes to enjoy herself. Unlike King Jupiter, who offers nothing but sternness or Mercury, who cares only about making money. No Artemis is fun and exciting. You can enjoy yourself with her. She likes to hunt, mess about with weapons and wild animals and shit like that. She is the lord and protector of the untamed wilderness."

"Really," Flavius said, raising his eyebrows. "I didn't know you were interested in hunting. I thought you were a man of books and archives, of learning, of watching the stars and moon at night. An astronomer. A scientist. I remember what Scipio told me - he said that you are one of the best educated men in Rome."

"It is true," Scoti said, raising his chin in a little haughty and conceited manner. "My reputation is growing among the educated classes. Scipio's description was accurate. I speak Greek and am well versed in astronomy, mathematics and the science of paleography among other things." Turning to Flavius, Scoti studied him for a moment. "But now that we are getting to know each other better," he continued, "you should know I was not always a book worm. There is a different side to me - of which you know nothing. When I was still just a boy, I would sometimes sneak away from my classes to go hunting - sometimes to even chase girls. I often got into trouble with my elders for doing that. I was a youthful rebel once."

"You were a young rebel. Oh, I am shocked," Flavius replied raising his voice in mock horror, while keeping a straight face. "You ran away from your classes. I am disappointed Scoti. I really am. As my secretary I would have expected more from you."

"I was young. I am not a rebel anymore," Scoti stammered hastily, failing to notice the twinkle in Flavius's eye. "I finished my education in the end. I did what my family wanted me to do."

"Fine - and as we are getting to know each other," Flavius continued raising his eyebrows as he pushed on deeper into the city. "Scipio assigned you to me, to act as my secretary, because he said you knew how to read and write. He told me that you are an experienced archivist with one of the best memories in Rome. But he also warned me that under no circumstances was I to allow you to touch wine or beer. Care to explain that before we meet our Massaliot hosts?"

"Yes, its best if I don't touch any wine at all," Scoti said, hurriedly looking away with a sudden embarrassed look. "No good will come from that."

***

Limping on down the Massaliot street, Flavius remained silent as he pushed on through the crowds towards the Temple of Artemis. Scoti was not a complete stranger of course Flavius thought, for he had known him from before, when Scoti had been part of Scipio's failed election campaign - in charge of winning the vote of the scientific community. But during their sea voyage from Ostia to Massalia, he had started to get to know Scoti better and to his surprise he had begun to like the man. Despite their vastly different backgrounds and social class, they were becoming friends. The astronomer had a vain conceited streak, an arrogance that came with his education, but it was just harmless vanity he had concluded. If one peeled away the layers of pride and haughtiness - there was a genuinely honourable person underneath. A bit like Archagathus had been. Scoti too appeared to have a brilliant memory, being able to recall the most insignificant details on virtually any topic. There was no doubt that he was going to prove indispensable, and to his surprise he had realised that the two of them made a good team. Had that been the reason why, out of all the people he could have chosen, Scipio had shrewdly insisted on sending Scoti with him on his diplomatic mission to the Tin islands?

Turning to gaze at the locals going about their business, Flavius took a deep breath. Things were going to be alright he thought. On his brief return home to his farm outside the frontier colony of Placentia in Boii country, before setting out on his diplomatic mission, he had been pleased to see how Caius, his eldest son and heir, had taken to managing the

112

farm. The young man appeared to have changed overnight. Raising himself out of the lazy unambitious stupour in which he had wallowed for years, Caius had finally started to take his duty and responsibilities seriously, like a man emerging from a long sleep. The boy could handle the farm and he could rely on Caius to protect his family. It was a secret relief and heart-warming to witness. Caius was finally coming of age. Agrippina had even mentioned that his son had set his eyes on a local girl. Despite the endless hardships brought on by the war, things on this particular front appeared to be looking up. His family were going to be alright while he was away on his mission to the Tin islands. But it would not stop him from worrying. The multitude of threats the colonists faced had not disappeared, nor did it seem likely that the war with Carthage would end soon. Attack, raids, kidnapping, starvation and pestilence remained real possibilities and life was lived constantly on the very edge of catastrophe.

"You look troubled," Scoti said, glancing at Flavius as the two of them turned into a street filled with the sweet scent of freshly baked bread.

"I was just curious," Flavius replied. "Why do you think Scipio chose you to accompany me on this mission? He could have chosen Laelius or Davido or that lawyer Platinus - but he settled on you. Any ideas as to why?"

For a moment Scoti did not reply, as he eyed the bakers' shops.

"Well apart from my obvious qualifications," the astronomer replied at last, with a little sniff. "It was not Scipio's idea to send me along with you. It was Tertia's idea. She said the two of us would make a good team. She convinced her husband to include me. That's why I am here."

"Tertia," Flavius exclaimed sounding surprised.

"That's right," Scoti replied, raising his chin. "That woman is as smart and cunning as an owl. If you ask me the best decision that young Scipio ever made was to marry her. Those two make a formidable couple. They are going to go far together. Mark my words."

Remaining silent, Flavius turned to eye the massive Temple of Artemis that lay ahead, perched on the high ground. It was the solemn duty and responsibility of every Roman citizen to fight for his family and his country, he thought. That ancient and sacred contract and commitment, handed down over time from one generation to the next was what had made the Republic into the great Empire it was today. So, he would do his duty to the Republic he had told Scipio, his young patron. He would accept the diplomatic task Scipio wanted him to carry out on behalf of the Senate. He would travel to the Tin islands and do his best to secure the flow of tin to Massalia and Rome remained uninterrupted. He would serve his country like before, like he had done all his life - first as a soldier, then a spy and now as a diplomat in the service of the Republic.

He had not expected to like his new job as "Legate of Rome." Flavius thought looking grave. It would take him far away from his farm and family and he had no experience of being a diplomat. Nor did he have a clue as to where the Tin islands were - other than that they were very far away beyond the sea to the north and west. But to his surprise the role had started to grow on him. The responsibility which had been entrusted to him was a grave and solemn one - but it also gave him a chance to defend his countrymen. To do something that might change the course of the long war with Carthage and alleviate the common suffering.

Young Scipio had arranged it all of course. His shrewd patrician patron, and his formidable wife Tertia, had lobbied the Senate to get him the position. They had supplied the necessary funds, opened doors, assigned Scoti to him as his secretary and got the official agreement from the Senate. As an ambassador, a legate, the Senate in Rome had formally agreed to delegate considerable power to him to negotiate diplomatic contracts on behalf of the Republic. Wrenching his gaze away from the grand temple - Flavius lowered his eyes. He had never before held such power. Nor had he ever pictured himself holding this position. It was a sobering experience - one which could easily go to his head if he was not careful. By the law of nations, his person as an envoy was protected and inviolate. None were allowed to harm him. He represented the dignity of Rome and how he conducted himself would reflect on the Republic. He could conduct and negotiate a new treaty with the tribes who lived on the Tin islands. He could do pretty much what the hell he liked, and Rome was paying.

Feeling the pressure and urge once again, Flavius came to a halt in the street, so abrupt that Scoti, looking startled, turned to glance at him in alarm. For a moment Flavius, frowned as he hurriedly reached out to steady himself against a wall. The constant thirst and accompanying need to piss, which he had first noticed some time ago, was not letting up and now he had also started to suffer from bouts of blurred vision. Supporting himself against the wall, he quickly shook his head and opened his eyes wide trying to focus. At fifty-one he was growing old, and his body was no longer working as well as it had used to do.

"You alright, Flavius?" Scoti said, concern etched into his voice.

"Can you keep a secret?" Flavius muttered. "From Scipio and from my wife if you ever meet her again. They must not know. No one must know."

"Sure. I can do that," Scoti replied with an uneasy look.

For a moment Flavius said nothing as he reached up to rub his eyes. Then he straightened up.

"No, I am not alright," Flavius said at last. "Before we left. In Rome. I went to see a doctor. He says that I am suffering from something called diabetes. That the constant thirst and need to piss all the time and now the blurred vision is a sure sign. Diabetes - it's a disease. I am told that it's not infectious, but there is no cure. I am just getting old, but I am still going to be able to complete our mission - understood. I do not want you to have any doubts about that. We are going to see this through to the end. We are going to do our duty to Rome."

**

Approaching the temple complex, there were fewer people about and the street was quieter and less congested. Pausing to glance about, Flavius noticed a woman sitting on the ground her back leaning against a wall. The woman was begging, a sleeping baby wrapped in a blanket around her chest, while just outside the doors to the huge stone building a prostitute was plying her trade. Spotting the two men patiently standing waiting for him on the stone steps leading up to the temple entrance, Flavius grunted and veered towards them, his walking stick tapping the paving stones with a little clacking noise. The two Massaliots were smartly and stylishly dressed, but as he and Scoti approached they regarded him coolly and without smiling. The elder of the two was in his early thirties, calm and business-like with jet black hair tied back into a ponytail like a woman. His fingers and arms devoid of any rings or amulets. His youthful companion looked no older than nineteen.

"Gentlemen, good day to you," Flavius called out, looking grave as he extended his hand to the elder of the two. "My name is Flavius. The Senate in Rome has appointed me as their Legate. I will be leading the mission to the Tin islands, and I am sorry that we kept you waiting. I am not as familiar yet with your fine city streets, as I would like to be."

"Welcome to Massalia," the older man replied in good Latin reaching out to grip Flavius's hand in a rather stiff and business-like manner. "My name is Pytheas and my colleague here is called Acco. My government has instructed us to be of service to you. The two of us will be accompanying you to the Tin islands. I have been briefed on your mission and who you are. You have the letters of power with you? The written instructions from the Roman Senate. I will need to see them before we continue."

"Of course we do," Scoti said swiftly, reaching for his satchel and producing two tightly rolled parchment scrolls. "See here and here are the seal and marks of the Senate. We are completely legitimate."

Studying the documents for a moment, Pytheas paused. Then he looked up and nodded.

"Good," Pytheas continued in a tight voice, showing no warmth or compassion. "Then we are all set. My government has instructed me to be your guide and principal adviser. I have been to the Tin islands before and have met with Queen Talwyn. I know the customs of the local tribes well. Acco here will act as our translator. He was born with a gift for languages. We are in luck. For he is the best translator in Massalia, perhaps in the world."

"I speak seven languages Sir - fluently," Acco said hurriedly, taking over the narrative in perfect Latin, as he eyed Flavius with an eager respectful expression on his youthful face. "Latin, Greek, Punic, Hebrew and several Celtic languages and dialects. Pytheas flatters me, but he is right. Few can do what I can do. There is a dwarf in Spain serving in the Roman army, who is also said to be a pretty good translator, but I have never met him." For a moment Acco paused, gazing at

Flavius as if he were observing a challenge. "It would be useful Sir," the young man continued, "if over the coming days you would speak to me as often as you can - so that I can get a feel for how you use and formulate words. If I know how you like to speak - it will make my job easier when we get to the Tin islands."

"I will bear that in mind," Flavius said in a graceful manner. "And I thank you and your government for providing this assistance and hospitality. Rome and Massalia are close allies and friends. Long may it last."

"We have common interests and a common enemy," Pytheas responded, dipping his head in a formal manner. "The alliance between our two peoples is a strong one. It has stood the test of time."

Gazing at the Massaliot diplomat, Flavius nodded. Despite his crisp business-like attitude and his words, he sensed that Pytheas was holding back, as if he did not yet fully trust him. As if he were not entirely sure about him. The man appeared to be suspicious - but why?

"Pytheas," Scoti exclaimed, breaking the awkward silence with a sudden curious gleam in his eye. "That is a famous name around here."

"Yes, it is." Pytheas replied turning to the astronomer. "I am named after my great grandfather - the famous explorer who went in search of the source of our Celtic trade goods. The first Greek to ever visit the northern lands and see the midnight sun. It was he who laid much of the foundations for my city's prosperity and commercial success. The book he wrote about his travels is widely read across the civilised world."

"You are Pytheas's great grandson!" Scoti exclaimed, as a little colour shot into his cheeks. "Oh my. This is indeed my lucky day. Your ancestor is a hero of mine. I read his book, when I was just ten."

"I am descended from his line, yes," Pytheas said, in his calm business-like manner, refusing to show any emotion. "My family are still active in the politics of our city. Do you know much about Massalia and her people?"

"I do," Flavius replied seizing his chance. "Fifty thousand inhabitants. The leading Greek colony along the southern Gallic coast. Founded by colonists from Phocaea and nearly as old as Rome. Your drachmas are admired and widely used among the Celtic tribes right across the continent. Your envoys and traders are highly respected for their impartiality and business acumen. But most importantly you have been a staunch ally of the Republic since the earliest days. Massalia has no love for Carthage. You have been competing with them for a share of the western maritime trade markets for centuries. The Carthaginian maritime blockade is why your great grandfather travelled overland to the west coast of Gaul and further north on his journey of exploration. I presume that we shall be following the same route to the Tin islands?"

"I see that you are well informed," Pytheas said eyeing Flavius stiffly and for a brief moment Flavius noticed a hint of respect in the Massaliot's eyes. "Yes, you are correct. My city's continued prosperity depends on our trade acumen and our alliance with Rome. Carthage has always been our great rival. For many years they blocked our ships and merchants from sailing west beyond the Pillars of Hercules because they feared we would discover their trade secrets. As for the route we will be taking, yes, we shall be treading in my great grandfather's footsteps."

"I had a good mentor on the voyage over from Rome," Flavius said gesturing at Scoti. "My secretary made sure that I was well briefed."

"I see," Pytheas replied, quickly glancing at Scoti before turning his attention back to Flavius. "Well, I am pleased that you have made the effort. Massalia demands little from her friends - except for people to respect us. That is important to us. Unfortunately, many who come to my fair city have little knowledge of my home and care even less about the history or welfare of my people. They treat us as if we were a backwater of no importance or significance."

"Knowledge is power," Flavius said gravely. "So, when do we start. Time presses. I have instructions to make my way to the Tin islands as soon as possible. I have been informed that the Carthaginians too are sending a diplomatic mission. We think they are going to try to persuade Queen Talwyn to embargo the trade in tin with us. We cannot allow that to happen."

"No, an embargo would be most unfortunate," Pytheas agreed. "We shall be leaving soon, in the next few days. Our journey will take us north and then west into the heart of Gaul until we reach the coast where we shall cross the sea by ship. You do not need to worry about the details. I shall be your guide. But before we leave," for a moment Pyheas paused, carefully studying Flavius, "tonight at sunset my government is going to hold a reception in the temple behind me. It's in our honour. A sacrifice to Artemis will be performed by the priests - for the success of our mission and to the alliance between our two cities. I would be most honoured if you would be able to attend. And if you do, my government would, expect you to give a short speech."

"Of course, we will attend," Flavius said gruffly. "If the reception is in our honour, then we shall be there. It would not do to start our mission under inauspicious circumstances, now would it. Rome keeps its word and its contract. And it will be a good opportunity for us four to get to know each other. We have a long journey ahead of us and the success of our mission will depend on us working closely together. Do you not agree?"

"That is good to know. I am pleased," Pytheas replied - quickly looking away with growing relief.

For a moment an awkward silence followed and once again, Flavius sensed that Pytheas was holding back. There was something that the man was not telling him. Some truth he was not sharing, which appeared to account for his attitude and mistrust. But what?

Chapter Nine - The Sacrifice

Lying across the stone altar that stood before the huge statue of Artemis, the pig was squealing, the frantic high-pitched noise filling the majestic, largely empty temple as the animal was held in place by two strong men. Looking on in silence, the small crowd of dignitaries and government officials remained silent, as the priest solemnly turned to face the statue and raised his hands calling out for the goddess to accept the sacrifice. Standing amid the gathered men, Flavius looked grave and dignified clad in his white Roman toga, while Scoti, Pytheas and Acco gathered around him. As the priest finished his plea to the goddess - the squealing abruptly ended, as the pig was killed, its dark red blood surging out onto the cold altar stone before dripping down onto the floor. Carefully pressing both his hands into the spilled blood, the priest came up to Flavius and with his fingers he slowly and reverently drew three blood red lines across his forehead before doing the same to Scoti, Pytheas and Acco.

"Great goddess Artemis," Flavius suddenly heard Acco whispering beside him, as the priest began to speak again in Greek. "Virgin daughter of Zeus. Lord of the Hunt. Protect these men as they embark on their long and dangerous journey. Smile on their endeavour. May they succeed and return to us safe and sound," Acco added, smoothly and flawlessly finishing his translation as the priest fell silent.

As the sacrificial ceremony came to an end and the group of dignitaries broke up into small groups, a murmur of voices began to fill the vast temple. Turning to look around at the gathering, Flavius hesitated as he carefully observed his hosts. Then finally he reached up to rub his clean-shaven chin, before turning to Pytheas who was also watching the assembled officials.

"Our ambassador to your city," Flavius said quietly. "Quintus Caecilius Metellus. He is not here? I would have expected him to be here. If for no other reason than to honour the alliance between our two countries."

At his side Pytheas drew a sharp intake of breath, his face suddenly looking troubled.

"I do not know where the Roman ambassador is," Pytheas replied in a stiff voice. "I am sure that he will have a good reason for not being here. He always does."

Glancing at Pytheas, Flavius eyed him for a moment. "I know the man," he continued at last. "I had dealings with Metellus before in Rome - before he was posted here to be our ambassador." Looking concerned, Flavius sombrely lowered his eyes as he remembered his last encounter with the man. "We are not friends, he and I," Flavius said speaking quietly. "Metellus did his best to make my life hell once, but he failed. He is a disgrace to his family and a first-class arsehole - unworthy of his position, if you ask me. If it were not for his supporters in the Senate, he would be dead by now. Did you know that he was accused by some of being a Carthaginian sympathiser in the pay of the enemy. He was once a spokesman for a faction in the Senate called the Patriots party - who were openly advocating for peace with Carthage, to be struck on Hannibal's terms. Metellus is lucky to have escaped with his life for such betrayal."

"So, I gather," Pytheas replied, refusing to look at Flavius. "I heard you investigated him a few years ago - when you were trying to capture Carthaginian agents operating in Rome. When you were still working for your patron Trebonius as a Roman spy."

Looking surprised, Flavius gazed at the Massaliot diplomat.

"You know I worked for Trebonius?" he exclaimed. "How do you know what I did before this. How could you possibly know that?"

"I think it is time that you gave your speech now," Pytheas said stiffly gesturing at the blood-stained altar. "It would not do to keep everyone waiting."

***

Flavius was just about to finish his speech to the assembled gathering, when there was a sudden commotion near the temple entrance. A moment later a bedraggled looking figure hove into view, staggering towards the dignitaries, swaying unsteadily on his feet. As the man approached Flavius saw that it was Quintus Caecilius Metellus. The Roman ambassador looked drunk, his tunic stained and reeking of wine. Turning to stare at Metellus, in horror, a mutter of disapproval arose among the gathered government officials but no one made any attempt to stop or confront Metellus as he staggered into their midst.

"What are you all staring at," Metellus called out, slurring his words. "Smile. I am here am I not. That is what you all wanted isn't? For me to attend this fucking boring party."

Among the Massaliot officials however no one spoke up in reply - the assembled men appeared to be too embarrassed to act. Standing before the grand statue of Artemis the temple priests too seemed to have grown highly uncomfortable at the intrusion, their eyes lowered.

"Metellus," Flavius's cried out, angrily breaking the tense oppressive silence as he advanced towards the Roman ambassador. "Get your act together man. This is no way to behave. You represent the dignity of Rome. You are a guest here among these people."

Catching sight of Flavius, Metellus came to an abrupt surprised halt, and for a moment he seemed paralysed by indecision.

"Oh, it's you," Metellus blurted out at last, raising his arm and pointing an accusing finger at Flavius. "Fancy that. You Flavius are why I was posted to this shithole in the first place. You destroyed my career. You are the reason why my family no longer acknowledges me. You were always getting in my way. It was always you. You. You. You. Well I am going to settle this right now, right here in front of all these good people."

But before Metellus could say another word, Flavius struck him on the head with his wooden cane and the force of the blow was such that it knocked Metellus to the floor where he lay groaning.

"Pytheas," Flavius said sharply turning to the Massaliot diplomat who was staring at the scene in growing horror. "Help me carry this arsehole out of the temple. His presence here defiles the goddess. We will dump him on the steps outside and let him sleep it off."

But in reply Pytheas hastily shook his head.

"No, I cannot do that," Pytheas said. "He is the Roman ambassador. By law none may touch him or harm him. The gods have declared him inviolate, and we must obey the sacred commands. I am sorry. None here will touch him. None will help carry him out of the temple."

"Great. Fine," Flavius exclaimed, looking exasperated as he hurriedly turning to Scoti. "But that law does not apply to me or Scoti. We are Romans and this prick is as inviolate as a maiden on her wedding night. Scoti - grab his legs. We are going to move him out of the temple."

For a moment the Roman astronomer said nothing, as he looked down at Metellus who was still lying on the floor groaning, his eyes closed. Then Scoti took a step towards the Roman ambassador and before anyone could stop him, he had kicked Metellus in the balls, eliciting an explosion of fresh writhing agony across the diplomat's face and body.

"Sorry Sir," Scoti said, as he hurriedly grasped hold of Metellus's legs, and together with Flavius lifted him up. "My foot seemed to have slipped."

Saying nothing, Flavius looked grim as he and Scoti carried Metellus out of the temple before unceremoniously dumping him outside on the stone temple steps. For a moment Flavius paused, catching his breath as he gazed down at the groaning man. Then he turned to Scoti.

"What did you do that for? Why did you kick him?"

"I know who he is," Scoti replied with sudden scorn, his eyes gleaming with a strange intensity. "I have heard about the Patriot party. I know what he was trying to do in Rome - peace on Hannibal's terms. Metellus was advocating for our surrender, but it was just not right Sir. I lost two brothers at Cannae."

As Flavius and Scoti prepared to re-enter the temple, however they were suddenly confronted by Pytheas and Acco at the entrance doors. Coming towards him, Pytheas was staring at Flavius with a wary look.

"I hope that I did not offend you and your companions in there," Flavius said, eyeing the Massaliot diplomat. "But I could not allow that man to sully the dignity of Rome by his disgraceful drunken behaviour. I am only sorry that you have had to endure his company for so long. That cannot have been easy."

"No, it has not been easy," Pytheas snapped as his mask cracked. "That man has been a source of endless frustration for my government. But there was nothing we could do about it except endure him."

"Did you think I was going to be like him?" Flavius said sharply. "Did you think I was going to be another Metellus?"

"I have my sources in Rome," Pytheas retorted drawing himself up into a defensive posture. "They, told me that you were a troublemaker. A man who did comply with the established rules of conduct. That you had no respect for authority. All Roman diplomats who I have met have belonged to the senatorial class. But you do not. You are just a carpenter, of no social standing. They told me that you have had no education, no diplomatic experience or skill and that you cannot even read or write. So yes, I was worried that I would be saddled with another incompetent Roman official, another Metellus. I had my doubts about you. I feared you would be just another vulgar and coarse man, who would make a complete mess of things. A man completely out of his depths who would possibly get us all killed. You cannot blame me for being suspicious and worried. This mission to the Tin islands is as important to Massalia, as it is to Rome."

"I see," Flavius growled. "Well, it appears that whoever briefed against me was not a friend of my patron Publius Cornelius Scipio. The assault on my character was really an attack on Scipio. But such is political life in Rome. So now that we have met - do you still think that I am a first-class arsehole?"

For a moment Pytheas did not reply, turning to look away into the gathering darkness of the evening.

"No, you are not," the Massaliot diplomat admitted turning to eye Flavius with a sincere and apologetic look. "I was mistaken and for that I apologise unreservedly. It was satisfying to see how you handled that arsehole over there. To see Metellus taken down a peg will have pleased many this evening and won you much respect in my city, even though none will openly admit to it. I see now that you are not the man that I was informed you would be. I am pleased it is so. If you will respect me and my city - then you and I Flavius will get on very well indeed."

"I respect you," Flavius said nodding. "I respect your city. And we should have no secrets here between us. It is true that I am of a lowly social class, but my patron Publius Cornelius Scipio felt I was the right man for this job and the Senate in Rome agreed. It was Scipio's idea to send me to the Tin islands, not mine. But I understand what we are doing here. I understand why it is important. You see," Flavius said taking a step towards Pytheas, his eyes gleaming. "I want to help end this war as soon as possible, so that I can get a last chance to see Julian, my youngest son again before I die. My son is serving in Spain, and I have not seen him in over seven years. It would be nice - to see my boy one final time. It would be really something. So, when we go to the Tin islands you should know that I am determined to succeed just like you are. We must all strive to bring this war to a successful conclusion as quickly as possible."

Gazing back at Flavius, Pytheas said nothing as he sullenly took in what had just been said.

"Fine," Pytheas said at last. "No more secrets between us. In that case you should know that Acco here suffers from gynophobia."

"What?" Flavius said with a frown as Acco looked startled.

"Gynophobia," Pytheas said nodding, his expression deadly serious. "I was going to tell you. It is an abnormal fear of women. The boy is absolutely terrified of coming face to face with women. He will bolt if he has to converse with a woman. The doctors say there is little they can do about the medical condition, but it is real. Just like a fear of heights or confined spaces or spiders. I am not making it up."

"Is that true?" Flavius responded turning to Acco who was suddenly looking very embarrassed. "You fear women?"

"I do Sir," Acco stammered. "I am sorry but the mere sight of them terrifies me. I have always had this fear since I was old enough to remember. It is hard to explain. It's like a dread."

"Jupiter's cock," Scoti swore softly, "sympathy and all with your condition, but if this is the case - why is he coming with us?"

"He's coming with us," Pytheas said in a patient voice, "because he is the finest translator in the city, and we need him."

"That may well be true," Flavius snapped, "but you do realise that we are going to be conducting our negotiations with a Queen. Queen Talwyn - a woman. I cannot be effective, if my translator bolts at the very first sight of her. How am I ever supposed to communicate with her in that case?"

"We will work on it," Pytheas said hastily. "We will get Acco ready for when he meets the Queen. We will make it work."

"And how are you going to do that?" Flavius asked in a sceptical voice. "Are you a doctor as well as a diplomat?"

"We will make it work," Pytheas said sharply, raising his voice. "Acco says he wants to try so, he is willing to confront his fears."

"It is true Sir," Acco said gazing at Flavius. "I know what I am signing up to. I want to make it work. Please Sir, give me a chance. I want to face my phobia. I want to conquer it."

For a long moment Flavius said nothing as he eyed the young man. Then at last he nodded in agreement.

"Alright But you are responsible for getting him ready for when we meet Queen Talwyn," he said turning to Pytheas. "I am counting on you to do that. Otherwise it's, going to be a fucking disaster."

"I will do my best," Pytheas replied in a sincere manner.

"Anyway," Flavius said, raising his eyebrows as he gazed back at Pytheas. "No secrets between us. So maybe now you would care to explain to me how come you know so much about me? I would really like to know. How come you are so well informed. How did you know about me and Trebonius?"

For a moment Pytheas hesitated, seemingly torn. Then making up his mind he shook his head.

"Not here," he snapped as he started out down the temple steps. "Follow me. I shall show you."

***

Ahead in the deserted street, Pytheas and Acco had come to a halt outside the doorway into a terraced building and were patiently waiting for Flavius and Scoti to catch up. It was getting late, and, across the sprawling city, darkness was rapidly setting in. As he limped up to the Massaliot diplomat Flavius frowned. What was going on? Where was his colleague taking him? Gazing back at him Pytheas looked strangely nervous and on edge as if he were doing something he was not really supposed to be doing.

"I must ask you," Pytheas began - speaking in a solemn voice, "that you keep to yourself what you are about to see. Foreigners are not normally permitted into this building, and I am going to need your word that you will tell no one, strictly no one about what you witness here. No one. Understood. It is a state secret. Now give me your word."

As both Flavius and Scoti replied giving the Massaliot diplomat their solemn undertaking to keep his secret, Pytheas knocked on the door, his knuckles appearing to rap out a specific code. For a long moment nothing happened. Then with a creaking noise the door swung open and a burly armed porter appeared in the doorway. Gazing at Pytheas the man appeared to recognise him. Gesturing at his companions to follow him Pytheas entered the building speaking a few words to the watchman as he did.

Following Pytheas down a corridor Flavius blinked as his eyes adjusted to the light. At the end of the passageway the building appeared to open up and suddenly he found himself in a large open room lit by a series of flickering torches attached to the walls. In the middle of the space was a large table and sprawled across it - a vast map made of stone, bronze and wood.

"Is that what I think it is," Scoti gasped as he caught sight of the stone map laid out across the table.

"Yes," Pytheas replied quietly as he came to stand beside the table. "It's a complete map of the western half of the continent of Europa. The lines drawn across the map denote tribal territorial divisions. The names of the tribes are marked in the stone as are their principal settlements, trade goods, estimated population numbers and war making potential."

For a moment Flavius said nothing as he stared at the map, trying to make sense of it all. He had never before seen a map so large and so detailed.

"What we have here," Pytheas said speaking quietly as he pointed at the map, "is a listing of every known tribe, kingdom, political federation, alliance, empire and trade route in the west. From the Carthaginian port of Gades in the south to the island of Thule in the far north where the sea turns to ice and the sun will shine at midnight. The map shows physical characteristics such as mountains ranges, lakes, trails and the course of rivers plus where they can be forded. It also shows the sources of metals, amber, slaves, hunting dogs and other trade goods. Tin here in the far west of Belerion. Gold, lead and silver deposits here. Amber here along the coast of the northern sea and slaves from these parts, here and here. You can see that this map gives us a very good understanding of the scale, challenges and distances involved in our trade with the indigenous Celts and peoples to the north. My government keeps this data up to date. As a great trading city it is important that we know exactly what is happening in our export markets and among our trade partners. This knowledge is of vital importance to the prosperity of my city so we take great care to gather our information and keep it updated."

"Wow," Scoti explained as he gazed at the map in astonishment. "Wow. It must take some effort to gather all this knowledge."

"It does," Pytheas replied turning to Flavius.

"Why are you showing us this?" Scoti exclaimed as his eyes swept across the vast map. "I mean its great from a trade point of view. But how is this relevant to our mission to the Tin islands?"

"Because they have a network," Flavius interrupted before Pytheas had a chance to respond. "A gigantic network of spies, like a spiders web. That's why he is showing us this," Flavius added looking grave. "The Massaliots have an intelligence network feeding them information that stretches across the continent. Is that not right Pytheas?"

"Yes - that's right," Pytheas replied gazing back at Flavius. "Over many years my city has built up and maintained an extensive web of informants, spies and sympathisers in every tribal community right across this map. It is these informants who are supplying us with a constant stream of news as to what is going on. We really rely on this knowledge. It means that we know exactly what is going on across half a continent. We know what individual tribes are doing and planning. We know their intentions, capabilities, dynastic quarrels, rivalries, traditions, challenges and problems. We have built up a huge-detailed understanding of who our trade partners are and we have armed our merchants with this knowledge. For knowledge is power after all. But it does not only concern trade but politics and war too. We know everything that is going on. Absolutely everything that is of importance to my city and we need to - if we are to respond effectively to changing circumstances. Rest assured nothing important slips by without us noticing it at some point." For a moment Pytheas paused savouring the moment. "You mentioned to me earlier today Flavius that knowledge was power," he added. "Well here is that power at it rawest and most intense form."

For a long moment Flavius did not respond as he stared at the map. Then at last he turned to Pytheas.

"It's impressive," Flavius replied looking grave. "Damn impressive. I see now why you knew about myself and Trebonius. So, tell me. On the Tin islands. Who is our contact? Who is your man there and are they any good?"

"His name is Morcant," Pytheas said quickly. "A nobleman at the Queen's court and yes he is good and very trustworthy. He will be on hand to help our cause when we get there."

Chapter Ten - The Art of Diplomacy

In the flickering reddish glow, emanating from the burning torches that were arranged along the enclosing defensive wall and earthen embankment, the Celtic hill fort of Carn Brea had taken on the look of an ominous, forbidding place Flavius thought. As if the spirits of the local people's ancestors did not want him to be here. As if he was a trespasser. An unwanted guest. Looking grave, clad in his mud stained and hooded travelling cloak, he stood waiting just inside the fortress gate. It was night and scattered across the sky over his head, were a few dozens of twinkling stars. Throughout the small settlement and cluster of thatched round houses all was quiet and peaceful, as if the inhabitants were hiding away. The glaring exception of-course were the rowdy and boisterous celebrations that were taking place inside the great hall, less than a stone's throw away from where he stood.

For a moment Flavius eyed the large building from whence the noise was seeping out into the cool dark night before turning to his three companions. Standing about next to their tethered horses, Scoti, Pytheas and Acco looked tense and nervous as they awaited their audience with Queen Talwyn.

They had finally made it to the legendary Tin islands. The journey from Massalia was an achievement in itself Flavius thought. The things he had seen and heard along the way had given him a thousand new ideas for stories to tell his young grandchildren. After a long and arduous ride on horseback right across Gaul - through the territory of several tribes, a ship had taken them across the narrow sea to the island of Belerion. The expedition had encountered no problems with the local tribes and that was largely due to Pytheas. The Massaliot diplomat had been able to call on a friend in every major Gallic settlement through which they had passed. And the more that he had seen of how the Massaliots operated across Gaul, the more impressed he'd become by the vast intelligence gathering, trade and diplomatic network which Rome's allies had created. It was truly awesome. The local help and knowledge they had received had proved invaluable. Allowing them to avoid blundering into war zones, famine stricken-regions, pestilence and trails that were known to be watched and preyed upon by bandits and outlaws. The local guides who Pytheas had hired had been competent and reliable, allowing them to make rapid progress.

And after crossing the mist shrouded sea - seeing the majestic white cliffs that had suddenly appeared, towering straight out of the sea, had been a most magical experience. The Tin islands were far larger than he had been expecting, their coast stretching for hundreds of miles. The islanders had not been that different to the Gallic tribes on the mainland he had observed. For in appearance, technology and in customs they appeared to all be Celtic, but Pytheas had pointed out the subtle tribal differences. The island on which they now found themselves, Pytheas had told him, sat right upon the edge of the world beyond which was nothing but the globe circling sea. The feared and brutal outer ocean, in whose depths great sea monsters were said to protect the home of the mythical Hyperboreans. And the closer to the edge of the world one lived, the wilder and more fierce the people became, Pytheas had claimed.

"Looks like they are having quite a party in there," Flavius murmured turning to Pytheas.

"Yes, it appears that what those locals down at the coast told us earlier is true," Pytheas replied in a stiff uptight voice as he gazed in the direction of the hall. "So, the Queen has been victorious. She has won her battle. This must be her victory feast. Good gods," Pytheas suddenly groaned. "They are all going to be completely stark raving drunk in there. Maybe we should have postponed our arrival until tomorrow. Have you ever visited a Celtic-hall full of pissed up warriors celebrating victory in battle before Flavius? It's not pretty. You are always just one insult away from causing a mass brawl and getting your head kicked in."

"No, I am not waiting for the morning," Flavius replied calmly. "We do this now. We have travelled a long way for this. As for brawling. I have some experience with these Celts. I fought them in battle at Telamon, when they were sober. That's how I got this limp."

"Yeah, well there are only four of us and I am not fighting anyone," Pytheas said with a sniff. "My brawling days are over."

"So if the civil war between wife and husband has indeed ended," Flavius continued, "then that is surely good news. It should make reaching an agreement that much easier. Now that she has won - the Queen will have regained control over all the tin mines and all the miners. We only have to deal with her. Otherwise, we would have had to strike two agreements. One with her and a second with her husband. That would be complicated."

"Yes," Pytheas muttered. "It would. You are right. It is good news that Queen Talwyn has emerged as the winner. We can deal with her. She is a known quantity - unlike her consort about who we know little."

"In the Republic," Flavius continued in his quiet and calm voice, "it is not customary for women to have any official public power, but here on these islands I see that they do things differently."

"The Celtic and Germanic tribes," Pytheas responded. "They are known to use women as peacemakers. To use women to negotiate peace treaties between warring tribes and clans. The tribes believe that the sexual wiles of women, the natural sanctity that they offer, makes them ideal for this work."

"Maybe," Flavius looking thoughtful. "Still for a woman - even here - to rise to such power and to hold on to it - that is quite an achievement. She must be a strong and formidable lady if she has survived this long."

"Oh, Queen Talwyn is formidable alright," Pytheas said. "She can smell weakness in men like dogs can smell a fox. And she just loves exposing her opponents weaknesses, making them submit to her will. She can be most ruthless when she needs to be. She has to be. The wolves are forever circling her throne waiting for their chance to knock her off it."

For a moment Flavius said nothing. Then he turned to look at Acco, who was nervously gazing down at his boots.

"You alright son?" Flavius said. "You ready to meet the Queen. You are not going to let me down and make a run for it?"

"Yes Sir," Acco stammered, quickly looking up at Flavius. "I can do this. I am ready to face the woman. I am prepared."

"Don't worry Flavius," Scoti said from the darkness. "I will be standing right behind him to catch him if he does try and do a runner. He is not getting out of this the easy way."

"Acco is going to be alright," Pytheas growled. "Leave him alone. You have all witnessed the work that we have put in together to reduce his phobia. If he says he is ready then he is."

"Alright son," Flavius said reaching out to lay a hand on Acco's shoulder. "I believe you. Just follow your training and do what Pytheas has taught you. Take your time, if you need to and don't let anyone upset you. I have your back. All four of us have each other's back. We're a team. You got that."

"Yes Sir," Acco stammered.

"I am just messing with you boy," Scoti said, his face hidden in the shadows. "We will look after you. We stick together, the four of us. That's what we do. We are all a long way from home, and we all want this mission to be a success. You are not going to be alone in there Acco."

Flavius was about to speak again when a figure suddenly appeared out of the gloom accompanied by a couple of armed guards. As the man approached, he called out in his native language, beckoning for them to follow him.

"He says that Queen Talwyn will see us now," Acco translated hastily. "We are to follow him into the great hall."

***

Limping into the hall, Flavius was immediately confronted by a fierce blast of heat from the burning torches and braziers and the sour smell of spilled wine, beer, urine, excrement and unwashed bodies. In the stale atmosphere, the odour was strong and decidedly unpleasant. The great hall was packed and swiftly Flavius found himself surrounded by scores of boisterous celebrating warriors, most of whom looked quite drunk and inebriated. A few appeared to have passed out and were lying slumped across the floor, while others were singing, arm wrestling and urinating where they stood. Struggling through the mass of bodies, holding two tankards, a young-serving girl was being repeatedly groped. Spotting Queen Talwyn Flavius led his three companions straight towards her in single file and as he appeared in their midst, a sudden hush settled across the hall, as all eyes turned to stare at him. Ignoring the suspicious hard-faced men with their tattooed bodies, wild beards, moustaches and hairstyles, Flavius kept his eyes on the Queen.

Sat upon her simple throne at the far end of the hall Queen Talwyn looked completely sober, yet her face was pale like milk, her body fragile - betraying that she was not well. In fact, she looked ill. Lying about at her feet were several huge savage-looking hunting dogs lazily gnawing on discarded bones, drool dripping from their open jaws and razor-sharp teeth. But if the Queen appeared frail in body, there was no such weakness in her eyes. For as he approached, Flavius suddenly felt her iron gaze upon him, fearless, penetrating and merciless as if she were trying to see right into his very soul. Meeting her eyes, Flavius found himself unable to look away, locked in a silent battle of wills. The Queen was trying to dominate him. To make him acknowledge his inferiority to her. It was just as Pytheas had warned him. Limping towards her, Flavius sensed the growing tension in the great hall. By now he had everyone's attention. There had better be a fucking good reason for disturbing and interrupting our party - the hall appeared to be telling him. And that had been the aim. To get their attention.

Halting before the Queen, Flavius paused before solemnly and respectfully inclining his head to her. At his side, standing so close he was almost clinging to him, Acco was staring at the woman in terrified horror, a bead of sweat trickling down his youthful cheek like a tear.

"Queen Talwyn. Rightful ruler of her people, mistress of the Tin islands. Congratulations on your great victory. Rome is pleased. My name is Flavius," Flavius began speaking in Latin, his face grave and serious. "I am a Legate of Rome. The Republic has tasked me with negotiating a new trade agreement with you and your people. The Senate in Rome wishes to reaffirm the bond of friendship that exists between us."

As Flavius finished speaking, he hesitated. At his side Acco remained silent, unable to speak, frozen by the sheer horror of having to face a woman. But before Flavius could react, Scoti had given the young translator a little sharp prod and the act seemed to work - for immediately, like a machine that had got stuck, Acco sprang back into life and began to speak, hurriedly lowering his eyes to the ground just as Pytheas had trained him to do.

When Acco finished translating, silence followed once more and the only noise throughout the tense expectant hall came from some snoring men and the hunting dogs gnawing and slobbering over their bones. Sat upon her throne, surrounded by her nobles and bodyguard, Queen Talwyn did not move. Nor did she say anything as she took her time scrutinising Flavius from top to bottom, as if she were purchasing a prize horse at the market. Still, she kept her silence. Her pale face giving no clue as to what she was thinking. Shifting her attention to Scoti and Pytheas, she gave them the same silent and intimidating treatment. Then at last she turned her attention back to Flavius and spoke, her voice steady as iron, her eyes filled with steel.

"The Queen says that we are welcome in her hall," Acco said, keeping his eyes rigidly focused on the ground. "She says that Rome is always welcome here in her domain although it has been many years since the Republic has bothered to send a Legate to negotiate with her."

"Tell the Queen that I am grateful for her hospitality," Flavius said eyeing her in a calm and dignified manner. "The Republic has not forgotten about her. The trade in tin is most valuable and has enriched both our peoples. Trade is good. Friendship and trade is even better. Rome wishes for good relations. It is a sign of how important the Senate views our diplomatic relations - that they have sent me half-way across the world to negotiate a new treaty in the midst of a war. We are ready to do a deal. I am here to do business."

As Acco translated, Queen Talwyn nodded before suddenly frowning and turning to stare at Acco as if she had noticed something.

"She asks you Sir," Acco translated as his face exploded into a furious blush. "Whether your translator is afraid of her? She wants to know why I will not look her in the eye. I am so sorry Sir."

"Don't be," Flavius replied quickly. "There is nothing to be ashamed of. Tell her the truth son. That you suffer from gynophobia. That you fear the sight of women. That it is a real ailment."

"Yes Sir," Acco muttered quietly, in a miserable voice.

But as the young man spoke, still refusing to look at the Queen, for a moment there was a stunned silence. Then throughout the hall the warriors burst into shrieks and loud peels, of laughter. As the merry noise continued, swirling around the four of them like a storm, Flavius looked unhappy as at his side Acco was physically trembling, from the public humiliation he was being subjected too. Then at last the laughter died away, the storm cleared and Queen Talwyn was gazing at Flavius with a sudden glimmer of amusement in her eye.

"She says, she has heard that the great war against Carthage is not going well for us," Acco rattled out in flawless translation. "She takes a keen interest in the conflict as some of her young warriors have signed up as mercenaries to fight for Carthage in Spain. She asks, if it true that Romans do not dare to fight against Hannibal? That Rome is terrified of him. That you are scared even when your forces outnumber Hannibal's army."

For a moment Flavius did not reply as he eyed the wily Queen. Then gathering himself together he spoke.

"Rome is going to win the war. Hannibal," Flavius exclaimed suddenly raising his voice, "is overrated. He knows how to win a battle, but he does not know how to end the war between us. He does not know how to finish what he started. That will prove to be his downfall. Time is not on his side."

"And Rome does," Acco translated the Queen's sharp mocking response. "Rome knows how to finish the war. How?"

"The same way in which we finish all our wars," Flavius replied in a stern voice as he stood his ground, his eyes gleaming in the flickering torch light. "When we have won and the defeated are down on their knees before us begging for terms. Only then will we stop fighting."

As Acco finished his translation, silence descended upon the hall. On her throne Queen Talwyn however, did not look pleased. For a moment she stared at Flavius before abruptly gesturing at his companions.

"The Queen says that she sees Massaliots among your party," Acco said quickly, his eyes fixed on the floor. "But that you do not appear to have brought her a gift. She says that it is customary and polite to bring the ruler of a people - a gift. She wants to know what you have brought her - so that she can see and make a judgement on the quality of what you have to offer?"

"A gift," Flavius said slowly nodding. "You mean a bribe. I am sorry but I do not deal in bribes. The Queen knows the quality of our products and those of our allies in Massalia. But we have brought a gift for the Queen. Something that I think she will find quite useful."

"Then where is it?" Acco translated as the Queen abruptly and theatrically opened her arms wide with a perplexed look that raised another round of laughter from the packed hall.

Looking unperturbed by the mocking laughter, Flavius stood his ground, calmly waiting for the noise to subside.

"The gift that we have brought the Queen," he called out last, "is not a physical object which I can show to her. It is far more valuable than that. Far more potent and powerful. Like I said it will be most useful."

For a moment, Flavius paused to allow Acco to catch up. Then, fixing his grave eyes on the Queen he continued.

"Queen Talwyn - you have many enemies, I am sure," Flavius said as he started to make his pitch. "A Queen can never be complacent to the threats that surround her - as I am sure you are only too well aware of. Inside your tribe, possibly even inside this very hall there are men who wish you ill. Also, beyond your borders - there are those who are actively plotting to take your throne. Your husband for instance. You have rivals, competitors. The nature of man is to covet what others have. To want what they have. To take it by force or stealth. Other, tribes perhaps will eye your lucrative trade with us with envy and jealously. They may so be inclined to take some of it for themselves. Rome is not your enemy Queen Talwyn. We protect and take care of our friends and allies. We can help you secure your throne. We can help you defeat your enemies. Rome's friendship is our gift to you."

As Flavius finished speaking Acco's lone voice filled the great hall. Then, when he too stopped speaking there was silence. Sat upon her throne, Queen Talwyn was staring at Flavius with a sudden and strange glow in her eyes and once again. Flavius sensed the iron in her will. At last, she spoke, her words cutting through the silence like a knife going through skin.

"How?" Acco stammered. "How can you help me?"

"The city of Massalia - Rome's ally," Flavius replied calmly, "has an extensive network of informants and sympathisers among every major tribe - right across these islands and beyond these shores. We know our trade partners and we know what is going on with them. We know what the Queen's rivals are doing. If a new preferential trade deal between us were to be agreed, we would be willing to share that information with you. It would give you some advance warning and understanding, as to who your enemies are and what they are likely to be up to. Such information could prevent another rebellion like the one your husband just instigated. Knowledge is power. Do you not agree?"

Upon her throne the Queen's expression had not changed, nor did she give any indication that she agreed with him, but Flavius was conscious that she was gazing at him with a new glimmer of respect.

"The Queen asks," Acco translated, as the Queen spoke again. "Why she, should trust you? She trusted her husband once and he tried to steal her throne. What proof can you offer that you have such resources?"

"If we were to agree a new trade agreement," Flavius replied in a grave manner. "It would be in our interest to keep you on your throne. That's only logical. The Queen protects our trade interests and Rome in return protects her. As regards trust. It must be earned. The Republic does not lightly enter into agreements but once we do, we keep our word. Contracts are sacred. They are not meant to be broken. Oaths and promises are not meant to be discarded. Such is the Roman way and woe to those who break their bond." For a moment Flavius paused, as Acco's voice rattled away in a well-practised manner, clear, eloquent and precise. "The informant network exists," Flavius continued, "but the Queen already knows this, or else I would be amazed that she does not. I am speaking the truth. Massalia has been trading with the tribes of these islands for hundreds of years. Our allies have not been idle. They have recruited an army of spies."

Staring back at him Queen Talwyn studied him for a moment, with a sudden wary look. Then she spoke.

"The Queen asks if you know of any men right here, in this hall," Acco said, rushing out the words as an angry upswell in muttering erupted throughout the packed hall. "Who are plotting against her right at this moment - and if so, she challenges you to point them out."

For a moment Flavius hesitated, quickly making eye contact with Pytheas as around him the angry tumult continued.

"The Queen knows her own hall," Flavius called out at last raising his voice. "She is no fool. These matters are however state business and best discussed in private which we are happy to do. What however is clear is that the Queen's consort had help in planning his rebellion. He did not do this alone. He had help and we know who helped him."

As Acco, finished translating the hall erupted in howls of outrage and Flavius was swiftly struck by a coin that was flung at him from the crowd. Stoically, he stood his ground as all round, angry threatening voices were raised, berating him for his temerity. Then abruptly Queen Talwyn rose to her feet. Her eyes sweeping across the hall, her face pale while she raised her hand for silence. Finally, as order returned, her gaze settled upon Flavius.

"She asks you," Acco said sweating profusely, "what trade terms does Rome offer?"

"The Senate in Rome is willing to agree generous trade terms," Flavius replied. "We are prepared to double the price we pay for her tin as long as the flow of trade to Massalia is not impeded in any way."

"Twice the usual price," Acco said, hurriedly translating as the Queen raised an eyebrow, her eyes fixed on Flavius with a mocking look. "She says, that Rome and Massalia can do better than that. She says that you sound desperate. Your offer is an insult."

"No, it is a fair offer," Flavius said shaking his head.

Gazing back at him the Queen paused. Then she leaned back in her seat and spoke, her words hard and sharp like flint.

"She says that your terms are not acceptable," Acco translated. "She says, that she has already made another trade treaty with Carthage. She has given them the exclusive rights to the tin trade. As of now an embargo exists on all tin exports to Rome and Massalia."

"An embargo," Flavius exclaimed, looking startled.

"Flavius. Flavius. Look," Scoti said hurriedly with a sudden sharp intake of breath. "Over there. Look. Carthaginians."

Turning to look in the direction his secretary was gesturing, Flavius's expression abruptly darkened as among the mass of Celtic warriors he suddenly caught sight of a smattering of men who appeared to be different to their hosts. Clad in unfamiliar clothing, they looked foreign. With their own distinctive weapons, the men seemed out of place, as if they too, like himself, did not belong here. The strangers looked like they were soldiers. All were of fighting age, tough, experienced men and each one was observing him with a tense hostile expression. Then Flavius froze as his eyes locked onto one individual. Standing among the crowd was a swarthy, splendidly clad man with black curly hair and a fine coat of body armour emblazoned with a black horse on a white background. Coldly glaring back at him with an unfriendly look, there was something strangely familiar about the man, as if he had seen him before. But where?

"Fucking Carthaginian mercenaries," Scoti hissed looking about in alarm. "They look like Spaniards. What are they doing here?"

For a long moment Flavius did not reply, his face hard as nails, his eyes gleaming like flint, his body rigid like a statue.

"That one over there is not a Spaniard," Flavius snapped coldly as he glared back at the enemy. "He's a Numidian and I have met him before - in Rome. Years ago when I was hunting a gang of Carthaginian agents who had robbed the state mint. That man over there was part of the group I was looking for. I believe his name is Gisgo. I have unfinished business with that man."

"Shit Flavius," Scoti muttered. "What are we going to do? There are only four of us, and I count at least twenty Carthaginians."

Ignoring Scoti, Flavius eyed Gisgo for a moment longer. Then calmly he turned his attention back to the Queen.

"Acco," Flavius said sharply, his voice like ice. "Tell, the Queen that a trade embargo against us is a most unfortunate development. Tell her that she has been badly advised on this matter. Very badly advised. But that it is not too late for her to change her mind. Tell her that she is making a mistake by siding with Carthage against us. A grave and terrible mistake."

As Acco translated, Flavius held the Queen's eye, allowing her to see his displeasure while anger flowed through his veins. There had always been a chance he would have come face-to-face with the enemy in this distant land, but now that it had happened the shock was both raw and powerful.

Gazing back at him, Queen Talwyn looked unimpressed, her expression hardening as she spoke in reply.

"The Queen asks you - why do you think she has made a mistake?" Acco said, trembling slightly on his feet. "She says, Carthage has helped her a lot. The men Carthage sent here have fought for her in battle. They helped defeat her husband and crush the rebellion. She is merely keeping her promise to them."

"She is making a mistake," Flavius growled, eyeing the Queen, "because she is backing the losing side. Rome is going to win this war and when we eventually do - Gades and all the other Carthaginian seaports with whom she currently trades, will come under our control. And when they do, the trade with Carthage will cease and she will discover that all roads lead to Rome. When we win the war, the Republic will become her only customer and there will be consequences if she has been seen to back Carthage over us. Rome treats her friends and trade partners with respect, but those found to have favoured the enemy will be regarded with suspicion and possibly worse. Rome may be distant, but our arm is long. The Queen should ponder on that before she makes her final decision."

"Sir," Acco groaned. "She is not going to like that. It's a threat."

"Just say it like I did," Flavius snapped in no mood for dithering. "The time for pleasantries is over. I have not come this far for our mission to end in failure. We are in the presence of the enemy."

As Acco began to translate, Flavius eyed the Queen and, as his words struck home for the first time, he saw what he thought was a small flicker of doubt appear in her eyes. Taking a deep breath, Queen Talwyn paused as one of her nobles stooped to whisper something in her ear. Then at last she raised her chin, as if in a challenge, before turning to Flavius with a wary look.

"The hour is late. It has been a long day for all, and these discussions will continue at another time," Acco translated, his eyes still fixed on the ground. "The Queen says that we are welcome in her hall. She will provide you with food and drink and a place to sleep. She says that the issues which you raise are important, but that she needs time to think about what to do. She will give you her answer when she is ready to do so. Until then we must be patient and wait."

As the great hall returned to its former rowdy celebrations and feasting, Flavius watched as the Queen stiffly rose from her throne and left the building, surrounded by her bodyguard and a few of her nobles. The audience was over, but the result was still unclear. Turning to his companions who were standing close together forming a tight little group, Flavius sighed and reached out to grip Acco's shoulder in a fatherly manner.

"Well done son," he said. "I thought you handled that well. Your translation was flawless."

"Thank you, Sir." Acco replied, relief clearly audible in his voice. "I am glad that I managed to see it through. The training we did - it helped."

"So now what?" Flavius muttered turning to Pytheas, while shooting a quick glance at the Carthaginian mercenaries standing about in the crowd. "We wait? We wait for the Queen to decide on what to do?"

"Yup," Pytheas said, looking tense as he too turned to look around at the boisterous crowd. "The good news is that she has not completely dismissed our request. The bad news is that it seems that Carthage got here before us. They got their bid in first which gives them an advantage. Do you really belief that stuff she was saying about them helping her win her fight with her husband?"

"Those men," Flavius said using his head to indicate the Carthaginians in the crowd. "They are mercenaries, fighting men. So yes, I believe they could have helped the Queen in battle. That one over there - staring at us right now. He's a Numidian prince. His name is Gisgo. He crossed the mountains into Italy with Hannibal. So no, we are not going to be able to compete with them on fighting skill, as there are only four of us and none of us are soldiers. But I am not giving up without a fight. Carthage be damned. We came here to get an agreement and that is what we are going to do. I am not leaving without what we came for. Screw them and their embargo. We are just going to have to convince the Queen to change her mind."

"That's going to be tricky," Pytheas said quickly. "Our arrival appears to have put the Queen in a difficult position. Now she faces a dilemma. She must choose between us and Carthage."

"Well, who said being Queen was easy," Flavius retorted as he turned to eye the crowd. "No, we wait and we use every opportunity, we get to convince her to change her mind and lift that embargo. And as for the Carthaginians. We stay out of their way. No point in picking a quarrel, if we don't need to. So," Flavius added, turning to Pytheas. "Come on. I have seen enough about how you operate. Where is our local man? Where is Morcant? If he is as good as you say he is, then we need him to help us. He should be here. Where is he?"

"I do believe he is approaching us as I speak," Pytheas said suddenly as he caught sight of a one-armed man picking his way towards them. "That's him over there. The man with one arm and the spiky hair. He only speaks Greek, so Acco you will need to translate for our Roman friends."

Turning to gaze at Morcant as the Celtic nobleman came up to their small group Flavius said nothing. Gripping Pytheas's proffered hand with a broad pleased grin Morcant spoke quickly in Greek, before embracing the Massaliot as if he were greeting an old friend, he had not seen for ages. Then as Pytheas replied, the Celt turned to look at the others, making no attempt to hide his public association with them. Gesturing at Flavius, Pytheas made a remark and in response Morcant's expression changed and became serious and respectful. Reaching out, the two men quickly and formally shook hands.

"Morcant says it is a great pleasure and honour to meet you Sir," Acco translated as he stood at Flavius's shoulder. "He says that you spoke well just now and that he is glad you are here. He is a friend of Rome. The future of the tin trade and his people's prosperity lies with Massalia and Rome - not Carthage. He says that you are right that Rome is going to win the war. He says that times here have been turbulent, and the arrival of the Carthaginian diplomats has not helped matters. He promises, he will do what he can to help us."

"Thank you," Flavius replied. "Tell him that we are grateful and yes we are going to need his help. As much as he can give us. Can you ask him what he knows about these Carthaginians and whether he thinks the Queen will change her mind about the tin embargo?"

As Acco translated, Morcant studied Flavius for a moment with a serious look.

"He, says it is going to be difficult. The Carthaginians and their leader, a man named Gisgo, have managed to make an impression on the Queen," Acco said. "They fought in battle for her and in return she promised them exclusive rights to the tin exports. She cannot now go back on her word. To do so would be a sign that she cannot be trusted. Not only the Carthaginians would see that - but our own people too. The rebellion by her husband, may have been crushed but the situation is still volatile and unsettled. Her husband has fled into exile and is still a threat. The Queen cannot afford to look weak or break her word to Gisgo. She has some hard decisions to make. And it does not help her that she is still recovering from being poisoned. You saw how pale and unwell she looked. Well, that is because someone tried to murder her a few days ago."

"Poisoned," Flavius exclaimed looking startled. "By whom?"

"It's still not entirely clear yet," Acco replied translating Morcant's words. "But another of her advisers - a man named Aed is suspected of doing the deed. He was her official taster. He had the opportunity to get close to her. If her food was poisoned, then he should have been affected too but he suffered no symptoms and he had a motive to kill our Queen."

"Aed," Pytheas said with a frown. "I know this name. Was he not supposed to be sympathetic to Carthage?"

"He is," Acco translated as Morcant spoke again. "He, along with myself are the Queen's principal advisers. Aed persuaded the Queen to look favourably upon the Carthaginians. He got her to agree to their embargo request. He's caused a shed load of trouble. And now he is under arrest and awaiting trial. The judgement is going to take place as soon as we get back to Caer Bran. If found guilty they are going to sever his head from his body."

"So that is good news for us then," Scoti interrupted glancing at his companions with a hopeful look.

For a moment none of the men in the small cluster spoke as Flavius and Pytheas, exchanged a quick look. Then, looking grave Flavius turned away, his eyes seeking out Gisgo across the crowded noisy hall. The Numidian Prince had not moved and was coolly observing him in return, the hostility on his face palpable and real, as if Flavius's unexpected appearance had ruined his day.

"It is our job. It is my job," Flavius said at last, turning back to Morcant, "to try and persuade the Queen to be favourable to Rome. We cannot accept a trade embargo. It would be a disaster. So, we cannot just sit here idly and patiently waiting for her to come to a decision. We need to get the Queen to change her mind and fast. So, I want ideas. Anything. Anyone."

"Fear not," Acco said translating, as across from him, Morcant suddenly grinned at him. "I have already thought about this before your arrival. I have a plan. The Carthaginians think they have already won by getting the Queen to agree to their embargo. They believe that they don't have to do anything further. But time, is not on their side. They arrived here by ship, and I know that they are keen to return to Gades before the weather turns for the worse. If they delay too long, they are going to get stuck here for the winter. So, all we have to do is stall the Queen. Play for time. We simply stay put and wait until they leave. Then we shall have the Queen, all to ourselves. Once the Carthaginians have left it will be much easier for us to get the Queen to change her mind."

Chapter Eleven - Judgement Day

Lying stretched out on the bale of hay that served as his bed, Flavius was woken by the sound of a barking dog. Sitting up, fully clothed, he quickly turned to look around. It was just after dawn and nearby Pytheas and Acco were still asleep, curled up in the hay, their cloaks acting as blankets. Crouching beside the open door, Scoti however was awake, peering out at the Celtic settlement of Caer Bran, his sleep deprived eyes red and swollen. Across his lap lay a knife. Noticing that Flavius was awake, the astronomer gave him a tired, sullen glance.

"You have not slept?" Flavius said as he joined Scoti at the door - peering out at the small settlement beyond.

"That's right. Not for one moment," Scoti growled. "I have been keeping watch all night. In case of trouble. Some-one has to. There are Carthaginians sleeping just fifty paces away from us. What is to prevent them from coming here during the night and knifing us all to death. They could do that easily. It would solve their problem and I doubt the Queen would do anything to punish them."

Saying nothing Flavius peered at the cluster of thatched round houses and the encircling embankment beyond. A few people were out and about going about their business, but apart from the barking dog the Celtic settlement was quiet and peaceful.

"You are wrong. It would not solve their problem," Flavius said at last, looking grave. "If Gisgo and his men were to kill us, Rome would just send another legate with similar instructions to us, and I think you underestimate the Queen. She is very much in control of her own domain. She will not take kindly to such a breach of diplomatic protocol. Her reputation would suffer."

"And we would be dead," Scoti murmured.

"I am going to go for a stroll," Flavius said. "Morcant says that today is the day of Aed's trial. Stay here and try and get some sleep. Get some rest Scoti. I am going to need you to be sharp and alert this afternoon when the proceedings take place. It's going to be an important day for all."

"If you are going out then take this," Scoti said offering Flavius his knife. "As protection. You never know when you may need it."

"No, that knife won't protect me," Flavius replied shaking his head. "You keep it. I won't be long."

"What's going on Sir?" Scoti said hurriedly, as Flavius was about to step through the doorway. "I mean I know we said we would stall the Queen until those Carthaginians had left, but those fuckers are still here. They don't look like they are in a hurry to leave either. Morcant said they were keen to return home, to Gades before the weather changes, but that does not appear to be true. What are they waiting for? Why are the Carthaginians still here?"

"I don't know," Flavius replied. "We must be patient. But we can wait it out, the whole winter if need be. The enemy cannot. Time is not on their side. Morcant is quite sure that they will leave soon."

"I do not like that man - Morcant," Scoti sniffed looking away. "I can't explain it but there is something not quite right about him. There is something of the night about him."

For a moment Flavius eyed Scoti with concern. "You need to get some sleep Scoti," he said at last. "I can't have you staying up all night again. I need that brain of yours to be fully functional."

"You think that the Queen will give us our reply today regards the new trade agreement?" Scoti said, looking tired.

"Who knows," Flavius replied with a shrug.

Emerging from his billet, Flavius turned to look around before limping off towards the edge of the protective embankment, that encircled the camp. Several days had passed since his audience with the Queen at the hilltop fortress of Carn Brea some miles away to the east. Scoti was right, Flavius thought - suddenly revealing his own worries. Gisgo and his mercenaries appeared to be in no hurry to leave for home. It was a disconcerting development. A stalemate had started to develop. The enemy had no business left to attend to and yet they were refusing to leave. The Numidian Prince seemed reluctant to leave him alone with the Queen, as if he had sussed out his plan. As if he feared the presence of the Roman delegation and was induced to stay in order to counter their diplomatic moves. To ensure that the Queen did not go back on their agreement. The Carthaginian was no fool Flavius thought, with grudging respect as he clambered up the embankment. For if the roles had been reversed, he would have done exactly the same. There was no way he could leave the enemy to play their games unhindered.

Reaching the top of the earthen embankment, he turned to look back across the small Celtic settlement of Caer Bran. Nestling within its confines, the small number of round houses with their thatched conical roofs and doorways - all facing away from the prevailing winds - looked neat and homely. Smoke was curling up into the blue sky from smoke holes and nearby, a fisher woman was hanging fish upon a wooden rack for them to dry in the gathering strength of the sun. Further away another woman was showing a young girl how to weave while beside them a man was sat on a stool carefully painting a clay pot.

Within the encircling embankment too, were three large ring cairns, burial mounds, that looked very old. The stone and earth platforms appeared to have a magical resonance with the locals - as if this place was different and special, a holy place - like a sacred grove or a temple back home. Eyeing the three ring cairns with a grave look, Flavius at last shifted his gaze. Caer Bran, he had figured out, appeared to be a tribal gathering place, a spot where important business and rituals were carried out. It was smaller than the powerful hilltop fortresses of Carn Brea or Trencrom and its views were less spectacular, which made it a less defensible spot. Yet the Queen had insisted that her entourage move here for Aed's trial. Such an important event, it seemed, could only be held here - with the spirits of the ancestors looking on in silent and eternal judgement.

Limping back towards the house in which he and his companions had been billeted, a loaf of bread tucked under his arm, Flavius had just come around a corner when he suddenly spotted the party of Carthaginians. Swiftly he came to a halt. The eight mercenaries were sitting about on the ground in between the houses. A couple of them were concentrating on a game containing small blue and white glass counters on a chequered board, while the others were chatting quietly together, their weapons hanging from their belts. Like the Roman delegation they too appeared to have nothing to do but wile away their time. As they spotted him however, their conversation abruptly ceased. Then slowly and ominously the mercenaries rose to their feet and moved to block his path, eyeing Flavius warily and with unconcealed hostility. Staring back at the enemy, Flavius too, said nothing and as the tension became palpable a few of the locals nearby stopped what they were doing to observe the confrontation. Then before anyone could say a word - Flavius calmly turned on his heels and walked away.

Entering the round house, still clutching his loaf of bread, Flavius immediately saw that something was up. Leaning against the far wall Pytheas looked cross and fed up, his arms folded across his chest, while in the hay, Scoti was fast asleep, snoring softly. Acco however was muttering to himself. Blushing furiously and looking very uncomfortable he was staring down at the ground. The source of his discomfort was not hard to discern, for standing just inside the doorway was a young Celtic woman. Her eyes too were down-cast and she appeared to be waiting for something or someone.

"What's going on? What does she want?" Flavius said, quickly turning to Pytheas for an explanation.

"She says that she has been waiting for you," Pytheas replied sullenly. "She says that she has been instructed to take you to meet someone. Right now. And only you and Acco. No one else. But she is refusing to say who it is who wants to meet or what this is all about. This could be a trap Flavius. Gisgo could be setting an ambush for all we know. I don't think you should go with her. Its too dangerous. The risk is too high."

"A secret meeting," Flavius exclaimed, quickly turning to eye the girl.

"She doesn't understand a word you are saying," Acco groaned as if in pain. "Why did they have to send a woman as the messenger. I was not ready. Someone is poking fun at me. Someone is having a laugh at my expense. Some cruel spirit did this on purpose - to humiliate me."

"She won't say who wants to meet me or what it is about?" Flavius repeated.

"No," Pytheas replied shaking his head. "Trust me. We tried, but she refuses to answer my questions. She just insists she was instructed to take you and Acco to the meeting place. She says she was told not to leave without your answer. She won't even say where you are to meet. Honestly - I don't actually think she knows what this is all about either. She is just a messenger."

Remaining silent Flavius eyed the girl who refused to meet his gaze. The woman was young, barely eighteen and strikingly pretty.

"Alright. Acco - on your feet son. I am going to need you to translate," Flavius said, at last making up his mind. "Let's go and find out what this person wants."

"You are going to go with her? But that's madness," Pytheas protested, looking visibly alarmed. "This could be trap to lure you into an ambush. Why else, all this secrecy? Why else refuse to reveal who is asking to meet? Anything could happen. I don't like it one bit."

"If Gisgo had wanted us dead," Flavius replied patiently, "he would have killed us already. He does not need to lure us out into a trap. He has the men to overpower us. He has that power but he has not used it."

"Maybe he wants your death to look like an accident, so that Queen Talwyn cannot blame him," Pytheas exclaimed. "Have you considered that? He could say you slipped over the edge of a cliff or hit your head on a rock. All he needs is a plausible excuse and for there to be no witnesses."

"I am going to find out what this person wants," Flavius said in a determined sounding voice. "If I am not back by nightfall you are in charge of the mission Pytheas. We talked about worse case scenarios. So see our task through to completion. You know what to do."

Then gesturing for Acco and the girl to follow him, Flavius stepped out of the house and into the daylight.

***

The wood was not far from Caer Bran and, as he followed the silent young woman across the field towards it, Flavius could hear the wind stirring and rustling the leaves and branches. Plodding along at his side, his eyes focused on the ground; Acco looked miserable. Entering the forest, Flavius turned to look about with a guarded expression but among the trees and undergrowth he could spot nothing suspicious. There seemed to be no one about. No warning signs that he was about to be ambushed and as he followed the girl deeper into the wood, he heard cheerful bird song. Whoever had asked him to meet way out here appeared to be keen to keep it a secret. But why?

Ahead, the girl had finally come to a halt beside a large boulder and as she did, she abruptly turned and called out to someone in her native language. For a moment nothing happened. Then Queen Talwyn suddenly appeared, stepping out from behind the massive rock, looking pale and unwell, clad in a white and long-hooded cloak. She was swiftly followed by a young handsome looking warrior, his face covered by the tattoo of a wolf, an axe hanging from his belt. The young, rugged man appeared to be no older than twenty, but he had the look of an experienced fighter. Hurriedly Flavius turned to check the surrounding trees and undergrowth but the Queen appeared to be alone with just her solitary bodyguard.

"The girl," Acco whispered. "She says she is the Queen's handmaiden Sir. I think her father is a druid. I have seen him about. He has a huge beard. Pytheas says that he doesn't like foreigners."

Saying nothing, Flavius eyed the Queen as she came up to him and gave him a careful and silent examination which reminded him of their first encounter in the great hall at Carn Brea. At last wrenching her eyes away from him, the Queen turned to Acco and as she did a cruel and mocking smile appeared on her lips as she saw the consternation her presence had caused.

"Ask her what she wants, son?"

As Acco hurriedly translated, with his eyes firmly fixed on the ground, the Queen's smile vanished and she turned her attention back to Flavius and spoke, her dark eyes gleaming with purpose.

"When you first arrived in my kingdom," Acco translated speaking in a clear and flawless manner. "When you first came to me at the fortress of Carn Brea. That night you told me that you knew who was plotting against me. I want to know everything. I want you to tell me who among my people is still supporting my husband. Who of my subjects wants me dead? Who was behind the plot to poison me? Was Aed, my adviser really involved?"

For a moment Flavius's eyes dueled with the Queen. Then abruptly he looked away.

"Tell the Queen," Flavius said sternly, "that I am glad that she has decided to believe me when I say that my Massaliot friends know what they are talking about. She is wise to trust me. Now we can do business together. Tell her Acco that we have informants and sympathisers among every tribe and nation with whom we do business. Knowledge is power."

Watching him with a wary look the Queen remained silent as Acco translated for her. Then she replied.

"She says she is aware that the Massaliots maintain a network of informants among the tribes," Acco translated. "She understands its value. Otherwise, she would not have bothered to call you out here."

"Good," Flavius replied seizing the initiative. "So, like I said, we are happy to work with her to secure her throne. We are happy to share information with her in exchange for a new trade agreement. The terms we offer have not changed. Most importantly the trade embargo against us, which she has agreed with Carthage, must be lifted at once. The flow of tin to Massalia must not be blocked in any way. If those conditions are met, then I am prepared to talk and tell the Queen what I and my colleagues know."

Gazing back at him, Queen Talwyn suddenly looked frustrated, while at her side the young tattooed warrior had begun to mutter to himself, his expression hostile and unhappy.

"The Queen says," Acco translated, "that you must give her something. If you want her to consider your request an act of good faith is required. Today is the day of Aed's trial. It's a very important day. If found guilty he will have his head chopped off. So there is not much time. A man's life is at stake. A man she has known all her life. She asks you again - she wants to know if you have evidence that he is guilty of poisoning her or not? She gives you one final chance, but if your answer does not satisfy her - she says we are no longer welcome in her kingdom. That she will send us back to Rome without any trade agreement and the consequences be damned. She does not care what Rome thinks of her."

"An act of good faith. Sure," Flavius retorted. "But first of all what does she think? Does she believe that Aed is guilty? I am curious. If she has known Aed all her life then surely she is a much better judge of him than I am. Why ask me? He is one of her subjects."

Eyeing him angrily from across the forest floor, the Queen however managed to contain herself as she fired back an answer.

"The Queen says," Acco dutifully translated, "that it is not your place to question her and that she requires an act of good faith from you before she will consider our request for a new trade agreement. She stands by her position. She wants to have your answer."

"Not before she tells me what she thinks. Does she believe Aed poisoned her?" Flavius said stubbornly standing his ground.

As Acco translated the Queen suddenly sneered at Flavius, furious that he refused to give way and submit to her will. Moodily she turned to look away and for a long moment the forest remained silent. Then at last the Queen spoke, the tone of her voice more emollient this time.

"As to whether Aed is guilty of poisoning her," Acco said hurriedly, "she admits to having doubts. So if you have something to say, now is the time to do so. The trial will begin and conclude this afternoon. She says you must decide right now whether you want her to be a friend or foe."

"Doubts," Flavius exclaimed, raising his eyebrows. It was the first time the Queen had offered him something, a subtle shift in her position. A hint at compromise. She appeared to want a deal, but how far was she prepared to go? For a moment Flavius studied the wily Queen with a grave expression, conscious that he now had to respond, that it was his move - that he had a decision to make. A huge decision - for his opinion would surely either save Aed or condemn him to death. At last, clearing his throat he nodded. He could not alienate the Queen by holding out. He had to give her something.

"Of course I am willing to talk," Flavius replied at last in a conciliatory sounding voice. "As an act of good faith. Rome is prepared to support you Queen Talwyn. We can help you secure your throne. In return all we seek is a mutually beneficial trade agreement." Allowing Acco to catch up Flavius paused before continuing. "My colleagues and I do not know for sure if Aed was behind the poisoning, but we suspect he was. There is evidence to condemn him. The conspiracy against you Queen Talwyn is wider and deeper than just your husband. Others, powerful men beyond your borders also now have an interest in your downfall. Pytheas my Massaliot companion says he has learned that your husband has had military and financial aid from some of the tribes to the east, whose kings covet your tin mines and wealth. He says your husband struck deals with these lords offering them a share of your people's wealth once he was in charge. What is undeniable is that someone aided your husband. We believe that Aed acted as the go between who set up the meetings with the other kings. We also believe that Aed met your husband in secret several times after the rebellion began. We do not know what they discussed, but the fact that they met is surely significant."

Staring at him as she listened to the translation, the Queen's eyes gleamed, her pale face hard as nails. Then abruptly she looked away, her chest rapidly rising and falling.

"The Queen wants to know how you know all this?" Acco translated. "She says it would be most convenient for you, if Aed was found guilty - considering that he is no friend of Rome."

"No," Flavius responded firmly shaking his head. "I have been honest with her. This is what my Massaliot friends tell me has happened and I am not at liberty to reveal my sources. I have been as cooperative as I can be. Quid pro quo."

His answer did not seem to please the Queen but again Flavius noticed her self-restraint. At last Queen Talwyn turned to him, with an unhappy brooding look.

"She says Sir," Acco said with a sudden hope, "that she is still considering what to do regards our request for a new trade agreement. She will give you her answer when she is ready to do so."

***

In the hazy afternoon sunlight a large subdued crowd had gathered around the three ring cairns inside the settlement of Caer Bran. Standing on top of one the burial mounds for all to see, guarded by two men - his hands tied behind his back,

Aed was staring at the horizon in silence. A tragic and sad looking figure, Flavius thought as he stood in the crowd of onlookers. The man still appeared to be struggling to deal with the devastating loss of his family. Aed had not said a word since he had been led out, calm and dignified to face his fate.

Sat upon a chair - surrounded by her nobles and bodyguard, Queen Talwyn too was looking on as the trial appeared to be getting underway. Shifting his gaze across the crowd, Flavius caught sight of Gisgo and his mercenaries. The Carthaginians were bunched together - easily identifiable by their appearance and clothing. They too had turned up to watch the proceedings.

"He is going to lose his head," Pytheas muttered. "I think he is guilty."

"You think so?" Flavius replied, refusing to be drawn away from Gisgo and his men.

"It is in our interests that he is," Pytheas replied coldly. "Aed supports Carthage. He is their man. Not ours. And once he is gone our influence with the Queen will only grow. It will be good for us, if Aed dies."

"Maybe," Flavius replied. "But the Queen is not yet fully convinced that he is guilty. She has doubts."

Pytheas was about to speak again when a sudden angry tumult arose among the crowd standing waiting around the ring cairns. The disruption was coming from the area where the Carthaginians had gathered. Frowning, Flavius suddenly caught sight of the figure of the druid, his distinctive clothing and long beard setting him apart from the crowd. The holy man appeared to have picked on one of the Carthaginian mercenaries and the two men were in what looked like the midst of a nasty argument and stand-off, which was threatening to turn violent. But just as things appeared to be spiraling out of control Flavius saw, Gisgo hurriedly intervening and appearing to calm things down. Moments later the Carthaginian mercenary was being hastily bundled away by his comrades.

"See. The Carthaginians have their own problems," Pytheas said with a gleeful smirk, leaning into Flavius and gesturing at the confrontation. "Gisgo's sea captains are eager to sail. They have a ship waiting for them down at the port of Ictis. The captains don't give a shit about this trade embargo. They just want to go home. They are putting pressure on Gisgo to leave for Gades. And that incident you just witnessed over there." For a moment Pytheas paused, looking smug. "Well, I have heard," he continued, "that one of Gisgo's men has taken a liking to the druid's daughter and that the druid is not at all happy about that. He is said to be very protective of his daughter. He hates foreigners. He wants them all gone from these shores."

"The Queen's handmaiden," Flavius said. "You mean the same girl who came to us this morning?"

"Yes. Same one apparently," Pytheas nodded. "Her father, the Druid, is an important man. He has influence with the Queen. He will never allow that Carthaginian mercenary near his daughter and if the man persists, there is going to be more trouble. Massive trouble. You don't mess around with the druids. It's all good for us though. The more problems that Gisgo has the better. It will teach that Numidian scumbag a lesson."

"He has access to the Queen?" Flavius said, suddenly looking thoughtful as he turned to study the furious Druid who was still waving his clenched fist around and being held back from going after the Carthaginian by some of the locals.

"The Druids are always a problem," Pytheas sighed. "They hate everything about us - Roman, Massaliot and Carthaginian. It doesn't matter. We're all foreigners and unwanted. The druids are always hostile to us - always counselling the tribal kings to refuse us trade rights. They are after all the guardians of their people's heritage, lore, religion and culture and they see us as competitors - but we must be careful. They are venerated among their people. Their power equals that of the warrior class. That man over there," Pytheas added gesturing at the druid. "He believes our presence here threatens his position and that we are corrupting the locals with our trade goods and foreign gods."

"Do you think he could have had something to do with the attack on the Queen?" Flavius asked.

"The Druid?" Pytheas said sounding startled. "Why would he try to poison his own Queen?"

"Because," Flavius replied. "He has a motive. The Queen has done nothing to stop foreign merchants from visiting her kingdom and trading with her people. Maybe the druid does not agree with that and is angry that the Queen refuses to listen to him. You said yourself that he hates foreigners' and the influence trade gives us. Maybe he thought it would end if the Queen were dead."

"Well, it's a possibility - sure," Pytheas exclaimed looking unconvinced. "But it is unlikely. Do you doubt the quality of the briefing I gave you before?" Pytheas added rounding on Flavius with a slight challenge in his voice.

"I do not doubt your word or the intelligence provided by your government," Flavius responded coolly. "But if the Queen has doubts then that is a concern. She knows Aed best of all. If she decides he is innocent we are going to look like fools or worse, liars. Just this morning I stuck my neck out telling her that we believe Aed is guilty so I just want to be sure that we got it right."

"We got it right," Pytheas said in a confident voice. "I doubt very much that the druid is working with the Queen's enemies.

He is an intelligent man and to all accounts he is loyal too. Think about it. The motive you raise does not add up. If the Queen died her husband would take over and he is not going to ban the tin trade either. Foreign merchants would still arrive because the Queen's husband needs the revenue from the trade just as badly as the Queen does. No. It is much more likely that Aed did it. The word is that Aed blames the Queen for the death of his wife and son. That is his motive. He is guilty."

For a moment Flavius said nothing. Then he shifted his attention back to Gisgo who was still trying to calm the tension with the druid. "Well, I think you are right," Flavius said. "The more problems Gisgo must deal with the better. That man should just leave and go home."

***

"He says that he is completely innocent," Acco rattled out-standing at Flavius's shoulder as the young translator squinted at Aed who was still on top of the ring cairn, his hands tied behind his back. "He says he did not poison the Queen. He swears this on the grave of his wife and son. He did not do it. He has been loyal to the Queen throughout."

Standing in the subdued crowd, Flavius looked grave. The trial had finally begun but being conducted in a foreign language he was completely reliant on Acco's commentary to tell him what was going on. Still a man's life was at stake and among the populace he could sense the tension and the anguish. Aed was not just anyone - he appeared to be a popular figure. Wrenching his eyes away from the prisoner, Flavius turned to gaze at the Queen. Sat upon her throne, Queen Talwyn was observing the trial in silence, her pale face giving nothing away. And standing behind her chair was the young-tattooed warrior he'd met in the forest, his alert watchful eyes darting about, picking out faces among the crowd as if he were searching for threats.

Turning his attention back to Aed, Flavius sighed. Standing upon the top of the cairn beside the defendant - the Druid was leading the prosecution, his face dark like a storm, his powerful accusing voice booming like thunder claps. On and on he went until at last, the druid stopped speaking and an ominous and expectant silence descended upon the crowd.

"Now the Queen must decide his fate," Pytheas whispered.

With the populace all turning towards her, Queen Talwyn did not move, her inscrutable eyes fixed on Aed who was gazing back at her. As the tension grew a silent look seemed to pass between the two of them. Then the Queen slowly rose to her feet and taking a deep breath she spat out a single word.

"Guilty," Acco hissed. "The Queen says Aed is guilty. He is to die."

As a stir swept through the crowd and a few lone voices of protest were raised, Flavius lowered his eyes. He was partially responsible for this outcome he knew - having told the Queen he believed Aed to be involved. So, he should have been pleased by the verdict. For Aed was Carthage's man after all - but strangely he could not bring himself to feel any satisfaction. This was an ugly business - ugly but necessary. Up on the cairn the two guards had seized hold of Aed and had forced him down onto his knees. Then with brutal swiftness one of them raised his axe and moments later hacked Aed's head off, before raising it and turning to show the gruesome sight to the watching populace.

The trial was over and as the people began to drift back to their homes and jobs Flavius spotted Morcant heading towards him. The one-armed Celtic nobleman with his greasy spiky hair looked triumphant.

"He says that the matter is now closed," Acco translated as, Morcant came up, beaming a smile. "The rebellion has been crushed and the plotters against the Queen have received justice. With Aed gone another obstacle has been removed. The Carthaginians have just lost their principal ally. Aed was not our friend. He was Gisgo's friend. And now that he is gone, our influence with the Queen will grow. This is a good day for us."

Standing beside Flavius, Pytheas too, looked unabashedly pleased. Stepping forwards to give Morcant a quick embrace the Massaliot diplomat was grinning from ear to ear.

"It was a hard decision, but the Queen chose, wisely in the end," Pytheas added turning to Flavius. "She acted decisively. If she had let him go it would have been interpreted as a sign of weakness. Clemency would have just encouraged others to try and kill her. Now no one can be in any doubt as to what to expect from her. That woman is made of iron."

"I know. Aed's death should help our case," Flavius replied refusing however to join in with his jubilant colleagues.

Then before he could continue Flavius froze as he spotted Gisgo approaching with a couple of his mercenaries. The Numidian Prince looked angry, his gleaming eyes blazing with determination.

"Oh boy, here comes trouble," Pytheas said hurriedly as he noticed Gisgo. Then the Numidian and his gang were standing before Flavius, their arms folded across their chests. For a moment no one spoke, as the two sides eyed each other with wary and sullen hostility. Then abruptly Gisgo raised his finger and pointed it at Flavius in an angry, accusing manner.

"Sir," Acco said nervously swallowing. "Gisgo says that you should be ashamed of what you have just done. You have made a terrible mistake. A mistake that had just cost an innocent man his life. You have just helped condemn an innocent man to death. The gods will be offended by such an act. They will set their will against you and curse you from this day forwards. For justice is beloved by all. And justice was not done today."

"Really," Pytheas snarled. "Acco. Tell this Numidian bastard that Aed was guilty and that if he doesn't like the Queen's verdict, he can fuck off back to Gades any time he pleases."

Eyeing Gisgo calmly, Flavius said nothing as he coolly refused to give any ground and Gisgo did the same.

Then Morcant took a menacing step towards Gisgo, eliciting a sharp aggressive reaction from the Carthaginian mercenaries whose hands quickly dropped to the weapons hanging from their belts. Looking unperturbed, subjecting Gisgo to a mocking look, Morcant thrust out his nose in an aggressive manner to the point where it was nearly touching the Numidian's face.

"Morcant speaks in Greek. He asks," Acco said hurriedly, "whether Gisgo wishes to take up his complaints about the trial with the Queen? He is welcome to do so. He asks Gisgo why he thinks Aed was innocent - setting aside of-course the fact that Aed was his friend and a Carthaginian ally."

Coolly standing his ground Gisgo did not give an inch and his eyes remained fixed on Flavius. At last he spoke ignoring Morcant with contemptuous silence.

"Gisgo replies in Greek. He says," Acco translated as the words tumbled out of his mouth. "That it was not proven, beyond reasonable doubt, that Aed was behind the poisoning. Gisgo says he listened to every word of that trial. That druid - the accuser. He offered no proof and no witnesses. It was a sham. A set up. The Queen needed a guilty verdict, in order not to look weak. But, it was the wrong decision. Gisgo asks whether it was Morcant who poisoned the Queen?"

In response Morcant drew back and laughed. Then he spoke in a sneering voice.

"Morcant says he is used to being accused of many things, by many people," Acco hurriedly translated - a bead of sweat trickling down his cheek. "But no, he did not poison the Queen. He did not even set foot in her hall that day she was poisoned. He is a loyal subject. Everyone saw that he fought for her in battle against her husband despite having only one arm. He says that Gisgo should be careful. He is a guest in a foreign land and the Queen's hospitality will not last forever. Her patience wears thin. He advises Gisgo to leave now while he still can."

In response however Gisgo, seemed unmoved. For a moment the Numidian's blue eyes lingered - blazing at Morcant with unbridled contempt. Then slowly he turned his attention back to Flavius.

"Gisgo says," Acco stammered nervously, "that if you hoped he and his men were going to leave and sail back to Gades, that you are mistaken. This morning he received word that his ship, which was waiting for him at the port of Ictis - that it sailed away. Apparently, the ship's captain would wait no longer. So, he and his men are now stuck here. Marooned. Abandoned. They have no way of getting home. He says you had better get used to his company for he is going nowhere. Nor is he going to allow the Queen to change her mind about the trade embargo. He is going to hold her to the promise she made to him."

As he patiently waited for Acco to finish speaking, Gisgo suddenly raised another angry finger pointing it at Flavius.

"And he says Sir," Acco said hurriedly, "that you and he are not going to be friends. He says you could not stop him in Rome all those years ago, and that you will not defeat him now either."

Chapter Twelve - Winning the War

Tearing across country, the two chariots swayed and rattled in the cool dawn light. Drifting across the fields, wisps of morning mist obscured the horizon, and the only noise came from the creak and bump of the wheels, the snorting horses and the pack of dogs, who were joyfully bounding along at their side - keeping pace with the vehicles. Standing bolt upright in one of the chariots, holding on tightly, Flavius felt the fresh air rushing across his face. Squashed in beside him on the narrow platform, Acco was grinning in delight while Morcant was holding the reins with his hand and calling out to his horses, expertly guiding them and keeping his balance with well-practised ease. The stump of his other arm pressed to his side. Over in the other chariot, squashed together with their driver, Scoti and Pytheas were smiling as they raced along, like boys enjoying a long-promised treat. It was the first time he had ever ridden in a chariot, Flavius thought, and he could see why his companions looked pleased. The sense of speed was intoxicating and the light, wood and wicker-framed – two-wheeled chariots were far more agile than he had been expecting. Still, as he gazed at the country ahead Flavius could not bring himself to join in with the general excitement. Looking sober and thoughtful - he appeared to have something else on his mind.

At last reining in his horses, Morcant called out to his hunting dogs and brought his chariot to a halt close to the edge, where the lush green grass abruptly gave way to a shallow open cast tin mine. As the second chariot trundled to a halt and the dogs milled about aimlessly, Morcant paused before he proudly pointed at a few miners who were already out and about, hacking at the cuttings with primitive shovels and pickaxes made from antler bone.

"This is the oldest tin mine we have," Acco said, quickly translating Morcant's words. "It is older than the city of Athens or Rome and it continues to yield a bounty. The mother goddess is most generous. Long may it last. The miners make cuttings in the ground and we exploit streams too. The tin is dug out by hand, hauled to one of the hill top forts where it is smelted into ingots before being transported to the port of Ictis where it is then stored until the foreign merchants come to buy it. That is the way it has always been done."

Standing in the chariot, Flavius nodded but remained silent, as he gazed at the mass of cuttings that crisscrossed the mine, like wounds in the earth. The mine looked huge, extending away into the morning mist. Hacking away at the ground on their small plots, the miners, men, women and children were ignoring the visitors; their backs bent; their faces grimy with sweat, toil and dirt.

Calling out to Morcant in Greek, Scoti was beaming, as he jumped down from his chariot and came over.

"Scoti asks," Acco translated. "Whether there are any underground mines?"

"Morcant says - yes we have those too, but not here. He says the underground mines are more difficult to build and expensive to run. If they can they prefer the open cast method. It's easier."

Upon the chariot, Flavius nodded but kept to his brooding silence.

"Something the matter Sir?" Scoti asked, catching the look on Flavius's face. "You have been awfully quiet since we set out."

"I have been thinking," Flavius replied, at last turning to his secretary. "About what Gisgo told us the other day."

"Well, he is wrong about Aed, if you ask me," Scoti said with a dismissive shrug.

"No, it's not that," Flavius said quickly shaking his head. "He said something else - that we were never going to be friends. It has given me an idea and if I can make it work - I think it may just allow us to win the war."

"An idea - to win the war?" Scoti exclaimed, looking startled. "Which war? The one here between the Queen and her husband?"

"No," Flavius said gravely. "The one between Rome and Carthage. I have thought of a plan," Flavius added, before turning to stare at the tin mine and the toiling miners with a faraway look. "A plan - but I need to make it work. Don't you see Scoti. I thought coming here at first - to these distant islands was a punishment. But now I see Fortuna's hand in all of this. The goddess has given us an opportunity and I think we need to take it."

"I don't understand Sir," Scoti said with a concerned look.

For a moment Flavius said nothing as he marshaled his thoughts. Then he turned to his secretary, his eyes gleaming with sudden determination.

"Gisgo made himself clear enough," Flavius said. "His ship has sailed away leaving him stuck here. He now has no way of getting back home. So, we cannot get rid of him like we had hoped. We cannot kill him either, for he has his mercenaries to protect him and there is nothing more which we can offer the Queen - to try and convince her to change her mind regards the trade embargo. I have already offered her everything that we can. So how do we defeat our enemy? How do we get what we want? There is only one option left."

"Which is?" Scoti said quickly.

Standing upon the chariot, squashed together with Acco and Morcant, Flavius took a deep breath.

"We make friends with Gisgo," he announced. "We befriend him. We turn him - from being an enemy into a friend - an ally. It will take time but that's how we will win the war."

"Friends," Scoti protested - looking surprised. "Hell Sir. You want to make friends with that Numidian scumbag?"

"Yes I do. It's the only logical way out of our predicament. Out of this stalemate," Flavius replied. "Think about it. There is more at stake here than just our trade agreement. See the big strategic picture. Gisgo is a Numidian. He is not a Carthaginian - although they are allies. If we get this right and make it work, it could change the course of the war. Gisgo is a Numidian Prince. He will be a powerful and influential man among his people. If we were able to make friends with him and convince him to change sides - to abandon Carthage for Rome - think about what that could possibly achieve."

Staring at Flavius in disbelief, Scoti appeared to have been stunned into silence. For a moment he struggled to formulate an answer.

"Right," Scoti exclaimed at last, frowning. "And how do you propose to make friends with Gisgo? You heard what he said. He seemed pretty hostile. How are we ever going to trust a man like that?"

"I did not say it would be easy," Flavius responded. "And I am going to need help, but I think it is worth a try. Hannibal has long tried to loosen the bonds that bind the peoples of Italy to Rome. Why can we not try and do the same with the Carthaginian alliance?"

"I still can't see how we are going to become friends," Scoti retorted, looking away with a skeptical expression. "Gisgo is the enemy. He is not just going to change sides because you ask nicely."

"I have worked out a plan," Flavius said patiently. "It may or may not succeed, but like I said, it is worth trying. First off though - we are going to need to prepare the ground. I need to know more about the man. Anything could be useful. We need to find something that we can use to persuade him to swap sides. We need to get to know Gisgo better before we make our move."

"So how do we do that?"

"There is a man among the party of Carthaginians," Flavius said quickly. "He is their translator. Acco here tells me that his name is Phameas and that he is also a Punic tin merchant and sea captain."

"Phameas is familiar with the tin trade," Acco said, nodding in agreement, turning to glance at Scoti with a confident look. "They say he has visited these islands many times. I have heard him speak and seen him about. But he's a poor and lazy translator. He only knows the native language and his own."

"I have also learned that he has a taste for young men," Flavius said. "Like the Greeks he does not seem to care much about gender - if you know what I mean. So Acco, I have a job for you," Flavius added turning to him. "I want you to approach Phameas tonight. Catch his eye. Lure him away. Use your charm. Flatter him. Get him drunk and then probe him for information. Try and find out as much as you can. Anything that we can use to persuade Gisgo to change sides would be useful. Anything! Phameas must know Gisgo fairly well. If we can learn something from him, that would be a good start."

"What?" Acco exclaimed, his eyes bulging in alarm. "You want me to do what?"

"You heard me," Flavius said, looking deadly serious. "I need you to do this for me. You are the only one of us who can. Seduce Phameas, and find out as much as you can. I am not accepting no as an answer. It's perfectly innocent. You will just be two translators - sharing notes in a foreign land."

"Sir," Acco protested - a blush spreading across his youthful cheeks. "I may suffer from gynophobia but that does not mean that I take a liking to men. I don't. I really don't."

"Then don't let him touch you," Flavius said sternly. "Don't let it go too far. You are in charge. But I really need you to get him to talk and reveal what he knows. All of us must at times do things that we do not enjoy."

Looking aghast, Acco turned to Scoti and then to Pytheas seeking support, but the two men remained silent and after a moment. Acco lowered his eyes and groaned in defeat.

***

It was dark and in-the-roundhouse the small fire was crackling, its flickering light casting shadows across the earthen floor. Sat with his back against the stone wall, Flavius was patiently gazing up at the wood smoke that was escaping into the cool night through a hole in the thatched roof. Nearby, in the straw a little animal was rooting about, while crouching at the doorway. Scoti was once again on guard, his knife lying across his lap. Lying stretched out on his bed Pytheas was trying to sleep, but Flavius could sense that he was still awake.

"Someone is coming," Scoti called out at last in a quiet voice, peering out into the darkness. Gripping his knife the astronomer hurriedly rose to his feet. A moment later Acco slipped through the doorway - hurrying into the firelight. The young man looked haunted as he turned to Flavius, his eyes bulging, his brow soaked in sweat. Stiffly rising to his feet, Flavius came over to him.

"I don't care what you say Sir," Acco whispered furiously. "I am never doing that again. I don't care what you threaten me with.

He tried to kiss me. He would have raped me if I had allowed it. It was awful. An absolutely dreadful experience. Never again."

At the door Scoti sniggered, looking away when Acco shot him a furious glance.

"So you got him alone?" Flavius said, calmly eyeing the young man. "You managed to have a chat with Phameas. What did he have to say?"

Turning his attention back to Flavius, Acco was momentarily lost for words. Screwing up his face in a frustrated expression he looked like he was about to scream. "I just want you to know Sir," Acco said struggling to control himself, "that I am doing my best to confront my phobia. I want to get over it. I really do and I know that I am making progress."

"We all know that son," Flavius said, looking serious. "And we all respect you for that. Now what did Phameas have to say?"

Looking away Acco hesitated.

"Not much," he muttered at last. "I tried to get him to talk about Gisgo but he wouldn't say much other than telling me that Gisgo is very wealthy and that he is the deputy to a Numidian Prince called Masinissa. That's pretty much all I could get out of him. He got drunk very quickly and I spent most of the evening fending off his groping hands."

"Masinissa," Scoti exclaimed, sounding surprised as he came up to Acco. "Are you sure he used that name?"

"Yes," Acco said guardedly. "I am sure. Why? Do you know this man?"

"I have heard of him, yes," Scoti said quickly turning to Flavius. "He is one of King Gaia's sons and an heir to the kingdom of the Massylii, the eastern Numidians. He is a very important man. A warrior. Masinissa stands a chance of becoming the next Numidian King and if Gisgo is his deputy…"

"It means our man occupies an influential position," Flavius snapped, finishing Scoti's sentence. "Good. Well done, Acco. This is most useful information. If we can turn Gisgo into an ally of Rome, we may be able to persuade Masinissa to do the same and in one stroke we could destroy the Numidian alliance with Carthage. If that does not help win the war, then I don't know what can."

"But it still does not give us a handle on how to persuade Gisgo to change sides Sir," Scoti said quickly.

"Are you really serious about going ahead with this plan of yours?" Pytheas called out quietly from his bed of hay.

"Yes, I am," Flavius said sharply. "I have to try. Fortuna has brought both Gisgo and I, here to these distant shores for a purpose. I can see that now. I need to take the opportunity that she is offering us. Think of the prize that awaits if we can get this to work. Think how this could change things. The Numidian cavalry are the most feared of all among Hannibal's army."

As Flavius finished speaking, silence descended upon the four men in the roundhouse as they considered what had been said. Then all eyes turned to the doorway, as Flavius heard a little noise. A moment later Morcant appeared, quietly slipping into the building with a guarded look. Spotting Flavius he hurriedly began to speak in Greek.

"Acco?" Flavius called out.

"Morcant says," Acco hurriedly translated. "Forgive the lateness of my visit but I have news. The Queen has come to a decision. She won't tell me what it is, but she is due to make an announcement tomorrow at the communal games. I think it is regards, the trade agreement. She is finally going to rule on the subject."

Hurriedly Flavius and Pytheas exchanged glances.

"Ask him," Flavius said at last, "what he thinks the Queen will do?"

As Acco dutifully translated, Morcant quickly shook his head. "He says he honestly does not know," Acco said. "All he knows is that she has come to a decision, and she will make it public tomorrow at the games. He wanted to warn you in advance. The games, they can get quite rowdy. They are quite competitive. There are going to be winners and losers. It's a bit like warfare but without weapons, if you know what he means."

Chapter Thirteen - The Ancient Game

Noisily congregating around the gate into the settlement of Caer Bran, their eager chatter punctuated by the barking of dogs, Flavius could see that the crowd were excited. An expectant party-like atmosphere had taken hold as all waited for Queen Talwyn to appear. It was morning and the sun was rising in a clear blue sky, powerful, unstoppable and majestic, its rays breathing warmth and life onto the spectacular green countryside. Standing together in a tight knot, looking rigid and awkward, Scoti, Pytheas and Acco were looking on nervously and Flavius could sense their apprehension. The Queen was keeping them waiting he thought. Looking sombre and grave, he turned his eyes to the eager people thronging the top of the earthen embankment. Morcant had been brief in his description - the Queen would announce her decision at the communal games. Today he was going to find out whether his mission had been a success or not. Shifting his gaze, Flavius took a deep breath as he suddenly spotted Gisgo and his mercenaries standing about in the crowd. The Carthaginians too looked sullen and uneasy - as if they were expecting to be confronted by bad news.

"What do you know about this game?" Flavius said, at last turning to Scoti. "Morcant only said that it was very popular in these parts."

"Not too much," Scoti said uneasily shifting his feet about. "From what I have gathered it is a simple game, a ball game Sir. They call it hurling. Two teams compete to carry a small ball across country and into their opponents goal. The first team that manages it wins. There are few rules and its rough. Tackling, brawling and punching are all allowed. But no weapons."

"I see," Flavius said. "A substitute for war but without bloodshed. This should be interesting."

"Where is Morcant Sir?" Scoti asked quickly.

"A good question. I don't know. He should be here. This is an important day," Flavius replied with a frown.

Scoti was about to speak again when a sudden hush descended upon the crowd and a moment later Flavius caught sight of Queen Talwyn striding out of the gate followed by a few of her nobles and bodyguards. Studying her, making her way through the crowd, Flavius could see that the Queen appeared stronger and healthier - the small-coloured glass beads in her hair and her white cloak reflecting the sunlight. She appeared to be recovering well from being poisoned and her face was no longer pale and gaunt. Hurriedly turning to look about, Flavius frowned again. There was still no sign of Morcant. Was his 'no show' a sign of trouble ahead? Had the Queen ruled against him?

"She looks awfully cheerful," Pytheas muttered.

"Is that a good or bad thing?" Acco asked.

"Who knows," Pytheas replied, biting his lip. "But I guess we shall have her answer shortly. Gentlemen, whatever the outcome, we did our best. We should be proud of that."

"I agree," Scoti said quickly. "We did all we could. No regrets."

Gazing at the Queen, Flavius said nothing as he watched her calmly climb onto her horse drawn chariot. A moment later the young warrior sporting the green face tattoo of a wolf, whom he had met in the forest, squeezed in beside her and took the reins, whilst another bodyguard steadied the horses. Then turning to the crowd, the Queen began to address them, her voice strong and clear and, as she began a great cheer of approval arose from the gathered spectators outside the gate and up on the embankment.

"She declares the day's festivities to have started," Acco said translating. "Now she is talking about the forthcoming match.

She says that the game between the men of Caer Bran and Chun Castle will heal the wounds that the recent civil war has wrought. She hopes that the game will close the divisions and end the bitterness - for all are her people. All must obey the common law. All are her-kinsmen, and she is their rightful Queen. She asks people to forgive those who fought for her husband and welcome them back. She asks people to be strong in heart and body, like the rocks that withstand the restless, mercenary sea. She says that we need to move on now in peace and prosperity and unity to a better future."

As Acco spoke, his voice flawless and eloquent, Flavius suddenly spotted the unmistakable figure of the Druid in the crowd. The bearded man was watching him with a cold and calculating look.

"Morcant's here," Pytheas said suddenly in a tight voice. "And he has brought his chariot. Looks like we are going for a ride again."

Quickly turning, Flavius spotted the one armed man standing bolt upright on his chariot as it swayed and bucked towards them across the uneven ground. Staring at the crowd Morcant looked strangely troubled.

"Sir. Sir," Acco was suddenly tugging at Flavius's sleeve, catching his attention. "The Queen she is now speaking about the trade agreement. She is addressing us and the Carthaginians."

Hastily Flavius turned his attention back to the Queen and as he did; he noticed that she had picked him out from the crowd and was beckoning to him. For a moment Flavius hesitated.

"Stay here," Flavius said curtly to the others as with Acco in tow, he began to make his way through the crowd towards the Queen. As he pushed towards her, he suddenly noticed Gisgo and a couple of his men doing the same. The Numidian looked tense and uncomfortable at the Queen's summons. He too appeared to be in the dark as to her intentions Flavius thought. It was a hopeful sign. A moment later Flavius was standing before the Queen, swiftly joined by Gisgo, Phameas and a couple of the Carthaginian mercenaries. As Phameas and Acco spotted each other, both broke into a furious embarrassed blush and hurriedly looked away without an exchange of words. Ignoring the Numidian Prince, Flavius eyed the Queen in a calm but grave manner. He was about to get his answer. The success or failure of his mission was about to be revealed. Standing upon her chariot, Queen Talwyn appeared to be in a good mood. Her eyes were twinkling in amusement but not in the manner of a friend and for the briefest moment Flavius thought he detected something mocking in her posture.

As the Queen began to speak, Flavius quickly glanced at Acco and was surprised to see that the young man no longer had his eyes fixed on the ground but had mustered up the courage to gaze back at the Queen. The boy had been speaking the truth about wanting to confront his phobia.

"The Queen asks us to enjoy this day," Acco said, translating as nearby Phameas did the same for Gisgo, speaking in a quiet voice. "It is a day of great celebration and unity. She says she has come to a decision regards the trade in tin, which she conducts with both Carthage and Rome. It has been a difficult decision, for she sees the benefits that trade brings and she has no wish to get embroiled in the great ongoing war to the south. Nor does she wish to offend anyone. So," Acco continued his voice betraying a rising tension, "she has ruled that today's hurling match between the men of Caer Bran and Chun Castle will decide the matter. She asks each of you. You Flavius and you Gisgo - to nominate one man from your party, who will join the opposing teams. A symbolic player who will compete for the ball like the rest. If the Carthaginian team win the game, the trade embargo against Rome and Massalia remains. If the Roman team wins, there shall be no trade embargo, and all shall be free to trade in her domain. She says that she will ask the gods and the strength of men to decide who is a worthy winner. For no one can argue against the will of the gods."

"What. Is she having a laugh?" Flavius exclaimed, looking startled as at his side Gisgo appeared to be having a fit - the Numidian's face rapidly darkening with anger and dismay.

"Gisgo is not happy with the verdict," Acco said, blushing once again, his mouth working rapidly and flawlessly as the words tumbled out. "He says that the Queen made him a promise. She cannot now go back on her word. He is calling this an insult. A disgrace. He and his men fought for her and some died for her. He insists that the Queen keep to her word. The embargo must stand."

In response the Queen stood her ground, her amusement only growing as she faced the two angry and shocked looking envoys.

"The Queen says she has made up her mind," Acco said. "Take it or leave it. This is her verdict. She says we should now go away and choose the man who will join the opposing teams. The game will start imminently, and the gods will be watching. She wishes each of us good luck."

For a moment Flavius did not move as he eyed the Queen, but she seemed deadly serious. At his side Gisgo appeared to be swearing. Then taking a deep breath, Flavius forced himself to bow to the Queen before abruptly turning on his heels and stalking back to his companions, his face looking like thunder.

Seeing him approaching, both Pytheas's and Scoti's faces abruptly fell, as they feared the worst.

"She is having a laugh," Flavius growled, as his anxious companions quickly closed in around him. "The Queen says

186

the success of our mission is going to be decided by this hurling match. She wants us to nominate one of our own to join one of the teams. If our team wins, we get what we came for. If the Carthaginians win, the trade embargo against us remains."

"What?" Scoti and Pytheas both exclaimed at the same time. "But that is insane," Pytheas continued. "I have never heard of something so outrageous. None of us have the slightest idea how this game is played. How can she allow a stupid match to decide such an important issue? It's not right."

"It doesn't matter what we think," Flavius snapped, quickly turning to look around at the anxious faces peering back at him. "She is the Queen. She is showing us who is boss around here and we have no choice but to accept. And what happened to you," Flavius added rounding on Morcant who was standing looking sheepish. "Where the hell have you been?"

As Acco translated, Morcant carefully cleared his throat, looking sombre.

"Morcant says that for some reason the Queen is not pleased with you right now," Acco said translating. "He does not know why, and he was only informed of what was happening this morning. Using the match to decide the issue is as much a surprise to him as it is to you. He says he did his best to try and convince the Queen as to the merits of the Roman proposal."

"His best. No he has been bloody useless as our agent," Flavius snapped direction his ire at Morcant.

Glaring at Morcant, Flavius's gaze lingered as Acco refused to translate his last sentence. Then with an unhappy scowl Flavius turned to stare at the Queen who was still standing upon her chariot.

"Fine," he said at last. "So be it. Come on then. Let's play her little stupid game. Who is best suited on our side to play in this match?"

For a moment no one spoke. Then slowly Flavius, Pytheas and Scoti turned to look at Acco.

"What?" Acco spluttered. "Me? But I know nothing about this game. I am just a translator. I couldn't possibly join the match."

"There is no one else," Flavius said in a grave voice. "You are the youngest. You are the fittest. It has to be you Acco. I am sorry. Just do your best."

***

Trundling along, standing upright on Morcant's chariot, with the one-armed driver guiding his horses, Flavius was gazing fixedly at the small groups of shouting men who were dashing about across the fields in a wild and confused manner. The players were indistinguishable from each-other, and it was impossible to know who was on whose team as they chased the ball. Except that the locals did seem to know who was on the opposing side. Many of the men already looked bruised and battered and a few were sporting nasty scrapes and cuts from where they had been tackled to the ground, kicked or punched.

"Who has the ball? Do we have the ball?" Scoti yelled, as he jogged along behind the chariot upon which Flavius and Pytheas were standing, squashed in together with Morcant, their driver.

"I don't know," Pytheas shouted back, his eyes glued on the fast moving game. "We had it a moment ago but I think the other team may have wrestled it back. Look at the runners. They are going in the wrong direction. One of them must have the ball."

The hurling match had already been going on for over an hour, with the contest swaying to and fro across the fields in a chaotic fashion. Starting at the midway point between the settlements of Caer Bran and Chun Castle there appeared to be no fixed playing field, no boundary but the sea. And no discernible rules. Tackling, brawling, running, kicking and throwing the ball - the rival packs of opposing players were struggling with each other in a brutal physical contest as they attempted to seize control of the small ball and run with it towards their opponents' goal. The game had appeared finely poised until just a few moments ago. Now, Flavius could see to his growing horror, the Carthaginian team appeared to be gaining ground, pushing towards the gates of Chun Castle, two miles away, which acted as one of the goals. If the Carthaginian team were able to carry the ball through the gates all would be lost.

Seeing the changing fortunes of their team, Pytheas groaned. The tension among the small group of spectators who were still following the game as it wildly plunged across the countryside was palpable. Catching sight of Gisgo and Phameas on the other side of the rival packs, Flavius took a deep breath. The Numidian Prince had somehow managed to get hold of a horse - which he was riding to keep up with the fleet footed players while Phameas, his translator, was sitting directly behind him clinging on for dear life.

"There it goes," Scoti shrieked, as one of the players hurled the ball towards a comrade who caught it and set off at a frantic pace. The ball carrier was instantly set upon by his opponents who surged after him like a swarm of bees, yelling and shouting.

"I do believe Sir," Scoti shouted with a sudden indignant voice as he drew level with the chariot, "that the Carthaginian team have more players than us. How can that be fair? I have counted them all and there is a definite imbalance in numbers. We have been set up."

"Oh great. Are you sure?" Flavius growled.

Sensing what they were talking about, Morcant suddenly spoke as he urged his horses on after the groups of running, shouting men.

"Morcant says there is nothing in the rules to state that the teams have to have equal numbers," Pytheas exclaimed, his face darkening. "He says that it quite normal for one team to field more players. He says in the end it is spirit, team work and fitness that is more important than numbers."

"Just like in warfare then," Flavius snapped.

Ahead, the Carthaginian team had appeared to have broken through and were streaming towards Chun Castle sat upon its rocky summit to the north. As the tired, looking Roman team gave chase, frantically trying to halt the ball runner, Flavius felt the chariot start to pick up pace. Thundering off in pursuit on the other side of the field Flavius caught a brief glimpse of Gisgo as his horse leaped across a small stream.

"Oh no," Pytheas groaned again, as the Carthaginian ball carrier broke free and flung the ball at a comrade who was completely unmarked. Catching the ball in a smooth motion the man sprinted away unopposed.

"Where is Acco?" Scoti yelled as he started to lag behind, his chest heaving from the exertion of keeping up with the game.

Where indeed was Acco, Flavius thought, as he stared at the packs of running men. He had not seen him all morning. Ever since he had reluctantly gone off to join the Roman team. Had he simply refused to take part and gone off to sulk? But as the game started to tilt decisively towards the Carthaginian side and the wild affray started to close in on the gates of Chun Castle; Flavius suddenly spotted him. Standing guard just outside the gates, Acco was alone and appeared to have manfully positioned himself as a last line of defence. To defend the goal. And with the swarm of battered and bruised men charging towards him, Flavius saw the young man brace himself to tackle the ball carrier and prevent disaster. Then the mob of screaming struggling men were upon him and abruptly Acco disappeared from view, lost in a chaotic tangle of moving bodies, mowed over by their savage momentum. A moment later a great victorious cry rose up as the Carthaginians scored and won the game. Hearing the triumphant cries Flavius sighed and lowered his eyes. He had lost. His mission had ended in failure.

As the victorious Carthaginian team celebrated - their defeated opponents halted, half bent over, looking around with despondent expressions, gasping for breath, their hands resting on their legs. Gazing at the scene, Flavius suddenly caught sight of Acco. The heroic young man was lying stretched flat out on the ground as if an unstoppable force had rolled right over him.

"I suppose that is that then," Pytheas muttered, looking glum. "We lost. We can all go home now," he added bitterly.

Standing upon the chariot looking sombre, Flavius did not respond. Turning to see an exhausted disbelieving Scoti struggling towards him, Flavius once again lowered his eyes.

"Come on. Let's go and see if Acco is alright," Flavius said at last gathering himself, together and raising his head. "He doesn't look too good."

It was a while later, with a bruised and shocked looking Acco sitting on a boulder, gingerly taking a drink from a water skin, with his companions standing around him - that Flavius noticed Gisgo sitting quietly upon his horse at the edge of the groups of celebrating victorious players. Catching Gisgo's eye, Flavius however saw that the Numidian looked strangely subdued despite his team having won. He appeared to be keeping his distance, refusing to take part in the celebrations. Standing beside the horse, Phameas had folded his arms across his chest as he too stared at the exhausted groups of players.

"Why is the bastard not looking more triumphant," Scoti snapped sullenly. "He has won hasn't he? Why is he not rubbing the fact in our faces. I know I would if the roles were reversed."

For a moment Flavius's eyes lingered - gazing at Gisgo.

"He's cautious," Flavius said at last. "Gisgo - he's a careful man. Have you noticed that he only speaks his mind when he knows he is right."

"You mean like earlier," Pytheas said, glancing in Gisgo's direction. "When he told the Queen she was a disgrace?"

"Yes," Flavius said nodding. "Exactly like that. He knows when to push his claim and when to hold back. It must mean that he is a reasonable man - a man who is willing to be swayed by good arguments."

"Maybe," Pytheas muttered looking doubtful.

"Well, here she comes," Scoti said in a weary voice, as he gestured at the Queen who was riding her chariot towards the groups of exhausted players, who were hanging about around the entrance to the fortified hill fort. "This is going to be hard to explain when we get back to Rome. Defeated by a stupid ball game. If it were not so serious, we would be laughed out of town and no offence to you young Acco. You did what you could. We all witnessed that heroic last stand of yours."

Sitting on his rock, his face battered and bruised, Acco nodded weakly, still looking a little disorientated from being flattened by the charging scrum. As the Queen rode up accompanied by a mounted entourage, Flavius stiffly got to his feet and turned to face her - conscious that Gisgo had dismounted and was leading his horse towards him. Upon her chariot, Queen Talwyn looked pleased, her eyes darting about at the bloodied and grimy players. Then she raised her arm and cried out, a smile appearing across her lips.

"She is hailing the victorious team," Acco said dully, as he manfully staggered over to be at Flavius's side. "She says she enjoyed the spectacle, a game worthy to be remembered for a long time. She says that both teams performed well and she is proud of all who participated. But as in life - there are always winners and losers. Tonight however all shall feast and drink together like brothers and your scrapes and cuts will be testament to your rugged self respect."

Slowly the Queen turned to Flavius and Gisgo with a strange gleam in her eyes and, suddenly unable to contain herself any longer, she chuckled. Staring back at her Flavius frowned. What was this? Sat upon their horses, the Queen's entourage had started to laugh as if they too knew about the joke. The joke that no one had told him about. They appeared to be laughing *at* him. Were they mocking him? Quickly Flavius glanced at Gisgo but the Numidian looked as surprised as himself.

"The Queen," Acco said, staring at her and speaking in a dull tone, "asks you - why the subdued, sorry faces? It was just a game. She says that you look like you have lost everything."

Standing his ground, Flavius did not respond, his face impassive as he waited for her to continue.

"She says that you should have more respect for her and her people. She says let this be a lesson for you," Acco continued as the Queen spoke again. "For she grows weary of Roman arrogance and Carthaginian greed. You demand much - as if you have the right to demand anything. You threaten her as if she were a mere vassal who must show obedience. But you are both in her kingdom now, and she is undisputed Queen and mistress of everything the eye can see. She is sovereign in her kingdom and she will not be bullied. She will not be rushed. Nor will she be forced to make important decisions without proper consultation. She says she has played a joke on you today and it has been most amusing to watch. The game was never going to decide the trade issue - only she as Queen can do that. She says you allowed yourselves to be fooled and that today you made yourselves look weak and pathetic. But how she enjoyed watching us race about as if the end of the world was near."

For a moment, Acco paused as he swayed unsteadily on his feet. Standing upon her chariot the Queen was now openly mocking both Flavius and Gisgo. "For she has not yet decided on what to do regards the trade issue," Acco continued in a dull tone. "She will give us a final answer, only after she has had a chance to consult with the other kings and the spirits of her ancestors. It is an important decision and must be done properly. At the feast of Samhain. To mark the start of the dark winter months and the end of summer, the tribes will gather at the great blue standing stones far to the east. It is the ancestral meeting place. A sacred spot. She says that in the next few days we shall accompany her to the great standing stones and she will give us our answer there."

And with that the Queen abruptly signaled to her driver and turning around, her chariot and entourage went clattering off down the slope.

For a long moment no one spoke as Flavius watched the Queen drive away.

"Jupiter's cock," Scoti exclaimed at last running, his hand through his hair. "She fooled us. She played us. You were right all along Flavius. She *was* having a laugh after all. Talk about a weird sense of humour. I get the impression that the

Queen would not mind it if we all just went away and left her in peace. She sure has a strange way of conducting diplomacy."

"Well, that is a relief," Pytheas said exhaling sharply. "We are still in the game it appears. So what do we now, Flavius?"

"Now," Flavius said, turning to eye Gisgo who was looking flabbergasted. "Now. I think the time has come for me to have a chat with our friend over there. Acco, with me please."

***

Glaring - looking decidedly unhappy - whilst tightly clutching his horse's reins, Gisgo turned to face him as Flavius approached with Acco dutifully trailing behind. Halting before the Numidian Prince and Phameas, Flavius paused as he carefully sized up his opponent.

"In Rome all those years ago," Flavius said to him, at last in a quiet voice. "After you and your crew had robbed the state mint. How did you manage to get out of the city with all that silver-bullion; it still puzzles me how you did it. That can't have been easy?"

As Acco translated, Gisgo stared back at him in stony silence, and as he refused to answer the tension grew more and more palpable. Then at last Gisgo spoke, his eyes gleaming, his lips curling in contempt.

"He says he got out through the Cloaca Maxima, the sewers," Acco translated. "The silver bullion was secretly loaded onto a waiting river barge, which then transported it down the Tiber and to the open sea beyond. He wants to know what happened to his friend - a Spaniard called Turibas. You caught him in Rome after the chase across the rooftops. He knows it was you who pursued him and his companions. He recognised you from your limp and blond hair. You were a spy once. He wants to know if you tortured Turibas before he died in your prison?"

195

"Turibas," Flavius responded raising his eyebrows. "The Spaniard. Your friend. Yes, I remember him. A brave man. Tough and proud too. He did his duty and protected you and your companions as long as he could. He did his job well. He even lied to protect you, telling us that you were dead. And yes we tortured him to get him to talk, but we didn't kill him. One of your own - an assassin named Kleptos - got to him first. Poisoned him in his cell, so that Turibas would not be able to tell us where you were hiding or what the plan was for getting the bullion out of Rome. But we captured Kleptos in the end and now he stews in the darkness and isolation of the Tullianum prison, without one of his hands. Kleptos however was acting on orders from Epicydes. I know about him too. Hannibal's spy master was the brains behind the operation, wasn't he? He planned it - the cripple who you carried around on your back. He is number one on our list of most wanted men and one day we are going to catch up with him too."

At the mention of Epicydes's name, Gisgo abruptly looked away, as if the mention of the name had triggered an unpleasant memory.

"Where is that amulet you used to wear," Flavius asked, pointing at Gisgo's neck. "The one with the three tiny painted heads on a cord. Was that to remind you of your wife and son? I managed to recover a similar amulet from a dead man in Rome whilst hunting for you, but now I suspect it was a duplicate. Did you have a copy made and worn by one of you associates - to give me the impression that it was you who had fallen to your death from that roof?"

Gazing back at him, Gisgo's eyes gleaming with hostile, sullen intent. Then at last he nodded.

"He says Sir," Acco translated, "that he used to wear such an amulet, but that he has since given it to his son. Much has happened since those days when you chased him through

Rome. He asks you why you are bringing up all these events from so long ago?"

"Because we have a mutual friend," Flavius continued, eyeing the Numidian Prince. "Two mutual friends in fact. Two women. But you should know that Caelina is dead. I knew her from before the war. I was close to her once - a long time ago, but I know she helped you in Rome. During the robbery of the state mint, I know she provided shelter and information to Epicydes. I know what she did. But I eventually caught up with her in the town of Nola. She was working with Kleptos when she killed herself. She preferred death to being taken alive and publicly condemned as a traitor. She died because she got mixed up with you lot. As regards the other woman," Flavius added sternly. "Amia is alive and doing well. She has remarried a friend of mine and she and her son are living on my farm. I have accepted them as part of my own family now and they are happy. They have a good life."

Subjecting Gisgo to a grave look, Flavius suddenly pointed at him. "I took care of Amia, after you abandoned her. She was your charge. You promised her you would come back for her but you did not. You turned your back on your friend's wife. That was shameful. It was I," Flavius said gently touching his chest, "who gave her a second chance. Me. So you owe me for that. You know you do. It was Amia who told me everything about you. How you lost your wife and son in an accident at sea. How your father's debts bankrupted you. How you joined Hannibal's army to seek a fortune."

Staring back at him, Gisgo appeared taken aback, unable to hide his surprise. Then at last he spoke.

"He says Sir," Acco said, "that he is glad that Amia has found a new home. He is happy for her and for Mastanabal's son too. But all of this happened a long time ago. He has moved on. He asks you what it is that you want from him? He says he has not come here to conduct idle chatter."

"What do I want?" Flavius replied. "You told me that we could not be friends. But I disagree. We can be both friends and allies if you wish it so. I have no personal animosity against you. You are a soldier doing his duty for his country - just like I am. Just like so many others. You fight for your comrades and your country. There does not have to be conflict between the two of us. One day this war between Rome and Carthage must end."

"Friends," Gisgo suddenly spat out, speaking in Latin and it was clear that the idea appeared abhorrent to him.

"Yes friends and allies," Flavius retorted, standing his ground, looking grave. "Why not? You are not a Carthaginian. You are a Numidian. Rome is going to win this war - so why not come over to our side. Why not fight beside our legions? Abandon Carthage. If you were to do so, Rome would look most favourably upon you and your people. We have a long history of respecting and defending our allies - hence the fact that my translator here is from Massalia. And when Carthage has been finally defeated, a new and independent Numidia could arise from the ashes - one that is not a vassal to Carthage, a slave to no one. A free nation. You would be a free people. Think about that. Think about what that could mean. Think about where your country's true interests lie."

Looking away - Gisgo blew the air from his cheeks. For a moment he hesitated. Then turning back to Flavius with a disbelieving look, he slowly shook his head.

"He asks you Sir," Acco translated looking grim, "whether you have the power to make this proposal on behalf of the Republic. Or whether you are just bullshitting him and spouting nonsense in order to trick him. He wants to know how you could possibly guarantee that Rome will agree to honour the existence of an independent Numidia after the conclusion of the war?"

"No, I am not bullshitting you," Flavius responded. "He is right. I alone cannot give him that guarantee, but I know the men in the Senate who can. I have important friends and patrons in high places. I could argue your case before them. I could get you those guarantees. It would be a start. Trust must be earned, and we would need to be sure you are not bullshitting us either. But it can be made to work. An alliance between Rome and the Massylii could exist. It would be a good thing, a decisive alliance and it could start right now - here with us, with the two of us. We are just two men. There is no reason for there to be conflict between you and me. After all that we have been through," Flavius said with gleaming eyes. "If we could learn to trust each other that would be an important first step. I am serious. I am willing to give friendship a go if you are."

But Gisgo appeared to be unconvinced. Shaking his head once again he spoke, his voice sounding surprisingly calm and reasonable.

"He says," Acco said quickly, "that he does not trust Rome or your Senate. The tricks and greed of the Romans are well known. His answer is no. You are the enemy and he and you will not be friends. He says that Carthage may have her faults but that he is not about to abandon their alliance. Too much blood has been spilled to justify such a betrayal. He has watched too many good men die for that to become a reality. He says switching sides now would be a dishonourable act - that would offend the gods and the spirits of his brothers. He will play no part in such a venture. But," Acco suddenly hesitated, peering at Gisgo as if he had misunderstood something. "He says Sir," the young man continued at last. "That he has a counter proposal for you. Gisgo says that he is willing to pay you handsomely, if you were to side with him and Carthage against the Senate in Rome. You would not be the first of your countrymen to do so. He says the war is by no means settled in Rome's favour and that he could make you a very wealthy man."

For a long moment Flavius said nothing as he stared at Gisgo. Then he shook his head in a sad and exasperated manner.

"No, I will not betray my countrymen," he said. "I have a son fighting in Spain. No amount of money will get me to change my mind. I do not fight for money like you do. I have a duty to serve the Republic."

Gazing back at him, looking equally exasperated, Gisgo remained silent. Then muttering something to Phameas he shrugged, turned and began to lead his horse away.

Chapter Fourteen - The Standing Stones

Across the gently rolling hills the green country stretched away, pleasant, rustic and undisturbed as if nothing had changed since the day it was created. For several days now the party had been heading east towards the meeting place, the great standing stones where the tribes gathered - to celebrate the feast of Samhain. It was late in the afternoon and, riding his horse, Flavius looked tired and unwell. The sickness, the diabetes, the constant thirst and need to piss, from which he was suffering was not letting up and the bouts of blurred vision appeared to becoming, more and more pronounced and frequent. His illness was making things harder and harder, conspiring with time, which was was not making him any younger. Up ahead, leading the way Queen Talwyn, clad in her white cloak, was standing upon her chariot as it crawled along heading eastwards across the fields, with the sun to her back. The chariot driver squashed in beside her was the same young warrior he'd met in the forest, Flavius thought. The man had to be the Queen's favourite, for he accompanied her everywhere. Following their Queen, the forty mounted guards, nobles and slaves, riding close together, were trotting along in silence. The warriors had slung their shields and spears across their backs and for the moment the only noise came from the thud of hooves, the whinny of the horses and the barking of the hunting dogs who were bounding ahead. Trundling along on his own, driving his chariot, the breeze playfully toying with his long beard, the druid and his daughter, the Queen's handmaiden, were gazing rigidly ahead. After their altercation, the Druid was studiously and contemptuously ignoring Gisgo and his small band of mercenaries. The Carthaginians moving on foot in turn were tacitly keeping their distance from him and the Queen's party.

Turning to gaze at Morcant, who was riding alone in his own chariot Flavius's moody expression darkened. Ever since the debacle at the hurling game, he had been annoyed with

Morcant. The man had not proved to be of much use anyway and the bitter enmity that existed between him and Gisgo was becoming a separate problem. If the objective now was to make a friend out of the Numidian, Morcant was getting in the way. Instead of an ally the man had become an obstacle. Noticing Flavius's prickly mood and guessing what it was about, Pytheas hurriedly reached up to scratch his forehead revealing his concern.

"We must remain united," the Massaliot diplomat said, quickly glancing at Flavius as he trotted along at his side. "Please. You cannot blame Morcant for disliking Gisgo. The Numidian is our enemy. He made that very clear. Nor can you blame Morcant for everything that happened at that hurling game. He could not have known that the Queen was going to play a trick on us. It was not his fault - and we still need him. We still need his help to make a success of our mission. He is our man."

"Well, he should have known," Flavius growled looking displeased. "It is his job to warn us of such things. Instead, we were made to look like fools. Everyone is laughing at us. I am sick of it. The dignity of Rome must not be sullied. We cannot afford to be made fools of. It puts us at a disadvantage. The only saving grace is that Gisgo too was made to look like a fool. You pay him, don't you?" Flavius added rounding on Pytheas. "Massalia pays Morcant a retainer for his cooperation. That's how you assure his loyalty?"

"We do," Pytheas admitted, looking away.

"Well Morcant should have done a better job then," Flavius snapped. "He should have warned us. He claims he has the Queen's ear. So why did he not know about her plan? Everyone else in her entourage appeared to know - except for our man. It's a disgrace. We were ambushed. It cannot happen again. Do you hear me."

"I will speak with Morcant," Pytheas said diplomatically. "I will see what I can do. But I am still right. We cannot afford to fall out right now. We still need his help."

"Well, we shall see whether that is true," Flavius muttered darkly. "And who are those men with him," he added irritably gesturing at a small group of riders who were accompanying Morcant's chariot. "I noticed that they joined us yesterday, but I have never seen them before. Where did they come from?"

"I think they are his kin," Pytheas responded cautiously, staring at the horsemen riding up ahead. "I think Morcant said something about them being his extended family. They are going to join us for Samhain."

"Great," Flavius said, glaring at the men as Pytheas tactfully allowed his horse to drop back. Mastering his prickly emotions, Flavius took a deep breath and licked his bone dry lips before turning to Scoti, who was riding beside him.

"I have heard of the feast of Samhain," Flavius said. "The Gauls along the Po - in Italy - they celebrate it too. The end of summer and the start of the dark time. From my experience though, Samhain always ends up as an excuse for one great piss-up and fornication fest. Everyone always gets roaring drunk at these feasts. But these standing stones, this meeting place; I have not heard about that. You are my secretary Scoti - what can you tell me about these standing stones. What do I need to know about them?"

"Well Sir," Scoti said carefully clearing his throat, "from what I have gathered, there are many many circles of standing stones in these lands. But the one to which we are heading in special. It's old for a start. Not even the locals know how old or even who made them. That knowledge has been lost. Morcant thinks they are as old as the pyramids in Egypt. So, a lot older than the cities of Rome or Athens. Aside from that, the standing stones are a tribal meeting place. I am told that each year the tribes send representatives who gather together at the stones - to celebrate Samhain. The feast is a useful place at which to exchange news, arrange alliances, trade deals, marriages and so forth. Or just to meet up with family and old friends. Once within sight of the standing stones, a general truce exists and war is forbidden. It's a bit like the way the Greeks use their Olympic games Sir. The other thing you should know is that the locals believe the standing stones hold magical powers. The sick journey to these stones in the hope of being healed and cured. And for the Druids', it is a very sacred place indeed."

"Well looks like I am heading to the right spot then," Flavius said in a sullen voice. "Maybe these stones will heal me too. Good. What else?"

"That's all I have managed to glean so far Sir," Scoti said with a shrug. "But from the respectful way the locals talk about them, these standing stones must be quite something to behold."

***

"There, Sir," Scoti said pointing, his voice quivering with excitement. Peering in the direction his secretary was indicating, Flavius frowned as he walked his horse across the fields following the others. To the east across the open plain with the large blood red morning sun rising on the horizon as a backdrop, a vast circular embankment had appeared protected by a deep ditch. The chalky earthen mound appeared to be protecting something within, but he could not see what it was.

"The standing stones must be inside the circle," Scoti said eagerly, craning his neck. "Good gods we must be one of the first Romans to ever see this place. It looks huge."

"My great grandfather visited the stones," Pytheas called out proudly raising his chin as he rode alongside Flavius, his eyes fixed on the vast circular earthen structure. "One hundred odd years ago now. He left us a description. He said he had never seen anything like it. The temple of the island Celts; he called it. He said the standing stones have significant cultural and religious importance. To the locals it is what the temple of Jupiter on the Capitoline Hill is to the Romans or the temple of Delphi to the Greeks. This is one of the great Celtic holy shrines. My great grandfather wrote that it was a place of pilgrimage."

For a moment Flavius's eyes lingered. Then he turned to gaze at the civilian encampment that stood on its own, separated from the circular earthen embankment by a straight causeway, that cut through the land in a straight line. It too was large, bigger than he had been expecting. The camp looked temporary, and they were not the first to arrive he could see. For thronging around the mass of crude wooden huts, shelters and camp fires, going about their business, were hundreds upon hundreds of people, men, women, children, warriors, Druids', traders - the young and the old. Even from half a mile out he could hear the excited festival-like noises drifting across the fields, the barking of dogs, the dull hammer of blacksmiths at work. Sniffing the air he caught the delicious scent of fresh bread, roasting meat and wood smoke. Seeing Queen Talwyn heading straight for the Celtic camp, Flavius licked his lips, once again feeling the pressure in his bladder.

"Looks like we shall be sleeping out under the stars again tonight," Flavius said, as he glanced up at the sky. "But I don't see any signs of rain. Scoti, maybe when we are finally settled in you can rustle up some food for us. It has been a long journey. And Pytheas," Flavius added turning to the Massaliot diplomat. "Tell Morcant that I want to speak to him. You are right. He's our man. It's time we cleared the air."

"Very well," Pytheas replied, looking relieved.

Turning to look around, studying the people thronging the noisy bustling encampment, Flavius frowned as his three companions silently moved about - tending to the horses, unloading their gear, cooking pots and blankets, while at the same time marking out the space where the four of them would sleep and eat. The camp appeared to be filled with people from dozens of different tribes and more were arriving every hour. The newcomers were coming in from every direction, entering the expanding camp on foot or horseback, lugging their belongings, tools and trade wares on their backs. Only the nobles and kings appeared to have chariots, but no one seemed to be in charge and the festival appeared to be a free-for-all. Watching the activity, the people setting up camp and the joyful reunions around him, Flavius could see that everyone seemed to be getting on just fine and a relaxed, if excited atmosphere was prevailing. Nearby the Queen and her entourage were doing the same as his own companions, setting up camp, but there was no sign of the Queen herself. She seemed to have gone off somewhere. Turning to eye, Gisgo and his small band of mercenaries Flavius again licked his lips. The Carthaginians had claimed a spot of grass at a discrete distance from the Queen and her people. For a moment, Flavius watched Gisgo issuing instructions to his men before he thoughtfully reached up to rub his chin. The Numidian Prince was doing his best to avoid confrontation with the Druid. To keep his men in check. He could see that. The budding relationship between one of his mercenaries and the Druid's daughter was causing him problems.

"The feast starts tonight and will go on for three days," Scoti said, as he paused from what he had been doing and came over to Flavius. "The main celebratory event however is tomorrow night, starting at sunset - the day of Samhain. For the Celtic day ends at sunset. The party is going to go on all night. It's going to get quite wild, I am told. Just to warn you Sir. We may not get much sleep."

"I was young once. If I wanted to sleep, I would have chosen a quieter spot," Flavius said, forcing a little smile onto his lips. "Don't worry. We need to remain close to the Queen - to remind her that we are still here. Look. Our Carthaginian friends are doing the same."

"Flavius," Pytheas suddenly called out in warning.

Turning - Flavius immediately spotted Morcant advancing towards him, accompanied by some of the men who had joined them half-way through their journey. Observing the newcomers Flavius's smile slowly faded. Morcant's kinsmen looked like hard men, warriors with unfriendly faces. Coming to a halt Morcant too looked edgy, as if something was consuming him.

"Morcant says," Acco said hurriedly moving to Flavius's side. "That you wished to speak to him?"

"Yes, I do," Flavius nodded. Pausing Flavius eyed the one armed Celtic nobleman with his drooping moustache and spiky hair. "Tell him Acco," Flavius said at last, "that I know things have been a little tense between him and I since the game. Tell him that I expect him to do the job for which we pay him. He should have warned us that the Queen was planning to play a trick on us. Tell him Acco, that I do not want another debacle like at the game. I do not want to be ambushed like that again, understood. Now," Flavius said, taking a deep breath, speaking in a more emollient tone. "We need to move on. There is no point in digging up old bones. What has happened has happened and we need to work together."

As Acco finished translating, Morcant was staring at Flavius, his expression cold and unforgiving. Then he spoke, spitting out the words as if they were knives, his eyes gleaming with sudden hostility.

"Morcant says," Acco stammered sounding taken aback, "who the fuck are you to tell him what to do. You are in his country now and no one orders him about. No one tells him what to do. He says that if you had wanted this trade agreement so badly - that you should have supported the Queen's husband. You should have hoped that he would win the civil war instead of the Queen. For the Queen's husband would have been much more favourably disposed to Rome and Massalia. He would have given you everything you wanted - so don't lecture him on how smart you are. It is you, who messed things up."

And with that Morcant turned on his heels and strode away followed by his kinsmen - leaving Flavius and the others staring at him in shock.

***

Gazing at the massive stones, standing in a circle like silent sentinels - erect and alone in the green grass, Flavius paused. The stones, standing at least thirteen feet high and seven across were connected by horizontal lintels that lay across their tops and through the gaps in the outer circle, he could see another inner ring of smaller standing stones. For a moment Flavius said nothing. Then slowly he exhaled. The temple was magnificent. A majestic, timeless construction. The simple dignity of the stones speaking to him without the need for words - telling him that this was a statement of faith, an echo from a distant past. The long-dead builders telling him that we were here once. We existed. We built this.

It was late in the day and there were few people about. Standing beside him Scoti, and Acco were gazing at the stone circle in humble silence. After having settled in at the Celtic encampment, a short distance away, the three of them had wandered down the causeway and passed through the chalky outer embankment to gaze upon the monument.

"Those stones look massive," Flavius said at last, breaking the reverent silence, studying the circle with a builders-eye. "How did they manage to move those stones and place them upright in the ground? That is a huge job. It would have taken hundreds of men years to do something like that."

"I don't think anyone knows," Scoti replied quietly.

"I asked about," Acco said staring at the standing stones. "I was told by the locals that the stones were brought here to this spot, long ago. They were brought here from the west. The builders too originally came from the west. That's all people seemed to know or were willing to tell me. But if you ask me Sir. I would say this is a sacred burial ground. I noticed burial pits on the way in."

"Nah," Scoti said shaking his head. "That's not it. This place. It's a temple. To the sun. They built it to worship the return, each day of the life-giving sun. Look at how the stones are all carefully aligned to the east. They are orientated to the sunrise. I am an astronomer, trust me. Whoever built this thing knew what they were doing. There is purpose and design here. They placed those stones exactly so that they are in a line with the rising sun. I would not be surprised if, on the summer solstice - the alignment becomes perfect. That's what this place is all about. Perfection. Design. Faith."

"Well, whatever its purpose," Flavius answered, "I have a feeling that the Druids' will know the answer. They are the keepers and guardians of all knowledge in these lands."

"I don't think it would be a good idea to ask the Druid about that," Acco responded turning to Flavius with a little smile. "He doesn't look too friendly."

"You noticed," Flavius remarked raising his eyebrows as he caught sight of Gisgo and a couple of his mercenaries. The Carthaginians had suddenly appeared nearby standing on top of the chalky embankment, as they gazed across at the circle of stones. The Numidian Prince appeared to have the same idea as himself, Flavius thought. To come and inspect the ancient monument. For a moment Flavius eyed him in silence but Gisgo, if he had noticed his presence, appeared to be carefully ignoring him. At last, turning back to his companions Flavius gestured for them to follow him.

"Come on. Let's get back to the camp," Flavius muttered. "It's getting late, and I need to take a piss."

***

Returning to the camp, Flavius immediately noticed that something was going on. A crowd had gathered around the spot where the Queen had camped. Eagerly craning their necks, Flavius could see that the men and women appeared to be trying to get a glimpse of something, but the mass of bodies was blocking his view. Catching sight of Pytheas standing among the multitude, Flavius veered towards him, quickly followed by Scoti and Acco. At last - pushing his way through the crowd Flavius came to a halt. A few yards away, with her warriors forming a respectful circle around her - Queen Talwyn was crouching and hugging two young children. The two girls looked no older than eight or ten summers and both of them were sobbing, clinging to the Queen, their heads buried in her embrace. It looked like a happy joyful reunion. Standing nearby the Queen's companion, the young handsome warrior with the wolf tattoo, was looking on gravely, clutching a bulging sack in one hand. Standing directly behind him were three hard-faced and tough looking warriors, who Flavius did not recognise. The armed men, clad in rough mud splattered cloaks had not been part of the party that had set out eastwards - days ago. They appeared to be strangers, newly arrived.

"What's going on?" Flavius murmured as Pytheas edged up to him.

"The two girls," Pytheas said quietly. "They are the Queen's daughters'. Her husband took them with him when he fled. After the battle. As hostages. But now they are back with their

210

mother. The Queen has not seen them since the start of the civil war. I am told that she feared that she would never see them again. See those three men standing behind Galchobhar," Pytheas added. "They brought the girls in just a few moments ago. They are bounty hunters."

Staring at the scene, Flavius said nothing. Then Galchobhar took a step forwards and spoke, catching the Queen's attention. Stiffly, looking emotional, the Queen rose to her feet and hastily wiped a tear from her face while the young warrior took the sack he was holding and opened it, dumping the contents at her feet. And as he did so a startled gasp arose from the crowd, as a severed human head rolled out onto the grass. For a moment no one spoke as all stared at the gory, bloody sight. Gazing down at the decapitated head, the Queen however remained silent, her composure unchanged.

"Is that what I think it is?" Flavius murmured.

For a moment Pytheas was unable to reply, as a little colour shot into his cheeks.

"Yes," Pytheas said at last, sounding decisive. "That is her husband's head. Looks like those bounty hunters got him too. So, the rebel is dead. The Queen's war is over. She has won."

Chapter Fifteen - Samhain

The Celtic encampment had descended into a riot of shouting, laughter, dancing and singing. Sunset had come and gone and in the darkness; the sky was lit by the reddish glow of hundreds of small campfires. Nursing a wooden cup in his hand, Flavius stood gazing at the festivities. All around him, filling the night with wild abandon, drunken people were staggering about and nearby a group had abandoned themselves to wild uninhibited dancing, their arms raised to the heavens as if in religious ecstasy. The singing was terrible. A choir of cats. An assault on his ears, but there was little he could do about that. Looking pensive, Flavius lifted his cup to his lips and took a sip of the sweet tasting honey Mead. There was no sign of his companions. They had vanished into the turmoil shortly after the partying had begun and for the moment, he was alone.

Slowly moving through the crowd, observing the men, women and children enjoying themselves Flavius suddenly came to a halt as through the din he heard a short high-pitched scream. The woman's cry had not been one of joy or happiness. It had sounded frantic. As if she was being attacked. Frowning, Flavius turned to look about but in the darkness and among the heaving crowds no one seemed to have noticed or cared and the partying, feasting, singing and dancing continued unabated. Then he heard the scream again. It had come from the edge of the camp. Turning, he started off in the direction from whence the sound had come before coming to a startled halt. A few paces away, illuminated in the glow of a campfire, the druid and one of Gisgo's mercenary's were standing facing each other, nose to nose in a ugly, tense confrontation while the Druids' dishevelled looking daughter, the Queen's handmaiden, lay on the ground, as if someone had had flung her there. The Druid was clutching his staff, steaming with anger. His long beard nearly raking the ground, his eyes gleaming - cold and hard like flint. Standing his ground, stubbornly refusing to budge, his nose just an inch away from the Druid, the Carthaginian mercenary appeared to be in a murderous mood, his hand resting on the hilt of his knife. The two men appeared to be on the verge of a physical fight. Blood was about to be spilled. The sacred code of Samhain - that no fighting was to take place, was about to be broken and it was not hard to see what it was all about. Lying on the ground the young woman was in tears, desperately imploring the men to stop before it was too late.

Staring at the scene, looking shocked, Flavius took a deep breath as he recognised the Carthaginian mercenary. It was the same man who had taken a liking to the Druid's daughter. The same mercenary who had been involved in the earlier altercation with the Druid. The Carthaginian looked like he could handle himself in a fight, an experienced warrior - his carefully braided hair different to the other Punic mercenaries. And by the determination of his stance, it seemed that the girl meant a lot to him for he was not backing down. Then with the tense confrontation rapidly spiraling-out of control a figure came rushing out of the darkness. Pouncing on the Carthaginian, Gisgo was suddenly dragging the man away in a frantic, powerful grip, yelling at him as he did. Taking an aggressive step towards the Carthaginians the Druid snarled before raising his staff in a threatening manner as Gisgo hauled his man away just in time.

Flavius too was moving. Limping over to the girl, he quickly reached down and helped her to her feet. Looking startled, her cheeks stained by tears, she turned to look at him and Flavius immediately noticed that she was sporting a fresh bruise across her cheek. Someone had hit her. Then before he could do or say anything else, the Druid loomed into view, his fury palpable. Snatching his daughter's-hand the Druid roughly yanked her away from Flavius and within seconds the two of them had vanished off into the night.

Looking pale and unwell, Pytheas was sitting cross-legged on the ground among their blankets and personal gear. Standing beside him, Flavius sighed as he turned to look about at the feasting people, still clutching his mug of honey Mead. The darkness was alive with wild abandon. The noise and rowdiness appeared to be growing as the party-goers became more and more intoxicated while the night still had a long way to go.

Abruptly Pytheas leaning forwards and was sick. Coughing and spluttering he brought up the contents of his stomach before gingerly wiping his mouth and spitting out the last remains.

"I think I must have eaten something that did not agree with me," the Massaliot diplomat groaned. "Oh, I feel awful. It must be food poisoning."

Looking concerned, Flavius glanced at his friend.

"You had better stay here then and guard our stuff," he said at last. "Get some rest. Have you seen Acco and Scoti?"

"No," Pytheas replied, shaking his head. Then once again he was sick, retching onto the ground, his whole body shaking.

"Oh this is shit," Pytheas muttered, wearily closing his eyes. "Never again. I am not normally affected like this. But right now my stomach is being turned inside out. It's like I have a knife in my guts."

"There was a confrontation just now," Flavius said changing the subject. "That Carthaginian who has taken a shine to the Queen's handmaiden. He and the Druid were facing off. It nearly came to blows - a proper fight."

"Really," Pytheas groaned looking up at Flavius, his hand pressed tightly to his stomach. "Too much Mead and beer. It always leads to problems. People don't know their limits or don't want to know. I spoke to the girl earlier though - before the feast had started."

"You did," Flavius said, quickly glancing at his friend.

"Yes," Pytheas said with a tight grimace, as he appeared to be struck by a sudden bout of cramp. "It was just a brief conversation. Her father. The Druid. He watches her like a hawk. He is never far away. So, I had to be quick. I was trying to find out if the Queen had come to a decision on the trade agreement."

"So, what did she say?"

"Oh, nothing much," Pytheas groaned closing his eyes. "Nothing useful. I don't think she knows either. But she talked briefly about Morcant. She says that the Queen is not pleased with him. There is disagreement between them. The girl said there has been tension between Morcant and the Queen ever since the night that the Queen was poisoned. She says she saw Morcant in the Queen's hall, that night. The two of them had a heated argument. But she didn't know about what. She said she does not make a habit of spying on her mistress. She is the kind of girl - you know," Pytheas paused for a moment, "who will not abuse the trust placed in her. I can see why the Queen chose her. She is loyal."

Gazing down at Pytheas, Flavius suddenly frowned. For a moment he did not reply as he reached up to rub his chin.

"She said she saw Morcant in the Queen's hall. The night the Queen was poisoned?" Flavius exclaimed. "You sure she said that?"

"Yes," Pytheas responded, looking up at him. "Why? Something the matter?"

"I don't know," Flavius replied suddenly looking troubled. "But I remember something. Morcant told me that he was *not* in the Queen's hall; that night. The same night that the Queen was poisoned. So, if the Queen's handmaiden saw him there - that would mean that Morcant was lying to us."

Sitting on the ground, Pytheas had no immediate answer. Then at last he shrugged.

"I don't know," Pytheas said evasively. "Could be an innocent mix up. Maybe he got the days wrong."

"Maybe," Flavius said turning to gaze into the darkness with a troubled look. "Or maybe Morcant has been lying to us. But if so, why?"

***

"Sir. Sir," Acco called out hurriedly, his voice revealing his alarm, as he appeared out of the gloom - hastening towards Flavius. "I am glad I found you. It's about Scoti. I think he has got himself into some trouble."

"What do you mean, trouble?" Flavius replied with a frown, as he stood beside Pytheas who was still sitting on the ground; looking miserable.

"I think he has drunk too much," Acco exclaimed looking worried. "I think he is drunk. He is over there - gambling with some of the locals Sir. I didn't want to leave him but I had to - in order to find you. I fear he is going to start a fight. You had better come at once. The locals Sir - I think they may misunderstand him. I fear they may think he is insulting them. He is lecturing them on astronomy and science but he is drunk. He is babbling to them in Greek and Latin, but they don't understand a word he is saying. He is going to get himself into trouble."

"He's been drinking!" Flavius snapped, looking startled as he quickly ran his hand through his hair. "Scoti has been drinking! Oh no - this is no good. The man cannot take his drink. He can't handle it. He has no tolerance. It all goes straight to his head. Where is he?"

"Follow me," Acco said hurriedly turning away into the darkness.

Scoti was sitting cross-legged on the ground close to a crackling camp fire facing three men who were doing the same. In his hand the Roman astronomer was holding a cup and rattling it about with a stupid grin plastered across his face. As Flavius appeared, hurrying into the firelight, he saw Scoti turn the cup upside down and scatter the dice across a wooden board that lay on the ground, separating the two sets of players.

"Ha!" Scoti called out triumphantly in Latin, dumping the cup in front of one of the Celts and leaning forwards to prod one of the men with his finger. "See if you can beat that my friend. Alea iacta est. The die is cast. A six. A three and a glorious five," he added slurring the last word.

Gazing back at him, facing him in utter silence, the three men looked unamused and they made no effort to respond to Scoti. They were physically big and strong warriors in the prime of life with full beards - their hard, rugged faces completely covered in blue woad that gave them a fierce-some otherworldly appearance. The men looked hard as nails. Staring across at Scoti, it was clear they had not understood a word he had been saying to them. Swiftly crouching beside Scoti, Flavius reached out to grip his shoulder.

"What do you think you are doing?" Flavius said quietly, his face creased with concern. "You know better than this."

"Flavius - my friend," Scoti called out his eyes lighting up as he saw who it was. "You are just in time to see me win the game. The fine gentlemen here have challenged me to a throw of the dice, and I am about to pick them clean of everything they possess. Lady luck smiles on me tonight."

"You have been drinking," Flavius snapped urgently tightening his grip on Scoti's shoulder. "Come on. You know what drink does to you. This is not wise. You are going to get yourself into trouble. These men. They haven't understood a word you have been telling them and if you start taking their stuff, they will think you are robbing them."

"Oh leave me alone," Scoti called out, trying to shake free, slurring his words again. "It was only a little sip, and I am enjoying myself."

"It looks like you are about to get your head kicked in," Acco said sternly as he stood over Scoti looking down at him. "Those men can't understand a word you are saying, and they don't look too amused."

Turning to look at the three Celts with their strange blue painted faces, Flavius could see that they were still trying to work out whether Scoti was insulting them or not. He had never-before, encountered such painted people before. Then Acco was speaking to them in their own language. A moment later one of them replied, looking suspicious.

"They say they are from the far north," Acco replied hurriedly turning to Flavius. "He, says he and his brothers are from the very northern part of the island - where the highlands end and, there is nothing but the crashing sea. It has taken them over a month to walk down here."

"Great," Flavius said. "Acco. Explain to them that our friend here means no offence. Nor is he insulting them. He just can't take a drink and tonight he has already drank far too much for what is good for him."

As Acco translated and Scoti swayed lightly from side to side, Flavius gazed at the three warriors with a guarded look. Would they buy the explanation? If it came to a physical fight he and Acco would be no match for the three of them. Then as Acco fell silent, the three painted men exchanged glances with each other before bursting out into roars and shrieks of laughter.

"Oh wonderful. Now look who is insulting who," Scoti retorted, crying out and throwing up his hands in disgust. Slurring his words, he looked offended as the three warriors rocked on their haunches. "Come on you bastards," Scoti cried out, reaching over to prod one of them with his finger. "Stop dicking around. Play the game. I have a six, a three and a five. See if you can beat that."

Calming down, one of the painted men turned to Scoti, subjecting him to a mocking and bemused smile before speaking, his strange language utterly meaningless to Flavius. But the sudden intent in his eyes was clear. Standing watching the exchange between the two sides - Acco stiffened and a sharp intake of breath followed.

"He says," Acco said, quickly swallowing "that he will play the game. He will take a gamble but that we have not yet agreed what the bet is about. He says that if he wins Scoti will continue to drink all night with them. To the moment he passes out or someone decides to beat the crap out of him. Either way he keeps drinking, if he loses."

"No," Flavius said sharply, but as he did one of the Celts guessing what he had said, leaned forwards and placed a warning hand on Flavius's arm.

Studying Flavius with a hard sober look, the other brother's eyes lingered for a moment before he slowly shook his head. "He says that this is not your call to make," Acco translated. "He says the die has already been cast and is now waiting for a response. It is too late to withdraw from the game."

"Fine," Scoti blurted out, raising his chin defiantly. "I accept. But if I win. They will give me their permission to name their tribe for all eternity. I will get the patent and copyright to name their people on all official Roman government maps and correspondence. Their Roman name will belong to me. That will be my prize. So, I shall name them after myself - the Scoti.

That is how I shall remember winning this game and this night. Agreed?"

Hesitating, Acco glanced at Flavius, seeking permission to translate. Shaking off the other man's restraining hand, Flavius took a deep unhappy breath before finally nodding his consent.

Sitting across from Scoti, the three warriors were eyeing him in bemusement as Acco translated his words. Exchanging glances with each other one of them finally nodded in agreement and reached for the cup and the three dice. Rattling them in the air for all to see, he paused for a dramatic moment before sending them clattering onto the wooden board.

"Yes," Scoti roared triumphantly raising his arms in the air. "Yes. I win. Take that you Scoti. My blue-faced friends."

***

Sitting - gazing at the wild, boisterous, and noisy party that was swirling around him, bringing the darkness to life, Flavius stoically took another sip of Mead from his cup. Nearby, rolling over the ground a grunting couple were having sex uncaring as to who could see them while further away, lying dangerously close to a roaring campfire a man was passed out from too much drink. It was already well into the early hours of the morning, but the great feast of Samhain was still going on. The appetite of the revelers' appeared undimmed and there was no sign that the shouting, singing, feasting and dancing was about to end any time soon. Glancing at Pytheas, who was lying curled up on the ground, softly groaning from his upset stomach, Flavius took another sip from his cup. Lying on the hard ground on the opposite side of their patch, Scoti was fast asleep, snoring loudly, making little pig-like grunting noises, his body covered by his blanket. How the astronomer could sleep with all the noise and activity around him was a mystery Flavius thought, as he slowly shook his head in bewilderment. Only Acco was absent.

The night appeared to have been one of constant crisis management. Of hurrying and lurching from one problem to the next. There had not been much time for him to enjoy himself, Flavius thought and now he was dog tired and once again in dire need of a piss. First Pytheas had fallen ill. Then Scoti had needed rescuing and now Acco had vanished, getting up to god's know what? Stoically gazing at the couple having sex, Flavius slowly took another sip of Mead before looking away. To his surprise however he had noticed that Gisgo too was having to deal with his own crises. The Numidian Prince was having a very similar night. For he too seemed to be putting out fires. First with the face-off between his man and the Druid that had involved the Queen's handmaiden. Then later he'd witnessed another altercation between a group of drunken men who had appeared to accuse two of Gisgo's mercenaries of stealing. Gisgo had handled that crisis too. Paying the accusers to move on and so deftly avoiding another incident.

Suddenly Flavius froze - before grunting in disbelief. Out of the gloom coming from the fires, a couple had suddenly appeared. The man and woman were dancing together but it was a rather slow, awkward and clumsy embrace. The woman were young, no older than fifteen and holding onto her with both hands was Acco. The boy appeared to have mustered up the courage to master his phobia, his fear of women. He had done it. He had conquered it - just like he had said he would. Staring at the two dancers - looking speechless, Flavius grunted again as at last a pleased smile appeared on his lips.

**

As the morning sun-bathed the green plain in light and warmth the Celtic encampment looked like a battlefield. Strewn across the grass and in between the blackened smoking campfires, the bodies lay everywhere. Fast asleep. Snoring. Comatose, exhausted, and out of it from too much drink and food. Here and there a person was staggering about as if mortally wounded. The feast and the uninhibited hedonism had finally come to an end and a strange soothing and subdued silence had settled across the camp. As if people were slowly starting to remember what they had got up to the night before. In contrast, the small group of onlookers, standing bunched together in a circle, looked sober and wide-awake. The group were staring down at a patch of grass in sombre silence. With a frown Flavius shifted his gaze to Queen Talwyn and saw that she too was looking troubled. Her arms were folded across her chest and her anxiety was reflected in the faces of her warriors. Nearby too, Gisgo, standing alone without his companions, appeared to be looking on in a concerned manner.

Crouching in the middle of the circle, carefully examining the personal belongings that had been thrown and scattered about across the ground, Galchobhar looked grim as he suddenly called out. Reaching for something, he turned to show it to the Queen and as he did a ripple of dismay passed through the onlookers. In the young warrior's hand Galchobhar was holding up a severed human hand. The dead fingers still had a ring attached to them.

"He thinks the hand belonged to the Queen's handmaiden, Sir," Acco said quickly translating as he leaned into Flavius. "Someone hacked it off. The young warrior says he recognises the ring on the finger. It belonged to the girl. And he says there are signs that there was a fight. A struggle."

Across from Flavius the Queen had gingerly taken the severed hand and was examining it closely, her face drained and pale. Then at last she nodded, handed the severed hand to one of her warriors and turned to look at the belongings scattered across ground.

"So, no one has seen the Druid or his daughter," Flavius muttered looking perplexed. "They have just vanished. Just like that. Into the night?"

"Yes. That's about the gist of it. That's what they are saying Sir," Acco murmured lowering his eyes. "They are trying to figure it out now."

"So, no one heard her scream when her hand was hacked off," Flavius continued turning to Acco. "We don't know whether she and her father are still alive? We don't know who did this?"

"That's right Sir," Acco said hesitatingly. Then lowering his voice the young man spoke again. "Should we tell the Queen about the altercation last night - between the Carthaginian and the Druid, Sir? Those two men nearly came to blows. It could be important. Maybe that mercenary came back later to settle things when no one was looking?"

Catching Gisgo's eye Flavius held it for a moment. But if the Numidian Prince knew anything, he was keeping it carefully concealed.

"No," Flavius said quietly. "We will keep that to ourselves for now. The altercation which we witnessed proves nothing in itself. No need to drop Gisgo into it if we don't have any further evidence. What are they saying," Flavius added gesturing at the Celts.' "What do you they think?"

"They are puzzled. No one saw or heard anything last night," Acco replied. "No one appears to know what has happened or who cut off her hand or why? The Druid and his daughter have disappeared, and the Druid's chariot has also gone. But they must have left in a hurry for most of their gear is still here. Why would they leave all their gear behind? It doesn't make sense."

For a moment Flavius said nothing as he stared at the grim scene. Then at last he took a deep breath. "I don't know son," Flavius said. "But somewhere, someone knows what is going on."

Chapter Sixteen - The Hunt

Trundling on down the grassy slope, standing, and holding onto the chariot as the vehicle bumped and rattled across the terrain, Flavius could see that the forest up ahead was vast. A wall of trees and dark undergrowth - a dense competing canopy of brown and green that stretched away to the horizon. It was afternoon, and across the blue sky the warm sun shone supreme. Ahead, two hunting dogs were bounding across the open country, their eager, excited barks drifting away on the gentle breeze. Glancing at Morcant, who was standing squashed in beside him on the narrow chariot platform, holding the reins and driving the horses, Flavius's eyes lingered before sliding away. Things were still a little awkward with Morcant. A strange tension he could not fully explain. Nor was he entirely comfortable with being out here pretty much on his own with just Acco for company, but in the end he had decided to go. If Morcant had something important to say to him he would listen.

Standing beside him, staring at the forest Morcant however looked relaxed, his posture betraying no aggressive intent, his stump pressed against his side. The invite to go hunting with Morcant had come as a surprise Flavius thought. He had not been expecting such an overture - not after his last encounter with the one-armed Celtic nobleman. But Morcant had claimed he wanted a fresh start. To clear the air between the two of them. Afterwards they would talk he had said - for there was something important that he wished to discuss. It would be a good opportunity too, Flavius thought - for him to probe Morcant about the lying claims, raised by the Queen's handmaiden. Twisting his head around in the tight confined space, Flavius saw that Acco was looking a little nervous. The young man was clinging on as the chariot rumbled and jolted down the hill. First however they would hunt together, Morcant had announced. They would enjoy the remains of the day. For the forest was well stocked and rich in prey and today was the last day of Samhain. Tomorrow the tribes would be departing for home.

Shifting his gaze to the two other chariots which were riding formation, Flavius spotted Gisgo standing upright on one of the vehicles which was being driven by two kinsmen of Morcant. "The Numidian must be a part of what I want to talk to you," about Morcant had cryptically told him earlier – explaining Gisgo's presence at the hunt. "It is time," Morcant had continued, speaking in a sober voice, "that we all sat down together. That we put away our differences and discussed a solution to the trade stand-off."

Gazing at the Numidian Prince now, Flavius could see that he was alone, having left his mercenaries behind at the camp. Whatever proposal Morcant had in mind, he thought, it was going to have to be something special, something extraordinary to reconcile the Carthaginian and Roman trade positions. But Gisgo too seemed prepared to listen for despite the enmity between him and Morcant he was here. And if Morcant could pull it off, Flavius thought with sudden insight - Morcant would at once be the hero of the hour, the man who had created a diplomatic triumph for his Queen. He could see why the man would want the glory.

The third chariot contained three more of Morcant's kinsmen, all armed with hunting bows, quivers and throwing spears. For a moment Flavius gazed at the men. Back at the encampment they had ignored him - quietly busying themselves by preparing the dogs and the equipment for the hunt. None had deigned to approach or speak to him and Acco. A close-knit group of kinsmen - they preferred to keep themselves to themselves.

With the chariots parked at the edge of the forest, the horses were idly standing about, their heads lowered to the ground, nibbling at the grass. In the field the men were quietly busying themselves - getting ready, while the two hunting dogs were excitedly chasing each other. Clutching the bow and quiver full of arrows that Morcant had given him, Flavius was squinting, testing the weapon as Acco stood nearby looking lost. Morcant had not bothered to give the young translator a weapon. A few paces away Gisgo was gripping the throwing spear he'd been given and gazing at the forest with a distant faraway look. Studiously ignoring the others, the Numidian had not said a word since the hunting party had dismounted. Shooting Gisgo a quick sideways glance, Flavius could see that he too did not appear to be overtly happy to be here. But Morcant had insisted and like himself, Gisgo had appeared unable to decline the invitation.

Hearing Morcant calling out to him, Flavius turned and saw him coming towards him. Sporting a serious look the nobleman was clad in his tight-fitting trousers, his torso covered by a woollen tunic and a short loose cloak, fixed at the neck by a bronze brooch. In his hand Morcant was holding a throwing spear and a small knife was tucked into his belt.

"Morcant says Sir," Acco said translating, "that I am to remain here and guard the chariots and horses. One of his men will keep me company. He says that he will lead the hunt. We will start by sweeping eastwards through the forest. Once the dogs have picked up a scent - we will form a kill line. You are then to remain where you are and wait for him and the dogs to drive the prey towards you. Kill at first sight. If he calls out once, it means the dogs have picked up the scent. Twice - and the prey is heading straight towards you - so get ready. If you get separated and lost out there, he will wait for you back at the chariots."

"I have hunted before," Flavius said in a soft chiding voice as he slung his quiver of arrows across his shoulder. "But fine. I know the drill. Good hunting."

For a moment, Morcant eyed him in silence, as if to make sure he had understood. Then he nodded. Turning to Gisgo he began to speak in Greek - appearing to relay the same instructions. Watching the two men conversing, Flavius at last turned to Acco, lowering his voice.

"See what you can find out from Morcant's kin while you are waiting," he muttered. "It would be good to know in advance what kind of diplomatic proposal Morcant has in mind. I don't think Gisgo knows either."

"I will try Sir," Acco said looking dubious. "But these men. They are not exactly the most talkative types."

***

Crashing through the undergrowth, Flavius could hear the barking, baying dogs. The excited beasts appeared to have caught the scent of prey and were chasing it through the forest. Gasping for breath, feeling his heart thumping wildly in his chest, an arrow notched to his bow, Flavius came to a halt beside a great oak. A moment later Morcant's solitary cry rang out, confirming that the hunt was on. Hurriedly Flavius turned to look around, but among the dense trees and undergrowth he could see no one. He was on his own. But the others could not be far away. They would be holding their positions, a line of silent hunters - waiting for the dogs and Morcant to drive the prey onto their waiting spears and arrows. Abruptly the forest fell silent, as if every living thing was suddenly holding its breath. Cocking his ear, Flavius strained to listen, his eyes trying to peer through the foliage and trees. But out in front, among the dense trackless forest all remained eerily quiet and peaceful. Coolly controlling his breathing, Flavius waited for the signal to confirm that the prey was heading towards him but it did not come. And as the silence lengthened, he frowned. Had the dogs lost the scent? Had something happened to Morcant? Had the prey managed to escape? Standing beside the great oak Flavius hesitated, his bow raised and ready to shoot at the first sign of the fleeing animal. But out in front of him nothing moved.

Suddenly a face appeared a few yards away, soundlessly rising into view from among the bushes. Recognising the man, Flavius felt a sudden pang of unease. It was Gisgo. The Numidian Prince had appeared from out of nowhere, like a wraith. But as he stared at Flavius, Gisgo silently raised his finger to his mouth, bidding him to remain silent. Freezing beside the oak, Flavius felt an ice cold shiver run down his spine. Gisgo looked alarmed. He was worried. Something was wrong. Something suddenly felt horribly wrong.

For a moment the Numidian did not move. Then carefully and silently he pointed at the forest to his left and right before slowly running his finger across his throat. Stealing soundlessly up to Flavius, clutching his throwing spear, Gisgo was taking short shallow breaths, his chest heaving.

"Morcant," Gisgo murmured in broken Latin, his eyes gleaming feverishly. "Kill us. He kill us now. You. Me. Dead."

"What?" Flavius muttered, his cheeks colouring in shock. Hurriedly he turned to look around at the forest but as he did, he sensed it too. It was all too quiet. Where was Morcant? Where were the hunting dogs? Where were the others? Turning to stare at Gisgo again with growing alarm Flavius was unable to speak as the horrible truth dawned at last. The Numidian was not lying. This was no trick. Gisgo had sussed it out. He was speaking the truth. He could see it etched onto the Numidian's face. Instead of being a hunter, he had become the prey. Morcant had lured him out into the forest not in order to clear the air - but to kill him. He and Acco were in mortal danger.

Suddenly there was movement among the trees. Catching it from the corner of his eye Flavius was just in time to yell a warning and shove Gisgo out of the way, before a spear came hurtling through the air and thwacked into the oak, embedding itself with a powerful thud. Without waiting to see who had just attacked them, Flavius turned and frantically shot away into the undergrowth. Behind him, the forest had suddenly come alive with voices and activity. The men were shouting to each other. They were horribly close and as he limped away, he heard the unmistakable sounds of a pursuit, of feet pounding the earth and bodies tearing through the undergrowth. Morcant and his kin were giving chase. A moment later Flavius heard-the-sound of barking. Groaning in panic, his eyes bulging, Flavius plunged on through the forest as fast as he could go. There was no sign of Gisgo. He had lost sight of him in the confusion. The Numidian had vanished. Lost among the trees and undergrowth, as he too ran for his life. Wildly Flavius careened onwards, swerving past trees, struggling to stay on his feet and contain his growing panic. He was never going to outrun his pursuers and Morcant appeared to have set his dogs on him. He could not outrun them. Nor could he hide. The beasts would have his scent by now. It was only a matter of time before they caught him. The two hunting dogs alone would be able to tear him to shreds.

"Acco," Flavius bellowed at the top of his voice as he hurled through the wood. "Acco. Run! Run! Get away. It's a trap! It's a trap!"

There was no way of knowing whether Acco had heard him. The distance back to where they had left the chariots was probably too great. But he had to try and warn the young man Flavius thought, gasping for breath - even if it meant giving away his own position. He had to give Acco a chance to get away. If it were the last thing that he ever did. For the boy did not deserve to die - all because he Flavius had been a fool. Because of his mistake. Catching his foot on a bush Flavius cried out as he went violently tumbling and rolling across the ground. Staggering back to his feet having lost his notched arrow, he snatched a glance over his shoulder and caught sight of movement among the trees - horribly close. Then he was limping away again, forcing himself to move as fast as he could. How could he have been so stupid - a voice inside his head was screaming at him. How could he not have seen this coming? How could he have allowed Morcant to play him for a fool? And why did the Nobleman want him dead. And Gisgo too?

Plunging onwards, the trees flashing past, Flavius groaned in despair and panic. He was tiring rapidly and he did not have the answers and his life was about to end. He was not going to last much longer. His chest felt as if it were about to explode and his legs felt loaded with lead. The relentless pursuit was gaining on him. In a few more moments they would surely be onto him. The dogs bringing him down, tearing him to pieces while Morcant and his kinsmen did not need to do anything else but look on with grim satisfaction.

"Acco. Acco. Run. Get away," Flavius roared again with the last of his strength as he hurtled through the forest. Up ahead the wood appeared to be thinning out, the edge of the tree line marked by glorious dusty rays of sunshine, beckoning to him as if he were already half-way to the next world. Floundering towards the sunlight, Flavius was still screaming as he burst from the forest and out into the open fields. To his surprise ahead of him, pounding the grassy slope that rose to a ridge, he caught sight of a figure. It was Gisgo. The Numidian, being younger and fitter, had a head start on him, fleeing with frantic energy. The next moment an arrow went whining past Flavius's head, missing him by an inch. Staggering on across the sloping field trying to keep up Flavius threw a look over his shoulder and groaned. Four men and two dogs had emerged from the forest and among his pursuers he caught sight of Morcant. The one-armed man had lost his throwing spear but he was unmistakable as he shouted at his companions.

Up ahead Gisgo had reached the ridge of the hill and had come to a halt, staring at something that Flavius could not see. Then as another arrow went whining past him, Flavius closed his eyes and came to a floundering halt. He was spent and could go no further. The chase was over. It was no use. He would make his last stand here in this field, on this grassy slope. With luck he might be able to take one of the men or a dog with him before he was overwhelmed and killed. Streaking towards him, rapidly closing in for the kill the two hunting dogs were barking wildly. Dumping his bow onto the grass, Flavius snarled as he savagely pulling his knife from his belt and braced himself for the impact of the attack. Lumbering towards him, spread out in a semi-circle, following the dogs - the four hunters had slowed their pace now that they saw that he had given up running. Instead Morcant and his kinsmen were closing in at a brisk walk, their weapons raised.

"Come on then, you bastards," Flavius roared as he raised his knife.

A moment later the first dog came leaping at him, its drooling mouth open, displaying a line of horribly large and razor-sharp teeth. Receiving the animal full on - the impact of the savage attack knocked Flavius off his feet and onto his back. Desperately struggling to prevent the beasts' jaws from sinking into his flesh and clamping shut, Flavius howled, finding strength he did not know he possessed. As man and beast struggled and rolled over the ground in a frantic vicious fight to the death, Flavius managed to free his knife hand and with a murderous series of blows he ripped open the dog's stomach, spilling its guts across the grass. Staggering back to his feet Flavius, gasping and spluttering, saw that the other dog had backed off and was instead darting about - barking furiously. The next moment an arrow embedded itself in Flavius's shoulder, the impact spinning him sideways and knocking him to the ground. Gasping in shock, he turned to stare at the shaft sticking out of his body. Shouting to each other Morcant and his men were rapidly closing in for the kill. Gasping - Flavius coughed up a little blood as he lay on his side, unable to move, staring up at the blue sky. Fortuna, he muttered his lips moving without speaking as his knife slipped out of his hand and his strength drained away. Fair goddess. Look after them. Please. I beg you. Protect them. Do this last thing for me. Ensure they survive.

Suddenly, Flavius was aware of the sound of beating hooves. The noise was rapidly drawing closer and with it came the cries of men. Sinking back onto the ground he stared up at the sky waiting for the end - but it did not come. Instead the grassy slope around him was abruptly filled with confused yells and shouts, the neighing of horses followed by an abrupt solitary scream. Moments later Flavius heard a voice shouting his name. It was Acco. Then the young man was kneeling over him, panting for breath as if he had been sprinting.

"Oh, sweet Aphrodite," Acco cried out in horror and dismay as he saw the arrow sticking out of Flavius's blood-stained chest. "Oh great Zeus. Hang in there Sir. You hold on Sir. You are saved. We are not going to let you die. You are going to be alright. You are going to be alright."

"What happened?" Flavius groaned. "Where is Morcant? Why am I not dead?"

Swiftly another figure was kneeling beside him. The man's bearded face was pale and stained with sweat and as Flavius saw who it was, Gisgo suddenly grinned, his face lighting up with relief. Looming over the Numidian, standing looking down at Flavius lying on the ground, another man too had appeared, his rugged, handsome face frowning with concern. It was Galchobhar. In his hand the Queen's young bodyguard was clutching a bloodied axe. Then as quickly as he had appeared the young warrior was gone but Flavius could still hear him, close by, shouting. A moment later the thunder of beating hooves shook the earth.

"He saved us all," Acco gasped, his eyes lighting up in triumph as he reached out to grip Flavius's hand in his own. "Galchobhar. He and his warriors arrived just in time. We heard you yelling. That's how we found you and Gisgo. Morcant - he and his kin have turned tail and fled back into the forest. But we got two of the bastards. Galchobhar's warriors are going after the rest of them now. You hold on Sir. Don't you dare leave us now."

"I don't understand?" Flavius whispered as pain wracked his body, making his eyes feel heavy and drowsy.

"It seems," Acco said in a hasty eager voice, "that unbeknownst to us the Queen has had her own doubts about Morcant for some time. So she ordered Galchobhar to keep an eye on him. Her warriors just told me. After we left - they followed us here at a discreet distance. They have suspected for some time now that it was Morcant who was responsible for poisoning the Queen but they lacked the evidence to prove it. So they used you as bait Sir. But Gisgo he was in on the plan from the start. He and Galchobhar are friends you see. Gisgo knew there was a chance he and you would get attacked today. But he still came. He had to be here to ensure that Morcant revealed his hand."

Gazing up at Gisgo who was still kneeling beside him Flavius coughed up some more blood.

"You knew," he murmured weakly. "I was bait and no one told me. Well that was not very nice. The bastards put an arrow into me."

***

It was late in the evening and in the sprawling Celtic encampment near the standing stones, the people appeared to be recovering from the previous night's festivities for a quiet, subdued atmosphere lay over the camp. Sitting in his chair beside the crackling campfire, a blanket draped across his body, Flavius looked tired, weak and in pain as he gazed up at the stars in the dark sky. A Celtic physician had managed to remove the arrow shaft and to clean and bind the wound with a fresh bandage. He was going to live, the woman had told him. But he had been lucky. Damn lucky. For the arrow had only just missed an important artery - which if it had been cut would have caused him to quickly bleed to death.

Standing around him, Pytheas, Scoti and Acco were observing the camp with sombre and unsettled looks.

"I talked to Galchobhar," Pytheas said at last. "He told me that Morcant's fate was sealed after the bounty hunters caught the Queen's husband. Apparently her consort talked after he was caught. Spilled everything he knew. Galchobhar said that the Queen's husband begged him to spare his life and in exchange he would reveal the names of his fellow conspirators. That is when he named Morcant as his colleague in crime. He claimed that Morcant was working together with him against the Queen all this time. Little good it did him in the end though," Pytheas added with a sigh. "Galchobhar still cut his head off."

"I still don't understand," Flavius murmured. "If they knew Morcant was involved why did they let him go on that hunt? Why not arrest him immediately? And why was I not warned but Gisgo was? It's an outrage. I could have easily died in that forest. The Queen is going to have some explaining to do."

"The Queen apparently needed more proof before she could act," Pytheas replied. "General suspicions and her husband's word were not good enough. Desperate men will say anything to stay alive and Morcant is still an important nobleman in her realm with resources. If she arrested him without proof it could lead to another rebellion against her rule. It would give the other tribes an excuse to intervene in her affairs and seize her mines. Which is the last thing the Queen wants after everything that has happened. So instead she decided to set a trap. She set Morcant a test and he failed it. She flushed him out like a fox. This is the point where you come in Flavius," Pytheas said with a little apologetic look. "Galchobhar told me that he and Gisgo concocted the plan together. Morcant was allowed to learn that the Queen's husband had talked and had named him as a co-conspirator. That part was true and intended to panic him into action. The second part of the plan was the set up. Galchobhar used the Queen's handmaiden to approach Morcant. The girl was to pretend to blackmail him. She was to tell him that she had witnessed him poisoning the Queen and that she had shared that knowledge with you as a guarantee of her safety. She was to threaten to inform the Queen if she was not paid in silver."

"So hang on," Scoti interrupted. "You are saying Morcant then rejected the blackmail and instead went after the girl and tried to silence her for good. That the handmaiden's disappearance, the cutting off of her hand - that was all Morcant's doing. That he was responsible for her disappearance and that of her father, the Druid?"

"No," Pytheas said quickly shaking his head. "Galchobhar is not sure. Something unforeseen appears to have happened. Sure Morcant could have been involved, in a bid to try and silence her but Galchobhar thinks that something else may have got in the way before he act. He thinks someone else is responsible for her and her father's disappearance. Cutting off a hand is a symbolic act. It is the punishment that is meted out to criminals who have stolen something. It is a warning to others who may be similarly inclined. Galchobhar doesn't know what happened but he doesn't think it was Morcant who cut her hand off. Someone else did. The Queen is still investigating. It remains a mystery."

"So the key moment then, that proved Morcant was guilty," Scoti exclaimed raising his finger, "was when he decided to go after Flavius and Gisgo. When he decided to have both of you killed. Because after listening to the girl he feared you would reveal his role in the plot to poison the Queen. Even though you had no evidence against him. Otherwise if he was innocent of the crime - why try and go to such lengths to cover his tracks. After all having a foreign legate assassinated is a grave act. By moving first and acting quickly he probably hoped to get rid of the threat and bury any remaining witnesses before they could damage him. He must have been in a right panic by this stage."

"Precisely," Pytheas said nodding vigorously. "He made a mistake. He panicked. Which is what Galchobhar hoped he would do. The moment Morcant attacked you Flavius was the moment he incriminated himself. For he had no other cause to harm you. He was our man after all. Maybe he was worried you would turn him in to curry favour with the Queen. Even if he wasn't certain what you knew he could not afford to take the risk and let you live. As for Gisgo," Pytheas said puffing out his cheeks. "Those two were at each others throats from the start. I can see why Morcant would want him dead as well. Maybe Morcant lured you both into the forest so that afterwards he could claim you and Gisgo had got into a fight and killed each other. It would be a neat and clean way of explaining your deaths and removing the threat to his position. I doubt the Queen would mourn your passing. It was just unfortunate that none of us were told about the danger in advance."

"Would you have believed Galchobhar or Gisgo if they had come to you with this plan?" Scoti said with a shrug.

"Well at least Flavius here would have been warned," Pytheas retorted. "Flavius is right. The Queen has some explaining to do. This was a massive breach of diplomatic protocol."

"So where is the one armed bastard now?" Flavius said quietly.

"They didn't find Morcant," Pytheas said quickly, turning to Flavius. "He seems to have got away. He is still out there. But by morning every bounty hunter in the land will be after him.

Finding a one armed man shouldn't be too difficult. Morcant will either have to go into exile overseas or lose his head. The Queen is absolutely furious about his betrayal. She is in a proper rage. It's not pretty. If she catches him, Morcant is going to have his body cut to pieces and tossed into the sea. The swine does not deserve anything less. Only the Gods know what he was hoping to get out of it all. Land, money, status, power - presumably. They did say that he was an ambitious man."

As the men fell silent, in the darkness the fire crackled and spat.

"We got it wrong," Flavius muttered at last wearily closing his eyes. "Why did we not see this coming?"

"I know," Pytheas said, lowering his eyes with sudden embarrassment. "I know. I failed. I got it badly wrong, and for that I apologise. To all of you. I shall take full responsibility. There is going to have to be an inquiry into how we did not pick up on Morcant's true motives and allegiance. How we did not see this coming. My government will want to get to the bottom of this. We pride ourselves on our network of spies and informants. The information they supply is of vital importance to our trade and its continued success. If the system is compromised - remedies will need to be made." Looking glum, Pytheas turned to Flavius. "Morcant has done huge damage to our diplomatic standing and reputation here. He was our man after all. Everyone knew that. It is going to take a long time for our reputation to recover and this debacle will surely effect the outcome of the trade negotiations. Lucky for us the Queen does not believe we four were working with Morcant against her. If she had believed that – well, we'd all be missing our heads right now."

"It is not solely your fault," Flavius said, gently gazing back at the Massaliot diplomat. "Morcant played us all for fools. I too am to blame. I failed to see what he was doing and I advised the Queen to execute an innocent man. Aed was innocent just like he said he was. It was Morcant who poisoned the Queen. He lied to us again and again. We know that now. The Queen's handmaiden alluded to it before, but I did not fully grasp the implications of what she was telling us."

"You had no proof Sir," Acco protested. "What could you have done?"

"No Acco," Flavius said softly. "I too must accept my share of the blame. I helped get an innocent man executed and for that I shall pay the price. The gods will not be pleased. It was a dishonourable act. A spiteful act. Just because Aed was working for the Carthaginians. He did not deserve to die. The gods," Flavius paused for a moment as he winced with sudden pain. "The gods," he continued at last with a soft groan, "could have had their revenge on me today. But Fortuna spared me. She spared me for a reason - because I still have something to do before I pass on into the next world. I see that now."

"You need to get some rest Sir," Scoti said with an anxious look. "That's what that doctor said. Your wound will heal only, if you give it a chance. There is still a possibility that it will get infected."

"Scoti's right," Pytheas said quickly. "You must recover your strength. That is your number one priority Flavius. We need you fit and healthy."

Suddenly there was movement away in the darkness and a moment later Galchobhar appeared, striding into the firelight, looking grim, an axe hanging from his belt. He was followed by Queen Talwyn, clad in her brilliant white cloak. For a moment no one moved or made a sound as the Queen coolly came up to where Flavius was seated. In the warm reddish glow coming from the fire, the carefully arranged glass beads in her hair and the metallic rings on her slender fingers gleamed with a cold purpose. Staring at Flavius in silence - at last she spoke, her voice cutting through the air like a knife.

"The Queen says Sir," Acco said hurriedly taking his place at Flavius's side. "That she has finally come to a decision. After consulting her fellow kings and the spirits of the ancestors - she has made up her mind. She says she will keep her word - for she is an honourable lady and what is promised cannot be undone. Her word is law and she does not give it easily or lightly. So, the promise she made to Gisgo will be honoured. The trade embargo in tin will remain in place. The embargo will remain in place for one year exactly and not a day longer. During this time Roman and Massaliot merchants will not be permitted to buy the tin from her mines. After the year has passed," Acco exclaimed turning to stare at Flavius, "she says the ban will be lifted and normal free trade shall resume in full. But Rome and Massalia shall from hence forth pay double the old price."

In the firelight, the Queen's eyes gleamed.

"She says Sir," Acco continued, his voice faltering a little, "so much for your vaunted intelligence network. It has proved to be nothing more than a joke. A puff of smoke. You appear not even to have known what your own man was up to. So she advises you to choose your friends with more care next time. Your close association with Morcant has done you no favours."

In the crackling firelight the Queen was gazing at Flavius, and as he took in what she had just said she suddenly smiled. Then softly chuckling to herself the Queen turned and followed by Galchobhar, she vanished off into the darkness, her chuckling turning to laughter.

Chapter Seventeen - Trust Must be Earned

It was morning and in the Celtic encampment the people were packing up their belongings, preparing to leave. Staining the green grass, the blackened camp fires had been put out and already parties of men, women and children could be seen trudging away across the plain - heading for home, carrying their belongings and leading their animals. Sitting in his chair amid the subdued activity, his woollen blanket wrapped around his shoulders, Flavius was gazing up at Gisgo. Gathered around him in a tense semi-circle the Numidian Prince, Phameas, Xenocles and a few other Carthaginian mercenaries were standing about with their arms folded across their chests. Their hard rugged faces were giving nothing away as to what they were thinking. Standing behind Flavius, backing him up, Pytheas, Scoti and Acco too were looking on in grave silence.

"Thank you for agreeing to listen to me," Flavius said speaking in a slow and strained voice as he eyed Gisgo. "The Queen has informed you of her decision?"

As Acco translated, Gisgo nodded but said nothing, carefully keeping his thoughts to himself. For a moment Flavius hesitated.

"Good," he said at last, gazing up at Gisgo from his chair. "But that is not what I want to talk to you about. There is something else that you and I need to settle before we go our separate ways. The gods have brought us together, you and I," Flavius said gesturing at Gisgo and himself. "I believe they have brought us to this distant land for a purpose." For a moment Flavius paused to allow Acco to catch up. "I have a farm and a family back in Italy," Flavius began. "My home is on the Po river on the frontier in Cisalpine Gaul. It is a beautiful place. The earth is fertile and the forests provide a wealth of timber and good hunting. I have been blessed with two strong sons and two beautiful daughters, a good wife and grandchildren too. But after I have passed and all who have known me have done the same, the march of time will erase everything that I have known, loved and worked to create. My descendants will forget who I was. They will not care about my name. My farm will eventually fall into ruin and be replaced. I shall be forgotten, just like as if I had never existed at all. Nothing lasts forever. Such is the fate of all men."

As he paused and only Acco's voice rattled on, Flavius gazed up at Gisgo from his seat.

"But now you and me," Flavius spoke again, solemnly gesturing at Gisgo. "We have been given an opportunity, a chance to write our own fate. To do something that is bigger and greater than the both of us. To make history. When I spoke to you earlier," Flavius continued. "I meant it when I said that we could be friends and allies. I meant every word and I still do. For an alliance between us. Even if it is just you and me at first - long standing enemies, bitter rivals but now friends and allies. Would that not be something? Would that not be something which would be recorded and celebrated in history as an example to all men? That things can change. Would that not be something magnificent?"

Again, Flavius paused to allow Acco to give his translation.

"It is not too late for you and your men to change sides and abandon your allegiance to Carthage," Flavius continued as he looked up at Gisgo. "To fight for Rome, as friends and allies of the Republic. So, I urge you again. Seize this opportunity. There is no reason why you and I cannot be friends."

Gazing back at Flavius, at last Gisgo stirred.

"Gisgo says," Acco translated, "that he saved your life back in the forest. He did not have to do so. He could simply have let Morcant kill you but he saved your life because he believes you - when you said you took care of Amia and her son. You are alive because of what you did to help her and now he and you are even. He says that he owes you nothing. He says he can see that you are an honourable man and he respects you for that. He trusts you," Acco continued, "and he agrees that there is no reason for you and him to be enemies. But he will not change sides and fight for Rome. He has already told you that would be a dishonourable act, a betrayal and he will not go there."

"As I recall," Flavius growled - staring back at Gisgo with a disappointed look. "It was I, who saved his life in that forest. I shoved him out of the way of Morcant's spear. He would be dead now if not for me."

As Acco fell silent an awkward deadlocked silence descended upon the gathered parties. Looking deflated, Flavius sighed.

"Fine. Alright. I understand," Flavius said speaking in a grave and sincere voice. "Tell him Acco. That I believe he too is an honourable man. He fights for his country just like I do and I respect him for that. I get it. But for this conflict to end we must continue on down the path of friendship and trust is the first step in that direction. I will not yield to doubt. Trust must be earned and yesterday it was. So I shall hold you to your word," Flavius added. "There is no reason why you and I Gisgo should be enemies. Let it be so. We will go from there."

Then with a painful grimace Flavius stiffly rose to his feet and gingerly stretched out his hand to Gisgo.

For a moment no one moved or said a word as if they were all holding their breath, suddenly conscious of the historic nature of what was about to occur. Gazing at Flavius's proffered hand, Gisgo did not immediately respond. Then at last reaching out the Numidian Prince grasped Flavius's hand in a firm grip.

"So," Flavius said in a changed voice, eyeing Gisgo, "now that our business here in the Tin islands has been concluded, I am sure you and your men will be keen to get home. Without your ship however you will have to return overland through Gaul just like us. Tell him Acco, that we are willing to share our resources with him and his men. He is welcome to join us on the road home. We can share the same route south until we reach Massaliot territory. After that he and his men can find there own way into Spain."

As Acco finished translating Gisgo hesitated before turning to Xenocles who was standing beside him. For a brief moment Gisgo looked despondent. Then he turned his attention back to Flavius and nodded.

"Gisgo says it makes sense to travel together," Acco said translating, unable to hide his growing excitement. "You are right. He and his men are indeed keen to get home and will come with us for part of the journey. But not all will go. The Spartan, his friend has decided to remain behind - to stay here in this land. He has decided to join Galchobhar and the search for the missing girl, the Queen's handmaiden. The Spartan will not be coming back with us."

Chapter Eighteen - Burn, Kill and Destroy. Let Nothing Pass

Spring 210 BCE - South of the Ebro, Spain

The Spanish village was on fire. Crackling and roaring - the hungry flames tore into the thatched rooves of the houses, sending columns of thick black smoke pouring into the overcast skies. Strewn across the ground, the bodies of the dead and dying lay where they had fallen, while the small settlement was rocked by the terrified screams and shrieks of the survivors. Moving about among the ruined, burning buildings, the parties of Roman soldiers were going about their destructive work with ruthless and brutal efficiency. Nothing was being spared. Those villagers who had tried to defend themselves and their property had been killed. Slaughtered without mercy. Those who had tried to escape had been ridden down by the cavalry and now lay scattered across the surrounding wheat fields. The survivors - mainly women and children were huddling together. Their eyes filled with tears, fear and panic as they watched their lives change forever. Standing over them, examining their latest acquisitions, the slave merchants were excitedly pointing and calling out to each other.

"Burn it all," a centurion bellowed as he strode through the chaos, clutching his blood-stained short sword. "Nothing is to be left standing. All the animals must die. Destroy the lot."

Sitting on his horse, observing the carnage in silence, Julian was clad in his mail coat of bronze body armour over which he had draped his blood-red tribune's cloak. The mantle was fixed at the throat by a fibula while his head was crowned by a magnificent, plumed Attic helmet with two broad cheek guards. Protruding from underneath his body-armour, a defensive skirt made of long leather strips protected his thighs and hips. Clustered around him, mounted upon their horses, his officers were looking on, their tough, battle-hardened faces revealing little compassion for the villagers' fate.

"This time we caught them by surprise Sir," one of the Roman officers called out sounding satisfied as he turned to Julian. "But I don't think we shall be so fortunate at the next place. By now the locals will surely be aware of our presence."

"Nothing is to be spared. Wrath and ruin is what they deserve," another Roman officer snapped in a bitter sounding voice.

Remaining silent, Julian turned to stare at the plumes of smoke rising along the horizon to the east. Burn, kill and destroy - let nothing pass. Those were the orders that the Roman expeditionary army's new commander in chief, Gaius Claudius Nero had issued to him. He was to take his thousand strong column cross the Ebro to the south and devastate the territory of the Llercavones. The Roman position in Spain was still tenuous and weak, hanging by a thread. He was to teach the Spaniards that to rebel against Rome was a futile and dangerous thing to do. He was, Nero had made clear - to restore Rome's reputation after the twin disasters from the previous year. He was to lay waste to the country of the Llercavones as a warning to the other Iberian tribes - a warning as to what they could expect if they too decided to renounce their allegiance to Rome.

In the ruined village a party of legionaries had set about slaughtering some pigs who were still locked up in their pen. The frantic panic-stricken squealing of the animals was horrendous as one by one they fell silent. Scattered about among the burning buildings - dogs, chickens and goats lay dead beside their human owners in an orgy of violence and blood, while out in the fields a herd of cows had been butchered and left to rot. Only the Spanish horses were being spared to be conscripted into Roman army service.

As a soldier hurriedly emerged from a burning house, carrying a small looted hand mirror, the slavers began to clamp the surviving villagers into leg irons - shouting and marshaling them into a column for the long journey back to the coast. Gazing at the miserable humanity, Julian sighed. The villagers would be sold in the great slave markets of Tarraco and Emporiae. They were unlikely to ever see their old home or families again. Such was their fate. Such was the deal that Nero had struck with the slave merchants. For after their great defeats of the previous year, not only was the Roman army in Spain desperately short of men, but also money. So in exchange for a fixed rate of silver for each man, woman and child taken, the slavers would be given free reign - able to take what and who they wanted. And now Julian thought sourly as he looked on - the merchants were the only ones directly profiting from the devastation he and his men were unleashing.

Staring at the slavers as they went about their job, Julian's expression hardened. Then abruptly he looked away. Nero had given him a grim and unpleasant task to do. He knew that. He was a soldier. Not a butcher. There was no glory or satisfaction in attacking defenceless villages and slaughtering, torching everything in his path, but those were his orders. To devastate the land. It was just something he was going to have to do and bear for it had to be done. War was not pretty or noble. It just had to be won.

Upon Nero's arrival to take command in Spain the previous autumn, he had been hoping that his position as acting military tribune, one of six who took turns commanding a legion, would be finally and officially confirmed. He had after all, only been promoted to military tribune because so many senior officers had fallen with the Scipio brothers at Llorca and Castulo. His, had been a temporary battlefield promotion, but upon his arrival Nero had said nothing. He had given no indication or hint as to what he intended to do about the matter. The new commander in chief had not told him whether his position was permanent or not. He had left him hanging and-in-the-dark - his future quite unsettled.

For a moment Julian turned to glance at Bion, who was sitting on his horse. The dwarf - the Spanish army's chief translator, a genius with languages, was silently staring at the carnage with a pale face, as if he was about to be sick. It had been Bion, his close friend, who had warned him. For just before he had set out for this punitive expedition from the Roman base at Tarraco - Bion had slipped him the news that he had competition for his job. Only men hailing from the equestrian class, from rich, well-to-do families, were ever promoted to military tribune, the dwarf had told him. And you do not belong to that class Julian - Bion had warned. You are just a carpenter's son. A nobody from the provinces. You will never be accepted by the ruling classes. And now the anomaly of his command had been noticed. For apparently a young knight from Rome, who had arrived with Nero had now stepped forwards and was gunning for his position as military tribune. According to Bion, who spent much time at army HQ, his rival was arguing that he Julian was not qualified to hold the rank. That the position should be given to him instead. Bion had not known the name of the young officer but the dwarf had claimed that the man was a friend of Nero's and that he had Nero's ear. His rival had influence and political connections which he did not have.

With a stoic look, his emotions carefully hidden, Julian shifted his gaze back to the burning village. He had resigned himself, to the reality that once he returned to Tarraco, if he was not killed or captured along the way, that Nero would have him demoted. Bion was right. Social class determined everything the higher up the army chain of command you went. It was not about skill or dedication. To believe otherwise was foolish. So, on top of the brutality of his orders, the harshness of the punitive campaign he had that to look forward to as well. But there was no point dwelling on the issue Julian thought, gathering himself. He just had to get on with the job at hand. As his father, Flavius back on his farm outside the colony of Placentia would no doubt have put it. He had a duty to serve the Republic. So, get on with it boy.

Seeing that the last of the buildings was alight and every living being was either dead or in captivity, Julian turned to his officers.

"We are done here. Form the men up into a column and let's be on our way. I want to make it to the next settlement before sunset. We must keep moving. Speed is of the essence."

"Very well Sir," a centurion growled, as a moment later the cornicen, trumpeter raised his long, straight tuba, trumpet to his lips and blew on it - the signal ringing out across the burning, shrieking village.

For a moment Julian watched as the parties of Roman soldiers, carrying their spears and large shields, began hastening back to their units. Rallying around their standard bearers, the men were stuffing their looted objects into their marching packs, while their officers hurried about shouting and forming the soldiers into an orderly marching column. His thousand strong task force was a mixed group of varying quality, ability and experience. The ninety or so equites, Roman cavalry, which he had been given were newly arrived in Spain - reinforcements who had come with Nero, their new commander in chief, the previous autumn. The knights were all superbly equipped and motivated. They hailed from wealthy backgrounds unlike most of the five hundred hastatii and principes, who formed the main strength of his column. The five maniples, companies of heavy infantry were nearly to a man-veterans who had survived the twin disasters of Llorca and Castulo. Men who had been in Spain from the beginning, eight years ago now - like himself. The remaining four hundred or so light infantry, slingers and javelin men, although fast on foot and ideal for skirmishing, were poorly armed with no shields, helmets or body armour to protect them. They would not be able to hold their ground against a determined enemy assault. About half of them were indeed rowers from the fleet with little or no battlefield experience.

"Does this bother you?" Julian said, turning to Caciro and his small group of native guides who were sat upon their horses beside his staff. "Does it bother you what we are doing here. Seeing the destruction of this village and all the others that we have passed through? These people, they are Spaniards after all - like yourself."

Looking composed, Caciro did not immediately reply, as he stared at the smoking devastation and the scattered corpses. The Iberian scout was in his mid-twenties, small, sturdy and barefooted - his forehead adorned with a tattoo of a snake. At last, the young guide turned to Julian and shrugged.

"If they did not want trouble," Caciro said speaking, quietly in accented Latin, "then maybe they should not have broken their alliance with Rome. This was their choice. Their decision. Now they pay for their leaders mistakes. What did they expect you to do? Carthage will do nothing to protect them. The Punics are treacherous like that. They promise the tribes the world if they will only support Carthage, but when it comes to it the Punics do very little to help. And they are not my people," Caciro added, gesturing at the village and spitting onto the ground. "I have nothing in common with these villagers."

For a moment Julian eyed his guide. Then he shifted his attention to the rest of his mounted staff.

"Burn, kill and destroy. Let nothing pass," he called out as he began to urge his horse towards the head of the infantry column. "Those are our orders. Let's go. We head for the next settlement."

But just as Julian, followed by his staff were passing through the deserted village on their way to join the column, above the roaring din of the flames he suddenly heard a baby's fierce cries. Piercing, shrill and demanding. Frowning, Julian came to a halt as a moment later, a lone figure emerged from out of the clouds of billowing smoke and came towards him. In the soldier's arms and slung around his neck the man was carrying a baby, still wrapped in its woollen sling blanket. As he recognised the big Roman soldier, Julian raised his eyebrows. It was Lucius. His best friend appeared to be in a world of his own. Absorbed by the baby, Lucius was cradling it in his arms, utterly oblivious to the world, the maniple's battered battle-standard casually slung across his back.

"Standard bearer," one of the officers cried out, looking displeased. "Why are you not with your maniple. Get back to your men at once. Did you not hear the signal. We are moving out."

Coming to a startled halt, Lucius looked up.

"It was abandoned Sir," Lucius cried out. "I found it in one of the houses. The slavers were not interested. They were going to leave it behind to die. But its so small. I can't leave it here. I can't let it die. It's not fair. It's not right Sir."

Sat upon their horses in stunned incredulous silence the Roman officers were all staring at Lucius.

"What do you think you can do, for that baby?" Julian said, calmly walking his horse towards Lucius before any of his staff could answer.

"It's a boy Sir," Lucius said turning to Julian. "I am going to take him with me. Little fella is as light as a feather. See, I can sling him around my neck. It's no problem. I am going to give him a chance to survive Sir. That is more than what we gave to his parents today here in this village."

Gazing down at Lucius from his horse Julian sighed before looking away. There had been a slight whiff of insubordination in Lucius's response, but this was normal and to be expected. Lucius was his best friend, fearless - a first class soldier. A veteran of the Spanish campaign and a year older than himself. The two of them had started together as raw teenage recruits in the Spanish expeditionary army. They had fought together and survived together, but fortune had eventually put them on different career paths and now Julian was his commanding officer. Lucius had however never been one to be afraid of his commanding officers. Nor was he afraid to speak his mind or offer an opinion. It was not in his indomitable nature to tolerate fools, and that attitude had often got him into trouble with his superiors. But Julian knew how to handle him. Turning to stare at the baby in the big soldier's arms, Julian slowly shook his head.

"Lucius," he called out sternly. "You cannot take a baby with you on campaign. How are you going to feed it, or look after it? This is madness. It's going to die. You cannot save it. It needs its mother, and she is not here."

"I can't leave it behind Sir," Lucius said stubbornly as he turned his eyes to the baby. "I just can't," he added with a shrug.

Swearing softly to himself, Julian stared at his friend as he saw that whatever he was going to say would not change Lucius's mind.

"Fine," Julian snapped at last in a resigned tone. "Take it with you then if you must. But you will be solely responsible for looking after that baby and I hope to the gods' that you find it a surrogate mother before it starves to death, or we run into any trouble. I can't afford to have you distracted. Understood. We are in hostile territory. No one around here likes us much. Now get back to your unit, standard bearer. We are moving out."

"Yes Sir," Lucius called out, smartly rapping out a salute before hastening away with the baby wrapped in its blanket slung around his neck.

Chapter Nineteen - The Plan

Night had come and with it the temperature had plummeted. Across the flat summit of the hill the makeshift Roman camp was quiet, as the men tried to get some sleep. Without their tents however, the soldiers had been forced to spend the night under the stars with only their blankets to warm themselves. There had been no time or suitable construction materials to build any defensive structures. Crowded together with their mates, cloaked in darkness, the mass of men, were lying curled up or sitting about, their heads resting on their marching packs, their weapons, and shields within easy reach. In the darkness not a single pin prick of light could be seen, and the only illumination came from the pale moon and stars. All was quiet and peaceful. Beyond the camp, the night hid the countryside under a blanket of still, impenetrable silence that was suddenly pierced by the lone howl of a distant wolf. Crouching in a huddle with his senior officers Julian however was not paying attention to the nocturnal noises as nearby the Roman cavalry horses snorted and nervously kicked their hooves about.

"Caciro informs me," Julian said quietly studying the faces peering back at him from the gloom "that the town is less than two days march from our current position. If we follow the river valley that is. It's a walled settlement perched on top of a hill, an important population and production centre. But Caciro says that the last time he visited the place the walls were in a state of disrepair. The defences have been neglected for many years and cannot be easily restored. He says we should not have any major problems in taking the town. It's a rich place too - there is a small silver mine nearby. The town's people are known for their skill at rearing horses. So, it would be useful if we could seize them too. You know how short of horses the army is."

From the darkness there was no immediate reply from his officers.

"We are short of everything," one of the Roman officers muttered at last. "Men. Horses. Supplies. Money. Is this an expedition to teach the Spaniards a lesson or a foraging party, Sir?"

"A place like that will be defended Sir," another voice spoke up. "And wall or no wall we will still have to fight our way in. How many defenders can we expect to encounter?"

"Maybe four hundred or so," Julian replied quickly. "That is what Caciro believes. So, this is the plan. At dawn we will advance down the river valley. We need to move fast so there can be no delays. If the town's people realise, we are coming for them, it will make our job harder. We must try and catch the enemy by surprise. Speed is of the essence. Faustus, you will lead the way as usual with your cavalry. Keep an eye open for trouble. I will follow with the heavy infantry. You Nonus will protect our flanks with your skirmishers. Once we reach the town we will not delay. If the Spaniards refuse to surrender, we attack immediately. The place is to be torched and the same goes for the nearby silver mine. Nothing of value is to be left for the enemy."

"And if the people in the town want to surrender, Julian?"

"Those who resist are killed. The survivors will be sold as slaves," Julian said calmly. "You all know the drill by now."

Again, silence descended upon the small group of officers.

"The men, Sir," one of his centurion's said at last speaking quietly from the darkness, "they are unhappy about the order to not light a campfire. We marched twenty miles today at least. And twenty yesterday and twenty more the day before that. The men are tired and now everyone has had to eat a cold dinner and tomorrow they are going to have a cold breakfast. We also don't have any tents. The men are complaining that if it rains we will have no shelter. Sodden and disgruntled men will not make good soldiers Sir."

"No. A campfire will give away our position," Julian replied shaking his head. "The enemy will be able to spot us from miles away. It's too great a risk. We are in the midst of hostile territory. We must do everything we can to prevent the enemy from learning where we are camped. So, no campfires. And regards the tents. You know the supply situation. There are massive shortages of equipment. So much kit was lost at Llorca and Castulo that we are just going to have to get used to sleeping under the stars for a while."

"Don't you think these Spaniards already know exactly, where we are Sir?" Faustus said, turning to Julian with a concerned look. "Those villages which we torched. The plumes of smoke could be seen for miles. There will also undoubtedly be survivors who managed to escape and warn their compatriots as to our whereabouts. I would be very surprised, if the enemy does not already have scouts watching us day and night."

"Faustus is right Sir," Nonus exclaimed. "That last village was deserted. The populace had fled to the hills, and they had time to take all their animals with them. They knew we were coming. By now every damn, Spanish settlement south of the Ebro will be aware of our presence. Those people are not going to be hanging around waiting for us. So how the hell are we going to surprise anyone? Isn't it just a matter of time before we blunder into a tribal force that is large enough to take us on Sir?"

"Some of the prisoners told us that the Iberians are mustering a large force at Hibera to intercept us Sir," another officer said sounding anxious. "They were talking about an army several thousand strong."

"Listen," Julian replied patiently, turning to his officers. "I hear what you are saying. But enemy reports of our location will be of no use, if we are no longer there. By the time they have mustered a large enough force of fighting men, we could be forty or fifty miles away. The strategy has been clear from the beginning. In order to do our job, we need to rely on speed and surprise. Our safety lies in the speed of our movement. We must use that to our advantage. We must keep moving. We must keep the enemy guessing as to our whereabouts and intentions. We must change the position of our camp daily so-as-to confuse the enemy. To keep them off-balance and unprepared. Under no circumstances can we allow ourselves to get cornered or bogged down. We are not here to fight battles, to capture territory or lose men. We only have a thousand soldiers. We will be massively outnumbered if the tribesmen are able to concentrate their full strength against us. And remember a fifth of our force are raw recruits who may or may not bolt at the first encounter with an enemy war band."

For a moment Julian paused as he gazed at his officers. "So we are going to do this my way," he continued. "We are going to hit hard and fast - burn, kill and destroy - we are going to cause mayhem. Then we vanish into the hills. So that the Spaniards do not know where we are going to strike next. If they do not know where we will attack, they will be unable to concentrate sufficient force to defend themselves. The enemy are divided. They may outnumber us, but their fighting men are scattered all over the place, trying to defend their homes. All we have to do is to keep moving and to avoid large hostile forces. If we can do that we can succeed."

Pausing again Julian turned to Faustus. "I am not worried about that army mustering at Hibera right now," he said at last. "For I have no intention of fighting a pitched battle with them. Let them gather an army. It will take them some time to do so and once they do start to move such a large force will be slow to intercept us. By then we should be long gone."

In the darkness his officers remained silent and as they did. Julian suddenly guessed what was on their mind.

"We have our orders," Julian said in a harsh voice preempting his officers. "We are not heading home until our work here is done. None of you were there at Castulo and Llorca last year when our Spanish allies betrayed us. When twenty thousand of our so-called friends deserted and handed us over to Carthage on a plate. I lost good friends in those battles and now it's payback time. This is revenge. We are the whirlwind. Today we are Nemesis. So, we are going to lay waste to this country and teach these Spanish tribesmen a lesson they will never forget. The Illercavones played their part in that sordid betrayal and for that, we are going to punish them. If the locals do not learn to fear us, we will never drive Carthage from Spain and I will not allow my friends to have died for nothing. So we are going to do our job, unpleasant as it may be."

***

Picking his way through the undisturbed darkness that lay over the sleeping camp Julian looked resigned, while moving along at his side, Bion was frowning - his face etched with concern.

"Has he still got it?" Julian murmured glancing down at the dwarf. "It's still alive?"

"Apparently so," Bion replied. "You know Lucius. He's stubborn. When he gets an idea into his head he will just not let go."

"No one has complained?" Julian muttered. "I could hear that screeching baby from the head of the column earlier, when we were on the march."

"There has been some muttering, yes. I am sure the men are not happy with the constant wailing. But it's Lucius," Bion said with a weary shrug. "It would take a brave man to object and tell him that to his face. No one picks a quarrel with Lucius, unless they want to have a fist rammed into their face. Besides everyone knows that you gave him permission to take the baby along with him."

"Shit," Julian murmured, looking away.

"He's..." Bion broke off for a moment as the two of them quietly moved on past the sleeping soldiers. "He's found a woman to wet nurse the baby," Bion continued at last. "A prostitute. One of the camp followers. He is paying her handsomely to look after the baby."

"He's paying her! Great. Resourceful as ever I see. Come on Bion. You are my eyes and ears as to what is going on. Why is he doing this? I have known Lucius for nearly eight years. He has never before shown any interest in babies.' Why save this particular baby? It doesn't make sense. Is this his way of making a protest? Is he not happy about what we are doing here? Attacking and torching defenceless villages is not exactly an honorable thing to be doing. Is it getting to him?"

"I think," Bion said slowly and carefully choosing his words, "that he may be doing it to piss you off Sir. He's clearly not happy about something."

Once again Julian softly swore to himself as he peered into the darkness. "Well, it's time that we settled this," he growled.

Lucius was sitting with his back leaning against a large rock. His eyes were closed as if he were asleep, while in his lap, balanced on top of the maniple's battle-standard, he was cradling the baby. The little fella was wrapped in its blanket sling and appeared to be fast asleep. As he heard Bion softly calling out his name, Lucius opened his eyes. Locating him among the sleeping soldiers, Julian and Bion quickly crouched beside their friend.

For a moment Julian said nothing, as in the gloom he turned to gaze at the tiny sleeping face wrapped in its blanket.

"You are keeping it alive I see," Julian said at last, speaking quietly.

"I am Sir," Lucius replied in an even voice. "Little fella is going to be alright. He's going to survive. I have given him a name. I have called him Gordianus."

In the darkness Julian stared at Lucius, his eyes gleaming and for a long moment there was silence.

"Gordianus - really?" Julian snapped.

"Yes Sir, that is his name," Lucius said, gazing back at his friend.

"Why are you doing this," Julian murmured. "What's the matter with you? Carrying a baby around while we are on active duty. I am sorry - but its just weird. I have never seen anything like it before. I need your mind to be focused on the job at hand Lucius. You are a first-class soldier. I need you. Your men need you to be fully engaged. This baby. It's going to be a distraction and I cannot afford to have my men distracted."

"Well, that is your problem Sir," Lucius replied breezily. "Like I said. I found him and I am going to make sure he survives. No one is taking him away from me. Over my dead body."

"Are you doing this to piss me off?" Julian snapped.

Eyeing him coolly from the darkness, Lucius paused for a moment.

"No, it's not that," Lucius said at last. "I keep you honest Sir. I don't want to lose my friend. That's my job - keeping you honest. To prevent all that power, you now have - from going to your head. It's for your own good too. It would be a great shame, now that you are a military tribune and all, if you ended up becoming a dickhead like some of those other officers."

Taking a deep breath, Julian looked away. No one ever talked to him like Lucius did. And now once again he was caught. Torn. Should he have his friend flogged for disrespecting a senior officer or let him get away with it - which in turn could open him up to charges of favouritism and undermine morale?

"Goddamn it, Lucius," Julian hissed, turning back to him. "What's this all about? Is this in protest at what we are doing out here. I don't like it much either, but this is war. Shit happens all the time. If it's not us, then someone else would be doing it. You know that."

"No," Lucius replied. "You still don't get it Sir. This has nothing to do with what we are doing out here. I don't give-a-shit about these tribesmen or their villages. Let them burn. But you see. My girl and I." Pausing Lucius turned to look about licking his lips. "I have been humping my girl for a while now," he continued, "but something is not working. Either it's me or her, but she is not getting pregnant. I want a child Sir and I am fairly certain that she does too. So now," Lucius added in a triumphant voice looking down at the sleeping baby in his lap. "I have got one. I have found myself a son."

Chapter Twenty - These Tricky Spaniards

Sitting on his horse, surrounded by his mounted staff and bodyguards, Julian had come to a sudden unexpected halt. It was afternoon and across the rolling hills the sun was sinking in a clear, blue sky. His fist raised in the air - still Julian did not move, as behind him the column of legionaries had come to a stop and were standing about along the dusty path, waiting for the order to continue their journey. The men's body armour, helmets and weapons gleamed in the sunlight, while their large shields were covered in dust partially obscuring the scorpion images painted onto the wood. Clad in his blood red cloak and his splendid-plumed Attic helmet, Julian was looking concerned. Sat upon his horse directly behind him, the battle-group's signifier was holding up the vexillation war banner of the Third Legion, the soldier's magnificent wolf pelt covering his helmet. For a while no one spoke and the only noise came from the horses and the nearby shallow river water rushing and splashing over the rocks.

Ahead, the valley was channeling, the road into a narrow winding pass through the hills. Wedged in between the steep rocky cliffs and the rushing water, the track had become barely a few yards wide. Faustus's cavalry troopers had already entered the defile in advance of the main Roman column and now, Julian could see they were hurrying back to him. Something was wrong. As he watched Faustus cantering towards him, Julian quickly turned to survey the tops of the cliffs but among the boulders, scrubs and stunted trees he could see nothing untoward.

"What have you seen?" Julian called out, as Faustus came towards him. The young officer's brow was laced with sweat and he looked worried.

"Nothing Sir," the cavalry decurion replied. "No one. Not a soul. But that's my point. I don't like this defile Sir. It's too damn quiet in there. I just can't shake this feeling we are about to ride straight into an ambush."

"An ambush," Julian replied, his face darkening.

"Yes Sir," Faustus nodded as his cavalry troopers milled about at the head of the Roman column. "Its a perfect spot for an ambush. I served with Nero before Sir - in southern Italy, fighting against Hannibal's forces. I have some experience of ambushes. It is the Carthaginian's favourite tactics, and they learned their craft here in Spain. This defile smells of an ambush. Those cliffs extend some distance into the gorge. A whole enemy host could be hidden up there just waiting for us to enter the pass. Once we are inside and strung out along that path, all these Spaniards would need to do is block both exits of the defile and annihilate us from above with their missiles. We would be trapped, defenceless and unable to escape Sir. They could butcher us to a man."

For a moment Julian gazed at his cavalry commander. Faustus was one of the young competent and ambitious officers who had recently arrived in Spain with Nero, as reinforcements for the severely depleted Spanish expeditionary army. Hailing from a well-to-do equestrian family the young officer was already proving his worth and fighting skills.

Then biting his lip, Julian turned to stare at the road ahead.

"Caciro," Julian called out. "Is there another way in which we can reach the town. One that does not follow the river? Another route that is accessible for men, horses and wheeled wagons."

"Yes Sir," the Iberian replied in accented Latin. "There is. We could cross the hills, but we would lose a half a day at least. The fastest and most direct route is along the river just up ahead."

"But can you do it," Julian said. "If you had to could you lead us across the hills to the town?"

Quickly the young Spanish guide turned to converse with his small group of local guides, before looking up to check the position of the sun. Then he turned to Julian and nodded. "Yes I can. But if we were to set out now across the hills, we would still be up there when it starts to get dark. We would have to make camp up in the wilderness and I know there is no water up there either. No water for men or horses Sir."

Swearing softly to himself, Julian turned his attention back to the defile conscious that his officers were watching him - waiting for him to make up his mind. He had a decision to make. A big decision - one that could lead to the destruction of his command if he got it wrong. For a moment he hesitated. He could risk the defile, speed was important. But moving across the hills, although the longer and slower route, was the safer option. Biting his lip again, Julian at last turned to Faustus and his staff.

"We will make camp here," Julian called out. "I want a guard detachment watching the entrance to that pass. And get the campfires going. See to it that the men and horses are well fed and rested."

"Sir," Faustus exclaimed looking startled. "You want to make camp here? But we still have several hours of daylight left. Did you not say that speed was essential for our safety. Would it not be better to keep moving?"

"Campfires Sir?" another officer exclaimed looking puzzled. "I thought you said that we were not supposed to attract attention to ourselves."

"No. We make camp here," Julian said. "And yes, I want campfires to be lit. The men are to get a good hot meal as soon as possible. Break out the emergency rations and see to it that all get their fair share. I want the men well fed and rested. The horses too."

As his staff began shouting their orders to the column of legionaries, Faustus looking perplexed - nudged his horse alongside Julian.

"Sir?" he said.

"If you are right and I think you are - the enemy should be watching us right now," Julian said quietly turning to gaze at the cliffs lining the road ahead. "We must be cautious. These Spaniards can be tricky. They excel at ambushes. So here is what we are going to do. We are going to remain here for a while. But as soon as it grows dark, we are going to slip away and cross those hills. We shall keep the campfires burning so as to give the enemy the impression that we are still here. With a bit of luck and if Caciro does not get us lost, we should catch these tribesmen by surprise and reach the town by tomorrow morning."

"A night march." Faustus muttered raising his eyebrows. "That is always difficult Sir. Especially across hilly terrain. Much can go wrong."

"It's our job to ensure that nothing does. The night march can be done," Julian said. "I have done it before."

***

Across the open country the Roman trumpet rang out again, clear, precise and urgent. It was morning and emerging from the forested slopes and ridge to his right, Julian could see the enemy. Storming the flank of the Roman line of march, were dozens of lightly armed tribesmen, clutching javelins, bows and slings. The Spaniards were moving fast and making a terrific racket as they came on in a bold and fearless fashion. Turning to face them the Roman officers were screaming at their men, as Nonus's light infantrymen rushed to form a fighting line, their javelins raised in the air, their slings whirling over their heads.

"Keep moving. Keep the main column moving," Julian yelled from his horse. "We must keep moving. They are just trying to delay us. To slow us down."

Out on the plain, the groups of Roman heavy infantry had paused to stare at the Spaniards. All thoughts of tiredness, hunger and thirst forgotten in the face of the rapid and unexpected attack. Swearing out loud, Julian hurriedly turned to check the column. The night march across the hills had gone without a hitch and up ahead perched on top of its hill - outlined against the red rising sun was their objective, the Iberian town. It could be no more than a mile away. But the unexpected assault on his flank had complicated matters.

"Keep moving," a centurion roared at the heavy infantry companies, as he brandished his vine staff in a threatening manner. "Move. Move, you lazy bastards. You heard the tribune."

"Watch out for missiles, boys," another voice screamed over the din.

To Julian's right the foremost Spaniards had come storming into range and within seconds the tribesmen had launched a ferocious barrage of missiles at the Roman troops. As the hail of javelins, arrows and lead bullets shot through the air, the Roman velites responded with a barrage of their own. Moments later - the air thick with whining, flying missiles, the Spanish attack hammered into the Roman line, knocking a few unfortunate men to the ground and eliciting some shrieks. But as he stared at the fighting Julian could see that the damage appeared to be minimal. The enemy javelins were too slow. The low speed was allowing his velites to spot the missiles in flight and to jump aside and dodge them. The same however was true for the enemy. Only against the speedy invisible bullets from the slingers and the archers arrows did no one appear to have any protection. Staring at the fast moving missile contest, Julian grunted in satisfaction as he saw that his light infantry were doing their job. Outnumbering the enemy - they were easily holding their ground. They were keeping the Spaniards away from his heavy infantry who had no answer to the ranged weapons of the fleet-footed light infantry and who would suffer from a prolonged bombardment.

Then as suddenly and swiftly as the Spaniards had attacked, they were retreating, racing back towards the protection and cover of the forested slope and ridge from whence they had emerged. Seeing their enemy in flight the hundreds of Roman velites raised a mighty victorious cheer and before anyone could stop them they had set off in pursuit of the fleeing Spaniards.

"Goddamn it," Julian bellowed, seeing what was happening. "Get those light infantrymen back into formation. Recall them at once. What the fuck do they think they are doing?"

"Sir?" One of Julian's centurions called out, looking confused. "We have the enemy on the run. We outnumber them. This is the time to finish them off."

"No. Recall them," Julian roared. "Don't you see. They are not retreating. They are trying to lure our men into those trees. Fuck knows how many more Spaniards are waiting for them, hidden behind that ridge. The enemy are trying to lure us into an ambush, into a killing zone. Recall them!"

As the Roman trumpet rang out sounding recall, Julian groaned as he saw that many of the half-trained and inexperienced rowers who made up the Roman light infantry were not heeding his orders. They were continuing their wild, triumphant chase as the withdrawing Spaniards carefully drew them towards the forest and the ridge beyond.

"Follow me. With me!" Julian roared as he dug his heels into his horses' flanks and thundered away towards the mass of running men. Galloping across the open country, his red cloak streaming behind him - Julian could hear his mounted bodyguards cursing as they struggled to keep up. Then Julian was among his running velites, screaming at them to return to their positions and listen to their officers. Charging through the multitude, his sudden appearance seemed to have the desired affect for abruptly, as if coming to their senses, the Roman light infantrymen slowed to a confused halt.

"Back," Julian roared at his men, looking furious. "Back! The order for recall has been given. Get back to your positions at once you fools."

As the velites started to comply and return to the main column with chastened looks, Julian turned to stare at the groups of Spaniards. The enemy too had halted at the edge of the forest and were gathered about in small groups as they gazed at the Roman infantrymen.

"Here they come again," a Roman voice suddenly yelled.

Staring at the enemy war bands, Julian bit his lip. Once again advancing towards the flank of the Roman column, the groups of Spaniards were coming on, at a slower pace this time, but their intent was clear.

"Fall back. Then form a line and hold your ground," Julian bellowed, as he trotted through the mass of silent and retreating velites. "The first man to disobey orders again will find my sword stuck in his back. Listen to your officers. Listen to the signals. When the enemy flees again - this time we will stay put. We will stay where we are. Do you hear me? Do not let them lure you towards that ridge. They are just pretending to flee. They are doing it on purpose. It's an ambush. They are trying to lure you into an ambush."

As he regained his position at the head of the main column, Julian turned to eye the small groups of Spaniards advancing upon his flank. He'd been right about their intentions, for there were not enough of them to halt his advance. Instead, they appeared to be trying to slow him down. Maybe to give the civil population in the town a chance to get out before it was too late. Staring at the enemy, he could see that they appeared to be more cautious this time, but as they once again came into range the inevitable clash erupted. Filling the fields with their shrieks and savage battle-cries, the opposing parties of light infantrymen were suddenly darting and rushing about - furiously throwing their weapons at each other across the twenty or thirty yards of open space. Wrenching his gaze away from the fighting, Julian turned to stare at the Iberian town ahead. Then his eyes fell on the small wood lying in between him and the town in the distance. It was small but the trees and undergrowth were densely packed together providing good cover. For a moment he stared at the wood as an idea suddenly came to him. Turning to Faustus, who was nearby riding with his men parallel to the marching heavy infantry companies, Julian called out to him, beckoning him over.

***

The town was less than half a mile away now. Staring at the settlement perched on the summit of the low hill, Julian could see that Caciro had been right. Large sections of the protective wall that surrounded the place had fallen into neglect or were no longer existent. The defences were full of holes. The stones that had once formed the wall had probably been stolen by the tribesmen to build their own homes. But now their shortsightedness was going to come back to haunt them. Wrenching his eyes away from his objective, Julian turned to stare at his own men and the parties of Spanish light infantry who were still harassing his flank. Low on ammunition, both groups of skirmishers had resorted to eyeballing and threatening each other as they continued to move in parallel. Sizing up the situation, Julian's face betrayed no emotion. His plan was working. The enemy had still not spotted the mortal danger they were in. Either through carelessness or desperation - the Spaniards had still not realised that they were being steadily drawn away from the protection and cover of the forest and the ridge.

"When Sir?" an anxious officer hissed.

"A little longer," Julian said in a patient voice. "We will let them come just a little further."

Sat upon their horses around him, his staff were gazing at the enemy as they and the heavy infantry maniples continued their advance upon the town. At last - as the tension among his officers became palpable - Julian turned to his cornicen and nodded.

"Sound the signal for the attack."

As the trumpet rang out, ordering the attack to commence, Julian turned his attention to the wood that was now to his rear. A moment later, Faustus and his ninety cavalrymen burst from their concealed position among the trees and went charging across the fields towards the parties of Spanish light infantry. Abruptly the scene was transformed. Racing and thundering into the fight, their horses' hooves pounding the earth - their weapons raised, the Roman equites were yelling their triumphant battle-cries. To Julian's right, the enemy had come to a ragged and horrified halt as they at last spotted the danger, but it was too late. Already the foremost horsemen were galloping into the gap between the forest and the Spanish skirmishers, threatening to cut off their escape route. At the same time the Roman skirmishers raised a mighty roar and charged at their opponents.

Seeing the Roman cavalry charging towards them - the Spaniards abruptly turned and started to run. Discarding any idea of fighting back or making a stand, their only thought now appeared to be to get away. To flee. But they had drifted too far from the protection and cover of the forest and as he observed the fighting, Julian heard his officers cry out in triumph. Moments later the Roman cavalry were in among the fleeing men, scything them down with their spears and long cavalry swords. As the Spanish shouts and yells turned to wild panic-stricken shrieks, Julian's looked on with grim satisfaction. Lacking shields, body armour and helmets the fleeing Spaniards were easy prey for the Roman cavalry. They were going to get butchered - cut to pieces.

"That will teach those bastards, Sir," an officer cried out with an elated expression. "They thought they were going to ambush us but instead we turned the tables on them."

Saying nothing, Julian's eyes lingered on the fighting. Strewn across the fields the bodies of the fallen Spaniards littered the ground while Faustus and his men were chasing the last few survivors into the forest. Here and there a badly-wounded Spaniard was crying out but the Roman skirmishers were in no mood for mercy as they picked their away across the battlefield, dispatching the enemy wounded and promptly robbing them of their possessions.

"Recall our cavalry," Julian called out. "No need for Faustus to lose any men unnecessarily. And fetch Nonus. I need to speak to him."

Staring at the carnage, Julian could see that the threat to his flank had been decisively dealt with. Now for the town itself. Shifting his attention, he peered at the settlement sitting atop the low hill as he rode towards it. As the main Roman column approached, Julian was able to start to pick out the defenders. The Spaniards had been warned of his approach, but their defences looked rudimentary. A mass of heavy infantry, clad in thick-leather body armour and helmets were standing about waiting, thronging the gaps in the defenses, forming a human wall, bristling with shields, swords and spears.

A few moments later Faustus and his cavalry came flooding across the infantry's line of march and, as they did Julian could see that the troopers were breathless with excitement after their successful charge.

"Sir?" Nonus called out, as he came hastening towards Julian on foot, looking tired, his face stained with sweat and some blood.

"You alright?" Julian called out seeing the blood smeared across his subordinate's cheeks.

"I am alright Sir," Nonus replied cracking a weary grin. "It's not my blood. Man standing beside me got hit in the head by a slingers bullet. It made quite a mess. You wanted to speak to me?"

"Yes," Julian said quickly pointing at the town now just a few hundred yards away up the bone-dry gravel slopes. "See that. Looks like they are going to make their stand there. The enemy have plugged the gaps in their fortifications with men. That is where they intend to fight. I would say they have about a few hundred heavy infantrymen at most. But there could be more hidden in the town."

"I see them, Sir."

"I want you to take your skirmishers and drive them from those exposed positions. Disperse the enemy," Julian said. "My guess is that we have just destroyed their light forces, but if any remain your attack should draw them out. Then afterwards, you are to support the main infantry assault. If the enemy, try to intervene. If they get up on all the walls and try to attack us from above, you are to pin them down with your missiles, understood."

"Very well Sir," Nonus said carefully eyeing the town. "But my men are low on ammunition. It will take us a while to recover enough weapons to launch another missile attack Sir."

"Alright. Get it done," Julian said patiently. "We will wait for you and your men to get into position. And Nonus - keep one maniple back in reserve. I don't think we have destroyed all the Spaniards who attacked our flank. There will be more of them hiding behind that ridge. I don't want them being able to interfere in the assault. Tell the men to keep a close watch."

With Nonus hurrying away, Julian beckoned to Faustus. As he approached, Julian could see that the young aristocrat's face was awash with youthful energy, his eyes blazing with excitement.

"Take your men right around the back of the town," Julian said, speaking calmly and clearly. "I want to make sure the enemy have no nasty surprises waiting for us there. If all is clear - signal me. Then I want you to hold your positions. Do not allow anything to escape or get into the town, understood. You are to seal it off and prevent those warriors up there from escaping."

"Yes Sir. We will kill them all," Faustus said eagerly before hurrying back to his horsemen.

Watching him go, Julian paused. Faustus was a first-class cavalry officer and a reliable soldier, but there was something about the man that bothered him. Something that made him uneasy. But he could not figure out what it was. Dismissing the thought, Julian turned to his senior centurion and deputy who was riding his horse beside him. The old, grizzled veteran, in his late forties, with dark patches around his eyes, was staring at the enemy with a hard and merciless expression - his tiredness forgotten.

"Titus," Julian said, pointing at the town, "once the light infantry have done their work you will attack those gaps in the wall over there with two maniples. I want you to break into the town and put the enemy to flight. At the same time, I will lead the two other companies and assault the town from over there. One maniple will be held back as a reserve. Keep your men close together and watch out for ambushes. If the assault succeeds, we should be able to catch the defenders in a pincer movement. Burn, kill and destroy. Let nothing pass. Understood?"

"No mercy," the old veteran repeated, his eyes fixed on the town. "Right you are Julian. And afterwards? Do the men have permission to loot the place before we torch and sack it?"

"Yes, like before," Julian replied.

For a moment Titus paused. "Its going to get awfully congested and chaotic in those narrow streets. Close quarters fighting," he said in a gruff voice. "It will become difficult for my men to distinguish fighters from civilians. You know how it is Julian. People get frightened and desperate. It's inevitable that women and children are going to get killed - which will not please the slavers. Should we not give the town a chance to surrender first? It would avoid a bloodbath."

For a moment Julian gazed at the Iberians thronging the gaps in the wall.

"It would. Although I suspect that they will have got their women and children out by now," Julian said at last. "That's probably why those Spanish skirmishers were so eager to slow us down. Fine. I will give them an hour to make up their minds while we get into position. But they don't look like they want to surrender to me. You have your orders," Julian added turning back to his deputy. "See that your men are ready to carry them out."

Chapter Twenty- One - Vae Victis

At the base of the hill, the two hundred Roman principes, heavy infantrymen had gathered for the assault. The soldiers, clad in their breast plates, mail shirts and helmets and clutching their large-emblazoned shields and throwing spears, were patiently awaiting the order to start the assault. Massed together in their tight unit formations, their officers stationed at the front and back, their proud gleaming battle-standards rising out of their ranks, the men were peering up the slope at the Spanish town less than a hundred paces away.

It was approaching noon and in the clear blue sky the sun shone supreme, glorious and unchallenged. Across the fields that surrounded the besieged hilltop town however, a grim silence had taken hold. Standing among the principes, who had gathered for the assault Julian had discarded his red cloak and plumed Attic helmet. Instead, he was gripping a large legionary shield in one hand and his gladius, short sword in the other. His head was protected by an ordinary bronze helmet, conical in shape with large cheek-guards and a raised central knob. The equipment and weapons made him look just like any other soldier. His bodyguard had insisted on the disguise. The decision to strip him of any distinguishing marks that could identify him as a senior commander was, for his own safety. His guards had argued - for otherwise he would become a prime target.

A few hundred paces away, across the gravelly slopes to his right, Julian could make out Titus and his men, poised and ready to storm the town. For a moment he eyed the mass of Roman infantry, their shields and cruel steel-bladed weapons reflecting the sunlight. The coming fight, if there was to be a fight, was now about pride. The Spaniards could have escaped. They could have fled to the hills, but they had chosen to defend their homes instead. To make a stand. Shifting his attention back to the two lone figures who were bravely trudging up the slope towards the Spanish positions, Julian sighed. In his hand Bion was holding up a flag of truce, while his companion, a centurion was holding a spear.

"Moment of truth Sir," one of his bodyguards muttered.

Saying nothing, Julian peered at the two men. As expected the Spaniards were letting them come on without interference. From their positions the enemy were eyeing the two Romans with silent poignancy. The truce - the symbolism - was a well understood and accepted tradition. Everyone knew what Bion and his companion had come to do. The choice they were offering was plain for all to see. During a siege the town's folk would traditionally have until the head of the first battering ram touched the city gates, to surrender. This was their last chance Julian thought. If the defenders did not act before then, their fate would be sealed. No mercy would be granted or expected. The fight would be to the death.

Up on the slope opposite the closed town gate, and the mass of defenders filling the gaps in the walls, Bion and his companion had finally come to a halt. This was it, Julian thought. The moment had come. Live or die. But as the silence lengthened, Julian heard no raised voices and from the Spanish ranks not a man threw down his weapon or stepped forwards. For a moment longer nothing happened. Then the centurion, standing at Bion's side raised his spear and flung it at the wooden gates where the weapon embedded itself into the wood with a trembling decisive thud.

"They refuse Sir," a voice cried out, as on the slope Bion and his companion began hurrying back to the Roman positions.

Staring at the town, Julian licked his bone-dry lips, all thoughts of tiredness forgotten.

"Sound the advance," he called out. "Let's get stuck in boys. They have made their choice."

As the Roman trumpet rang out, signaling the start of the assault a company of velites came rushing passed the Roman heavy infantry. Storming up the slope towards the defenders, the skirmishers had raised their javelins and slings in a menacing manner and suddenly the slopes were alive with shouting and yelling. Waiting for them by their wall, the Spaniards could do nothing but stand their ground and bellow their defiance. A moment later the air was thick with missiles as the Roman light infantry raked the defenders, forcing them into a hurried retreat behind the cover of the walls and buildings.

"Company will advance. Let's go," Julian roared, starting forwards as he saw the results of the attack.

Moving at a brisk and steady walk, the Roman legionaries came on, a solid phalanx of shields, spears and gleaming swords. As the men began to advance up the slope towards the defenders Julian hurriedly turned to check that Titus had heard and seen the signal to attack. And he had - for the second Roman assault group too, like an armoured beetle, was now closing in on the town.

Up ahead, identifiable by their magnificent-plumed helmets, the two senior Roman centurions were leading from the front, grimly clutching their shields and short swords. They would undoubtedly be the first into contact with the enemy - leading their men by example. Their valour and contempt for danger would be witnessed by all. Following directly behind the foremost ranks, Julian suddenly felt his heart thumping away in his chest. The fear of combat and death never went away, but it could be controlled by training and discipline. He had been in combat so often before but he could not become careless. There was always the possibility that this would be the last thing he ever did. In perfect silence the Roman infantry began to close in on their baying, yelling opponents, and as they did the skirmishers swiftly started to fan out to protect their comrade's flanks and keep the Spaniards from sallying down the slope.

"Light Pilum," a Roman voice yelled. "Prepare."

A moment later with the gap down to ten yards, an officer bellowed an order and with a great roar the Roman ranks sent a hail of spears at the defenders. Looking on Julian caught sight of an unlucky Spaniard being swiftly struck by two, then three spears. The impact sent the man staggering and crashing backwards against a wall before the lifeless body slumped to the ground. The bombardment was quickly followed by a second volley of spears that scattered and drove the remaining defenders from their positions and back into the town.

Then without the order needing to be given, with a great savage cry the Roman infantry pulled their short stabbing swords from their belts and charged. Storming forwards, the legionaries surged up the final part of the slope and through the gaps in the wall - pouring into the town like an incoming flood. Following his men into the town, Julian gasped as he abruptly found himself in a narrow-congested street, boxed in by dry-stone buildings. To his right and left, a furious melee had broken out. Ringing out down the street, Julian could hear the crash and thud of metal against wood, the yelling and the horrible high-pitched shrieking of the wounded. On the ground the bodies of the dead and dying lay scattered about - some killed by missiles other showing brutal stab wounds to their faces and necks. However, in the furious hand to hand combat in the crowded, confined urban space, the experienced legionaries, veterans to a man, appeared to be in their element. Working together in a scrum, supporting each other in a well-practised drill, they were using their large shields as battering rams as they relentlessly pushed the Spaniards back. Sheltering behind their shields from the furious enemy blows that were raining down on them, the Romans responded with their short stabbing swords. Jabbing and punching at the enemy their murderous short swords were starting to inflict terrible damage on their less well-armed and trained opponents.

Sticking closely to his men as they slowly began to advance down the street and deeper into the town, his sword raised above the rim of his shield, Julian suddenly caught movement from the corner of his eye. Crying out a warning, he tried to raise his shield but it was too late. A moment later a hail of stones and bricks came clattering into the tightly-packed Roman ranks. The barrage was swiftly followed by a bold, shrieking figure who came leaping down from a roof to crash into the midst of the Roman formation. The Spaniard was semi-naked, armed only with a sword and as he frantically lashed out at the Romans around him, Julian barged into him, knocking him to the ground with his shield. Moments later the man was set upon by the legionaries, dying from a multitude of stab wounds. Looking up, Julian was just in time to be hit by a stone that struck his face. Wincing and staggering back in shock and pain, he spotted a woman standing on the roof of a building across from him. The woman was furiously hurling stones, bricks, roof tiles and pots at the Romans in the street below. But before Julian could do anything the woman was hit by a javelin, that impaled her and toppled her into the street where she hit the ground with a sickening thud.

Wiping the blood from his nose, Julian grimaced as the Romans pushed on down the street. Ahead, the legionaries were in no mood for mercy. Their brutally efficient teamwork steadily cutting a path through the enemy ranks, splitting the resistance into smaller isolated groups as the enemy were driven back down alleys and side streets. Excelling at this kind of close quarters fighting, the superior Roman equipment, discipline and training was beginning to tell. Pushing the Spaniards back towards the heart of the town, the Roman scrum appeared unstoppable as more and more Roman infantry squads began to fan out down the alleys and side streets in pursuit of the defenders. As he followed, bleeding from his face, Julian's eyes darted about, warily keeping an eye on the dark doorways, alleys and the rooves of the buildings. The town was not large but it was a confusing maze of narrow alleys and streets lined with stone buildings. Every intersection, doorway or building could be concealing an ambush.

Suddenly from somewhere in the maze of alleys and buildings, he heard Roman shouts. The soldiers appeared to be in trouble. They were crying out for help. Turning down an alley, surrounded by his squad of eight bodyguards, Julian hastened towards the noise. Ahead, the street was deserted but as he pressed his body up against a stone wall and cautiously poked his head around a corner, he spotted a party of Spaniards with their backs turned to him. Trapped in the alley beyond, surrounded by a furious mob - was a Roman infantry squad. The principes were doing their best to hold off the furious Spanish attacks that were coming in from all sides. but their the situation was desperate and getting worse. They were not going to last much longer. Quickly sizing up the situation Julian took a deep breath. Then with a cry he and his men came charging round the corner. Storming down the street to their comrades' aid, Julian and his men launched themselves at the Spaniards. Caught by surprise some of the Spaniards fled - howling and darting into the doorways of their homes, whilst others turned to face the new threat. Ramming his shield into a man, Julian shoved his opponent backwards against a wall before driving his sword into the man's exposed neck. Then his bodyguards were pushing the remaining Spaniards backwards, their steel blades flashing and stabbing in a frenzy of violence. And now it was the locals who were trapped between two Roman units. As desperate screams and shrieks started to fill the alley, the Romans cut the remaining men to pieces.

Once again wiping the trickle of blood from his face, Julian hurriedly crouched beside a badly wounded Roman soldier who was sitting on the ground - leaning against a wall. The man was groaning, grimacing in pain as his comrade tried to tend to him. Both his hands were pressed to an ugly wound in his lower abdomen from which black blood was seeping out. Seeing that there was nothing he could do, Julian gripped the man's shoulder before hurriedly rising to his feet and turning to survey the carnage. Sprawled along the street, lying in pools of blood, the bodies of the dead and wounded were everywhere along with a mass of discarded weapons and shields. As another Roman squad came running past, their heavy hobnailed boots pounding the paving stones, Julian gestured at his bodyguard to follow him.

Rounding another corner, Julian came to an abrupt halt as he caught sight of the elderly man and a boy. Both Spaniards were alone - calmly sitting on the doorstep of a house as if they had been waiting for the Romans to arrive. The man looked old, well into his fifties with a long beard, while the boy, his grandson perhaps, could be no older than twelve summers. In their hands both were clutching pathetic-looking wooden staffs apart, from which they were unarmed. Spotting the Romans, the older man appeared to say something to the boy. Then calmly both rose to their feet, their staffs raised, their intent to defend their home clear. For a moment Julian hesitated as he stared at the two Spaniards. What was this? Against the heavily-armed Roman troops these two stood absolutely no chance. Yet they seemed determined to defend their home with their pathetic sticks.

In the narrow street the Roman soldiers were slowly advancing towards the two Spaniards. The soldiers' eyes were darting about - warily on the lookout for an ambush that could come in from the rooves or doorways. But none came. Flinging aside a flimsy barricade of broken tables and chairs that was blocking the narrow street, the Romans came on, their steel blades gleaming in the sunlight. Staring at the scene, unable to look away, Julian watched as grandfather and grandson make a futile lunge at the Romans with their sticks. They were defending their home - a brave but hopeless gesture. Swiftly and ruthlessly the soldiers fell on them, easily killing the pair with their swords.

For a moment Julian stared at their bodies lying in the street. Then shaking his head he turned away. Across the town the shrieks and cries were starting to die down and all he could hear now were Roman voices. The fight was nearly over. The town was his. He had won. A moment later he heard someone calling out his name. Spotting Titus advancing down the street towards him with a party of his men, Julian quickly raised his sword.

"We have cleared the enemy from our half of the town. None are left. You good?" Titus called out as he came up looking concerned.

"I am good," Julian responded with a little nod. "I got hit by a stone. It's nothing. Well done. Then we have taken the town."

"We certainly have. Vae victis," Titus said, turning to look around at the carnage as around him the eager Roman soldiers began to slip into the buildings and homes searching for loot and riches.

***

Looking sombre, his arms folded across his chest, Julian stood watching the Roman wounded and dead being carried out of the town and down the slope where they were being carefully laid out in a line on the grass. Moving about among the wounded, his medical staff were doing their best for the men. But they could not save all, and as he looked on Julian could see the doctors were marking those who could be saved and those who could not. It was early evening and to the west the red tip of the setting sun was just about visible against the mountainous background. Gathered across the fields below the town in a makeshift camp, hundreds of Roman soldiers were trying to get some rest and sleep - exhausted after the night march and the subsequent fight for the town. Gazing at his wounded, Julian could see that his casualties had been mercilessly light. The same however could not be said for the Spaniards. For few survivors had been found inside the town and the slavers haul had been meager. The defenders had fought to the death. Shifting his attention back to the silent deserted town, Julian's face hardened. He had given the soldiers free reign to loot the place and tomorrow he would rest his men before torching the town, burning it to the ground.

"Sir," a voice called out.

Turning, Julian saw one of his cavalry troopers trotting towards him.

"Sir," the man called out again as he rode up to him. "Faustus says that you are to come at once. There is something that you need to see. Faustus says its urgent. He has found something Sir."

"Found something?"

"Yes Sir. He says its important."

Staring at the horseman Julian hesitated. Then he turned to stare to the west in the direction of the setting sun. He had sent Faustus on ahead to take control of the nearby silver mine. It was less than a mile away from the town.

"Fine. Show me. Let's go," Julian said, springing into action as he strode back to his horse and his bodyguards hurriedly rose to their feet.

As the small Roman party cantered across the rolling fields heading for the mine, Julian frowned, peering at the country up ahead. Faustus was not in the habit of calling him out if it wasn't really important. What had he found? At last, catching sight of the Roman cavalry squadrons sitting about on their horses guarding the mine entrance Julian slowed his horse's pace. The mine was not open-cast but a proper underground mine and as he eyed the dark entrance, like a cave mouth in the rocks, Julian spotted Faustus hurrying towards him. Riding up the young equestrian officer looked excited.

"Well, what have you found?" Julian called out. "What is so important?"

"Sir," Faustus said quickly. "The mine. When we got here we found that the Spaniards had tried to block the entrance and conceal it with boulders, wood and rocks. But we saw through that and have managed to get it open again. The shaft goes quite far into the mountain."

"Is that it?" Julian said sternly.

"No Sir," Faustus said smoothly. "Follow me. We found something else nearby. You need to see this."

Trotting over a rise with Julian and his men following, Faustus came to a halt and pointed to a large dried out riverbed. Strung out along the old water course, guarded by Roman cavalry troopers was a line of pack animals, mules, all tied together by ropes, side panniers slung across their backs. The animals were standing about in stoic silence.

"We found them hiding here," Faustus exclaimed in a triumphant voice. "A mule train. They were being guarded by a few Spaniards Sir, but we chased them off. The panniers on those mules are filled with silver. There is a galley worth of it down there and now it belongs to us. A nice addition to our empty coffers, Sir."

"Silver," Julian said as he eyed the mule train. "So that was what the Spaniards were protecting. That is why they were trying to slow us down this morning. Not to protect their town, but the mine. Maybe they were hoping to get this assignment away before we arrived. If so they failed. Well done, Faustus."

"Thank you, Sir." Faustus said quickly shaking his head. "But it's not all good news Sir."

Without explaining himself the young officer urged his horse down the bank and into the dried-up and concealed riverbed - casually trotting towards a band of emasculated looking men who were sitting together watching him from some rocks. Following Faustus down into the riverbed, past the stationary mule train, Julian stared at the men sitting about in their filthy, soiled and torn clothing. The strangers looked to be in a truly pitiful condition.

"They are Roman prisoners. Slaves Sir," Faustus exclaimed gesturing at the band of men. "We found them chained up in the mine. The Spaniards had left them to die but we freed them. They told us some important news."

"Roman prisoners?" Julian exclaimed looking startled.

"That's right Sir," one of the emasculated men called out. "I fought at Castulo last year. First maniple of principes, 2nd Legion. All of us, here were taken prisoner after the battle. The Carthaginians handed us over to these tribesmen who set us to work in their mine."

For a moment Julian remained silent as he stared at the Roman ex-slaves in astonishment.

"Are there any more of you?" Julian called out at last.

"There were to start with Sir," one of the Roman prisoners replied before lowering his head. "But they died."

"Sir, a word please," Faustus said quickly urging his horse alongside Julian. "When we liberated them, these men told us that this mule train - it is supposed to be heading south. The silver is meant for Carthage. The prisoners told me that a

Carthaginian cavalry force is already on its way here to pick up and escort the mule train to its destination. The prisoners told me that the Carthaginians are expected to arrive at any moment."

Chapter Twenty-Two - Retreat

Sitting on his horse on the summit of a small hill not far from the Roman camp, with his principal officers clustering around him, Julian was gazing at a line of hazy hills to the south that were just visible on the horizon. It was morning and-in-the fields directly below, the silent deserted Iberian town; the Roman camp was preparing a cold breakfast. The soldiers appeared to be in a relaxed and unhurried mood as they went about their business. At the edge of the camp, where Faustus's cavalry had tethered their horses, the mule train was being guarded by mounted pickets. The mules were standing about in stoic silence, still roped together with the side panniers full of precious silver strapped across their backs. Watching Julian in stoic silence, waiting for him to speak - his battle-hardened Roman officers were revealing little as to what was on their mind.

"Alright. Listen up," Julian said turning to his officers. "The capture of the mule train has changed our plans. The silver, those animals are carrying is worth a fortune and as you all know the army is very short on funds right now. So, we are going to retreat northwards and cross the Ebro. We are heading back to Tarraco. If we can get that haul of silver back to our base, it will be a major boost to our finances. This war is not only won by men and arms. It is also won by money. Money which we can use to sway the tribes to our side. To purchase supplies. Without money, we cannot fight and win."

"You want to retreat," Titus said, reaching up to rub his chin.

"Yes," Julian said. "I am calling an end to our expedition. We did what we came to do. We're heading back to base. For the rest of the day, however we are going to remain camped here. The men and horses need a rest after everything they have been through. We shall set out for the Ebro tomorrow at dawn."

As silence descended on the "O group," the officers quickly exchanged glances.

"Sir," Faustus said at last, looking troubled. "Are you sure that is wise? To remain here for an additional day. The prisoners whom we liberated from that mine have warned us that a contingent of Carthaginian cavalry is heading right for us. They could appear at any moment. We have no idea how strong they are going to be. Would it not be wiser to set out for the Ebro this very morning? To put some distance between us and them. We still have a long journey ahead to get to the river and if we move now we could avoid the Carthaginians."

"Faustus is right Sir," another officer said. "Maybe we should set out today. You did say earlier that speed of movement was our best defence. This extra day's rest - it could come back to haunt us if those Carthaginians catch up with us. Once those Punic bastards realise that we have their silver, they are going to want it back. They are going to come for us."

"No," Julian said firmly. "I know what I said. But the men and horses need the rest. And the doctors inform me that an extra day will make all the difference to some of our wounded. It's going to be difficult enough transporting them back to Tarraco with the resources we currently have. So we are going to stay here until tomorrow. But I am not indifferent to the threat posed by this Carthaginian cavalry force. We will take precautions. Faustus," Julian said turning to the young equestrian officer. "I want you to organise a series of mounted pickets to the south-east and west. They are to keep watch and give us early warning, if the enemy are spotted."

"Very well Sir," Faustus said lowering his eyes, his unhappiness with Julian's decision clear for all to see.

Ignoring his cavalry commander Julian turned to Nonus.

"And Nonus. Before we leave tomorrow," Julian said, pointing at the Iberian town. "I want you to take two maniples of light troops and torch that town. Burn everything. Burn the place to the ground."

***

Idly watching his men, Julian stood in the midst of the Roman camp eating, and enjoying his porridge with the aid of a wooden spoon. It was a beautiful evening and in the big skies overhead, the light was playing colourful tricks - the strange reddish and orange clouds stretching away to the horizon. Nearby, a group of soldiers were bartering and haggling with each other over looted objects which they had taken from the town and further away Julian could hear peels-of laughter. For a while, Julian observed his men before his eyes finally settled on Caciro and his small band of native guides. The Spaniards were sitting together. They had made it a habit of keeping apart from the ordinary Roman soldiers. Despite their aloofness however, Caciro and his men had proved invaluable Julian thought. Their local knowledge and ability to lead his task force along little-used paths - a formidable advantage. When he finally got back to Tarraco, he had resolved to commend Caciro for his work. The man was fast becoming a friend too - his loyalty and commitment to his friends never in doubt.

For a while, Julian's eyes lingered. He'd first met the young Spanish guide on the march to Castulo the previous year, when together they had scouted for a suitable camp site for the Roman army. Then later - after the disasters of Castulo and Llorca, where the Scipio brothers had lost their lives, to everyone's surprise, Caciro had reappeared at Tarraco asking for a job in the Roman army. The man was no friend of Carthage and so it had proved. For the Carthaginians had raped and murdered his sister. But as he studied the Spaniard, a little secretive smile crept onto Julian's lips. Caciro's only fault appeared to be that he was utterly oblivious to the dark mutterings that went on behind his back. He was completely blind to the fact that he considered himself to be a very funny man, while everyone else thought the exact opposite. When Caciro announced to his friends that he had a funny story to tell - it was a sure and reliable way of making his audience disappear.

Finishing his dinner, Julian was about to tuck his spoon back into his tunic when he suddenly spotted the horsemen. The two riders had appeared out of the forest to the east and were galloping straight towards the Roman camp, as if chased by Hades himself. Frowning, Julian peered at them and as they drew closer, he saw that they belonged to one of Faustus's squadrons.

"Where is the commander! Where is the tribune!" one of the riders, yelled as he raced up to the camp.

Hastily Julian raised his arm. "I am here," he shouted.

Hurriedly veering towards him, the two scouts slowed their pace as they came trotting through the camp towards Julian. Nearby - noticing the horsemen, Titus rose to his feet from where he had been trying to get some sleep.

"What is going on?" Julian called out, as he was quickly joined by his deputy.

"What is it son. Carthaginians?" Titus exclaimed, his eyes knotted into a sudden concerned look.

"No Sir," one of the men gasped. "Worse."

"Sir," the other rider said hurriedly, his face streaked with dust and sweat, his chest heaving. "We were out on picket duty to the east. We came as soon as we could. There is a Spanish army camped not seven miles from us. We didn't get too close but from what we saw, I would say they have at least three thousand men. Maybe more."

Staring at the two Roman equites, Julian's face coloured in shock.

"This must be the army that was mustering at Hibera to intercept us," Titus said, quickly turning to him with a grim look. "They have advanced faster than we had expected."

"Three thousand men," Julian snapped as he recovered. "Cavalry. Were they accompanied by Carthaginian cavalry?"

"We didn't see any Carthaginians Sir," the scout replied. "All local tribesmen. Most of the Spaniards looked like swordsmen and light infantry, but it's possible we did not see their whole force Sir. We did not dare to get too close. When we left them, they were hunkering down for the night."

"Could be a trick," Titus growled, again turning to Julian. "If they are just seven miles away, they could reach us with a night march - hoping to take us by surprise. The darkness would mask their approach."

"Shit," Julian swore softly, his mind racing. The appearance of the Spanish army had become a grave and unexpected threat. If the numbers were true, he and his men would be outnumbered three to one.

"What are we going to do Julian?" Titus said quietly - eyeing him.

For a moment Julian did not respond as his attention was fixed on the forest to the east. Then at last he turned to the two scouts.

"Where are your two colleagues?".

"We left them watching the Spaniards Sir."

"Good. Then ride back to them. Keep an eye on the enemy and if they start to move return here at once," Julian said. Then he turned to Titus, his face grave but calm. "Find

Faustus and tell him that I want the cavalry pickets to be reinforced. I want eyes on that Spanish army at all times. They are to shadow the enemy as long as possible before rejoining, us. No need to panic. We are going to stick to the original plan. The infantry should be ready to depart at dawn."

"Julian - what about the threat of a surprise night attack?"

"They are not going to attack us tonight," Julian said sharply. "We stick to the original plan. I am not going to exhaust the men by keeping them up all night."

For a moment Titus sucked air into his lungs, his aged face creased with concern.

"It's a two-day march to the river from here," Titus said at last, his eyes gleaming. "We are still a long way from safety."

"I know," Julian said in a sudden resolute voice, turning to eye his deputy. "But I have made my decision. See that those orders are carried out and then report back to me."

***

To the south - in the direction of the Iberian hilltop town, the massive plumes of black smoke were still rising into the deep blue skies. Sat upon his horse, ignoring the spectacle, Julian, clad in his red tribune's cloak and Attic helmet looked sombre and pensive as he led the main Roman infantry column northwards across the open and gently rolling countryside. It was just before noon, and around him the rhythmic crunch and scrape of the Roman soldiers hobnailed boots rang out. The men, holding their large shields, their throwing spears and marching packs slung across their shoulders, appeared to be in a subdued mood. There had been no permission requests for marching songs, nor could he hear the usual banter that accompanied the troops on the march. Instead, an oppressive silence had taken hold as if everyone had been given a piece of bad news.

Glancing at his light infantry armed with their missile weapons, Julian watched them moving parallel to their comrades, massed in their unit formations, guarding the plodding mule and baggage train that was carrying the wounded. For a moment, his eyes lingered. Then he turned to stare at the squadron of Faustus's cavalry scouts who were just visible, far ahead, specks in the distance. He had not been able to take all his wounded with him. Some had been too weak to be moved and he had been forced to leave them behind. It had been a tough decision, but he could not afford to have them slow him down. One of his medical orderlies had bravely volunteered to remain behind with the men.

"Sir," one of his officers riding nearby, suddenly called out pointing with his finger. "Look."

Twisting in his saddle Julian turned to look to the south, back the way they had come. Then he frowned. Beyond the main infantry column, maybe a mile away, figures on horseback had appeared and were racing towards him, throwing up small clouds of dust. For a moment Julian studied the approaching horsemen.

"Looks like Faustus and his men Sir," one of the Roman officer's declared.

By now every rider around Julian had turned to peer at the approaching horsemen, their faces looking worried.

"It's Faustus Sir," another voice quickly called out at last. "And it looks like he is bringing all his men with him. That's our entire rearguard. Aren't they supposed to be keeping an eye on the enemy army?"

Softly Julian swore to himself, as he peered at the Roman equites thundering towards the column. His officers were right. What was Faustus doing? He'd given the young knight the task of covering the rear of the column, and reporting back on the movements of the Iberian army that was by now undoubtedly coming after them in pursuit. Then before Julian could speak or act - around him - there was a sudden and sharp collective intake of breath. Along the ridge to the south more figures had appeared, enveloped in clouds of dust. The newcomers too were riding horses and there were dozens of them.

A few moments later as the stunned looking Roman officers stared at the newcomers, Faustus and his men came charging up the side of the plodding infantry column.

"Carthaginian cavalry," a Roman voice screamed. "Carthaginian cavalry on the ridge to our rear."

"What did you see?" Julian bellowed as he spotted Faustus riding towards him. The young officer's face was coated in sweat and dust.

"Carthaginians Sir," Faustus yelled as he approached. "It must be that contingent that was sent to collect the mule train. They have finally caught up with us."

"In what strength?" Julian cried out.

"Hard to say Sir," Faustus gasped, as he finally drew level with Julian, his chest heaving, his horse's flanks glistening and slick with sweat. "They were on top of us before we knew it. Little fast moving Numidian bastards on small horses. I would say about two hundred strong."

"Numidians," Julian growled, as a groan of dismay swept across the officers around him.

"Yes Sir," Faustus nodded quickly.

Wrenching his eyes away from Faustus, Julian turned to stare at the distant figures massed along the ridge, as his mind worked at a feverish pace. The Carthaginian cavalry, however were making no immediate effort to set off in pursuit of his men. They appeared to be content to just watch the Roman column - staying where they were for now.

"Julian," Titus called out, turning to him, looking increasingly concerned. "If those Numidians decide to work together with the Iberian army which is pursuing us, we will be in real trouble. All those horsemen have to do is slow us down and allow those Spanish infantrymen to catch up with us. Once they do, we will be outnumbered at least three to one. We will never be able to out-run those horsemen or shake them off. Those Numidians are experts at this kind of delaying warfare. They will be able to harass us all the way to the river. Faustus and his cavalry will never get near them if they don't want to be caught."

"I know what they are capable of," Julian retorted angrily. "But I am not going to allow them to slow us down. The column keeps moving. We are not going to play the Numidian's game. Not this time. Faustus," he added, hurriedly turning to the cavalry officer. "I want you to bring in your all cavalry scouts. All three squadrons. Mass all your men on our flank over there. But keep your distance from the enemy. Do not under any circumstances allow yourself to be drawn away from the main column. The enemy will try and trick you into following them. They will try and lure you into a rash pursuit. Don't let them, understood?"

"Yes Sir," Faustus replied quickly, nodding that he had understood.

"And someone," Julian shouted turning away. "Fetch Nonus - hurry."

"What are you doing?" Titus growled, eyeing Julian with a perplexed look.

"You will see," Julian snapped - his face darkening. "These Numidians are not the only ones who can play pretty tricks."

In the afternoon sky, the sun beat down on the dusty arid and open country. Still leading the main Roman column from his horse, surrounded by his officers and bodyguards, Julian was peering southwards at the Numidian cavalry force, which was shadowing them from a safe distance. The enemy horsemen appeared to be in no hurry as they easily kept pace with the plodding Roman column. Moving northwards, the Roman troops appeared to have picked up the pace. For a moment, Julian broke away to gaze at the infantry companies. No one had ordered them to go faster but, seeing the danger to their rear the Roman legionaries had picked up the tempo on their own accord. Hurrying along, the men remained silent, their faces grim and tense, while out on the flank, the mules carrying their precious cargoes of wounded men and silver were being pushed to go faster too.

"This had better work, Julian," Titus growled, riding beside him as Julian shifted his attention back to the Numidian horsemen, a quarter of a mile away. "See that dust cloud to our rear. That must be the Spanish advance guard closing in. They are hot on our heels. We can't afford to delay. If those three thousand Iberians catch up with us we are done for. It will be over."

Saying nothing, Julian stared at Faustus's cavalry. The Roman force had positioned itself in between the Numidians and the main Roman column, as if to try and shield their comrades from attack. Moving forwards at a walk, the Roman equites were sticking close together, forming a dense impenetrable mass of men and horses, partially obscured by fine clouds of dust. But as he watched, Julian could see that the Roman formation was slowly falling further and further behind, as Faustus skillfully maneuvered to cut off and push the enemy away from the infantry.

"Come on. Come on. Take the fucking bait," an officer muttered, tension etched into his voice and face.

Stoically Julian observed the two slow moving cavalry forces who were carefully and tensely eyeballing each other from across the short distance that separated the two sides. Still the Numidians did not attack. What were they waiting for? Licking his bone-dry lips, he tried to swallow - abruptly feeling the stress and crushing pressure bearing down on him, making his legs feel dreadfully heavy and leaden. He was taking an awful risk. If Faustus miscalculated for just one brief moment or the men disobeyed orders, the fight could end in disaster. The Numidians outnumbered his own cavalry two to one and with their faster horses and massed javelins volleys they could do untold damage.

But it was too late now to change the plan he thought. He was committed. He would see it through to the end.

Suddenly out on the flank a few Roman cavalry troopers broke away from the main force. Shattering the tense silence with their battle-cries they made a few mock attack-runs at the Numidian force. Staring at the scene, Julian immediately understood their purpose. Faustus was trying to provoke the enemy. Trying to goad them into action. For a moment the Carthaginians however did not respond. Then without warning and with terrible swiftness the Numidians finally pounced. Raising a dreadful bellowing cry the small, lightly-armed African horsemen broke away and charged at the Roman cavalry with their javelins raised above their heads. The speed at which the enemy came on was something to behold, but as they came racing and screaming into range, Faustus and his men turned and broke formation rapidly fleeing back towards the main Roman column. And as they did - they revealed what they had been concealing amid their ranks. Needing no encouragement, Nonus's hundred odd light infantry who had been hiding among the Roman cavalry leaped forwards. Clutching large infantry shields borrowed from the heavy infantry, without hesitating they sent a volley of javelins straight into the mass of charging Numidian horses. The missile attack caught the enemy completely by surprise. At that range, with the Numidians unable to change course and with no protective armour for both men or horses, the spears could not miss. Looking on Julian gasped as he saw dozens of enemy horses go tumbling down to the ground, their riders flung headlong from their mounts and into the screaming chaotic confusion.

As the Roman light infantrymen bravely stood their ground, hunkering behind their large infantry shields, they sent another volley of javelins hammering into the Numidian cavalry at point blank range, causing more and more enemy horses and men to go crashing and rolling onto the ground. The unexpected missile assault had thrown the enemy into utter confusion. Then before the Numidians could recover, Faustus was rapidly wheeling his riders around and moments later, the Roman cavalry came thundering back in to join the attack. Seeing the equites charging towards them - the few surviving Numidians broke, turned and fled in panic-stricken haste. Accompanied by frenzied, bolting, riderless horses they left more than half their comrades lying behind in the dust.

"Fuck yeah," an officer close to Julian cried out, raising his fist in savage triumph and satisfaction.

"I don't think they are going to be bothering us again Sir," a triumphant Roman voice called out.

Seeing the devastation that Nonus's light infantry had wrought, Julian exhaled with relief. For a moment he gazed at the carnage. The Numidian force had been pretty much destroyed in just under a minute. Out on the flank, Faustus had already given up chasing the fleeing survivors and was rallying his riders, while the light infantry picked their way across the blood-soaked carnage, swiftly finishing off any of the living and wounded.

At last Julian turned to Titus.

"That was revenge for what they did to us at Castulo last year," Julian said coolly. "For all the good friends, that I lost."

Chapter Twenty-Three - Evacuation

"How far behind are they?" Julian yelled, twisting in his saddle as the Roman rider came galloping up.

"A few hours," the man cried. "They are moving fast Sir, as if Hades himself is using his whip on them."

It was early evening, and the countryside was bathed in a glorious golden sunset.

Looking grim, Julian turned to stare at the Spanish horsemen who were shadowing his column from a safe distance. The Iberian riders were too few in number to intervene or slow his troops down, but they were keeping his men under observation and that was bad enough. Their presence meant that he could not change course or vanish into the hills without the enemy infantry knowing about it.

"Looks like we are in a race to get to the river," Titus said sourly.

Peering at the distant Spaniards, Julian muttered something to himself. Then he shifted his attention to the Roman column that was hurrying across the plain. Among his soldiers the earlier elation at seeing the destruction of the Numidian cavalry force had quickly given way to trepidation. The vast dust cloud to their rear was unmistakable and ominous. The men did not need to be told that speed was of the essence now. Fear lent them strength. With three thousand vengeful Spaniards in pursuit; no one was under any illusions as to what their fate would be if they were cornered. Quickly Julian bit his lip. But his soldiers were getting tired, and every mule and spare horse was already overloaded with stragglers and wounded. How long could they keep up this pace? The relentless pursuit was creating casualties and it was putting everyone under growing pressure. At some point he was going to have to decide whether to ditch the silver carried by the mule train or leave his growing number of stragglers behind. To decide to run or fight. But whatever he decided to do he had to get it right. It was his responsibility. His soldiers were counting on him as their commander. If he got it wrong - men would die.

For a moment, Julian's eyes lingered on Faustus's equites strung out in a wide protective line as they brought up the rear of the Roman battle-group. The good news was that the Numidians had not reappeared. There had been no sign of them after the beating they'd received.

"Sir," one of his officers suddenly called out. "Horsemen?"

Quickly Julian turned his attention back to the hazy line of hills to the north. Galloping towards the Roman column was a small band of riders. As they drew closer, Julian recognised Caciro. The Iberian guide was accompanied by some of his own men and the Roman cavalry scouts who had ridden on ahead.

Slowing his horse to a walk Caciro quickly fell in beside, Julian who gave him a questioning look.

"Trouble ahead," the Spaniard said in his accented Latin, looking strangely unperturbed as he gestured at the hills. "We scouted the road. To make sure that it is safe and no ambush. There is a pass through the hills which we must take. It's the quickest way to the Ebro. But when we approached the pass, we saw that it is blocked by enemy tribesmen. They occupy the high ground and are in a formidable position. They are waiting for us."

"They are blocking the pass?" Titus exclaimed, his face darkening. "How many men?"

"We saw a few hundred," Caciro said calmly turning to Titus. "Swordsmen massed along the road. Slingers on the high ground. They know that we have to move through the pass in order to reach the river. By the looks of their camp I would say they have been there for some time - waiting."

"Then we are trapped," an officer exclaimed.

On his horse Julian reached up to thoughtfully rub his chin, as his officers looked despondent.

"It's the same tactics as those employed by the Numidians," Titus growled, turning to Julian. "They are trying to slow us down again. To give their comrades a chance to catch up and finish us off. If we have to fight a way through that pass it could cost us time, which we do not have."

"Then we will go around and avoid the pass," Julian said. "Caciro - is there another way to get to the river. Across those hills?"

"There is another way yes of course," Caciro replied looking deadly serious. "One of my men knows a path across the hills but its narrow and difficult. It will cost us time and this track is an even better ambush spot than the main pass. We will be vulnerable. The track is too narrow and steep for wheeled wagons and the men and horses will need to move up in single file." For a moment Caciro paused, as he eyed Julian. "These tribesmen are not stupid," he continued. "This is their homeland. They will know the country like the back of their hands. They will probably have placed sentries along the track to warn their comrades if we attempt to go that route. They will spot us before we have even entered the hills."

"If we have to leave the wagons behind, how are we going to carry the wounded and the stragglers?" An officer riding nearby, exclaimed looking worried. "My brother is among them Sir."

Ignoring his officers, Julian gazed at Caciro with a calculating look.

"How long will it take us to cross those hills and when we get beyond them," Julian said. "How far to the Ebro?"

Turning to one of his native guides, Caciro briefly spoke to him in his own language.

"Several hours to cross the hills if nothing goes wrong or slows us down," Caciro replied at last. "After that - maybe fifteen to twenty miles to the river," Caciro added with a shrug. "Once we are across those hills the country is easy to cross and we should make good time."

"Julian," Titus said intervening, "say we did get across those hills. We still have to cross the river. The Ebro is not some trickle of piss. There are no bridges or fords that I know about and it's as wide as the Po. How are we going to get the men and beasts across with the enemy hot on our heels? Would it not be better if we found a suitable defensive spot, say the summit of a hill and prepared to make a stand there, while sending Faustus north to get help."

"We cannot fight," Julian said in a patient voice turning to his deputy. "Even if we did send Faustus ahead across the Ebro for help - it would take Nero some time to marshal a sufficient force and march to our aid. By then it will be too late. Either the enemy or lack of water will have got us."

For a long moment Titus glared at him - a strange accusing glint in the older man's eyes that appeared to be silently screaming - you either do not trust Nero to come to our aid or Faustus for seeking it. What's the matter with you?

Ignoring Titus, Julian turned to gaze at the golden sun to the west and as he did, he was suddenly reminded of the fighting retreat he'd led years ago when he and his company had ended up at the Lusitanian port of Olisippo in the far west. It seemed a lifetime ago now but he could not shake the thought that the experience had somehow been preparing him for his current predicament. Shifting his gaze to the hills ahead Julian suddenly felt calmer. He had got his men out alive then and he would do so again now.

"Alright listen up," Julian called out at last. "We are going to cross the hills using the alternative path. We are going to go around this blocking force. Caciro, you will lead us to the mountain track and get us across the hills. We are going to do this. We are going to get across the river and back to Tarraco. We are officers in the Roman army and I do not want any of you to show doubt in front of the men. Morale must be maintained. I do not want to hear any hopelessness. We have hope. We are going to get home."

"Julian," Titus said crossly, "what about the risks? How are we going to get across those hills without being detected? You heard Caciro. The enemy will most likely have sentries watching that mountain track. If the enemy catches us strung out in single file there will be a massacre."

"We will cross the hills at night," Julian replied coolly. "Under the cover of darkness. By my calculation we should reach those hills just as it goes dark."

"Another night march Sir?" An officer exclaimed.

"Yes," Julian said with a nod. "We will cross the hills in darkness. That will give us a chance to slip away. Then once we are in the country beyond we will rest for a few hours before setting out for the river at dawn. It can be done. With a bit of luck it will confuse the enemy long enough for us to get away. So see that the men are prepared."

"What about our wounded Sir," the officer who had spoken out earlier said. "If we must abandon the wagons - how will we transport them? You are not thinking of leaving them behind are you?"

"No we are not leaving anyone else behind," Julian replied, turning to the officer who had spoken out. "We are going to dump the silver carried by the mule train. That will free up the mules to carry the wounded and the stragglers. Titus," Julian added turning to his deputy. "When we reach those hills I am going to entrust you with finding a suitable spot where we can bury the hoard in the ground. Take a squad of men to help you and memorise the location. We can then come back later and retrieve the silver at our leisure."

For a moment Titus gazed at Julian as if he were about to protest. Then abruptly changing his mind, he nodded and remained silent.

***

Shrouded by darkness the silent column of Roman soldiers, horsemen and mules crept up the steep winding path that led higher and higher into the hills. Leading his horse on foot, his hand tightly clutching the reins, Julian anxiously peered into the darkness trying to spot the warning signs that they were about to walk straight into an ambush. But there had been no sign of the enemy and the night remained peaceful and quiet. Ahead - leading the way Caciro, and his small band of guides were slowly and cautiously moving forwards, pausing now and then to quietly check their bearings and that they were still on the right path. Strung out behind Julian, in a long single file the Romans were following at a snails' pace. The men hardly daring to breath or make a noise as each soldier held onto the shoulder or marching pack of his comrade in front of him. The men's tiredness and exhaustion after the day's march had been momentarily forgotten - overridden by the strong desire to get away and escape, to avoid capture by the Spanish.

"All good," Julian whispered as Caciro, abruptly hove into view.

"Yes," the Iberian guide muttered. "A few more hours and we should be across and into the plain beyond. We keep moving."

Julian was about to speak again when suddenly the silence of the night was shattered by a baby's piercing cry. As they heard the wail in the darkness, the whole Roman column came to an abrupt and horrified halt. For a moment, Julian stared at Caciro in disbelief before closing his eyes in dismay. At his side the Iberian guide groaned. Then as the baby's solitary cry rose again, demanding to be heard, it was cut off in mid-flow as if someone had muffled the noise. But the damage had already been done. There was no way a watching enemy sentry could not have heard the sound of the baby's cry. Turning towards the darkness around him, Julian held his breath, his free hand resting on the pommel of his sword. The mountain track was a horrible place from which to fight. But as the seconds ticked by nothing happened and the darkness remained undisturbed. Slowly, Julian exhaled as he felt his heart thumping away in his chest.

"Lucius - he get us all killed," Caciro hissed angrily raising a finger.

"Let's go," Julian whispered softly pushing the Iberian guide up the path. "We need to keep moving."

***

"The river. The river," the joyous cry went up among hundreds of voices as the Roman troops at last caught sight of the wide placid waters of the Ebro gleaming in the afternoon sunlight.

Looking pleased, Julian allowed himself a smile.

"Well done Sir," Titus called out with grudging respect from his horse, as the exhausted Roman column moved towards the ribbon of water like thirsty men staggering out of the desert. "But we still need to get across and time is short. We may have fooled those Spaniards in the hills but they are still coming after us. They will be here soon. We must hurry. Or else we shall find ourselves trapped with our backs against the water."

Turning to look to the south the grin on Julian's face faded. The clouds of dust kicked up by thousands of boots were still there - an ominous vengeful portent of destruction and death. The pursuing Spanish army had to be only a few hours behind and they were moving fast. He'd instructed Faustus and his cavalry troopers to cover his rear and to give him any advance warning of unexpected trouble. But Titus was right, Julian thought. Crossing the river as broad as the Ebro was not going to be easy and they needed to hurry.

For a moment Julian's eyes lingered on the plodding mule train, the attendants and the spare horses who were carrying his wounded and the stragglers who could not walk. The men had done magnificently to remain on their feet, to keep up the pace and to get this far despite what little rest they'd had. They were not going to give up now when they were so close to safety.

Then surreptitiously, Flavius glanced at his deputy. Titus had done as he had asked and had buried the silver in the hills telling him, he had marked the spot. But his deputy had said no more than that - as if he did not trust his commanding officer with the secret. Suddenly looking sombre Julian turned away. Titus may be a grizzled veteran, nearly old enough to be his father, but the officer had not distinguished himself during the expedition. Nor had he proved to be a friend. The constant questioning and challenging of his orders was beginning to irritate. When he returned to Tarraco, he was minded to-lodge a complaint about Titus with Nero. But they still had to get across the Ebro. Forcing all other thoughts from his mind Julian's gaze quickly swept across the little copses' of stunted green trees and bushes that lined the banks of the river ahead.

"Nonus," Julian called out turning to the officer who was striding along nearby. "I understand you were an engineer in civilian life. So I want you to take your men and start cutting down those trees over there. We are going to make rafts to ferry the heavy infantry across the river. How long do you think it will take you to make the rafts."

"Very well Sir," Nonus replied, casting an eye at the small copses along the riverbank. "But I built roads, not rafts Sir."

"I am sure you will manage," Julian said patiently from his horse.

"Let's see," Nonus exclaimed licking his lips. "To get a thousand men across the river would require a large number of rafts. With all my men at work and if we have enough supplies of rope and axes we could probably do it in half a day. But then there is the river current to consider, and the wounded will take up more space than the not wounded."

"We don't have a half a day," Julian said sharply. "We have a few hours at most before the enemy arrive. That is all the time you have got. So, hurry. Get your men to work at once. And I am going to need a party of your best swimmers to swim across the river to the northern shore right away. They are to tie a rope across the width of the Ebro. Secure it at both ends. We will use that to help ferry the men across and combat the effects of the current."

"Yes Sir. I will do my best," Nonus replied, quickly rapping out a salute before hurrying away, shouting to his men.

"We are never going to get all the men across, in the time we have," Titus said in a brooding manner as he stared at the broad waters of the Ebro, now just a couple of hundred paces away. "If it comes to it, we shall all have to swim."

"Faustus and his cavalry will be able to swim their horses across the river and the mules can do the same," Julian retorted. without glancing at his deputy. "I am not worried about them. But most of our soldiers do not know how to swim and the heavy infantry will go straight to the bottom with all

308

their body armour. So swimming is not an option for them. No. Our best chance is with the rafts. Once the first is complete we will start ferrying the heavy infantry across. They will get priority. The heavy infantry go first."

"That will leave us defenceless if the Spaniards appear," Titus growled. "And what about the wounded Julian - should they not be sent over first?"

"I want you to cross the river with the first group of men," Julian said in a patient voice ignoring his deputy's comment. "Take command of the operation on the northern bank. We should be safe once we have crossed but you had better set up a perimeter just in case. That's an order Titus."

For a moment Titus gazed at Julian, surprised by the sudden harshness in his commander's voice. Then he turned to look away.

"Very well," Titus said at last before riding off.

Silently watching his deputy depart as he headed towards the water's edge, Julian suddenly felt relieved to be without Titus. He had tried to work with the man. He had tried to foster a spirit of collaboration among all his officers. For smooth cooperation between the battle groups two most senior officers was vital for the success of the expedition but in the end he and Titus had just not got on.

"Come on. Let's move. Let's get these rafts built," Julian cried, abruptly turning to his officers and men as the Romans surged towards the riverbank. "Hurry. We do not have much time."

Trotting down to the water's edge to let his horse drink, Julian turned to observe the feverish activity that was now taking place along the riverbank. The men did not need to be told a second time that they were in a race against time. Setting to work on felling the trees parties of light infantrymen were fanning out along the embankment, the sound of their axes thudding into wood, drifting away across the placid still waters. Close by, with Nonus shouting instructions at them, another party of men were hurriedly stripping naked before splashing into the river with coils of rope draped around their necks. For a moment Julian watched them battling with the current as they swam across to the northern shore. Then urging his horse up the rocky embankment, he rode over to where the companies of heavy infantry were sitting about resting after their long journey. The men's faces, bodies and weapons were covered in dust and dirt but as Julian appeared among them, a few of the men raised a ragged hopeful cheer.

Dismounting beside the mule train carrying many of the wounded and those unable to walk, Julian hurriedly led his horse to where the senior doctor was getting his staff to carefully lay the wounded out on blankets on the ground.

"I cannot send the wounded across the river right away," Julian said, speaking quietly as he took the doctor aside. "They will have to wait their turn. But we will try and get everyone across."

"I understand Sir," the Greek man replied. "But I will need help carrying them down to the water's edge when the time comes."

"Fine. Do your best for them," Julian said, quickly patting the doctor on the shoulder before moving off again.

Sat upon his horse on a small rise above the riverbank, surrounded by his staff and bodyguards, Julian was observing his men at work when Lucius suddenly came hurrying past clutching his unit's battle-standard, his baby son still strapped in its blanket sling across his chest. Spotting Julian, the big man broke into a furious guilty blush before hurriedly averted his eyes and continuing on his way.

***

It was early evening and across the river Roman shouts rang out. Out on the water, a line of crude wooden rafts packed with soldiers were being slowly pulled across to the northern bank. Sitting upon his horse on the southern shore, Julian was peering at the convoy and the long series of thick ropes, tied together, that spanned the width of the Ebro. The soldiers were using the line to drag themselves across and prevent the current from pushing them downstream. But the process was agonisingly slow. Clustered around him, sat upon their horses, his officers were looking increasingly worried. The tension palpable. Breaking away from the spectacle out on the river Julian turned to gaze at the remaining men thronging the southern bank. He had managed to get all his heavy infantry across the river. Most of the wounded and the mules had gone too plus some of his light infantry but there were still hundreds of men waiting to cross.

"It's too damn slow," an officer snapped in frustration. "We need more rafts or they need to hurry it up."

"There is no time," Julian said irritably, venting a little of the pressure he was under. "Goddamn it. Instruct Nonus to order those of his men who are able to swim into the water. If they can swim, they should not be on a raft. Space on the rafts should only be allocated to those who cannot swim - damn it. We should have thought about that at the start. Now it's too bloody late - the space it would have freed up has been wasted."

"Yes Sir," one of the officers said, before hurrying away.

Looking tense, Julian watched as down at the water's edge a few of the light infantrymen, unencumbered by heavy body armour, helmets, shields and clutching only their javelins, gingerly waded out into the water and began to swim towards the northern shore. Everyone was tired and tired men made mistakes he thought including himself. But it was clear from the reaction that most of the men were either incapable of swimming or were preferring to wait for their turn to cross on one of the rafts.

"Goddamn it," Julian snapped again. "They should teach every soldier who joins the army how to swim from now on. This is ridiculous."

Around him, none of his remaining officers or bodyguards said anything as they gazed at the evacuation. Then suddenly one of them called out, sounding alarmed as he pointed.

"Sir. Sir. Look."

Hurriedly turning to look in the direction the officer was pointing a collective groan of dismay broke out among the men gathered around Julian. Across the plain to the south, less than half a mile away, horsemen had appeared and were galloping towards the Roman position along the riverbank. The thud of the pounding hooves beat the earth kicking up small clouds of dust. And swarming on behind them at a run, like an army of advancing ants, were large masses of tiny figures.

"It's Faustus and his men," an officer cried out. "And they have company. Looks like the enemy skirmishers are finally here."

For a moment, Julian stared at the horsemen racing towards the river pursued by the mass of Spanish light troops. Lacking the equipment of their more heavily-armed comrades the skirmishers could run at pace, carrying just their javelins and slings. And now they were closing in rapidly on his position in overwhelming numbers. Intent on ending the evacuation before it could be completed. Once they got into range they could wipe out his remaining force with their missiles. Suddenly Julian spotted Faustus dashing towards him. The young knight was nearly standing up in his saddle, his cloak flying behind him.

"The enemy are here," Faustus screamed, shooting past Julian, as if he needed to explain himself. "It's now or never Sir."

And without another word, stopping for no one, Faustus and his troopers, horses and all went straight into the river, crashing and splashing into the water. Moments later with the equites desperately trying to cling on to their mounts - the horses - their heads bobbing up and down just above the waterline, began to swim towards the northern shore. Along the water's edge the remaining Romans too had seen the rapidly approaching threat to the south and within moments pandemonium had broken out and all order and discipline evaporated. Suddenly it was every man for himself. Plunging headlong into the river scores of soldiers were yelling and shouting as they frantically tried to get away while others went sprinting off down the riverbank in a hopeless search for a ford.

For a moment Julian's eyes lingered on the panic-stricken chaos and confusion at the water's edge. The rafts were still on the other side of the river and would never get back across in time. In the water, terrified men were thrashing about, their arms raised, and it was clear that many were going to drown. But others had caught hold of the rope that still spanned the river and were using it in a desperate attempt to drag themselves across and keep themselves afloat. Taking a deep breath, Julian quickly turned to stare at the advancing Spaniards. He had done his best. There was nothing more he could do for his men.

"Alright time to go," Julian yelled at his guard as he urged his horse down the bank and into the water. "Follow me."

Chapter Twenty-Four - A Supporter of the Fabian Strategy

Pointing at the large parchment map that was spread out across the table Gaius Claudius Nero, supreme commander of all Roman forces in Spain, carefully cleared his throat, his bald head somehow reflecting the sunlight that was pouring in through a window. It was morning and inside the building housing the Roman HQ at Tarraco the tension was palpable. Silently observing his boss from the back of the large room where he'd been told to wait - Julian could see that Nero appeared to be irritated although he was doing his best not to show it. Meanwhile the three man delegation from the Senate who were standing around the table did not look pleased either. The three distinguished looking senators clad in their fine white togas with purple stripes running along the borders were frowning, their arms folded across their chests.

"The situation to the south - here along the Ebro is precarious," Nero continued quickly tapping the map with his finger. "Opposing us are at least three Carthaginian field armies. Hasdrubal is camped here protecting the approaches to the city of New Carthage. Mago is here in the interior defending the silver mines and the latest intelligence suggests that Gersakkun has retreated to the far west, here just north of Gades to gather new recruits. Prince Masinissa and his Numidians are thought to be with Gersakkun and King Indibilis has vanished. No one knows where he is. The Iberian tribes here to the south of the Ebro are in an open state of revolt against us. After last year's disasters at Castulo and Llorca the bastards have been persuaded to switch sides. Carthaginian agents are at work among the tribes. All the work that the Scipio brothers achieved has been undone by those defeats. It's a proper shit show south of the river."

"Well I still don't see why you cannot cross the Ebro in force and attack the Carthaginians to the south," one of the senators exclaimed pointing at the map. "We gave you ten thousand reinforcements last year. What have you been doing all this time?"

Turning to the senator Nero fixed his beady eyes upon the man as if he were gazing at a lunatic and for a brief moment Julian expected his commander in chief's scorn and contempt to explode into the open. With a mighty effort Nero however appeared to master himself.

"I cannot attack the Carthaginians," Nero snapped, "without first securing my rear. To act before then would be rash. That was the folly that the Scipio brothers made. I do not intend to make the same mistake. We must be cautious and advance one small step at a time. The Spanish tribes south of the Ebro must first be pacified and brought back into the Roman alliance. They need to be punished for their betrayal after which their loyalty and support must be secured. Only when that task has been completed can I entertain the idea of moving against the Carthaginian cities to the south. But its going to take time."

"So you have done nothing for six months?" the senator who had spoken earlier retorted.

"No," Nero said coolly shaking his head. "We have not been sitting on our arses doing nothing. The strategy for subduing the Spaniards is simple and effective as I explained in my last correspondence to the Senate. Those tribes who refused us were given an ultimatum. Either hand over money and hostages and rejoin the Roman alliance or face our wrath. Those that chose war we managed to isolate from each other through diplomatic means. Then at at the start of the year I sent three battle-groups across the Ebro to devastate the territory of those Spanish tribes who still remain hostile to us. Our columns struck here, here and here," Nero added jabbing at the map with his finger. "Their task was to burn, kill and destroy everything in their path - to bring death, panic, terror and destruction into every Spanish home. To teach the Spaniards to fear us - to fear Rome. This they did most successfully."

For a moment Nero paused as he turned to gaze at the three senators. "Don't you see," he said at last with the whiff of a challenge in his voice. "At the moment our prestige in Spain is low. We need to recover our prestige. Only then can we expect the Spanish tribes to fall into line. The Iberians need to learn to fear us again. Fear is good. Men respond to fear."

"By creating a trail of devastation and terror across their country?" One of the senators exclaimed looking unimpressed. "Some may wonder whether you are just here to enrich yourself."

"Oh for heavens sake - terror is an accepted tactic of war," Nero roared slamming his fist down on the table and thrusting out his nose as he finally lost his cool. "This is not some fancy political debating club banquet in Rome. This is a fucking war. We are fighting for our very lives here. We are only just hanging on here in Spain. The situation is desperate. I barely have twenty thousand men. Many of them are poorly trained levies with no or little combat experience. Morale is not great. We are short of money, horses, basic equipment, supplies and every maniple in the fucking army is under-strength. I am being expected to prevent Hasdrubal from marching on Italy and at the same time you want me to drive Carthage from Spain. How am I supposed to do that when the enemy outnumber us three or more to one? What do you expect me to be able to do with the resources at my disposal? It's a goddamn joke that is what it is."

For a long moment silence reigned in the room. Standing at the back Julian lowered his eyes. In the six months or so that he had served under Nero he had come to know his commander in chief as a good soldier but Nero was infamous for his temper - his ability to silence a room unmatched. He had seen his boss reduce officers to tears.

"Alright, alright," one of the senators said at last raising both hands in a soothing manner. "I think we all need to calm down. Nero - the Senate in Rome is well aware of the precariousness of the position in Spain. But the situation in Italy is difficult too. Hannibal remains a major threat even after the recapture of the city of Capua. Most of the south of Italy is still in his camp. So I am afraid that no additional troops or money can be spared for the foreseeable future. You are just going to have to do the best you can with the resources you have. But you must understand that there are many in the Senate who want to know when we will resume the offensive again in Spain. They are growing impatient. We would not be doing our duty if we did not press you on this point."

"Forgive me my lords," Nero replied in a sullen but more dignified manner. "But it is important that I impress on you the scale of the challenge we are facing here in Spain. Since I took command last year I have been busy reorganizing and reforming our forces after the great disasters that we suffered. Our army is still not ready to take on even one of the Carthaginian armies without risking disaster. If the city fathers back in Rome wish to have an answer - then tell them that I will not be able to take the offensive for at least another year. That is my considered assessment of the military situation."

"A year," one of the senators exclaimed looking incredulous.

"Yes a year," Nero retorted bluntly. "I am not prepared to throw away my men on a rash and hasty advance that could end in another disaster. We must bide our time and rebuild our strength just like we did after Cannae. So I am going to hold my army north of the Ebro for now. Fortunately it seems that the Carthaginian generals do not get on with each other. They are refusing to cooperate and coordinate in driving us from our positions north of the Ebro. Which is just as well for if they did we would be hard pressed to hold them back. So when we do finally move south to confront the Carthaginians we will do it properly or not at all. I am the commander in chief in Spain. That is my decision. Now my lords," Nero added as a gleam appeared in his eyes, "would one of you please care to tell me why the Senate has in its wisdom sent you here? I am no fool. Commission of inquiry - my arse. What is really going on back in Rome? Something is afoot, I sense."

In the room the three senators quickly exchanged glances and as they did Julian suddenly lifted his head. Nero was right. Something appeared to be afoot.

"The Senate," one of the senators said at last, eyeing Nero gravely, "has received complaints about you Nero. Our delegation has been sent here to investigate and establish wherever they hold any merit."

"Complaints?" Nero snapped arching his eyebrows in surprise. "Who has been making complaints against me?"

"A number of allied Spanish kings and tribal chieftains," the senator replied. "They have written to their intermediaries in Rome who have brought the matter before the Senate. Our Spanish allies claim that you are treating them with unnecessary harshness. They complain that you have unilaterally increased the quota's of money and supplies which they must deliver to us. They are particularly incensed by the lack of diplomacy you have shown in your dealings with them - which in their own words borders on the insulting."

"I did not insult anyone," Nero sneered. "These are ridiculous claims. As for the money and supplies, yes we need them. So what?"

Once again the three senators exchanged silent glances.

"Nero," the leader of the delegation said at last turning to him and speaking in a patient, quieter voice. "I am one of your supporters. You know that. So listen to me when I give you this friendly warning. I like most of my colleagues voted for you to be given the post of commander in chief in Spain but the politics in Rome has changed since you left for Spain. Maybe you are not aware, being stuck out here on the edge of the world - but attitudes in Rome have shifted. Decisively so. The political wheel has moved. You and I are supporters of the Fabian war strategy. Maybe once it was an effective way in which to deal with Hannibal but now Fabius and his strategy have fallen out of favour. The people and the Senate in Rome have had enough of Fabian caution and attrition warfare. They have rejected the defensive frame of mind. Instead they now clamour for action and the offensive spirit. People are tired of this long war. They want to finish it. They desire victory. In the Senate the faction hostile to Fabius are now in the ascendancy. They are demanding action to bring the war to a speedy conclusion. They have the numbers in the chamber and the support from the people."

"Quintus Fabius Maximus Verrucosis saved Rome during her darkest hour," Nero said sharply, his eyes blazing. "If it were not for him we would have surrendered and Rome would have been finished as a great power. His is still the right strategy for dealing with Hannibal. I will hear no bad word spoken about Fabius in my HQ."

"No. You are missing the point," the senator replied shaking his head. "I am talking to you as a friend. Listen to me Nero - Fabius and his supporters are out of favour. You and I are a minority now. There are going to be political consequences for all of us if we don't adapt to the new reality. The politics in Rome has changed and we must change with it. The Senate is growing increasingly restless at the lack of action in Spain. They want you to take the offensive as soon as possible."

For a moment the room remained silent as Nero gazed down at the map. Standing at the back Julian braced himself for another outburst but it did not come. Instead to his surprise Nero nodded, looking strangely and uncharacteristically calm as if he had decided to deceive the senatorial delegation instead.

"I hear your words my friend," the commander in chief said. "Fine. We shall discuss the matter later tonight again at the banquet and entertainment that I have arranged for you. But for now if you will excuse me I have some other important and urgent matters to attend to."

As the three senators bade farewell to Nero and trooped past Julian and out of the room one of them gave Julian a stern inquisitive look as if to ask who the fuck are you and what are you doing here?

"Julian," Nero snapped beckoning for him to approach. "Report."

Moving up to the table upon which lay the map Julian saluted. He and his men had only just arrived back at the Roman base at Tarraco that morning and he was still dog tired from the long journey. Nor had he yet had a chance to see Sicounin and his children. But he was nearly there. Carefully choosing his words he began to recount every detail of what had happened during his punitive expedition to the south. Gazing back at him, his beady, crafty eyes gleaming intently, Nero remained silent throughout. Then at last the commander in chief stirred.

"Casualties?"

"Light during the actual campaign Sir," Julian responded. "But during the crossing of the Ebro homeward bound ninety-five men went missing - presumed drowned in the river."

"So I heard," Nero growled.

Frowning - Julian looked confused.

"You heard Sir?" he said. "How? This is the first chance that I have had to speak to you since my battle group returned."

Taking a deep breath Nero placed his hands on his hips and fixed Julian with an unhappy look.

"I know because one of your officers has raised a complaint against you and how you handled your battle-group," Nero snapped. "They came to me this morning. The charge against you is that you willingly and knowingly placed the men under your command in mortal danger against the advice of most of your officers. You delayed your departure from the last Iberian town which you sacked by a day and this delay nearly cost everyone their lives. Did I or did I not instruct you at the start of this campaign to try and minimize our casualties?"

"One of my officers has made a complaint against me?" Julian said as the colour faded from his cheeks. "Who Sir?"

Glaring at Julian Nero did not immediately respond as he paused before turning towards the window and the fresh sea breeze that was streaming into the room.

"Show him in," Nero called out at last in a loud voice.

A moment later a door opened and Faustus marched into the room halting before Nero and snapping out a smart salute.

"You," Julian exclaimed staring at Faustus in shock. "It was you." Then it suddenly dawned on him. The young equestrian officer Bion had warned him about. The ambitious soldier who had served with Nero in Italy before and who was actively seeking to steal his job as military tribune. The knight who had claimed that he Julian was not from the right social class to hold such senior command. It was Faustus. It had been Faustus all along. Faustus was his rival.

Ignoring Julian completely Faustus was gazing at Nero with an impassive expression.

"I understand that you have lodged an official complaint," Nero began eyeing Faustus, "against your superior officer here. Will you please repeat the charge here so that all us are clear as to what is going on?"

"Certainly Sir," Faustus responded. "Whilst we were encamped below the last town which we sacked the tribune delayed our departure from the town by a day. He claimed the men needed a rest despite knowing that enemy forces were rapidly closing in on our position. I have witnesses to the order Sir. And that day's delay nearly allowed the enemy to catch up with us and destroy our column. The tribune knowingly put his command in danger. In my opinion he does not deserve the responsibility that has been entrusted to him Sir. There are better more capable men deserving of his position."

"Faustus," Julian barked in dismay but as he did Nero swiftly held up his hand for silence.

"So do you still wish to go ahead with your complaint?" Nero said.

"I do Sir," Faustus said staring back at the commander in chief. "The tribune is not fit to lead his men into battle."

"Thank you," Nero said quickly nodding at Faustus. "That will be all. You may go."

Rapping out a salute and blanking Julian, Faustus swiftly and smartly turned on his heels and marched back out of the room.

"I cannot ignore it when one of my officers is accused of recklessly putting his men and his whole command in danger," Nero snapped turning to Julian. "I am sure that you will agree."

"I got most of my men home Sir," Julian retorted angrily. "As commander I take full responsibility for everything that happened out there. It was my call and if I had to do it all again I would do it exactly the same way. With all due respect

Sir you were not there. My men were exhausted and if I had not rested them that extra day I doubt many would have made it back to the Ebro. We were harried all the way by Numidian cavalry and Iberian tribesmen. We barely slept for two days on the retreat northwards."

"Alright," Nero said looking displeased. "Alright. I get it. I am not a total idiot. You were there. You will have your reasons Julian and you did seize that silver which we still need to retrieve. That was good work." Gazing at Julian Nero paused. Then he sighed. "I shall take these mitigating factors into consideration. But the charge still stands and cannot be ignored. I am going to talk to the other witnesses and after that I will have to think about it. I will give you my verdict when you return to Tarraco. In the meantime these are serious charges you understand. The consequences if the complaint is upheld will be severe."

"I understand Sir," Julian said. Then he frowned. "What do you mean *when I return to Tarraco?*"

"Yes I have another mission for you," Nero declared carefully rubbing his hands together as if he were washing them. "It seems only fitting that you should carry it out as I understand it was you who captured her. Sophonisba," Nero exclaimed fixing his eyes onto Julian as he produced a tightly rolled parchment scroll. "Daughter of the Carthaginian general Gersakkun. Princess of Carthage - a feisty woman if ever there was one. You managed to take her alive last year during the defence of Tarraco when you overran her father's camp. Well we have finally agreed a prisoner swap with the Carthaginians. Sophonisba is going to be exchanged for some of our officers taken after the battle of Castulo and I want you to do the swap. Your orders therefore are to escort Sophonisba to the agreed meeting place and make sure that the prisoner exchange is successfully completed. You are authorised to take a small mounted escort with you. All the instructions and authority are in here," Nero added handing Julian the sealed scroll. "I am going to give you a week's leave to be with your family before you set out. Starting today. Use the time to reflect on what you want to be in my army for when you get back you and I are going to have a chat about your future. I am minded to send you back to Rome."

"Back to Italy," Julian exclaimed as anger edged into his voice. "In an honourable fashion or a dishonourable manner Sir?"

"You have your orders tribune," Nero responded looking displeased and ignoring the question. "See that they are carried out. That will be all."

"Sir," Julian snapped stiffly and awkwardly saluting. Then he turned on his heels and stalked from the room, his face like thunder.

"And Julian," Nero called out just before he was about to step into the hall beyond. "If there is any danger that Sophonisba will escape before the exchange has been completed - I want you to kill her. The bitch tried to gouge my eyes out the last time I tried to interrogate her."

Chapter Twenty-Five - Swimming Lessons

Standing in the doorway of the hall in his home in the officers quarters of the Roman base just outside the Greek colony of Tarraco, Julian was watching his son Corbulo playing with Daleninar, his daughter. The little boy, seven years old was shrieking with laughter as he tried to tickle his sister's feet. In response Daleninar, who was not even two, was kicking at her brother in protest as she lay on the bed. Then as the inevitable crying started, Ana rushed into the room. Scolding Corbulo with a few words the thirteen year old slave girl hurriedly picked Daleninar up in her arms before gently swaying her about as she tried to stop the piercing cries. Gazing at the scene Julian allowed himself a little contented smile. He had purchased Ana last year so that she could help Sicounin his wife while he was away. With no family around to help out Sicounin needed the support while looking after two young children and the other household duties. Neither he nor Sicounin had ever owned a slave before and it had all been rather awkward to start with. Ana was from the far west of Spain but apart from that and her age he knew nothing about her. The girl did not like to talk about herself or how she had become a slave. Still they had treated her well and she had not run away.

"Here let me," Julian said reaching out with both his hands. Saying nothing, her features revealing no emotion, Ana quickly handed Daleninar over to him and for a moment Julian gazed down at his daughter who had abruptly stopped crying and was staring back at him with large innocent and inquisitive eyes.

Touching her nose with the tip of his finger Julian smiled again. Then he turned to little Corbulo who was sitting on the bed eagerly watching him. He could see that the boy was pleased that he was back. For him it was a treat. He was home at last Julian thought as he finally allowed himself to relax. His family appeared to be doing well. It was a blessing. Then suddenly without warning he remembered the destruction and terror that he'd witnessed in the Spanish settlements which he and his men had sacked. Swiftly the haunting images returned, accusing and relentless, determined to be seen and heard. The bodies of dead children lying in the streets and in their homes. The pools of blood. The desperation of the villagers torn away from their families. The shrieking and wailing. The lines of chained slaves. The abandoned toys. The sound of the crackling flames and the stink of smoke and death. Looking haunted, his hand trembling slightly, Julian quickly turned away unable to look at his own children.

"Ana, there is work to do," Sicounin said sternly as she came into the room. Continuing in her native Iberian language Sicounin appeared to be giving the slave girl instructions. Then as Ana hurried away Sicounin turned to Julian carefully studying him with her smoldering coal black eyes before affectionately placing her hand on his shoulder. At twenty-four with three births behind her and two young children to look after, Sicounin had lost none of her natural vigour and fearlessness. A strong willed woman who knew what she wanted - her straight black hair was tied in a bob above her head and her appearance was immaculate.

"Welcome home Julian," she muttered softly pressing her head against his back. "I am so glad you are alright. We heard the stories of what has been happening in the south. Now that the soldiers are back the market is filled with their news. I have been listening to some of them this morning. How are you?"

For a moment Julian said nothing grateful that he did not have to explain what he had been doing. For he doubted that he would be able to. Sicounin knew him inside out however. She could tell his mood from a single glance.

"Relieved," Julian replied lowering his eyes. "Relieved it is all over but I have to go away soon again. Nero has given me a week this time."

"A week," Sicounin murmured. "Well then we shall have to make the best of the time that we have got."

Forcing himself to look down at his daughter whom he was cradling in his arms Julian nodded. Standing behind him her face pressed against his back, her hand resting on his shoulder he could feel his wife's hot breath through his tunic. For a moment no one spoke.

"I want another child," Sicounin said at last.

"Another one," Julian exclaimed.

"Yup."

"Alright."

"You heard about Lucius," he added. "He has finally got himself a baby son."

"How?" Sicounin said sounding surprised as she abruptly lifted her head from his back and turned Julian around so she could look him in the eye. "I know Lucius's woman. She is my friend. Those two have been trying for a child for ages. But Lucius has been with you all this time. How is it possible then that he now has a son? I don't understand."

"There was a lot of looting," Julian replied glancing at his wife. "Some men came away with silver and precious stones. Lucius however took an abandoned baby from one of the villages which we passed through. He carried it all the way back here. He told me he wanted a son."

"And the baby lived?" Sicounin said staring at Julian with her deep black eyes.

"Yes. Lucius looked after it. He would not let anyone near his son apart from a wet nurse who he paid to feed it. I have never seen him being so protective over something. He has changed."

"So Lucius the great shagger has finally been tamed," Sicounin said with a twinkle in her eye. "Well I am pleased for him and his woman. She will be delighted even if the baby is not her own. It doesn't matter."

Scrutinising him with her beautiful eyes, Sicounin paused.

"So what does Nero want from you this time," she said folding her arms across her chest. "What is so important to our commander in chief that he has to take my husband away from me again? Go on Julian. Something is bothering you. I can tell. What is it?"

"There is to be a prisoner exchange," Julian replied reaching out to gently touch Daleninar's nose again with the tip of his finger. "It's straightforward enough. The Carthaginian princess Sophonisba is going to be swapped for some of our officers. I am to handle the exchange. But Nero - he is a tricky man," Julian added with a sudden frown. "I have to be careful. The last thing Nero told me this morning was that I was to kill Sophonisba if there was a danger she would escape but there is no mention of this in the written orders which he gave me. They are ambiguous. His orders are therefore not clear. And there is something else," Julian said in a despondent voice. "One of my officers has made an official complaint against me. Nero says he is going to have to think about what to do. However if the complaint is upheld its likely we will have to move out of these quarters. Nero told me he is minded to send me back to Italy. I think he means to give me a dishonourable discharge from the army."

"A complaint," Sicounin said looking startled. "Who? Which officer made the complaint against you?"

"Faustus."

"Faustus," Sicounin cried out her eyes suddenly ablaze. "I know his wife. I am going to have a word with her about this. You are a fine soldier Julian and I will be damned if I am going to let Faustus get away with this."

"No. I don't want you getting involved," Julian said quickly shaking his head. "There is nothing you or I can do about it. Faustus and Nero know each other from before in Italy. They are buddies. The complaint is unjustified but Faustus is ambitious. He is not going to withdraw it."

Looking frustrated and angry Sicounin shook her head.

"So what then," she said. "You are going to just let them get away with this. If Nero sends you back to Italy what are we going to do? I though you did not want to go back to Italy. The army is your life Julian and you have not seen your family in nearly eight years."

"We are not going back to Italy," Julian replied. "I will think of something before it comes to that. This place. Tarraco is our home and this is where we are going to stay - in Spain. We were two young runaways once. You were sixteen when I met you. Remember those days," he added gazing at Sicounin with sudden fondness. "Hiding from your father and brothers when they came looking for you - when they tried to take you back. And what did we promise ourselves. That we would make our own way in life. That we would build our own home. That we would create our own family and that we would not be in debt to anyone. Well we have done that and no one is going to take that away from us. No one."

With a sigh Sicounin placed her hands on her hips. Then she lowered her head to the ground.

"I never liked Nero," she muttered. "Many of the officers wives don't like him either. He's arrogant and he rubs people up the wrong way. Surely there is something that we can do to stop this madness."

"I will think of something," Julian said gently laying his daughter back down on the bed. "I won't let Nero kick me out of the army. No way."

Turning to study her son who was sitting on the bed quietly playing with the small wooden toy sword that Lucius had made for him Sicounin was silent for a long moment.

"You need to spend some time with your son," she said at last. "Corbulo does not get to see his father very often. When you are away he is always asking when you are coming home. The boy is surrounded by women all the time and that is not always good for him. He needs his father. So why don't you take him out for the whole day tomorrow. Just you and him."

Gazing at little Corbulo Julian nodded. "Alright," he said. "Would you like that son? A day out with your dad?"

"Yes father," the boy replied eagerly.

"Good. Then I have an idea," Julian continued. "Tomorrow you and I will go down to the sea and I am going to teach you how to swim. Every Roman boy needs to know how to swim. It may save your life one day."

Chapter Twenty-Six - The Prisoner Exchange

Sat beside the fire amid the remote mountainous wilderness Julian was clad in a mud splattered poncho, his hood drawn over his head against the coldness that had descended from the high mountain peaks. It was night and darkness cloaked the land blotting out both the moon and the stars. Out of sight the gentle splash of running water tumbling over rocks could be heard and nearby tethered to their four wheeled wagon the horses were snorting and softly stamping their feet, steam rising from their flanks. Sat huddled around the fire Lucius, Bion, Caciro and six of the eight Roman guards assigned to prisoner escort duties were finishing their evening meal. All of them were dressed in long riding cloaks, hoods and ponchos, hiding their weapons beneath their clothes.

In their midst sitting bolt upright beside the crackling fire with both her hands tied behind her back Sophonisba was moodily gazing into the flames which were creating dancing shadows across her face and body. The beautiful Carthaginian princess had not said a word since they had left Tarraco. Eyeing her from across the fire, his hood drawn over his head Julian remembered the night the previous year when he had taken her prisoner. When her father, the Carthaginian general Gersakkun, had fled leaving his daughter behind to fend for herself. Sophonisba however had proved more than capable of being able to look after herself. Her proud, feisty and fearless character had quickly revealed itself when she had tried to slash open his throat when he had got too close. There was no doubt that the lady was dangerous and unpredictable. A formidable enemy of Rome who made no secret of her hatred for him and his men. For that reason he had decided to take no risks. He had kept her tied up. Feeding her himself and accompanying her everywhere. However on the long ride from Tarraco to the spot where the prisoner exchange was going to take place she had so far given him no trouble. Perhaps the realisation that she was going to be exchanged.

That she was being freed and going home - had finally calmed her down.

"Sir," Lucius piped up casually pointing his spoon at Julian. "Question. You know that silver horde which we buried in the mountains during our retreat to the Ebro. Did Titus ever tell you where he buried it?"

"He did not," Julian replied shifting his attention to Lucius. "But I am reliably informed that he did tell Nero where it can be found. All I know is that the silver is in a hole in the ground close to a tree. Apparently Titus marked the tree with two letters AS to indicate the spot."

Across the fire Lucius frowned.

"Well that's not very smart," the big man growled. "What happens if someone chops the tree down. Then the marker will be lost and why use those two letters. How does AS tell you there is silver buried in the ground?"

"Titus said he marked the tree right at the base of the trunk," Julian replied. "Anyway it doesn't matter. That silver is not going to remain in the ground for long I guess. I am sure that Nero will be sending a party to retrieve it when he can. Why do you ask?"

"AS you moron," Bion said digging his elbow into Lucius's side with a little contemptuous shake of his head. "The first two letters of the Greek word for silver. If you had a brain my friend you would have known that."

Letting the dwarf's jibe pass Lucius gingerly reached up to rub his chin as he gazed at Julian from across the fire.

"Well I was just thinking Sir," Lucius began. "What if we were to make a detour and liberate that silver. Take it for ourselves. That would make us pretty wealthy. To hell with this war I say. We have done our bit. I am fairly certain I have seen more than my fair share of fighting. If we took that silver we could retreat to some nice sunny Carthaginian colony in the south and enjoy the rest of our lives."

"I can't see you holding onto any of that money," Bion said quickly. "Lucius you will have spent your share before the end of the month. You just wouldn't be able to help yourself. When it comes to money, you are still a child."

Sat beside the fire Julian was coolly observing his friend. "Lucius," he said at last as the fire crackled and a shower of spark shot away into the darkness. "You once told me that it was your job to keep me honest. That you wouldn't allow me to turn into an arsehole now that I had become your commander. Well it is my job to keep you honest as well. To stop my good friend from becoming another corpse nailed to a cross - the punishment for desertion. So let me do my job and you concentrate on doing yours. Does that sound fair enough?"

At the edge of the fire Lucius smiled. "You got me Sir," he said. "Just looking out for my old mate as always. Making sure all that power you have does not go to your head. Don't worry I will tell you when you are being an arsehole. But the truth is Sir that I never really intended to go looking for that silver. Nah I just wanted to see your reaction."

For a moment Julian studied Lucius with an accommodating look as the band of Romans around the fire quickly glanced at each other before a few cautious smiles appeared.

"You are all damn lucky to have me as your commander," Julian announced at last raising his chin. "Another man may take you scoundrels the wrong way and then you will be pining for the days when I was in charge. You will see."

"Sir," Bion said quickly turning to him. "So its true what Nero has said. There has been a complaint made against you? So its true that Faustus is gunning for your job. I never did like that arrogant prick. He is all smiles and laughter until he rams his knife into your back."

"It's true. I may not be in command for much longer," Julian conceded glancing at Bion. "Nero is talking about packing me off back to Italy. A dishonourable discharge I suspect. I am to find out when I return to Tarraco after this mission. I may not be around for much longer."

"Shit Sir," Lucius exclaimed suddenly looking troubled. "Back to Italy. You never told me it was that bad."

"Well it is," Julian said forlornly turning to look at the fire. "Faustus is standing by his complaint and he and Nero are friends. They served together in Italy before. This may be the last time that I am in command. So all of you had better get used to the idea that you may have a new commander soon."

"Faustus," Lucius growled. "Oh good god. Not him. Please."

But before Lucius could speak again Julian had shifted the conversation to Caciro who was silently and carefully cleaning his spoon with his tongue and fingers.

"Bion here," Julian said calmly gesturing at the dwarf, "is one of the most intelligent and educated people that I know. He knows every language in the west and then some. He may be small but his brain makes up for his lack of size. He if originally from the Tin islands and ended up here in Spain as a slave but one day he is going back home as he promised his mother he would. Lucius over there," Julian continued, keeping his eyes on the Spaniard, "is a butcher's son from Rome. He is my oldest friend in the army. He has bedded more women than their are ships in the Carthaginian navy. But you Caciro. You never finished telling us your story. Why don't you tell us how you managed to end up here with this bunch of cutthroats and roughnecks?"

Gazing at his spoon Caciro however did not immediately reply and for a while the silence was disturbed only by the crackle of the flames and the splash of the mountain stream. Then the small young Iberian guide looked up at Julian with a deadly serious expression, the flickering light playing tricks with the snake tattoo across his forehead.

"You wish to know Sir?"

"I do," Julian said in an encouraging voice.

For a moment Caciro hesitated.

"Before," Caciro began and as he spoke in his accented Latin a hush descended among the men sitting around the fire. "I lived in my village with my father and two sisters. My father taught me to be a hunter. I would go up into the mountains with him to hunt deer. My sisters made clothes and sold them to the traders from the coast. We had enough. Then one day Carthage came to our village. They were Spaniards, mercenaries with Punic officers. Bad men. They came demanding food and money but we had none to give."

For a moment Caciro paused - brooding. "Carthage came to our house too. They were drunk," he continued. "My father was away. The soldiers they made me stand and watch. They gave me a choice. I was to choose which of my sisters they would rape and if I didn't choose they would kill them both. So I chose. I pointed my finger and they raped her and afterwards they murdered her anyway. They were laughing when they left. So since that day I have sworn revenge on Carthage. I cannot rest until I have had vengeance for what they did to my sister. Nothing else matters - but that."

As Caciro finished speaking silence descended across the little camp and Julian lowered his eyes towards the fire.

"Hell. That is some serious shit that you are carrying around Caciro," Lucius exclaimed at last gazing at the Iberian guide.

"But it was not your fault. You had no choice. Your sister will have understood that."

"Maybe," Caciro said sombrely glancing at the big man. "My sister who was murdered was called Stena. She was funny. She was always telling funny stories and jokes. She made us laugh. She was our heart. The centre of everything with her joy for life. She was very good at making us laugh. So maybe now that she is with the gods she whispers her stories to me in my sleep for like her - I too can be very funny."

"Graceful gods," Bion muttered under his breath, rolling his eyes.

"I don't think now is the time for another story Caciro," Lucius said hastily as the blood drained from his face. "I think we had better all get some rest instead. It's been a long day."

***

Sitting on his horse Julian gazed out across the tranquil river to where a small island divided the current. It was afternoon and to the west along the beautiful river valley a wall of dark storm clouds were building on the horizon. Far from the coast as they were the Ebro was much narrower than it had been nearer to the sea. The small island that sat in the midst of the river was nothing more than a sand bank with a solitary tree stuck in the middle. Shifting his gaze to the southern shore for a moment Julian studied the steep banks. The dense tree cover came right up to the water's edge and he could see no one about. Yet this was the agreed spot. The place where the prisoner exchange was to take place. Quickly Julian glanced up to check the position of the sun. They were early so he could afford to wait. Mounted on their horses surrounding the wagon upon which Sophonisba was seated his eleven companions were gazing out across the river.

"It's the correct place Sir," Caciro called out at last.

"I know," Julian replied.

"Sir, look," one of his men suddenly cried. "Over there."

Staring across the river Julian too had caught sight of movement among the trees. A few moments later a small party of horsemen appeared cautiously descending down the bank to the water's edge. As they reached the river the horsemen halted and gazed across at the Romans in silence.

"Carthaginians Sir," Lucius called out. "At least they are wearing Carthaginian clothes. Looks like they have been waiting for us."

Studying the strangers Julian said nothing. Lucius appeared to be right. Then as he looked on another party emerged from the forest on the opposite side of the river. The second group of riders were leading four men on foot. The walkers looked dishevelled, their clothes in ruins, their bearded faces grimy and haggard. Their hands were tied behind their backs and all four men were bound together by a thick rope as if they were on a chain gang. Leading the men to the water's edge the Carthaginians joined their comrades and halted.

"Are they our boys?" Julian called out.

For a moment the Romans in his party, who had been specifically chosen to accompany him because they personally knew the officers who were to be exchanged, remained silent as they peered at the figures across the river. Then at last the men stirred.

"Yes Sir. That's him," one of the men replied. As the others confirmed the identities of the remaining officers Julian nodded, looking satisfied.

"Alright," he said turning to Bion. "Get Sophonisba up on her feet so that they can see we have her."

"Shall I cut her free?" Bion asked as he turned towards the wagon.

"No," Julian said sharply. "She is not free until the exchange has been completed. Until then she remains bound."

"Four of ours for one Carthaginian princess," Lucius muttered as he sat on his horse beside Julian. "Someone over there must really want her back. Good riddance if you ask me."

Studying the party of Carthaginians on the opposite side of the river Julian remained silent as on the back of the wagon Bion spoke to Sophonisba in Punic. A moment later with infinite grace and pride, looking composed and calm like a statue, the Carthaginian princess rose to her feet.

For a moment nothing more happened as the two parties of horsemen carefully eyeballed each other from their respective sides of the Ebro. Then abruptly four of the mounted Carthaginians turned and leading the Roman officers they entered the water and started out for the sandbank. Their horses slowly swimming and wading out into the river. As the four Romans staggered and spluttered through the placid water that came right up to their necks, struggling to stay on their feet, the officers were pulled along by the rope. Staring at the riders swimming towards the island Julian frowned as he suddenly spotted a strange sight. Clinging to the back of one of the half submerged Carthaginian horsemen, his hands tightly clasped around the man's neck, was another smaller man, a cripple by the looks of it.

"Ask Sophonisba if she recognises the men on those horses," Julian said quickly turning to Bion.

Glancing at the Carthaginian princess as Bion spoke to her Julian saw a little smile of recognition and relief appear on her face. The first time he had ever seen her smile.

"She says," Bion replied at last shooting Julian a quick glance. "That the cripple being carried across the river is called Epicydes. Sophonisba says that she is a friend of his son, Chariton."

"Epicydes," Julian muttered. The name meant nothing to him. For a moment longer he gazed at the Carthaginians who had by now reached the sandbank and were emerging from the river.

"Alright. Listen up," Julian said quickly turning his horse towards the wagon where Sophonisba was still on her feet gazing at the southern shore. "Lucius and Bion, you are with me. The rest of you stay here and keep your eyes open for trouble. Let's get this done."

With Sophonisba sat directly in front of him, his arms wrapped tightly around her midriff to stop her from falling off, Julian carefully urged his horse into the river. As the cold water surged up to his waist his horse snorted in protest. But the river was not too deep and soon half submerged, they were swimming across towards the sandbank where the party of silent Carthaginians and their prisoners were waiting for him. As he and his companions finally emerged from the river and onto the sand bank, water cascading from the flanks of his horse, Julian halted, gazing at the Carthaginians from under the hood of his poncho. The four Roman officers looked exhausted and had collapsed onto the ground, their ruined clothes soaked. The men hardly seemed to have the strength to look up at their colleagues who had come to rescue them. The Carthaginians however were gazing back at him with tense guarded expressions and as Julian's eyes came to rest on the cripple clinging to the back of the rider their eyes met.

For a long moment no one spoke. Then at last Epicydes called out to Sophonisba speaking in his native tongue.

"He is asking her if she is alright," Bion muttered. "He is asking her if we mistreated her at all."

As Sophonisba replied, her voice betraying her emotion at being freed, Julian stared at the cripple who to his surprise and despite his physical weakness and deformity appeared to be in charge. And as their eyes met again Julian suddenly sensed the presence of a cunning and highly intelligent mind. This man was dangerous. Highly dangerous and as he held Epicydes's piercing gaze an involuntary chill abruptly ran down his spine.

"We make the trade Roman as agreed," Epicydes suddenly called out to him speaking in Latin.

Saying nothing Julian swiftly cut the bonds that had tied Sophonisba's hands behind her back. Then without ceremony he shoved her off his horse where she landed in a pool of muddy water with a little startled squeal. Staggering back to her feet she shot him a furious look before hurriedly stumbling across to her countrymen. At the same time one of the Carthaginians had cut the ropes binding the Roman officers together and kicking them to their feet the Romans shuffled over to where Bion and Lucius were waiting.

Ignoring Sophonisba, who reaching her own people, had turned around and was spitting at him, Julian warily kept his eyes on Epicydes. Clinging on to the back of the man carrying him - the cripple's eyes were twinkling and gleaming as if he was amused by something.

"We're done here," Julian called out at last. "The exchange has been made. Let's go," he added quickly glancing at his companions.

"Not quite," Epicydes said.

A moment later one of the Carthaginians tossed a sack towards Julian.

"What's this?" Julian snapped as he quickly gazed at the sack that had rolled to a stop at his horse's feet.

"A little present for you," Epicydes replied. "A warning."

As one of the Roman officers gingerly picked up the sack, opened it and glanced inside he immediately recoiled in horror. Silently the officer turned to show the contents to Julian and as he saw what was inside the blood drained from his cheeks. Gazing back at him with sightless eyes was a human head.

"His name was Honorius," Epicydes called out with sudden glee. "He was a Roman spy. A double agent pretending he was one of us when in reality he was working for that little fat master of his - Trebonius. But I saw though his scheme. I caught him and now you can bury him. When you get back to Tarraco tell Nero that if he sends any more Roman agents into our territory that they shall meet the same fate. Now get the fuck out of my sight."

***

Riding his horse at a walk Julian looked tired and sombre as he led his small band of men on the final stretch towards the Roman fortress. They were nearly home. His mission had been a success but he did not feel elated. Behind him creaking and jolting across the rough stony track the four wheeled wagon carrying the Roman officers was being pulled along by a driver and two horses while the rest of his men were riding along side.

It was just after noon and in the distance the walls and watch towers of the Roman base rose up out of the coastal plain with the sea as backdrop. Thinking about what had occurred Julian turned to gaze at the sack with its grim contents that was lying inside the cart. There had been a time years ago when he and his company had been inserted into the south of Spain. When he had been instructed to cause unrest among the Numidian mercenary troops serving Carthage during the start of the Numidian civil war. It had been there - hiding out in the mountains that he had been approached by a man named Honorius who had claimed to be a Roman spy. Honorius had come to warn him. It had to be the same man. The spy had told him that a Numidian named Gisgo had discovered what he was up to. Gisgo was intent on capturing him and putting an end to his operation. It had been Honorius's timely warning that had allowed him to initially avoid his pursuers. Then after a long and difficult fighting retreat he had finally succeeded in leading his men to safety in Olisippo in the far west.

With a sigh Julian turned to study the fortress ahead. In a way he owed Honorius everything. Honorius had saved him back then and he had barely known the man and now he never would. It was a quirk of fate. Of chance and luck. How different life would have been if Honorius had not intervened and had allowed Gisgo to capture him instead. He and his comrades would probably be sweating it out as slaves in some god awful Carthaginian mine if not for that man. But instead he Julian had remained free and he had made it to the rank of military tribune. Sombrely Julian lowered his hood to his shoulders. Epicydes had been cruel in only returning the man's head. There would now be no peace for Honorius. With his head separated from his body - with no final resting place - his spirit would be lost forever. It was a sad end to a brave man. But that was the price the gods had demanded in exchange for his own good fortune. When he returned to base he had resolved to make a sacrifice to the gods - for Honorius's spirit. For in this war the names of many of those who served and were lost would forever remain unknown but their deeds were immortal.

As the party of horsemen neared the gates leading into the Roman fortress a crowd of off duty soldiers had started to gather. The men - curious to witness the arrival of the former prisoners - were lining the track, calling out and showering Julian and his men with inquiries and comments. Recognising the centurion strolling towards him from the gates Julian hailed the officer.

"Centurion," Julian cried raising his hand. "Send a runner to inform Nero that the prisoner exchange was a success. I shall be along shortly."

"No Sir," the centurion called out. "I can't do that."

"What?" Julian cried frowning. "Why not? Are you refusing to carry out an order."

"No Sir," the centurion replied smartly. "I can't because Nero is no longer here and he is no longer our commander in chief. He was recalled while you were away. The Senate have summoned him back to Rome. He left two days ago by ship. Seems some of the city fathers were not happy with old Nero. But that's politics for you. The news is that there are going to be fresh elections in Rome. They are going to send us a new commander in chief."

Coming to an abrupt halt Julian stared at the centurion in disbelief. Then a moment later Bion was at his side, his cheeks flush with excitement.

"Oh my word. Don't you see what this means. It looks like you are off the hook Julian," Bion exclaimed in a breathless voice. "With Nero gone Faustus has lost his protector. Without Nero that complaint against you. It's going nowhere. Everyone here knows your qualities as a leader. I do believe. I do believe you are going to keep your job."

Chapter Twenty-Seven - Rome's Great Gamble

Late Summer 210 BCE

Stretching along the road leading north to the Greek coastal colony of Emporiae a vast and eager crowd had gathered to welcome the newly arrived Roman troops. Standing at the side of the track thronging with noisy spectators, Sicounin and his children by his side, Julian was watching the approaching column. Clattering down the track towards him at a brisk walk the Roman cavalry vanguard, freshly arrived from Italy, four ranks wide, came on through the cheering crowds. The equites armour, shields and helmets dazzled and reflected the sunlight while the stern faced riders ignored the people.

"Where is he father?" little Corbulo cried out jumping up and down with excitement unable to contain himself as he held onto Julian's hand. "Can you see him? Can you see him?"

"Not yet," Julian replied in a patient voice.

"They say that he is barely older than I am," Sicounin said eagerly craning her neck to get a better view of what was coming down the road towards them. "That he is still only twenty-five years old. Is it true that no one stood against him during the recent elections in Rome?"

"So I heard," Julian said staring at the Roman equites as they started to move on passed heading for the Roman fortress.

"You met him once before didn't you," Sicounin cried out quickly turning to her husband. "Back in Italy?"

"I did. Yes briefly in Rome when I was there."

"Isn't he a bit young to hold this position?" Sicounin continued. "I mean all the others have been much older."

Standing beside his wife Julian did not reply as he carefully concealed his own doubts. Sicounin was right. Electing the young Publius Cornelius Scipio to the supreme command in Spain was a massive gamble. One that had caught most of his fellow officers by surprise when they had first heard the news. What were the people of Rome thinking when they had cast their votes. The young Scipio he'd met briefly at his father's house in Rome all those years ago had had courage. There was little doubt about that but at the age of just twenty-five Scipio had absolutely no experience of commanding a Roman field army or leading one into battle. The young man was a complete novice. But the election had been decisive he had been told. None had stood against him. The Roman people had decided to place their trust in the young patrician whose father and uncle had been killed at Castulo and Llorca the previous year. And now Scipio had finally arrived in Spain bringing with him ten thousand reinforcements for the Spanish expeditionary army.

"He bears a famous name," Julian said at last as he caught sight of the first of the infantry columns marching towards him - eight abreast - as they followed on behind the cavalry vanguard. "Let's hope he is a chip off the old block. If he is anything like his father or uncle we should be alright."

"Gnaeus and Publius Scipio respected you," Sicounin said quickly, her eyes fixed on the marching soldiers. "Maybe young Publius will do the same and treat you well. At any rate he can't be worse than that old sack of bones Nero. Gods, I am so glad that man was recalled."

Suddenly up the road the intensity of the cheering crowds rose to a fever pitch and moments later Julian caught sight of a cluster of senior officers mounted on horses riding towards him. The officers plumed helmets, blood red cloaks and fine coats of chain mail body armour were unmistakable - making them stand out. And riding at their head, leading his staff in a dignified and composed manner - handsome and youthful - was Publius Cornelius Scipio.

"There he is. I see him," little Corbulo shrieked pointing with his free hand. "That's him. That's him."

Gazing at the new Roman commander in chief Julian said nothing. Holding onto his seven year old son's hand - with his other hand he was suddenly rummaging in the pocket of his tunic. As his fingers closed around the small hard object that lay inside a sombre expression appeared on Julian's face. Carefully producing the signet ring from his pocket he stared at the small gleaming metal band. He still had it. The ring he'd taken off the elder Publius Scipio's finger as the general lay dead - killed during the battle of Castulo. For a moment Julian stared at the ring as he remembered that dreadful day. He had resolved - when the time was right - that he would return the ring to his former commander's son. And now that day had arrived. Sooner than he had been expecting.

"Father," little Corbulo called out. "Look. See the standard bearer. He is wearing a wolf's head."

Slipping the ring into his pocket Julian turned his attention back to the party of officers who were now just a dozen paces away - coming straight towards the spot at the edge of the road where he and his family were standing. Behind Scipio and his principal officers was a standard bearer, a splendid wolf's pelt draped over his helmet. The officer was holding up a proud battle-standard while massed behind him came Scipio's mounted entourage clad in long brown cloaks with hoods. The solemn faced officers were ignoring the crowds, their eyes fixed on the Roman fort ahead. For a moment Julian gazed at the riders as they approached at a walk, their horses hooves ringing out among the cheering crowd.

Then suddenly Julian froze and his heart skipped a beat. A few yards away among Scipio's mounted entourage a rider had come to a sudden and unexpected halt at the edge of the road. The blond and deeply tanned figure appeared to be in his fifties and he was staring back at him as if he had seen a ghost. And as he recognised the man Julian eyes widened in shock.

"Father," Julian blurted out in disbelief.

Standing at her husband's side Sicounin suddenly looked confused as she noticed the look of shock on Julian's face. But before anyone could do or say anything Flavius had slid from his horse. Raising both his arms in the air in silent joy he came limping towards Julian before clasping his arms around him in a fierce bear hug. For a moment father and son held onto each other. Then abruptly Flavius broke away and as he took a step back, gazing at Julian, his body and arms were trembling, his face flushed.

"Son," Flavius said in a hoarse voice. "It's good to see you Julian."

Flavius had aged Julian thought as he stared at his father. Considerably so. Nor did the old man appear to be in particularly good health. But it had been eight years since he had last seen him. Eight years!

"Father," Julian responded struggling for words. "This is a surprise. I had no idea you would be arriving with Scipio."

"I work for Scipio now," Flavius said before abruptly halting. "The last time I saw you," Flavius gasped. "I let you go. Remember that night in the colony. Cassia your sister warned me just in time. You were going to run away. You were about to do something stupid by going off to join that band of Gallic mercenaries. But I got to you in time. I told you to go to Rome instead. I told you to go and join the Roman army. And you did. And I still thank Fortuna that you had the wisdom to do that. That you listened to me. Glorious Fortuna," Flavius exclaimed with a hoarse voice. "The army made a man out of you. I am so pleased, Julian. We did not know if you were dead or alive but here you are."

"Father," Julian said biting his lip. "It is good to see you too. This here is my wife Sicounin and my two children, Corbulo and Daleninar."

As Julian gestured at her, Sicounin blushed and overcome by the emotion of the unexpected meeting a little tear trickled down her cheek. Then before anyone could stop her Sicounin quickly turned to Flavius, formally bowed her head and taking Flavius's hand in hers she kissed the ring on his finger.

"Father," she said in a respectful manner.

Standing at Julian's side little Corbulo was staring up at Flavius with an inquisitive look while Ana just looked uncertain as she held Daleninar in her arms.

For a moment Flavius remained silent as he gazed at Sicounin. Then reaching out to her he quickly drew her into a tight hug and as his eyes shifted to the children a happy smile appeared across his lips.

The Romans

Flavius's Family

Agrippina, Wife of Flavius

Atia, Agrippina's mother, Flavius's mother-in-law (deceased)

Caius, Oldest son of Flavius and Agrippina

Octavia, Oldest daughter of Flavius and Agrippina (deceased)

Julian, Youngest son of Flavius and Agrippina

Cassia, Youngest daughter of Flavius and Agrippina

Sicounin, Julian's Spanish wife

Gallus, Cassia's Gallic husband

Little Corbulo, Julian and Sicounin's son

Little Daleninar, Julian and Sicounin's daughter

Little Corbulo, Cassia's and Gallus's first-born son

Little Hortensia, Cassia's and Gallus's daughter

Little Laela, Octavia's daughter

Little Mastanabal, Amia's son

Friends of Flavius and Julian

Amia, Victorix's new wife, former wife of Mastanabal

Victorix, Cenomani hunter and friend of Flavius

Gallus, cousin of Victorix from Turin, Cassia's husband

Trebonius, Patrician patron, Roman spymaster. Magistrate

Plato, Trebonius's freedman and secretary

Aemilia, Trebonius's sister

Lucius, army friend of Julian

Gordianus, army friend of Julian (deceased)

Manus, Julian's commanding officer in Spain (deceased)

Bion, army translator and friend of Julian

Papiria, Roman agent recruited by Flavius (deceased)

Caciro, Iberian guide and tracker

Roman citizens, soldiers and allies

Archagathus, Greek doctor and Trebonius's personal physician (deceased)

Gnaeus Cornelius Scipio, brother of Publius Cornelius Scipio (deceased)

Publius Cornelius Scipio, Military Tribune and later Consul of Rome (deceased)

Publius Cornelius Scipio, the younger, Son of his father by the same name

Marcus Claudius Marcellus, Roman general, known as the sword of Rome

Titus Manlius Torquatus, Roman general assigned to command in Sardinia

Tiberius Sempronius Gracchus, Consul of Rome in 215 BCE

Quintus Fabius Maximus, Consul of Rome in 215 BCE, known as the Shield of Rome

Quintus Caecilius Metellus, Roman plebeian aristocrat and relative of Velio

Velio, Roman land commissioner at Placentia

Quintus Naevius Crista, prefect of allied forces, victor of the battle of Apollonia and Capua

Quintus Fulvius Flaccus, Consul in 212 BCE, Pro Consul 211 BCE, Conqueror of Capua

Appius Claudius Pulcher, Consul in 212 BCE, Pro Consul 211 BCE, Conqueror of Capua (deceased)

Gaius Claudius Nero, ancestor of emperor Nero

Lucius Marcius, Roman knight and soldier in Scipio's army

Platinus, Scipio family lawyer

Scoti, astronomer friend of young Scipio

Davido, entrepreneur friend of young Scipio

Gaius Laelius, soldier and childhood friend of young Scipio

Aemilia Tertia, young Scipio's wife - grandmother of the famous Gracchi brothers

Pytheas, Massaliot diplomat

Acco, young Massaliot translator

Roman Glossary

Acta, News reports

Achaean League, the city states of Corinth, Argos, Sicyon and Megalopolis in the Peloponnese

Adyton, small holy room at the back of a temple which was never open to the public.

Aemilii, Roman aristocratic family/clan

Aesculapius, the God of healing

Aesculapius temple, on Tiber island, Rome, dedicated to the God of healing and medicine

Aetolian League, city states of Elis, Messene and Sparta

Agora, the central marketplace

Alpheus, god of rivers

Amposta, modern Castell D'Amposta, Spain

Aoos river, now known as Aoos or Vjose river, northern Greece and Albania

Aphrodite, Goddess of love

Apollo, God of healing and music

Apollonia, Greek speaking city on the Illyrian coast, now known as Pojani, Albania

Appian Way, road connecting Rome to Capua

Apulia, region in south eastern Italy

Aquae Appia, the oldest of Rome's aqueducts

Achaean league, Greek city state defensive alliance

Arethusa, Syracusan nymph, water spirit

Arevaci, Celti-Iberian tribe

Argiletum, the street in Rome of the booksellers

Ariminum, modern Rimini, Italy

Arno river, still called the Arno and it flows through the city of Florence

Arpi, ancient town in south eastern Italy

Artemis, Greek Goddess of the hunt, the Roman goddess Diana

Arx, the most northerly of the two summits of the Capitoline hill.

Asses, simple Roman coinage

Atanagrus, capital city of the Ilergetes, in the region of modern Lleida, Spain

Atellani, Iberian tribe

Athena, patron goddess of Athens

Atrium, the open-living-space at the heart of a fine Roman house

Aufidus, now known as the Ofanto river, Italy

Aufidena, now known as Alfedena, Italy

Augur, fortune teller, religious priest

Bacchus, god of wine, liberation and a good time, otherwise known as the Greek Dionysus

Baebulo silver mine, mine location near Linares, Spain

Baetis river, now called the Guadalquivir

Balearic slingers, slingers from the Balearic Islands

Belerion, ancient name for Cornwall

Belli, Celti-Iberian tribe

Beneventum, Latin colony, now known as Benevento, Italy

Boii, Gallic tribe living in the Po valley, Italy

Bononia, now known as Bologna, Italy

Brundisium, a Greek speaking city in the far south of Italy, now known as Brindisi

Brutians, ancient peoples living in southern Italy

Calabria, region in southern Italy

Calatini, ancient Italian tribe

Campanians, people from the Italian region of Campania

Candida, the official clothing of a candidate up for election

Canusium, modern Canosa di Puglia, Italy

Capitoline Hill, one of the hills in ancient Rome

Capua, Campanian city close to Naples

Carales, capital of Roman Sardinia, now known as Cagliari

Caer Bran, West Cornish iron age settlement

Carn Brea, West Cornish iron age settlement

Carnyx, boar headed Celtic war trumpets

Castra, fort

Casilinum, stood on the spot where now stands modern Capua, Italy

Castulo, near modern Linares, Southern Spain

Celtici, Celti-Iberian tribe in southern Portugal

Cenomani, a Gallic tribe in northern Italy, who were friends and allies of Rome.

Chakka, a small handheld mill stone to grind grain into flour

Chun Castle, West Cornish iron age hill top fort

Cis-Alpine Gaul, Roman name for the Gallic lands in northern Italy between Alps and Apennines

Cispadana Gaul's, Gauls living south of the Po river

Cissa, small ancient town just north of modern Tarragona, Spain

Clastidium. now known as Casteggio, Italy

Clepsydra, a Greek time keeping machine, a water clock

Cloaca maxima, the old sewage system in central Rome

Cloacina, the goddess of cleaning

Colline Gate, Rome's most northerly gate

Comitium, the circular public space right outside the Curia Hostilia in Rome

Consul, highest elected Roman war leader and magistrate

Corcyra, Greek speaking city on the Illyrian coast, now known as Corfu, Greece

Cornicen, trumpeter

Cornus, town on the west coast of Sardinia, now known as Caglieri

Cryptologist, code breaker

Cremona, Cremona, Italy

Croton, now known as Crotone in southern Italy.

Cumae, now known as Cuma, close to Naples

Curia Hostilia, the Senate house in Rome

Decimomannu, now part of the city of Cagliari, Sardinia, Italy

Decurion, Roman cavalry officer

Demeter, goddess of the harvest

Diana, Goddess of hunting otherwise known as Artemis

Dilectus, the conscription process by which Roman military tribunes would choose new recruits for the legions during the Republican period.

Dimale, Greek speaking city on the Illyrian coast, now near modern Krotine, Albania

Discordia, Goddess of strife and discord

Drepana, modern Trapani, Sicily

Druid, Celtic holy man

Dugouts, canoes

Emporiae, modern Empuries, Catalonia, Spain

Epidamnum, Greek speaking city on the Illyrian coast, now known as Durres, Albania

Equestrian, Roman social class, just below the senatorial class

Equites, Roman cavalrymen

Etruria, Tuscany, Italy

Etruscans, tribe of Tuscany

Factionalism, old-fashioned party politics and personal rivalries.

Faesulae, town of Fiesole, Italy

Falacrinum, Roman village near town of Rieti

Falcata sword, curved Iberian sword

Fasces, the bundle of rods symbolising the power of the office of the consul.

Firedogs, a bracket support on which logs are laid for burning

Focale, Neck scarf

Fortuna, Goddess of Fortune/Luck

Forum, central market square

Forum Boarium, the ancient cattle market of Rome.

Forum Romanum, the ancient Roman forum

Gades, Cadiz, Spain

Garum, fermented fish sauce

Gaesatae, Feared professional Gallic mercenaries, from north of the Alps

Gaul, France

Geronium, ancient town in Molise, Italy

Gladius Hispaniensis, double-edged, pointed sword

Grumentum, now known as Grumento Nova, Southern Italy

Gwenap, settlement in West Cornwall

Hades, the underworld

Hamae, ancient sacred grove, only three miles from Cumae

Hasta, Roman spear

Hastatii, Roman infantrymen, formed the first line of a Roman army

Herdonia, modern Ordona, southern Italy

Hibera, modern Tortosa, Catalonia, Spain

Hippocrates of Kos, father of medicine

Hirpini, ancient Italian tribe

House of Aemilia, Roman patrician aristocratic family

Ictis, modern St Michael's Mount or Plymouth - location still uncertain

Ilergetes, Spanish tribe living around modern Lleida, north-east Spain

Llercavones, Iberian tribe

Illyria, modern coast of Croatia, Montenegro and Albania including the old cities of Apollonia, Oricum, Dimale, Epidamnus, Pharos and Lissos

Impluvium, basin set in the floor to catch rainwater

Insubres, Gallic tribe living around Milan

Insulae, apartment blocks in Rome

Juno, Wife of Jupiter and Queen of the Gods

Juno Moneta, temple housing the state Mint

Jupiter, Rome's patron god

Klepsydra, a Greek water clock

Lacetani, Iberian tribe in northeast Spain

Lares, the guardian spirits who protected the household.

Latinitas, citizen without the right to vote in the public assembly

Latium, region of Lazio around Rome

Lebbade, Punic cap

Leontini, Lentini, Sicily

Liburna, small, light and fast ships with a single rowing-bench and twenty-five oars on each side.

Lictors, attendants to a Roman consul

Ligurians, tribe living around Genua, Italy

Lilybaeum, modern Marsala in Sicily

Llorca, located near modern Cartagena, Spain

Locri, now known as Locri in southern Italy.

Lucania, region in southern Italy now called Basilicata

Lucanians, ancient peoples living in southern Italy

Luceria, Latin colony, now known as Lucera, southern Italy

Ludi Consualia, the festival of the harvest.

Lusitanii, Celti-Iberian tribe living around Lisbon, Portugal

Maniple, Roman army unit of up to 120 men

Mars, God of war

Massalia, Marseille, France

Massaliot, people of Massalia

Messana, modern Messina, Italy

Messene, town in southern peloponnese, Greece

Mount Eryx, mountain in western Sicily

Narnia, modern Narni, central Italy

Naupactus, now known as Nafpaktos, Greece or Lepanto

Neapolis, Naples, Italy

Nemesis, the winged goddess, the collector of dues.

New Carthage, now known as Cartagena, Spain

Nola, still called Nola, Italy

Okilis, now known as Medinaceli, Spain

Optio, second in command of a maniple unit

Oricum, ancient city in Albania

Ortygia – the site of the original colony at Syracuse, Sicily

Ostia, ancient port of Rome

Paenula cloak, Poncho

Parthini, city on the Illyrian coast, now known as Dimale, Albania

Patrician, Roman aristocratic class

Pella, historical capital of Macedonia

Peloponnese, southern Greek mainland

Persephone, wife of Hades, co-ruler of the underworld

Pharos, city on the Illyrian coast, now known as Stari Grad, Croatia

Phocaea, Greek speaking area on the west Anatolian coast

Phrygian helmet, ancient helmet

Picenum, region of Italy

Pila, Roman spear

Pisae, Roman town now known as Pisa

Placentia, now known as Piacenza, Italy

Plebeians, commoners

Plebeian tribune, Magistrate tasked with championing and looking after the political interests of the common people

Pontifex Maximus, the Roman High Priest

Poseidon, Greek God of the sea

Praetor, Consul's military subordinate

Prefecture, the administrative building housing the colony's authorities and public records

Principes, second line of Roman infantrymen

Principia, Roman camp HQ

Pro-praetor, Roman magistrate, commander and official

Pugio, army knife

Punic, Carthaginian

Quinquereme, heavy warship propelled by sail and five banks of oars

Reate, Rieti, central Italy

Revetments, banks to hold river water back

Rhegium, modern Reggio, Calabria, Italy

Rion, straights of Rion, Greece, western entrance to the Gulf of Corinth

Robigus, Roman god of agricultural disease

Rostra, a wooden elevated platform from where Rome's magistrates would traditionally address the people

Sabine country, region north east of Rome

Saguntum, Sagunto, near Valencia, Spain

Salapia, now known as Salapia, Italy

Salaria, old Salt road

Samnites, Italian peoples living in south central Italy

Sandaracha, a gold coloured mineral from which arsenic dust was derived

Saturn, God of plenty and wealth

Saturnalia, festival of Saturn in december, comparable to Christmas

Scorpions, bolt-throwers mounted on tripods

Scutum, shield.

Sentinum, now known as Sassoferrato, Italy

Sicyon, now known as Sicyona, Greece

Signifier, officer who keeps a unit's banner

Sora, modern Sora, Lazio, Italy

Spolia opima, Rome's highest military decoration,

Spoletium, modern Spoleto, Italy

SPQR, Senate and People of Rome

Strategos, Greek commander in chief

Stylus or styli, Roman pens

Sibylline books, the books of destiny

Stoa, a Greek style covered walkway with stone columns supporting a high tiled roof

Stylus, iron-tipped pen

Subura, slums in the heart of Rome

Syracuse, still known as Syracuse, Sicily

Tabula Valeria, painting in Rome depicting the Roman victory against Hiero of Syracuse and Carthage in the first Punic war

Tarentum, modern Taranto, Italy

Tarquinia, now known as Tarquinia, Tuscany, Italy

Tarraco, modern Tarragona, Spain

Taurini, Gallic tribe living near modern Turin

Taurasia, Turin, Italy

Terra Mater – the mother earth goddess, called Gaia in Greek

Tesserarius, the watch commander

Tharros, town in Sardinia

Thrace, modern Bulgaria

Ticinus river, modern Ticino

Tifata, mountain above Capua, Italy

Toga candida, specially whitened toga worn by candidates during elections

Torc, Celtic neck ring, denoting high social status

Tramontana wind, local wind that blows in the Apennines

Trebia river, modern Trebbia

Trencrom, hill fort in West Cornwall

Triarii, Third class of Roman infantrymen. The most senior and experienced class of heavy infantry

Triplex acies, Roman battle formation comprising three battle lines

Triremes, ancient warship

Tullianum, Rome's central prison

Tumultus Gallicus, A state of emergency referring to a Gallic invasion

Turma, Squadron of around thirty cavalrymen

Umbria, Italian region of Umbria

Ushant, island off the west Brittany coast

Utica, Carthaginian colony on the coast of Tunisia

Velites, Roman light infantry - skirmishers and javelin throwers

Venusia, Latin colony, now known as Venosa, Southern Italy

Vestal virgin, female priestess dedicated to the goddess Vesta

Via Aurelia, Roman road from Rome to Pisa, Italy

Via Flaminia, Flaminian way, ancient Roman road

Via Salaria, the old salt road, in Rome

Victoria, goddess of victory

Villa Publica, building where the censors had their base and where the public records were held. Stood on the fields of Mars.

Volturnus river, now known as the Volturno river, Italy

Vulcan, god of fire and carpenters

Zeus, Greek king of the Gods, Roman Jupiter

The Carthaginians, Spaniards and Gaul's

Gisgo's family, five blood brothers and friends

Gissa, Gisgo's wife (deceased)

Metzul, Gisgo's son by Gissa

Eliza, Gisgo's daughter by Hanna

Mastanabal, Numidian deputy commander (deceased)

Xenocles, Greek mercenary commander

Ablon, Iberian head of family

Korbis, Ablon's son (deceased)

Turibas, Ablon's son in law (deceased)

Asha, prostitute friend of Gisgo in Carthage

Caelina, Flavius's ex-girlfriend and Punic sympathiser (deceased)

Bostar, Punic doctor and friend of Gissa

Jezebel, Gissa's sister and Gisgo's sister in law

Donis, Phoenician sea captain and owner of the Punic Star

Hanna and Arishat, friends of Gissa, fellow captives and priestesses of Baal Hamon

Honorius, Roman double agent (deceased)

Galchobhar, Cornish Celtic warrior, new blood brother of Gisgo and Xenocles

Carthaginian soldiers, commanders and allies

Epicydes, Hannibal's spymaster

Kleptos. Assassin and Carthaginian agent

Hamilcar, Hannibal's father (deceased)

Hannibal, supreme commander all Carthaginian forces in Spain until 218 BCE

Hasdrubal, older brother of Hannibal

Indibilis, Iberian king of Llergetes tribe who had allied himself with Carthage

Mago, younger brother of Hannibal

Maharbal, Hannibal's cavalry commander and deputy (deceased)

Bomilcar, commander of the elite African infantry and Gisgo's rival

Hanno, Hannibal's nephew

Magilus, Gallic chieftain of the Insubres

Hanno, the Great, Carthaginian Suffette, political rival of Hannibal

King Gaia, King of the Eastern Numidians

King Syphax, King of the Western Numidians

Hasdrubal the Bald, Carthaginian commander of the invasion of Sardinia

Hampsicora, leader of the Sardinian rebels (deceased)

Hiostus, son of Hampiscora (deceased)

Gersakkun, Hasdrubal Gisco, Carthaginian general

Sophonisba, daughter of Hasdrubal Gisco (Gersakkun)

Masinissa, son of king Gaia of the Massylii, eastern Numidians

Carthaginian Glossary

Addax, white desert antelopes

Agora, a central market square

Ariminum, modern Rimini, Italy

Arno river, still called the Arno and it flows through the city of Florence

Arretium, modern Arezzo, Italy

Allobroges, Gallic tribe living around Lyon, France

Astarte, immortal Carthaginian god

Astrolabe, early navigational device

Baal Hamon, Carthaginian god

Bagradas river, now the Medjerda river, Tunisia

Barcid faction, Carthaginian political faction supporting Hannibal Barca

Bargusii, Iberian tribe living in Catalonia, Spain

Bastulo, Iberian tribe in southern Spain

Blessed islands, possibly the Canary Islands

Brutians, people living in the deep south of Italy

Byblos, ancient Phoenician city in Lebanon

Byrsa hill, ancient heart of the city of Carthage, Tunis, Tunisia

Canaan, the Levant

Carthage, near modern Tunis, Tunisia

Carpetani, Iberian tribe living around Madrid, Spain

Cassiterides, Tin islands, possibly the Isles of Scilly, Cornwall, UK

Castro, fortified Spanish hilltop village

Clastidium, now known as Casteggio

Cork oaks, Oak trees from which the bark makes cork for sealing bottles

Cothon, Inner circular harbour in the city of Carthage

Council of 104, 104 leading Carthaginian senators, government

Chretes river, river in Africa, which one is disputed

Cydamus Road, trans Saharan caravan route

Cydamus, oasis town, now known as Ghadames in south western Libya

Djenne, Known today as Djenne, Mali, West Africa

Dragoman, Gallic intermediary

Ebro river, Ebro river, Spain

Emporium, Greek colony just south of Barcelona, Spain

Eshmun, Carthaginian God of healing

Etruria, Tuscany, Italy

Etruscans, tribe of Tuscany

Falcata, Iberian style sword

Felsina – Cis-Alpine Gaul, now known as Bologna, Italy

Gades, Cadiz, Spain

Garamantes, ancient people who lived in the Sahara Desert

Guadalquivir river, main river of southern Spain

Gauloi, ancient type of Punic ship

Ghat, modern Ghat, Libya

Hippo, now known as Annaba, Algeria

Insubres, Gallic tribe living around Milan

Kerne, now possibly known as Arguin Island, West coast of Mauritania, Africa

Lebbade, High peaked Phoenician cap

Lilybaeum, town on Sicily now called Marsala, Italy

Lixos, near the modern seaport of Larrache, Morocco

Lusitania, Portugal

Malaka, modern Malaga, Spain

Masaesylii, western kingdom of Numidians

Massylii, eastern kingdom of Numidians

Melqart, immortal Carthaginian god, Lord of Tyre

Mogador, modern Essaouira, Morocco

Mutina, town of Modena, Italy

New Carthage, modern town of Cartagena, Spain

Numidia, home of the Numidians, northern Tunisia and Algeria

Olisippo, modern Lisbon, Portugal

Oppida, Gallic town

Po, the longest river in Italy that runs across the northern plains.

Porretta pass, the modern Passo della Porretta

Port, left hand side of, or from, a ship

Punic, Carthaginian

Sacred band, Elite Carthaginian cavalry force

Saguntum, modern Sagunto, Spain

Samnites, ancient mountain dwelling peoples living south east of Rome

Saturnalia, major Roman festival in December

Starboard, right hand side of, or from, a ship

Suffete, Highest of the elected Carthaginian magistrates

Syracuse, an independent city state in Roman times on Sicily, and still called Syracuse

Tanit, Carthaginian goddess. Protector of the city of Carthage, consort of Baal Hamon

Tartessos, ancient port in southern Spain

Taurini, Gallic tribe who lived around Turin

Ticinus, a tributary river flowing southwards into the Po, Italy

Tingis, Tangier, Morocco

Tophet, Carthaginian Cemetery

Tuareg, tribe of desert nomads

Veneti, Celtic tribe living around area of modern Venice, Italy

Volcae, Gallic tribe living either side of Rhone river, France

Printed in Great Britain
by Amazon

69570431R00214